T0110620

Praise for
The Dragons of Chiril

"Have you ever looked at a painting from a distance and thought it beautiful, only to draw nearer to it and realize it was more exquisite, complex, and wonderful than you ever imagined? *The Dragons of Chiril* by Donita K. Paul is like that. I began reading and liked it. As usual, I found myself happily enveloped in a vivid world full of emerlindians, tumanhofers, and dragons. But then, just when I thought the work was beautiful, something deep within me started to tingle… and I began to see that *The Dragons of Chiril* was far more than simple entertainment or escape. I had one 'aha!' moment after another. Clues everywhere, right in front of my eyes, blossomed into truth, until at last I put down the book and swam in the rich waters of adventure, peace, and blessed melancholy—the rare state revealing that you've been touched by the story of an inspired author. *The Dragons of Chiril* is sure to be loved by readers and re-readers of every age."

—WAYNE THOMAS BATSON, best-selling author of the
Door Within Trilogy, *Isle of Swords,* and *Isle of Fire*

"Donita K. Paul never fails to satisfy the imagination and delight the soul. In *The Dragons of Chiril,* she takes us beyond the boundaries of her beloved DragonKeeper chronicles and opens up vast new realms of wonder. The adventure of Tipper, the sculptor's daughter, will strike a responsive chord in the heart of every reader who has ever faced a seemingly impossible challenge. This is fantasy that truly illuminates reality!"

—JIM DENNEY, author of the Timebenders series

"*The Dragons of Chiril* is a delightful tale of otherworldly adventures laced with heavenly meanings. Author Donita K. Paul skillfully transports you to a fantasy world populated with emerlindians, tumanhofers, speaking grand parrots, wizards, and magical librarians; where flying dragons communicate and mysterious portals whisk you across the world. Readers young and old will love journeying along with the enchanting questing party on their mission to save the world and discover a loving God."

—MEGAN DIMARIA, author of *Searching for Spice*
and *Out of Her Hands*

"Stunning beginning to a new series! Rarely does an author recapture the exquisite charm and the bold freshness first discovered in her initial series. Donita K. Paul fans are in for a treat as they uncover new wonders and enchantment in the world of Chiril. New readers will revel in the magical blend of mischief and mayhem woven with wittiness and intrigue throughout this engaging tale. From the zany disposition of Lady Peg to the spirited charm and wit of Tipper, her youthful daughter, *The Dragons of Chiril* tingles our most fervent emotions of love, joy, and hope. An exciting complement to the DragonKeeper series, and a fantastical adventure for inaugural audiences of all ages."

—ERIC REINHOLD, author of *The Annals of Aeliana,*
Ryann Watters and the King's Sword, and *Ryann Watters*
and the Shield of Faith

The Dragons of Chiril

OTHER BOOKS
BY DONITA K. PAUL

DragonSpell
DragonQuest
DragonKnight
DragonFire
DragonLight
Dragons of the Valley

A Fantastic Journey of Discovery for All Ages

Donita K. Paul

A NOVEL

The Dragons of Chiril

WATERBROOK
PRESS

THE DRAGONS OF CHIRIL
PUBLISHED BY WATERBROOK PRESS
12265 Oracle Boulevard, Suite 200
Colorado Springs, Colorado 80921

Scripture quotations are taken from the New American Standard Bible®. © Copyright The
Lockman Foundation 1960, 1962, 1963, 1968, 1971, 1972, 1973, 1975, 1977, 1995. Used by
permission. (www.Lockman.org).

The characters and events in this book are fictional, and any resemblance to actual persons
or events is coincidental.

ISBN 978-0-307-73011-4
ISBN 978-0-30745-787-5 (electronic)

Copyright © 2009 by Donita K. Paul
Illustrations copyright © 2009 by Rachael Selk

Published in association with the literary agency of Alive Communications Inc., 7680 Goddard
Street, Suite 200, Colorado Springs, CO 80920, www.alivecommunications.com.

All rights reserved. No part of this book may be reproduced or transmitted in any form or by any
means, electronic or mechanical, including photocopying and recording, or by any information
storage and retrieval system, without permission in writing from the publisher.

Published in the United States by WaterBrook Multnomah, an imprint of the Crown Publishing
Group, a division of Random House Inc., New York.

Previously published as *The Vanishing Sculptor* in 2009.

WATERBROOK and its deer colophon are registered trademarks of Random House Inc.

The Library of Congress cataloged the original edition as follows:
Paul, Donita K.
    The vanishing sculptor : a novel / Donita K. Paul. — 1st ed.
        p. cm.
    ISBN 978-1-4000-7339-9 — ISBN 978-0-30745-787-5 (electronic)
    I. Title.
    PS3616.A94V36 2009
    813'.6—dc22

2011—First Revised Edition

147028622

God has blessed me by bringing young people into my life. The days would be so boring if I dealt only with adults. This book is dedicated to my readers. They keep me on my toes and motivated to write.

Jessica Agius
Mary Darnell
Hannah Johnson
Alistair and Ian McNear
Rachael Selk
Rebecca Wilber
Kayla and Joshua Woodhouse

Contents

Acknowledgments

"Where there is no guidance the people fall, but in abundance of counselors there is victory" (Proverbs 11:14, NASB). Each of these people, at one time or another, offered wisdom, encouragement, practical help, or inspiration to me in developing *The Dragons of Chiril*. Thank you.

Mary Agius	Paul Moede
Jessica Barnes	Jill Elizabeth Nelson
Evangeline Denmark	Aaron Pieffer
Kory Denmark	Joel Rauser
Michelle Garland	Faye Spieker
Dianna Gay	Darren Stautz
Jack Hagar	Tiffany and Stuart Stocton
Jim Hart	Case Tompkins
Shannon Marchese	Beth and Robert Vogt
Lyndsay Gerwing	Holly Volstad
Beth Jusino	Peggy Wilber
Krystine Kercher	Kim Woodhouse
Shannon and Troy McNear	Laura Wright

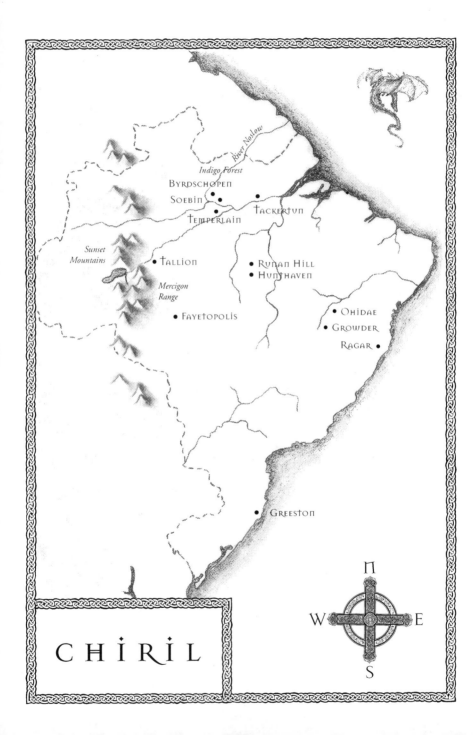

River Noslow

Indigo Forest

BYRDSCHOPEN
SOEBIN • •   • TACKERTUN
    • TEMPERLAIN

Sunset
Mountains   • TALLION   • RUNAN HILL
                                              • HUNTHAVEN
Mercigon
Range
        • FAYETOPOLIS   • OHIDAE
                                         • GROWDER
                                      RAGAR •

                          • GREESTON

CHIRIL

N
W   E
S

A View from a Tree

Sir Beccaroon cocked his head, ruffled his neck feathers, and stretched, allowing his crimson wings to spread. The branch beneath him sank and rose again, responding to his weight. Moist, hot air penetrated his finery, and he held his wings away from his brilliant blue sides.

"Too hot for company," he muttered, rocking back and forth from one scaly four-toed foot to the other on a limb of a sacktrass tree. The leaves shimmered as the motion rippled along the branch. "Where is that girl?"

His yellow head swiveled almost completely around. He peered with one eye down the overgrown path and then scoped out every inch within his range of vision, twisting his neck slowly.

A brief morning shower had penetrated the canopy above and rinsed the waxy leaves. A few remaining drops glistened where thin shafts of tropical sun touched the dark green foliage. On the broot vine, flowers the size of plates lifted their fiery red petals, begging the thumb-sized bees to come drink before the weight of nectar broke off the blooms.

Beccaroon flew to a perch on a gnarly branch. He sipped from a broot blossom and ran his black tongue over the edges of his beak. A sudden breeze shook loose a sprinkle of leftover raindrops. Beccaroon shook his tail feathers and blinked. When the disturbance settled, he cocked his head and listened.

"Ah! She's coming." He preened his soft green breast and waited, giving a show of patience he didn't feel. His head jerked up as he detected someone walking with the girl.

"Awk!" The sound exploded from his throat. He flew into a roost far above the forest floor, where he couldn't be seen from the ground, and watched the approach of the girl placed under his guardianship.

Tipper strolled along the path below, wearing a flowing golden gown over her tall, lean body. She'd put her long blond hair in a fancy braid that started at the crown of her head. A golden chain hung from each of her pointed ears. And she'd decorated her pointed facial features with subdued colors—blue for her eyelids, rose for her lips, and a shimmering yellow on her cheeks. Beccaroon sighed. His girl was lovely.

The bushes along the path behind her rustled. Beccaroon's tongue clucked against his beak in disapproval. Hanner trudged after Tipper, leading a donkey hitched to a cart. The man's shaggy hair, tied with a string at the back of his neck, hung oily and limp. Food and drink stained the front of his leather jerkin, and his boots wore mud instead of a shine. The parrot caught a whiff of the o'rant from where he perched. The young man should have carried the fragrance of citrus, but his overstrong odor reminded Beccaroon of rotten fruit.

A tree full of monkeys broke out in outraged chatter. Tipper, when alone, walked amid the animals' habitat without causing alarm.

"Smart monkeys," said Beccaroon. "You recognize a ninny-napconder when you see one." He used the cover of the monkeys' rabble-rousing to glide to another tree, where he could hide at a lower level. He had an idea where Tipper would lead Hanner.

"Here it is," said the pretty emerlindian. She pulled vines from a clump, revealing a gray statue beneath. "My father named this one *Vegetable Garden*."

Hanner pulled off more vines as he made his way slowly around the four-foot statue. "*Vegetable Garden*? Mistress Tipper, are you sure you have the right one? This is a statue of a boy reading a book. He's not even chewing a carrot while he sits here."

"Father used to say reading a good book was nourishment."

Hanner scratched his head, shrugged his shoulders, and went to fetch the donkey and cart. Tipper's head tilted back, and her blue eyes looked up into the trees. Her gaze roamed over the exact spot Beccaroon used as a hidden roost. Not by the blink of an eyelash did she betray whether she had seen him. Hanner returned.

Tipper spread out a blanket in the cart after Hanner maneuvered it next to the statue, then helped him lift the stone boy into the back. Hanner grunted a lot, and Tipper scolded.

"Careful... Don't break his arm... Too many vines still around the base."

They got the statue loaded, and Tipper tucked the blanket over and around it. She then gave Hanner a pouch of coins.

"This is for your usual delivery fee. I couldn't put in any extra for traveling expenses. I'm sure you'll be reimbursed by our buyer."

He grunted and slipped the money inside his jerkin.

Tipper clasped her hands together. "Be careful. And give Master Dodderbanoster my regards."

He tipped his hat and climbed aboard the cart. "I always am. And I always do."

She stood in the path until the creak of the cart wheels could no longer be heard.

Beccaroon swooped down and sat on a thick branch wrapped with a leafless green creeper. The vine looked too much like a snake, so he hopped to another limb.

"Was that wise?" he asked.

"I don't think so either, Bec, but what else can I do? I sell the artwork only as a last resort when we need quite a bit of cash. The well needs re-digging." Tipper pulled a tight face, looking like she'd swallowed nasty medicine. "We've sold almost everything in the house. Mother sees our things in the market and buys them back. Sometimes I get a better price for a piece the second time I sell it, and sometimes not."

Beccaroon swayed back and forth on his feet, shaking his head. "She never catches on?"

"Never." Tipper giggled. "She shows remarkably consistent taste. When she spots something that was once ours, she buys it, brings it home, shows it off to me, and tells me she has always wanted something just like it. And she never notices pictures gone from the walls, rugs missing in rooms, chairs, tables, vases, candlesticks gone. I used to rearrange things to disguise a hole in the décor, but there's no need."

The sigh that followed her explanation held no joy. Tipper looked around. "There never is a place to sit in this forest when one wants to plop down and have a good cry."

"You're not the type to cry. I'll walk you home." Beccaroon hopped down to the path.

His head came up to her waist. She immediately put her dainty hand on his topknot and smoothed the creamy plumes back.

"You're the best of friends. Keeping this secret would be unbearable if I didn't have you to confide in."

Beccaroon clicked his tongue. "No flattery, or I shall fly away."

They moseyed back the direction Tipper had come, opposite the way Hanner had departed.

Beccaroon tsked. "I don't like that greasy fellow."

"I know." Tipper gently twisted the longest feather from the center of Bec's crest around her forefinger.

The grand parrot jerked his head away and gave her his sternest glare. She was his girl, but he still wouldn't let her take liberties. She didn't seem to notice he was disgruntled, and that further blackened his mood.

"Hanner is all right, Bec. He takes the statues to Dodderbanoster. Dodderbanoster takes them to cities beyond my reach and gets a fair price for them. Sometimes I think the pouch Hanner brings back is way too full."

Beccaroon clicked his tongue. "Your father is a master artist. His work is worth a mighty price."

"Hanner says sometimes Dodderbanoster sells them to a dealer who takes them even farther away, to thriving districts. Wealthy patrons bid to own a Verrin Schope work of art." She held back a leafy branch so Beccaroon could strut by with ease. "Late at night when I sit in my window and think, I hope that Papa will see one of his sculptures or paintings in a market in some far away metropolis.

"I imagine the scene. He exclaims with shock. He turns red and sputters and shakes his fists. In fact, he's so angry he comes straight home and yells loud and long at his daughter who dares to sell his masterpieces."

Beccaroon rolled his shoulders, causing his wings to tilt out, then settle against his sides. "What of your mother? Does she ever mention your father's absence?"

"No, why should she? He's been gone for years, but she still sees him. She talks to him every night after his workday is done. Promenades through the garden with him. Pours his tea, and just the other evening I heard her fussing at him for not giving enough money to the parish."

"I suppose she dipped in the household funds to make up for his neglect."

Tipper sighed. "Yes, she did."

They went on a ways in silence.

Tipper picked a bloom, savored its spicy odor, then placed it behind one pointed ear. "Mother has an idea in her head."

"For anyone else, the head is a splendid place to keep an idea. For your mother, she should just let them go."

"She's determined to visit her sister." Tipper raised her eyebrows so that the upside-down V was even more pronounced. "She'll go if she manages to pack her long list of necessities. Some of the items are quite unreasonable."

Beccaroon snatched a nut from an open shell on the ground. He played the small nugget over his tongue, enjoying its sweetness, then swallowed. "And you? Is she taking you?"

"No, I'm to stay here and make sure Papa is comfortable and remembers to go to bed at night instead of working till all hours in his studio."

"I don't like you being alone in that house."

"I don't either."

"Of course, there are the servants."

"Only two now."

Beccaroon ruffled his feathers, starting at the tuft on top of his head, fluffing the ruff of his neck, proceeding down his back, and ending with a great shake of his magnificent tail.

"It seems I will have to move into the house."

"Oh, Bec. I was hoping you'd say that."

2

Needed: One Painting

Tipper walked up the wide veranda steps and crossed to a wrought-iron table where her mother sat sipping a tall cool drink and reading a book.

"Is that you, Tipper?" her mother asked without looking up from the page before her.

"Yes, Mother."

"You've been in the forest?"

"Yes, Mother."

"There are snakes in the forest. Big ones."

Tipper poured some frissent juice from a pitcher and took her glass with her. She leaned against the carved granite railing and peered up at her home. Byrdschopen had been in the family for generations. Eldymine Byrd had married Brim Schope and brought an astonishing wealth to his bounteous landholdings. Both husband and wife lived extravagantly and built Byrdschopen to accommodate their pleasure. Three stories, an attic, and a flat roof designed for entertaining. Massive stonework. One hundred seventy-six windows. Guests came from all over Chiril to visit. Servants crowded the quarters designed just for them. The family grew as seven sons and four daughters joined Eldymine and Brim.

Those days were long gone.

The extended family dwindled. Tipper's mother and father had one child. The wealth slipped away. No one visited.

Byrdschopen remained, but housed only four people.

Tipper glanced back at the rich forest. "I didn't see any snakes today." Sipping the sweet liquid from her glass, she let the coolness ease the tension in her throat.

Her mother puckered her lips in a moue of disapproval. "You could at least take Zabeth with you."

Tipper smiled at the long, lazy minor dragon sunning herself on the balustrade. "Zabeth is afraid of snakes."

"Just as she should be. You should be too."

"But I'm not."

Her mother looked up with a puzzled frown. "Not what, dear? That wasn't much of a sentence, and I haven't a clue what you're talking about."

Rather than explain, Tipper stroked Zabeth's green back. The warm scales glistened with different hues. The minor dragon looked up, winked, and curled her tail around Tipper's wrist, pulling her hand back to continue the gentle rub.

Mother cleared her throat. "I want you to speak to your father, Tipper."

"What's he done now?"

"It's what he hasn't done. I've asked him time and again to do a little painting of the garden there." She pointed to a fountain surrounded by a gravel walkway. Blooms fringed the pleasant sitting area with splashes of unbridled color. Every shade of pink dotted the dark green foliage. Spots of large yellow blossoms captured the sun. Tiny fibbirds with their purple and rose plumage flitted among the smaller flowers, drinking nectar.

"But you know how he is lately. He turns a deaf ear. Whatever project has captured his interest keeps him in his studio far too many hours." Her mother's plaintive tone touched Tipper's heart.

"I know, Mother. It's very hard."

"If he didn't come to me at night, I'd die of loneliness."

Tipper nodded sympathetically.

"So you will ask him. He always does as you request. You're his favorite daughter. I wish to take the picture with me to show your aunt." Her mother gathered up her things—a book, a fan, and a handkerchief. She left the glass and stood. "So comforting to know you'll take care of it. I'm tired now and will take my afternoon nap."

She came to kiss Tipper's pale cheek. Her complexion was only a few shades darker, and her hair still glowed a honey yellow. On her hand she wore a simple gold band declaring her married state. Her only other jewelry adorned her hair. A thin gold circlet had shifted to one side but was in no danger of falling off since a few shining braids wrapped around Lady Peg's head and secured the emblem of royalty.

Lady Peg wrinkled her nose at the dozing dragon. "Come, Zabeth. You've exerted yourself too much today. We'll go where it's cool and rest."

The dragon rose, stretched, then flew to the older woman's shoulder.

"That's right," said Mother. "I'll carry you. You must be exhausted."

Tipper whispered, "Lazy!"

Zabeth turned her elegant head, bestowed a dragon grin on Tipper, and stuck out her tongue.

Tipper chuckled and sat in her mother's seat. A bowl of fruit in the center of the table released a tempting fragrance. She plucked a cluster of grapes and popped one into her mouth.

The crackling voice of their butler, Lipphil, interrupted the pop of the fruit as she chomped it between her teeth. "Mistress Tipper?"

She choked. The ancient o'rant in shabby formal attire rushed forward. He almost pulled one of her arms out of the shoulder socket as he stretched it straight up and pummeled her back. "Perhaps you had better stand, Mistress."

She stood more because he hauled her to her feet than because she was following his suggestion. Lipphil thumped her between the shoulder blades.

She sucked in a breath. The butler let go and poured more juice into her glass. She sipped and nodded her thanks. This man had walked her at night as a colicky baby, bandaged her knees, and wiped tears from her cheeks when her father disappeared.

He stood at attention until she recovered. "Mistress Tipper, there is a young man here to see your father."

She tilted her head. "Send him away."

"He won't go."

"Well, he won't see Papa."

"Perhaps if you would tell him so. In the meantime, I'll trot down to Rolan's and have him come up to throw the young man off the property."

The thought of her ancient friend trotting almost caused Tipper to laugh out loud. With effort she kept a solemn face and said, "Certainly."

Lipphil left and returned, trailed by the unwanted guest. Tipper straightened her spine, lifted her chin, and tried to look as regal as her mother did when she received a guest. Thankfully, the tumanhofer couldn't see her insides shaking like a quiverbug before a rainstorm.

The butler announced the visitor. "Graddapotmorphit Bealomondore of Greeston in Dornum."

Tipper nodded. "Have a seat, Master Bealomondore." She gestured toward a chair at the table.

Lipphil poured a glass for the guest, then discreetly disappeared. Tipper noted that the butler had summoned a rather old minor dragon to be her protector. Junkit sat on the step into the house, looking alert and proud to be called to duty.

The short tumanhofer pulled himself up to his full height, perhaps four feet, clicked his heels together, and gave a jerky bow.

Tipper sat. "Please." She smiled and gestured to the other seat.

After flipping up the tails of his coat with a flourish, the young man sat. His eager expression showed in his eyes, while a grin stretched across his clean-shaven cheeks.

"I make my appeal to you, dear daughter of the celebrated Verrin Schope. I am an artist, and I have come all this way to offer myself as an apprentice to the great master. I saw his statue *A Morning in Time* in Brextik. I was struck with his genius, as was all of the city. I found another statue, by chance, in the home of an old family friend in the Valley of Chester. That one was *Dream Night*. Are you familiar with it?"

Before Tipper could affirm that she was, he went on with an air of enthusiasm that tired her. "Of course you are." He put his fingertips to his lips, made a smacking noise, then flicked his fingers into the air as if sending his blessing to the heavens.

Tipper sighed heavily and leaned back in her chair.

Bealomondore's eyes focused on something far, far away. "And the painting. Ah, the painting. A woman beside an ocean, a ship at sea, a cloud hovering in the distance, and the bird flying from vessel to shore with a message in its beak. The poetry of line, the color of emotion, the tenderness of technique."

His eyes riveted on Tipper. "I must study under Verrin Schope. I am capable. Let me speak with him. Let me show him my work. Let the master decide whether I am to slave for him and learn at his feet."

"He won't see you, Master Bealomondore. He is a total recluse."

"So I have heard. But if his precious daughter were to make my plea…?"

Tipper examined the aspiring artist with more interest. The precious daughter currently had a problem. Could the man actually paint? She looked beyond him to the fountain. How long would this obsession with having a likeness of the garden hold her mother? Would she forget in a day like she sometimes did?

No. From long experience, Tipper knew this was one of the times her mother would harp on a point until her daughter felt like screaming. The tumanhofer presented a way to avoid days, weeks, even months of nagging, pouting, and silent despair. Her mother's performance would drive Tipper to distraction. Perhaps the daughter could act as well.

Sighing dramatically, she said, "You have come such a long distance, across the entire continent. I hate to turn you away with no hope."

He leaned forward, keen to hear her words, his face practically torn with expectation. His earnestness almost made Tipper forsake her sudden plan. But Mother would want that painting day after day for months, until she inexplicably forgot about a picture from her husband's hand.

There was the trip to see her sister. Perhaps when her mother came back, the picture would be of no importance. No, it was more likely Lady Peg would postpone the trip until she had the painting. Then there would be two topics for her mother to worry to death—the delayed trip and the fountain depiction. The thought of her mother's nagging pushed aside Tipper's last hesitation.

"You have seen my father's work?"

"Many times." He reached across the table as if to touch her but withdrew his hand. "I have searched out every piece I could find. Twenty-nine statues, fifty-three paintings."

Tipper raised her eyebrows. She hadn't sold that many. Perhaps her father still produced his masterpieces, wherever he was. She scowled.

Tipper pointed to the fountain. "Paint that. Paint it tomorrow and be done by nightfall. Paint it in such a way that your very art proves you have already studied my father's style and genius. I will show it to my mother, and if she approves, then she will petition my father to give you an audience."

"Thank you," the tumanhofer gushed. He slid out of his chair and down on his knees before her, grabbed her hands, and bestowed a flurry of kisses on them. "Thank you. Thank you. You won't regret this kindness."

Tipper cleared her throat and tried to pull away. Junkit flew to her rescue, batting his blue wings against the effusive man's face.

He cowered. "Excuse me, I beg you. I am zealous for my ultimate dream to come true."

"Yes, well." Tipper glanced around. Her second servant stood in the door, a worried expression marring her usual serenity. "Gladyme, how good of you to appear at just the right time. Master Bealomon-dore will be staying the night and the morrow. Please show him to a room."

Gladyme gave a curtsy but looked doubtfully at the fancy-dressed guest. Nevertheless, she escorted the tumanhofer away.

Tipper collapsed in her seat, expelling her relief with a puff of air.

A few minutes later, Lipphil arrived with Rolan.

"Is everything all right, Mistress Tipper?" he panted.

"Yes, but I fear we shall have to do something with Mother to-morrow. I've allowed the artist to stay to paint the picture mother wants of the fountain. Even in her hazy state, I don't think we can let her watch the stranger at work and then tell her the result is a gift from Papa."

Rolan scratched his head. "I'm taking my wife to Soebin tomorrow to visit the market. I know it's not convenient for Lady Peg to go shopping, but it would get her out of the house."

Tipper jumped to her feet and squeezed the marione farmer's arm. "Just the thing, Rolan. You've saved us."

"Not if she spies that huge clock I took away last week and has me haul it back home."

Tipper narrowed her eyes and pressed her lips together in a straight line before speaking. "We'll have to chance it. Surely Boscamon will favor us with one more lucky circumstance."

Boscamon, the unseen ruler of fate. She knew better than to rely on a myth, but the phrase had slipped from her lips as if it had meaning.

It would be nice to have a mother or a father who took responsibility for regulating each day's events. Tipper would even accept a being without shape or form such as the "hero of the universe" legend if he would only show some dependability.

But Boscamon provided a convenient way to explain what could not be explained. Shifting blame for awkward situations onto the shoulders of Boscamon created a sense of relief without solving any problems. But Sir Beccaroon had taught her to carry her own burdens.

Tipper's body sagged as if a weight bore down on her. She recognized the threat, squared her shoulders, and lifted her chin. "Whatever tomorrow brings, we'll plow ahead. Determination isn't a choice. It's a necessity."

3

The Proper Light

Beccaroon cocked his head and critically examined the painting developing under the hand of the young tumanhofer Bealomondore. The grand parrot waited to comment until the artist pulled his brush back from the canvas. "You're good."

The man jumped and turned abruptly to face Beccaroon. "I didn't know you were there." He dabbed his paintbrush on his palette, then waved its green tip at the mansion. "Do you live in the house?"

"No, I'm visiting."

"Friend of the family?"

"Yes." He lowered his head, his version of a courtly bow. "I'm Beccaroon."

The tumanhofer put down his brush, wiped his hand on his artists overcoat, and extended it to shake.

Beccaroon tilted his head. The feathers above one eye ruffled up like an eyebrow.

Bealomondore withdrew his hand. "Ah! You don't…um. Pardon me. I'm not accustomed to…um… Pleased to meet you. I'm Graddapotmorphit Bealomondore, at your service." He clicked his heels together and bowed.

Beccaroon nodded and turned his attention back to the likeness of the fountain on a six-by-six-inch canvas. "I'm impressed with your replication of Verrin Schope's style."

The tumanhofer picked up his brush and rolled the slim handle between his thumb and forefinger. His brow furrowed as he studied the foliage surrounding the scene and then his work. He dabbed a few strokes of shading to the bushes, then stood back and glared at the fountain. "I haven't had the pleasure of meeting Lady Peg or Verrin Schope."

Beccaroon clicked his black tongue against his beak. "I doubt you'll meet either."

The artist whipped around again, facing the parrot with a scowl. "Is my talent not great enough? Do not say so! I am the best of the best."

"Then why do you seek tutelage under Verrin Schope?"

The tumanhofer's demeanor changed in an instant. His head hung, and tears welled in his eyes. "Because no one takes me seriously. I am a man of infinite talent but no occupation. I can speak with a golden tongue, but no one listens. I am a fop in the eyes of my friends and relatives."

"Well, you can't do a thing about your relatives, but you can choose better friends, ones who appreciate your gift."

Bealomondore shrugged, wiped his wet cheeks on his sleeve, and returned to his painting. "If Verrin Schope believes I have talent, then there will not be a soul to contradict him."

Beccaroon clicked his tongue again. "Verrin Schope is extremely involved in his current project. It could be that you will be denied your apprenticeship because the time is not right. While your talent would prove sufficient, Verrin Schope's availability could be…nonexistent."

"Then I'll wait," said the painter. Using his brush, now tipped in vermillion, he pointed to one of the ground-level windows. "Mistress Tipper is trying to get your attention. I assume she doesn't want to speak to me."

Beccaroon turned his head a three-quarter rotation. "She does, indeed, seem to be summoning me. What an unusual means of communication she's chosen."

The tumanhofer made a guttural sound. "Whenever I turn toward the house, she pops behind the curtain. She should realize an artist is a keen observer."

"Perhaps she does not want to disturb you when you are so nearly done."

"Perhaps she is avoiding me altogether, as are her mother and her father."

"Well, well," said Beccaroon as he stretched his glorious scarlet wings. "No need to imagine affront. I'll go see what ails the girl."

He flew to an entrance near the window where Tipper lurked. He waited a moment before she opened the door and gestured for him to enter.

"Is he done?" she asked.

"Almost. He's perfecting the shading and highlighting the flowers. His work is very good. Your father would be interested in the young man."

"*If* he were here."

"I can't think it is right to take this aspiring artist's painting and then just send him on his way. I also think you may have a hard time getting rid of him."

Tipper bit her lower lip and peeked through the heavy brocade drapes. "He *is* determined." She turned away from watching the artist and put a hand on Beccaroon's shoulder. "Mother could come back any minute."

"And she might not come back for several hours," Beccaroon countered. "Rolan knows you want her occupied for a greater part of the day." He sighed. "You want me to check, don't you?"

"Yes, please."

"I'll return shortly."

They crossed the room and went through a hall to the main foyer, where Tipper opened the massive front door. She kissed Beccaroon on his forehead, right in front of the golden plumes that formed a substantial crest.

He didn't acknowledge the affection but strutted out the door. Tipper's habit of stepping over his personal boundary should not be encouraged. He took flight without comment and soared high above the surrounding forest, following the wide path that wandered toward the market town. He flew over Rolan's farm and saw the crops standing in neat rows, almost ready to harvest.

He continued his journey, searching the road and several taverns along the way for any sign of Rolan, his wife, and Lady Peg. He squinted his eyes at a group of men camped by the River Noslow. He'd send someone to keep watch over these strangers. People had been going missing closer to the coast. Most agreed they'd been taken for slave trade. A nasty business, and Beccaroon would not let it get started in his territory.

Circling Soebin, he had a good view of the merchants folding up their tents, packing their wagons, and heading for home. Rolan and his lady passengers were nowhere in sight.

He flew back by a different route and finally spotted the wagon pulled by a large dapple gray workhorse. Rolan had placed a two-seater sofa in the wagon bed. The ladies tilted their parasols against the setting sun and chattered away.

Beccaroon swooped down and landed beside Lady Peg and Rolan's wife, Zilla.

"Oh, Beccaroon," exclaimed Lady Peg. "Just look what we've found." She pointed to a tarp-covered rectangular box around six feet tall. "You'll never guess."

Tipper shielded her eyes from the bright sun with a hand propped against her brow. She stood on the covered balcony that ran along the second floor of the mansion's west side. Rolan's farm lay beyond the forest. The road that led to the village passed by his front gate. So far she had not spotted any activity along the winding lane. No sight of a wagon bringing her mother home.

She dropped her hand to clasp the other and wrung her fingers together. "Oh, I do wish this day were over."

"I'm finished." The tumanhofer's voice startled Tipper.

She jumped and turned quickly. He scowled at her.

Pressing her lips together against saying something foolish, she kept her thoughts to herself. Why did the man have to be so prickly? Had he figured out he was not going to get his position of apprentice? He'd have the right to be even more unpleasant when she sent him packing without meeting her father. "You don't look very pleased about being done."

The muscles in his face tightened a fraction more. "One naturally prefers to execute a painting in one's own style. Still, I am pleased with the results."

"Well." Tipper paused, fumbling for words that would answer this touchy coxcomb. None came to her. "Shall we go see it?"

He blocked the door to the upstairs hall, and she waited for him to move aside. With her head held high in imitation of her mother's regal stance, she brushed past the shorter man. Walking briskly, she headed toward the main staircase, a showy affair that curved down from two points to the high-ceilinged foyer below.

In the hallway to the back of the house, Bealomondore displayed his small painting on a console table flush against the wall.

"The light is not good here," he complained. "I would like to present the piece with a full complement of candles. Perhaps two branches to the side and a shallow row in front."

"Yes, yes." Tipper picked up the painting, touching only the sides.

The smell of fresh oil paint reminded her of sitting in her father's studio while he worked on a masterpiece in progress. He would hum at times while making slow, deliberate strokes. Other times his hand moved so quickly the air seemed to buzz as it did when a fibbird flew past. She remembered the excitement of an image exploding out of a mundane background.

She tilted the canvas in her hand to catch the dying sunlight from the west window. She gasped. The exquisite detail of flowers, foliage, and a spray from the fountain captivated her. How could she declare this piece inferior and not worthy of her father's attention? Tears sprang to her eyes. Bealomondore had captured the vibrancy of Verrin Schope.

Why had her father had to withdraw from his family, abandon them? Anger surged through her, washing away sentimentality and destroying her appreciation of fine art.

She turned to the stiff tumanhofer, her face feeling like a frozen mask. "It's an interesting interpretation of my father's style. I shall show it to my mother and have your answer by tomorrow at breakfast. She will be tired after her venture to market. I suspect she will have dinner in her room and go early to bed, but I promise you I'll seek an audience this evening."

For a moment, the young artist's composure slipped. His eyes rounded in astonishment. "You seek an audience with your own mother?"

"My mother never forgets she is the second daughter of King Yellat." Tipper quickly turned away to hide her thoughts. Her mother had trouble remembering the day of the week but never the fact that she had worn a circlet crown of finest gold from the day she was born.

Tipper replaced the painting on the table. "I'll ask Gladyme to bring you all the candles you require. I'm afraid you will have your dinner in solitude again this evening. I will attend my mother in order to find an opportune moment to present your request."

"Your father?"

"As is his custom, he will not appear in the main house while there is a stranger present."

She heard his sigh. She could not look back lest she lose her resolve.

4

Impropriety

Beccaroon circled the main house in the fading light. The rosy rays of sunset tinted Verrin Schope's home so that the building looked made of pink marble. Beccaroon landed on the decorative parapet surrounding the flat roof of the mansion. Covered archways protruded from the patterned tiles of the floor. Each of these charming cupolas led to a stairway. Steps descended through the attic of the manor to the third floor.

The colorful bird strutted across the band of elaborate design that surrounded a smoother surface used for dancing. He remembered the many cotillions and summer concerts that had once been part of the grand house's activities. It had been years since friends had gathered to dance on this roof. So long ago that Tipper probably did not remember the spectacular events.

Beccaroon clicked his tongue against his beak and entered between pillars supporting a painted gable in the nearest cupola. At the bottom of the dark stairwell, a heavy wooden door blocked his path.

"Doors," he muttered under his breath. "Confounded nuisances."

At least Verrin Schope had had the courtesy to remove the knob and replace it with a bar handle. The parrot grabbed the metal lever with his beak and pulled down. The latch clicked, and he maneuvered the door open. Entering the dim hallway, he cast a grim look at the odious slab of wood. Obligation compelled him to pull the blasted thing shut. He sighed and reached for the handle.

"I'll get that," said Tipper from the shadows behind him. She breathed heavily as she glided past him. Her shoes made no sound as she hurried across the carpeted floor. "I saw you fly in and came to meet you. Where's Mother?"

"Behind me by five minutes at the most."

Tipper gasped. "I must find Bealomondore and make sure he doesn't cross paths with Mother."

"I don't approve of this scheme of yours, Tipper."

"I don't either, but sometimes one has to do what is distasteful."

"Does one?" asked Beccaroon as his girl raced away.

"Yes!" she called back over her shoulder. "If you have a scatter-brained mother and an absent father, the answer is yes!"

She disappeared around a corner. Beccaroon followed in his stately stride. "I believe," he said to the empty corridor, "that Boscamon will teach my young friend the efficacious nature of truth."

He ruffled his neck feathers, the image of a juggler throwing balls into the air disturbing his calm. The traditional view cast Boscamon as a mysterious conjurer manipulating daily circumstances. A circus performer who tossed balls into the air had never appealed to Beccaroon. Surely if someone had the power to control the universe, he would be more caring. As the magistrate, Beccaroon took his duties seriously.

He leaned toward there being a deity. Obviously, order came from somewhere beyond the scope of the temporal races. Although great minds could detect design in nature that had to be intelligently created, no one explained the phenomena to his satisfaction.

Nevertheless, in the end, balance was maintained. He pictured truth as a chunk of ice in a pond. One could push it beneath the water, but it would bob to the surface. He had instructed Tipper on the reality of choices. Action created reaction. There would be a reckoning for Tipper's deception. Experience would teach her the validity of his observations.

He strutted down the hall, following his girl, and muttered, "I hope the lesson doesn't hurt too much."

Tipper's thin leather soles beat a rapid rhythm on the wooden servants stair. She'd chosen the quickest route to the parlor, where she had last seen Bealomondore sipping a glass of wine and reading a book from her father's library.

Outside the door, she took a moment to slow her breathing and run through the lines she would use to put off the tumanhofer. After squaring her shoulders and lifting her chin, she swept into the room.

"My mother is about to arrive."

Bealomondore jumped to his feet. "I will be allowed an audience?"

"No, not tonight. I've explained. I will use the best of my diplomacy to present your case in a favorable light. Popping up out of nowhere and surprising her is the worst tack you can take. Please, avoid her at all costs. In the morning, at breakfast, I will tell you what I have accomplished."

The artist scowled, and Tipper held her breath, wondering if he would accept her terms. Finally he let out a sigh that seemed to deflate his shoulders.

"All right." He scooped up the book he had been reading. "Mind if I take this to my room? I doubt I will sleep tonight waiting for the verdict."

"Of course, Master Bealomondore, take the book. And if you would like, I will have Gladyme check on you before she goes to bed. Perhaps you would like her to bring you a light refreshment later?"

The tumanhofer bowed. "You are too kind."

Tipper hesitated. Was that a snide remark? No matter. She would have the artist out of the way.

She curtsied. "I fear we are not an easy family to get to know. My father is very much immersed in his work. My mother is of a nervous nature and doesn't like to have her routine disturbed. And I have not studied the social graces. I beg you to forgive us our inhospitable ways."

Bealomondore frowned again, but there was a touch of compassion in his gaze. "I fear that your family suffers at the hand of your habits."

Tipper felt her back stiffen and her chin come up. This tumanhofer had no business passing judgment on how they lived. "We are mostly content," she countered.

"Perhaps you have nothing to compare your present circumstances with, but surely your parents are aware that to squander a life is foolishness."

A rustle preceded the words pronounced behind Tipper. "Squander? Foolish?"

Horrified, Tipper whipped around to find her mother standing in the doorway.

"Do you already know of my purchase, Tipper?" Lady Peg looked over her shoulder. "Here they come now."

Grunting accompanied the arrival of something heavy. Rolan appeared in the doorway with a familiar grandfather clock angled on his back and shoulder. He held a rope to keep it from sliding.

Lady Peg gestured toward the far wall. "Right there, Rolan. Thank you so much. I've always wanted such a clock for that space, and this is just the thing. I do admit it was a bit dear. But perfect, don't you think, Tipper?" She gestured toward Bealomondore. "Give Rolan a hand, won't you? Help him ease it down to the floor. I'm so glad Rolan is strong. He's the best of neighbors, as I am sure you are aware."

Bealomondore shot across the room to give aid.

Lady Peg's face folded into lines of confusion. "I don't believe you *are* a neighbor, sir. Do I know you? Do you know Rolan? What are you doing in our house? We generally do not accept visitors. Company disturbs my husband."

Tipper's mother turned a worried look upon her daughter.

"This is Master Bealomondore, Mother. He's respectable and from a fine family on the coast, beyond the Sunset Mountains."

The tumanhofer faced Lady Peg and bowed deeply. "Madam, is the clock in precisely the right location? Do you want us to shift it left or right?"

"To the left three inches so that it is exactly between those two bookcases." Lady Peg tapped her finger against her chin. "No, no, I don't remember any Bealomondores. I don't know you at all."

Rolan and the tumanhofer shouldered the clock to one side. Bealomondore stepped back to eye the symmetry of the new location. Rolan cast Tipper an apologetic look.

She nodded, knowing full well the good farmer had tried his best to delay her mother's arrival.

"Is this satisfactory, Lady Peg?" Bealomondore nodded toward the clock.

"Not at all."

The tumanhofer turned back to gaze at the position of the huge piece. "I believe it is centered, Madam. Would you like us to obtain a measuring stick?"

"What *are* you talking about?"

"The clock. Precisely, the clock's position in relationship to the two bookcases."

Tipper's mother squared her shoulders and looked the visitor in the eye. "Young man, clocks do not have relationships with bookcases. At least not in my house. The whole idea is preposterous and, I believe, most improper. Tipper says you are respectable, but I am not convinced you even have an acceptable understanding of what is decent and upright."

Rolan stepped forward with humor barely concealed by his twitching lips. "Lady Peg, we must be reasonable. The clock is upright. I don't believe the young tumanhofer is completely off kilter."

The lady frowned. "You are right, and generally I respect your opinion. But I do not know any Bealomondores, Rolan. You can't say I do."

The gentleman farmer nodded. "But Mistress Tipper knows one, Lady Peg."

Her mother turned to Tipper. "You do? Which Bealomondore are you acquainted with?"

Tipper threw propriety to the wind and pointed to their guest. "That one."

She waited for the reprimand.

"Don't point, Tipper. There is no call to lower our standards of decorum."

Lady Peg glanced over the tumanhofer one more time. When her gaze returned to Rolan, her smile blossomed.

"Rolan, you are ever the good neighbor. Thank you for my excursion to Soebin. I enjoyed the company of your good wife, Zilla." She patted his brawny arm. "But please excuse me now. I'm tired, and there is a Bealomondore in my house. I must find Verrin Schope and inform him of this intrusion. And then I am going to bed. Tipper, have Gladyme bring me toast and warm milk, please."

"Yes, Mother."

Lady Peg strolled out of the room, looking very much like a regal noblewoman who was not one bit tired.

As soon as the door closed behind her, Bealomondore clapped his hands together.

"Does this mean I shall see Verrin Schope tonight? Will he come here to investigate the intrusion when Lady Peg informs him I am here?"

"Not a chance," said Rolan at the same time Tipper commented, "I doubt it."

Bealomondore looked from one to the other. "Does anything ever proceed in a natural manner in this household?"

Rolan and Tipper both answered, "Never."

5

Somewhat Truthful

Tipper stirred her tea, the tiny silver spoon ringing against the delicate porcelain cup.

"You're nervous, my dear," said Beccaroon.

"It's your fault."

Beccaroon tilted his head, and his eyes widened.

"Yes, you," said Tipper. She frowned and then imitated his voice. "'I don't approve of this scheme of yours, Tipper.'" She jabbed a fork into her sausage. Grease splattered on her plate as resentment laced her words. "The voice of conscience coming from a feathered friend. You kept me up most of the night."

Beccaroon returned to nibbling on a seedcake.

Tipper's next words froze on her lips as the door to the hall was flung open. Bealomondore came in with a light step and a smile on his face.

"Beautiful morning," he proclaimed and proceeded to take the chair directly across from his hostess.

His air of expectancy nearly crushed what little appetite Tipper had mustered this morning. She popped the bite of meat into her mouth, trying to deny the man's effect on her.

Beccaroon glanced out the tall windows. "The weather is, indeed, fine."

The tumanhofer smiled at the parrot. "Fine, yes, very fine." His eyes turned back to Tipper. She forced herself not to squirm under his steady gaze. She slowly chewed the morsel in her mouth and refused to look up.

Bealomondore sighed. Disappointment flowed into the room and surrounded them all.

Tipper swallowed, put down her fork, and folded her hands in her lap. "I am sorry, Master Bealomondore. It was impossible to show my father your fine painting."

"Perhaps today?" He spoke softly.

Tipper shook her head. "I regret that I have deceived you by allowing you to think that I would ever be able to win for you the post of apprentice."

She lifted her eyes enough to catch the shift in position of her guest. He pulled back, anger replacing the listlessness of remorse.

She hurried on. "My father is not in the position to take on a student at this time."

"You knew this yesterday?"

She nodded.

"And the day before?"

She nodded again.

Bealomondore stood, his chair scraping harshly across the floor. "I do not understand your motives, nor do I wish to. Good day, Mistress Tipper. I ask Boscamon to bless you and your family. Your needs are greater than mine."

Tipper's head jerked up. The artist was halfway to the door. "What do you want me to do with your painting?"

He did not turn. "Keep it. It is not my talent displayed but a copy of another's."

The door closed firmly behind him.

"And," said Beccaroon, "the paint is still too fresh to transport."

"Father put his oil paintings in a deep wooden frame." She sniffed.

"He packaged them to travel faceup, but in such a way that nothing could smear the picture." She raised the napkin to wipe away a tear. "I remember sitting on the bench in his studio, smelling the paint, watching him construct the box, wishing I could draw pretty pictures too."

The door opened again, and Tipper lifted her head, hoping to see the tumanhofer. Another apology might ease her conscience.

Her mother entered the room, gliding to the table with yards of gossamer fabric in shades of yellow and orange floating around her.

"I spoke with Master Bealomondore in the hall. He is leaving us." She sat in her place and rang a silver bell by her glass. "Such a pity too. Your father wanted to meet with him tonight. He's actually heard of the young man. Tipper, why didn't you tell me he is a promising artist?"

Gladyme came into the room with a plate of scrambled eggs, muffins, and sliced fruit.

"Here you are, Lady Peg. I'm sorry there's no cream for your brew this morning. The cow's gone off with thieves during the night."

Lady Peg picked up her fork and nodded as she gazed with delight at her meal. "Oh, this looks delicious, Gladyme. Never mind the cow. She was a most contrary creature without a lick of sense."

Tipper couldn't keep her face from twisting into a grimace. They needed the cow. Milk, cheese, cream, butter. What would they do without Helen, the crotchety brown cow? Where had the barn dragon been? She turned her look of dismay to her parrot friend.

Beccaroon leveled a beady eye at the housekeeper. "Thieves?"

"Yes, Sir Beccaroon. Lipphil's out looking for clues at this very moment. Tracks or an open gate is what he expects to find."

Beccaroon hopped down from his chair. "Excuse me, ladies. I shall go investigate."

Lady Peg smiled his way. "Thank you, dear friend. It is so nice to have someone around who takes charge and investigates. Investigating is not Verrin Schope's strongest pursuit. Research, yes. Creating, yes. Inventing, yes. But investigating domestic irregularities rarely interests him." She took a bite of melon. "Having the local magistrate at breakfast on the day the cow takes off is most convenient."

"Yes, Madam." Beccaroon bowed. "I shall report back when I have something to tell."

"Oh, that isn't necessary," said Lady Peg. She smiled as a thought came to her. "Perhaps you should tell Tipper."

Beccaroon passed through the door to the veranda. "Certainly, Lady Peg. As you wish."

Gladyme poured tea into her ladyship's cup, then removed the parrot's plate and bowl. She bustled out the door to the kitchen.

"Now tell me, Tipper," said Lady Peg, "why you are so gloomy. I see the trace of a tear on your cheek. Your father will be in here in a flash if I tell him his darling girl is unhappy."

"Mother, Papa never comes in a flash. I've been unhappy for years."

"My goodness, I think that must be an exaggeration. Years? I would have noticed, dear one. And your father would have noticed for sure. He is much more perceptive about emotions and problems and impending doom than I am."

Tipper felt fresh tears push from behind her eyes. She batted her eyelashes quickly to force them back. If only she, too, had a pretend relationship with her father, she would dump all her troubles on him and let them disappear. But Tipper was obliged to live in reality.

"Mother, you didn't tell Bealomondore that Papa wanted to see him this evening, did you?"

"Tonight, not this evening. Your father will still be working in the evening."

"Did you tell him?"

"Who?"

"Bealomondore."

"What?"

"That Papa wants to see him."

"Now what would be the point in telling him? The man is leaving, so of course he cannot meet with your father. Tipper, honestly, sometimes your logic runs around chasing rabbit tails."

"Rabbit trails."

"Your own tail, like a dog. Where are the dragons this morning?"

"Sunning themselves."

"A good occupation. Keeps them out of trouble. If they aren't moving, they can't be into mischief." Lady Peg dropped her hands to the table, a knife loaded with butter in one and a muffin in the other. "Tipper! Were you crying over Master Bealomondore's departure? This will not do, you know."

She didn't give Tipper a chance to answer but continued while waving the buttery knife. "I don't know any of the Bealomondores, and though your father seemed acquainted with the family, this young man did not have the courtesy to delay his departure long enough to speak with your father. And if he wants to court you," she said, gesturing wildly with the knife, "he must speak to Verrin Schope. It is only right."

A blob of butter sailed from the tip of Lady Peg's knife and landed on the tablecloth beside Tipper's plate.

"He didn't want to court me, Mother."

"Good. I'm leaving this afternoon to visit my sister. The picture you gave me last night is lovely. Your father liked it too, though he said he didn't paint it. He did make me a box to transport it in." She sighed, picked up her napkin, and dabbed the corner of her mouth.

"We couldn't have Bealomondore hanging around, trying to win your affections without a proper chaperon, and your father certainly isn't that."

As she wiped up the dab of butter, Tipper spent a moment wondering how her mother had acquired a box. Had Lipphil made it? Had she found an old one in the studio? She bit back these questions and presented one that might possibly elicit a straight answer. "Mother, how did you know that Bealomondore is a promising artist?"

"You must attend more carefully when you are spoken to, Tipper. Your father told me."

"He did?" Tipper's eyes narrowed as she thought. Gladyme and Lipphil would not have mentioned the tumanhofer's talent. Rolan and Zilla wouldn't have either. Sometimes her mother baffled her.

Obviously unaware of her daughter's confusion, Peg sipped her tea. "Yes, your father expressed his good opinion in no uncertain terms. And, of course, Bealomondore did do an excellent rendition of the fountain and the flowers around it. But if you correspond with your suitor, my dear, urge him to develop his own style instead of copying your father's."

"He is not my suitor, Mother."

"The tumanhofer may not suit you, dear one, and I can't say I blame you. There was that bit of nonsense about the furniture, but you must be open to the idea of someday accepting some man as your bemused."

"Betrothed."

"Generally when a man falls head over heels in love, he is befuddled. A more polite way of saying that is bemused. Befuddled implies a simpleton, and I don't think your father would allow marriage to a simpleton. Not that simpletons can't be rather nice. But he would rather announce your befuddlement to a man with a bit of brains."

"Engagement."

"Oh, I do hope you don't have a day filled with engagements. I need you to help me get ready to depart."

Tipper pushed back her chair and rose. "I'll help you, Mother."

"That's nice, Tipper. But let's postpone that until after we pack. I really don't have time to dally today. I'm going on a trip."

6

Dreams?

Tipper sat on a stone bench, let her slippers fall from her sore feet, and wiggled her toes. She sniffed the soothing fragrance of the giant pordimum blooms. Evening always brought out the perfumes in the garden.

Given the lazy atmosphere, she had to fight the urge to stretch out on the bench and close her eyes. She couldn't remember ever being so tired. She did recall the last time she sat for more than one minute. It had been at breakfast when her mother announced her intention to depart that very day.

Beccaroon perched on the edge of the fountain, eying the gold, ruby, and sapphire fish swimming in the circular pool.

Tipper gazed at him fondly, knowing the swishglimmers were safe. Her friend would never stoop to snatching an ornamental fish for a snack.

Overwhelming fatigue banished the urge to get up and fling her arms around the big bird. She loved him, but he didn't like displays of affection, and her body ached from running hither and yon for her mother, lifting and carrying and sorting. She was also weary of holding her tongue. It did no good to argue with Mother, just as it did no good to argue with Bec.

She frowned, considering all the fuss they had gone through today because of her mother's odd disposition. Lady Peg had once been Princess Peg. She'd been banished from the royal city, and Tipper secretly believed the action had been for the good of the country.

Sir Beccaroon, on the other hand, had the personality for leadership. Tipper remembered why she had sought him out. He'd taken many burdens off her shoulders that day.

"Thank you for all your help," she said.

He turned his head until he almost faced backward. He nodded in her direction. "You're welcome."

"And thank you for arranging the use of Lord Pinterbastian's carriage, horses, and servants to tend to Mother on her journey."

"You're welcome again, and no need to go into all the other incidentals I arranged today. You know I enjoy a list of things to do and the satisfaction of getting them done."

"Did you find out anything about our cow?"

"Helen is back in her stall."

She raised her eyebrows. "How ever did you manage that?"

"I didn't really." He turned to face her. His elegant tail dipped into the water. A throaty growl revealed his displeasure. He raised the feathers, shook a fine spray of droplets back into the small pool, and flew the short distance to her bench.

Tipper leaned against him. "How did we get our cow back?"

"When I went looking for your mother yesterday, I noticed a camp of unfamiliar people. This morning I sent several rangers to keep watch over them. Your dragon Trisoda was already there, chittering and scolding from a safe distance at the top of a tree. The men found the tiny beast's clamor quite amusing until the rangers showed up. The louts were arrested, and Trisoda coaxed Helen home."

"I should tell him thank you."

"Trisoda?"

"Yes."

"Do you think he'd understand you?"

"Sometimes I think the domesticated dragons do understand us."

Beccaroon chortled.

Tipper sat up and scowled at her friend. "Really, Bec. Sometimes I think they would speak if they could—that words are formed in their minds but there's no way for them to vocalize." She clasped her hands in her lap to keep from shaking a finger at her friend. "Zabeth, in particular, has a very expressive face, and she often reacts to what I say."

Beccaroon clicked his beak. "Your heart is too tender, Tipper. You give a beast attributes that belong only to thinking creatures."

She bristled. "Dragons have personality, a sense of humor, character, and can be cunning. Why do you say they don't think?"

"Awk! A young girl's romantic notion. Next you'll be telling me that hens gossip."

The emerlindian lass lifted her pointed chin. "Perhaps they do."

"If they do, that would make them a less palatable choice for your next meal."

Tipper stood. "Oh, really! I have never eaten a dragon, nor will I. Chickens and dragons are entirely different."

"One's a pet, and the other is food."

"I'm not even sure you can say a dragon is a pet. They seem entirely too independent to be ranked with a dog or cat."

"You're tired and fanciful." Beccaroon pointed to the manor. "Go eat the sandwich Gladyme is making for you and go to bed."

"What are you going to do?"

"I will check my territory for intruders before I turn in."

"I'll leave your bedroom window open." She leaned over and kissed the top of his head. "You don't know how relieved I am that you'll be here until Mother returns."

Beccaroon ruffled his feathers until his neck bulged twice as large as normal. He squinted one eye, looking very indignant. "Perhaps in that time I can teach you to treat my person with more respect."

"You won't indulge me a few kisses?"

"Awk!" He spread his wings to fly away, but Tipper stopped him.

"Look at this, Bec. Isn't this odd?"

He came to her side and examined the row of rocks providing an edging to a flower bed.

"What?" He peered where she pointed.

"The rocks are the wrong color."

"A trick of the light."

"No, these should be almost white, and they are not. You can see how dark they are, can't you? Almost black."

"Perhaps, but I can't remember how light they were before. Check them in the morning, Tipper. I can't believe this portends something other than that someone carelessly spilled something on them. Good night, now."

He turned and flew away, over the lush forest and out of sight.

Tipper picked up one of the rocks and noted how very light it was. The surface didn't feel sticky. She dropped it back where it belonged and left the mystery unsolved. Her brain could not handle anomalies tonight.

She visited the kitchen but could eat only half of her meal.

When she rose to go to bed, the housekeeper shook her head. "You'll have bad dreams on an empty stomach."

"I'm sorry, Gladyme. I'm too tired to appreciate your fine food."

"Off to bed then." Gladyme made shooing motions with her hands. "I'll have a hearty breakfast ready for you in the morning."

Tipper smiled her thanks and left the cozy kitchen. She made a detour to open the window in the chamber where Beccaroon would roost when he returned, then went to her bedroom.

While she brushed out her long hair and rebraided it for the night, she gazed at the family portrait on her vanity. She was the ghost-white baby in her mother's lap. All emerlindians came into the world ex-quisitely fair, and as they aged, their skin reflected the benefits of maturing. Wisdom, experience, and knowledge all revealed themselves on the outside of an emerlindian in a glorious brown complexion.

Although twenty years had passed, Tipper's mother looked exactly the same as she did in the portrait—wide-eyed, full of wonder, with just a hint of authority in the tilt of her chin. No matter how inane her commands might be, her mother was accustomed to complete compliance.

Of course, Verrin Schope had painted the portrait. When he fin-ished the likeness of mother and daughter, he painted himself as if he stood behind them the whole time.

"Just as it is now, Papa." She picked up the picture and tapped her father's image on the chest. "You were not really there as you are not really here. Why do we keep up the pretense for the general public?"

She knew the answer to her question. It was for her mother's peace of mind that they pretended Verrin Schope still manned the helm of their family ship.

She frowned at the picture. "What are you doing that you cannot tend to your wife, daughter, and home?"

She did not know the answer to that one.

Tipper blew out her candles and crawled in between clean, cool sheets.

The creak of hinges brought Tipper out of a pleasant sleep. She lis-tened, but the silence of the room allowed her to sink beneath con-sciousness once more.

Again she roused. Breathing. Not her own. She lay very still, con-centrating. Nothing.

I'm dreaming that bad dream Gladyme warned against.

She opened her eyes. Darkness draped the furniture, the curtains, the walls.

Nothing's here.

A rustle disturbed the quiet. Tipper moved her eyes toward the direction of the sound. In the round mirror above her vanity, two eyes peered into the room.

She stared. The eyes blinked. She swallowed.

A mouth below the eyes opened, grinning.

"Are you awake, Tipper?"

"No."

"Come, now. I don't have much time."

The eyes and mouth shifted, moving out of the mirror frame. The bed behind her sank as if someone sat on the edge. She realized the image had been a reflection. The person, a very real person, patted her on the shoulder, giving it a squeeze, then a shake.

"Tipper-too, get up!"

Only one person called her Tipper-too, and that person had not been around for a very long time.

"Papa?"

"Well, it better not be any other man in your room in the middle of the night."

She sat up and twisted around to face him. He wore black from his neck down. A robe of some kind. His complexion had darkened considerably. She reached for him, tentatively touching his arm. In a swift lunge, he enveloped her in a strong embrace.

"My girl, you're a young woman now. Beautiful, just as your mother said."

Tears streamed down Tipper's face, and she sniffed loudly. "Have you come home for good?"

He leaned back and looked her in the eyes. "I've been living a very complicated life, but I do believe I have solved the mystery that will end my constant journeying."

He wiped tears from her cheeks with his thumbs. "I have only a minute or two before I fade again. Tell me, where is your mother?"

"She went to see Aunt Soo."

"Dribbling drummerbugs, that puts a twist in my string for sure."

"Papa?"

"Yes?"

"My arms are sinking into you."

"Rather, going through me, Tipper. Not to worry. I shall try to return tomorrow night."

The space before her was empty. "Papa?"

Tipper jumped out of bed and ran down the hall on bare feet. She stopped at Beccaroon's bedroom and pounded on the door.

"Aaawwk! Come in!"

She wrenched the handle down and rushed into the room. "Papa was here. In my room. I spoke to him. He's gone."

Beccaroon shook his head. "Dreaming."

"I was not!"

The bird tilted his head, and moonlight glinted in his wide eyes. "Were the lights on?"

"No."

"What were you thinking about before you went to bed?"

Tipper remembered the portrait, Gladyme's comment about having dreams, and her strong desire to ask her father questions. She didn't answer Beccaroon.

The bird nipped her arm.

"Ouch!"

"Did you remember to pinch yourself to see if you were awake?"

Tipper rubbed her arm. "No, but I felt Papa's arms around me. He hugged me."

"And you hugged him back?"

"Yes, but—"

Beccaroon cocked his head. "But?"

Tipper's chin sank to her chest. "My arms went through him, and he disappeared."

The bird remained silent.

"He did say he'd try to come back tomorrow night."

Beccaroon stretched his wings and let them settle to his sides. "We'll sit up together and wait for him."

"You believe me."

"I want to believe you."

"Was I dreaming?"

"Maybe. Maybe not."

In Disarray

Beccaroon perched on the back of a chaise longue and surveyed the view from the nearby window. Moonlight bathed the veranda, muting the pinkish tinge so that the marble took on a bluish-gray color. He sighed over the sharp contrasts showing in the dark vegetation of the rain forest beyond. He'd much rather sleep in the canopy. At least Tipper had opened the window so the night fragrances danced in with the slight breeze.

His girl gave an indelicate snort and shifted position where she lay on the chaise. She had intended to stay awake and await the arrival of her father.

To occupy the time, Tipper had sung for him. She played a harpenstead, holding it across her lap and strumming chords or plucking the strings. Her soft, clear voice filled the lonely room with cheer. Beccaroon knew she had no idea how her music calmed those who heard her. Or if she sang a rousing tune, her audience responded with vigor. With proper training, her talent would outshine the greatest singers on any metropolitan stage.

Her tunes became mellower. Her voice deepened with emotion. At last, she put her instrument down and chose conversation. After three hours of small talk and yawning, she'd finally succumbed to natural fatigue.

The moonlight touched her as well. Her pale blue dress fairly glowed with the lavish luminosity from the sky. Her fair skin and hair glistened as if kissed by a shimmer of starlight.

Beccaroon sighed. Tipper's gift of voice and musical ability astounded him. The best warblers in his forest did not surpass her. He doubted she comprehended the extent of her talent. She should have been given the opportunity to excel, not left under the guidance of an old bird in a tropical jungle.

Circumstances could not be changed. Bringing up the sweet child without the aid of a fully witted parent in residence had been a trial, but Verrin Schope had charged the big bird to stand in his stead should something happen to him. Three days later, the artist had disappeared.

The parrot clicked his black tongue against his beak, then preened, cleaning his chest feathers. He stopped midmotion and tilted his head toward the door. Voices in the hall approached Tipper's bedroom.

Beccaroon stretched his wings. The two minor dragons in the room roused from their slumber. Junkit shook his head as if to force himself awake. Zabeth came to her feet and arched her back like a cat before settling and staring at the door.

The handle rattled and clicked as the latch released. Three indistinct figures walked through and paused in the semidarkness. The two dragons hissed. Junkit batted his wings, threatening attack.

"You said she was expecting us?" A rumbling voice came from the shortest and roundest of the three.

A lean figure in voluminous robes twitched his hand in the air. "Lights, lights, a bit of starlight and moon glow." The air in the room suddenly held bits of shining material giving off miniscule beams. One orb the size of a fist floated over the empty bed. It looked exactly like a small full moon, right down to the gray shadows along the face.

In the light, Beccaroon recognized the third person as his missing friend. He opened his beak to speak, then clamped it shut. Had Verrin Schope returned in the company of friend or foe?

"Oh dear, tut, tut," said the old o'rant who produced the twinkling lights and miniature moon. He shook a finger at Junkit and

Zabeth. "Behave and greet friendly visitors with some vestige of courtesy."

The dragons chittered and relaxed as if reassured by the gruff command.

Beccaroon watched with narrowed eyes. Perhaps these were friendly visitors, perhaps not.

The tall man gestured, and lunar moths escaped from his sleeve. The flimsy bits of pale gray fluttered about the room before following the moonbeams out the open window. The man seemed not to notice the insects and addressed the chittering dragons. "Much better. You have good manners, and I deeply regret that you are summarily ignored by most people. But of course, I am not most people. What is it, Librettowit?"

He bent to listen to the shorter man's interruption. "Harrumph!" He turned and bowed to the dragons. "My sincere apologies for startling you." He gestured toward Tipper. "There's the girl and a bird. This is the guardian, I take it. Pleased to meet you, Sir Beccaroon."

The parrot inclined his head but managed to pin Verrin Schope with a glare. His voice scratched the night air. "Welcome home, Verrin Schope. It's been a long time."

The emerlindian spoke softly. "Unavoidable."

Beccaroon waited for more information, but his friend remained silent.

As if the old o'rant could read Bec's thoughts, he jumped into the lull in conversation. "Yes, exactly, explanations!" he said. "Tut, tut, oh dear. We've disturbed the natives."

Verrin Schope strode across the room and knelt beside his daughter. He gently touched her shoulder. "Tipper, wake up."

She stirred and sat up, directly into her father's arms. He held her for a moment with his eyes closed, breathing deeply as if the scent of her replenished his soul. Beccaroon blinked his eyes and wondered at the love between them after the extended separation.

After a long, quiet moment, Verrin Schope stood, taking his daughter by the hand and pulling her to his side. He beamed at the assembled company.

"Gentlemen, this is Tipper, my daughter." He gestured to the guests. "These esteemed scholars have aided me in returning to you. Wizard Fenworth and his librarian, Librettowit."

Tipper curtsied.

Verrin Schope inclined his head toward the grand parrot. "And as you have guessed, this is Sir Beccaroon, a cherished friend of the family."

Librettowit and Wizard Fenworth bent at the waist, acknowledging the introduction.

Beccaroon bowed. "My pleasure."

"Papa, the lights." Tipper's face reflected the wonder of the miniature night sky suspended in her room.

"Fenworth is a renowned wizard in his country, Amara."

Tipper gasped. Her mouth dropped open, and she closed it with a snap. "That's on the other side of the world. How—?"

"Through a contraption they call a gateway."

"A gateway," Beccaroon repeated the unfamiliar word. "Where is this gateway?"

Verrin Schope rubbed his chin. "Actually, the gateway is in Lady Peg's closet."

"Mother's closet?" Tipper glanced around the room, peering at each of the men. "You came through Mother's closet?"

Beccaroon watched the two strangers nod. The librarian's face showed his embarrassment. The wizard shook leaves from his straggly gray hair.

The parrot cocked his head and quickly analyzed his response to the situation. Of course, he was pleased. His secret concern that Verrin Schope had met an untimely end vanished. The artist breathed, of that Beccaroon could testify.

He felt relief that Tipper had not hallucinated the visit from her father. The thought that perhaps the daughter had begun to exhibit the eccentric tendencies of her mother had crossed his mind.

But these strangers? Who were these unusual men who claimed to be from Amara? The hazardous journey to the other side of the world virtually cut off communication. Knowledge of civilization from that distant shore consisted mostly of seafarers' wild tales, speculation, and a generous dose of fabrication, all for the sake of a good yarn.

The men held Verrin Schope's esteem, but could it be that his old friend was enthralled by some magic? The elderly man scattered tiny stars into the air with a flick of his fingertips. Could he also scatter a normally intelligent man's wits?

"Papa." Tipper pulled on Verrin Schope's sleeve. "We must make our guests comfortable."

Beccaroon did not miss the quick, searching look Verrin Schope cast at the wizard.

The old man nodded. "We'll stay. Have to, don't we? The three of us shattered the gateway when we came through. Probably Librettowit's width, wouldn't you think?"

The tumanhofer librarian sputtered. "A gateway's an unreliable portal when the base has been disrupted. That's why we came, isn't it? To restore the base?"

The wizard's expression stretched lengthwise into a mournful mask of woe. "Disrupted the universe by tying the ends to a piece of stone destined to be carved into statues. But how were we to know? How? It's as much Verrin Schope's fault as our own." He twisted his sorrowful expression into a glare and aimed it at his librarian.

"Don't you go accusing me! I'm not the sculptor. I'm a librarian, not a wizard either. Seems you should have surmised the danger."

Fenworth glowered. "Wizards do not predict the future."

Librettowit scowled. "But it was a wizard who chose the anchor for the gateway. If I had anything to do with it, it was only that I did as you told me. 'Hold this tight!' 'Stick this through that loop.' 'Twist this together with that.' Do I even sound like I know what's going on? No! And I don't. Theory, I understand. Application is all up to you, Fenworth." He shuddered. "Don't give me any of this 'we' disturbed the universe."

"Excuse me," said Beccaroon. "Could we start at the beginning?"

"Good idea!" The wizard shuffled toward the vanity bench. "Mind if I sit while you explain?"

"No, not at all," said Tipper. "May I get you a drink?"

He turned a speculative gaze upon his hostess. "Do you have any water dripped through a mannacap shell with a twist of pure parnot in a tall Izden glass?"

"No." Tipper shook her head, looked at her father, and raised an eyebrow.

Verrin Schope shrugged and whispered, "Don't worry overmuch about it."

The wizard sank to the bench, sighing. Beccaroon thought he heard twigs snapping as the man bent. Fenworth reached into his robe. "Never mind. It seems I remembered to bring my own."

He pulled out a yellow glass containing a bubbling liquid. He took a sip, swished it around in his mouth, swallowed, and smiled.

"Now," he said, "the bird was going to explain. From the beginning, I believe. I'm ready." He nodded benevolently at Beccaroon. "You may begin."

"Are you related to Lady Peg by any chance?" Beccaroon asked.

"Never met her. Of course, we could be related without ever

having met. But no, I believe we are not, other than we are both dwellers of the world we inhabit." He frowned at the parrot. "Are you stalling?"

"Not at all. I have no intention of beginning."

"Then why am I sitting? Why am I drinking?" He held up a finger. "Don't tell me. I know. I am sitting because I am old and tired. I am drinking because I am thirsty." He let his hand drop to his knee. "Enough about me."

Librettowit sat on a short footstool in front of an upholstered wingback chair. "Fenworth, the parrot is not the one explaining but the one asking for an explanation."

"I thought he might want to tell us what has been happening here."

The librarian sighed. "I'll explain."

Verrin Schope and Tipper sat down on the chaise.

Librettowit glanced at the wizard, who was occupied picking a tangled lizard out of his long beard. Apparently satisfied that he would not be interrupted, the librarian began. "Twenty or so years ago, Fenworth and I endeavored to construct a gateway that would reach farther than any had ever reached before."

"Ambitious," muttered the wizard. "Tumanhofers are known to be ambitious."

Librettowit twisted his mouth in an annoyed grimace at his cohort but continued. "At Fenworth's insistence, he took my architectural drawings and applied them to a complicated weave, which he further elaborated upon."

"Ended with a preposition," said the wizard as he let the lizard go. "Scholar and all, and he still ends a sentence with a preposition."

"Fenworth anchored the gateway to a stone," Librettowit explained.

Verrin Schope cleared his throat. "An exceptionally fine piece of marble."

"The weave was too tight," said Librettowit.

"The stone was too loose," said Fenworth.

"The marble tumbled into the gateway and landed in my studio," said Verrin Schope. "I thought it had been delivered while you, your mother, and I were away visiting her relatives."

Librettowit looked apologetically at Tipper. "Fenworth and I were called away on a rather urgent bit of business for Paladin and didn't immediately discover the accident."

Fenworth dipped his finger in his drink and pulled out a twist of fruit. "Thwarted a plague."

Librettowit shook his head. "Brought rain to the farmers."

Fenworth popped the bite in his mouth and sighed, "Plague."

"Rain."

"Plague."

Librettowit turned back to Tipper and Beccaroon. He mouthed the word *rain*.

The wizard blew puffs of cloud out of his mouth like smoke rings. They formed into letters spelling *plague* and floated above his librarian's head. Librettowit took off his oversized hat and waved it through the word, dispensing the small clouds.

"Bah!" He slapped the soft, mangled cap back on his head. "We didn't get back for a couple of years, and soon after we did, Verrin Schope stepped through the gateway."

"Only part of him," corrected Fenworth.

"True. Only part of him."

"The gateway was functioning at a substandard efficiency," put in Tipper's father. "The entry had slipped, moving from some point in my studio, through the house, and stopping in your mother's closet."

Tipper turned to look at her father. Her eyes widened. "You're becoming transparent."

"Yes, I'm slipping, moving back toward the gateway."

Tipper sputtered. "B-but you said the gateway shattered."

Fenworth tipped his glass up and drank the last drop. "He should be all right."

"Should be?" asked Beccaroon.

"In theory, he will bounce off the closed entry and return here reassembled."

"Theory?" whispered Tipper.

"Goodness, girl," Fenworth blustered. "We just broke the gateway, so that theory hasn't been tested yet. Sit tight a minute, and we'll find out if we've got it right or not."

Beccaroon turned to ask Verrin Schope for clarification. Unfortunately, his friend had already vanished.

Tipper jumped to her feet with a tiny screech.

"Excitable child," said the wizard. "If he doesn't return, that's when you should holler."

Healing

Tipper stood, clenching her fingers into a tight fist, then releasing them to stretch her hand into an open gesture of helplessness.

"Where is he?" she asked no one in particular.

No one answered.

She turned to the wizard. "Should I go to Mother's room? He could be hurt, right? He could be in the closet, crumpled on the floor, in pain, alone!"

She started for the door. Junkit and Zabeth flew above her head.

Fenworth's voice followed her out of the room. "Great imagination. Creative, like her father. Is there a draft coming from the hall? Shut the door!"

Tipper picked up her skirts and ran down the hall. She burst into her mother's dark bedroom and raced to the closet door. Both Junkit and Zabeth screeched. The door swung open and whacked her in the face, knocking her to the floor.

"Tipper!" Her father knelt beside her. "Are you hurt?"

The minor dragons landed beside her and shifted nervously as they tried to sidle closer.

She struggled to sit up. "Are *you* hurt?"

"Me? No." The darkness concealed his expression, but she recognized confusion in his voice. "Why would I be hurt?"

She sighed and relaxed against the floor, giving up any effort to rise. "That wizard and his librarian didn't say one word that encouraged me to believe you'd come back alive."

"You'll get used to them. They have an odd way of communicating, but both are extremely intelligent."

Tipper felt tears welling up and sternly suppressed them. She would not cry like an incompetent numskull. Instead, she focused on her injury, putting a hand to her forehead.

Only a narrow path of light invaded the room from the open doorway. Verrin Schope gestured toward the dragons. "Back up a bit, please." Junkit and Zabeth scooted out of the way. Her father placed his hand over hers. "We need better light."

A glowing globe appeared above his shoulder. Tipper gasped. "What? How?"

"Let me see that bump." He gently pried her hand away from her forehead.

Tipper winced as he touched the sore spot, but her eyes studied the eerie light. "Did you do that?"

"I didn't mean to."

"Not my head. The light."

"That's going to be black-and-blue in the morning. We need some ice." He reached under his coat into his tunic and pulled out a small, blue pillowlike object. "Hold this on the bump."

Tipper took it. "It's cold."

"Yes. Do you feel dizzy?"

She shook her head gingerly.

"Let me help you up." He put one arm around her waist and placed his hand in hers. With seemingly no effort, he had her on her feet. "Pain?"

"A little."

"Where?"

"On my forehead, of course, and…"

He let her go and rummaged through his pockets. "Yes, dear?"

"Well," she hesitated. This man might be her father, but she really didn't know him very well. It had been a long, long time since she'd ridden on his shoulders or sat in his lap or had his help changing into her nightgown.

"Oh," he said and chuckled. "Shall we say the other pain is on your 'sit-down cushion'? Yours is not very well padded."

She remembered this tone of voice, and warm memories flooded her heart. She laughed.

Verrin Schope glanced at her and smiled, then pulled something from an inner pocket. "Here he is."

In her father's hand sat the smallest green dragon Tipper had ever seen. He was half the size of Zabeth, who was a great deal smaller than Junkit. The two dragons flew into the air, circling her father and eying the petite creature on his palm.

With one hand on her elbow, her father guided her to a chair. "Just sit here, and Grandur and I will ease your discomfort."

Tipper sat. "Grandur?"

"This is a healing dragon, and yes, his name is Grandur. I realize it is a bit incongruous, but they are born with their names already in place. Grandur informed me of his name right after he hatched."

Tipper put her face in her hands. "I think I hit my head harder than I thought."

"Are you dizzy now? Do you feel sick to your stomach? How's your vision?"

"The last is my problem." She raised her head. "I see a light that cannot be there. And a dragon named Grandur. And I'm hearing a voice that sounds like my father's, but my father never talked nonsense, and this voice is relaying all sorts of absurd bits of absurdity."

He lifted one eyebrow and looked sternly at Tipper. "Tipper-too, 'absurd bits of absurdity' is redundant."

She grinned up at him, remembering the silly banter they'd enjoyed when she was small. Wrinkling her nose at him, she responded as she would have fifteen years earlier. "Nonsensical bits of nonsense."

"That's my daughter. You haven't lost your sense of humor. As long as you have a wit to call your own, you will be just fine."

He turned her hand over in her lap and put the tiny dragon in her palm. Grandur hopped several times, then nestled into her cupped hand. She expected him to be cold and rough skinned, but instead his little body radiated a comforting heat, and smooth, velvety skin covered his feet and stomach.

Her father kept one hand over hers and placed the fingertips of his other on the swollen knot on her forehead.

"Just relax. This will only take a moment."

Tipper took a deep breath and let it out slowly. The pain eased from the bump. A tingle spread from the top of her head to her toes. She smiled.

The anxiety in her mind dissipated. Her father producing light out of thin air would be explained. The important thing was that he had returned unharmed after fading away. The little dragon was not so unusual, just a dragon in a smaller version than she normally saw. Not that she saw many dragons. Having two in their home and one in the barn was three more than most families possessed. And the Grandur-naming-himself thing...? Father would explain.

The restorative procedure that took away the pain on her forehead expanded to include some core of her being. She felt the contentment that had eluded her for so many years. For one moment, she thought she could reach out and gather into her hand something that held peace and love and joy. She opened her eyes and saw only her father, the green dragon, and her mother's vacant bed. Her eyes widened. The empty bed pierced her contentment, leaving a disturbing hole.

Her father patted her hand and spoke to her concern. "Concentrate on the glimmer of hope. Focus not on the shadows of dismay." Peace again flooded her.

When Verrin Schope drew back, Tipper reached up and felt her forehead. No bump. No soreness to the touch. Grandur moved from her hand to her knee and peered at the other two dragons.

Her father cleared his throat. "Do you want us to repair the damage to your backside?"

She giggled and shook her head. "It's better. I think it will mend on its own."

Grandur jumped off her lap and flew to Junkit and Zabeth. The three chittered as if communicating. To Tipper it sounded like a conversation in some whistling, chirping language.

"Were Junkit and Zabeth born with names?" she asked.

"Probably. But no one with the ability to understand them captured the name. Subsequently, no one has called them by their birth names. They may have forgotten," said her father. "I'll ask."

He fell silent, and all three dragons turned toward him, stopping their chatter and looking for all the world as if they were paying attention. But her father said nothing.

He smiled. "They did have other names, but they have grown accustomed to the names given to them and would not change now." He laid one of his long-fingered, fine-boned hands on her shoulder and squeezed. "They assure me that you are the best of mistresses, even though your ability to communicate is somewhat stunted."

"I'm their mistress?"

"A formality only. A courtesy title. No one is really the master or mistress of a dragon. Only a fool would believe he has anything but the privilege to request cooperation from one of these magnificent beasts."

Junkit, Zabeth, and Grandur must have understood his comment. They stood straighter and puffed out their tiny chests. Tipper grinned at their antics as Junkit swaggered in front of the other two. Then a thought wiped the smile from her face.

"Do they understand everything you say?"

"Yes."

"And everything I say?"

"Yes."

"Oh dear."

Her father's arm slipped around her shoulders. "Would you like to tell me whatever it is that you would rather Zabeth and Junkit did not let slip?"

"I think I would."

"And it's about?"

"Having money to live on for over fifteen years without you."

Verrin Schope rubbed his hand over his chin. "And?"

Tipper blinked back tears and looked at her hands folded in her lap. "And your art."

She heard his sharply indrawn breath, but he gently took her hand. "My intuition tells me that this is something of great import. More than you could surmise, not knowing all the circumstances." He hooked her arm in his and started for the door to the hall. "We shall need wise counsel. Shall we rejoin Fenworth, Librettowit, and Sir Beccaroon in your room?"

Tipper allowed her father to lead her. Wise counsel? A crazy wizard, a prickly librarian, and a grand parrot? Yes, they should ask Beccaroon what course was best to take. If only she didn't have to confess to her father before Bec could offer his advice.

Verrin Schope gave her arm a tug. "Come, child. March forward. Problems are never as big once you've faced them head on."

Tipper sighed. Her experience proved that problems could multiply in the wink of an eye, even while you tried to stare them down.

9

Unbalanced

They sat in the silent bedroom, Tipper's room, but now it felt more like a judge's chambers, and she was the criminal. Beccaroon might be her advocate. The two men from Amara would be the jury. And her father? He would be the judge. The certainty of who played what roles added to her tension.

She didn't know what to expect from the strangers. Bec would most likely allow her to weigh her crimes herself, using the strict standards he'd instilled in her. But how would her father react? With rage?

After her explanation of her dealings with Hanner and Master Dodderbanoster, Tipper expected her father's temper to explode. Over the years, this image of his anger had been at the back of her mind many times. She had even hoped the discovery of her pilfering among his treasures might bring him home. But the reality before her loomed larger than any scenario she had imagined. She held her breath as her father digested the news.

He spoke his question calmly, quietly. Too calmly. Too quietly.

"You sold my artwork, the pieces I had hidden in the jungle so no eyes would behold them until I deemed it necessary?"

She nodded but didn't look up. Squeezing her eyes shut, Tipper waited for the explosion. Instead, silence pushed against her. She opened one eye and peeked at the men sitting across the room. They stared at her father, obviously shocked by her admission.

Verrin Schope patted her and gave her a little squeeze. "How many have you sold?"

"I lost count."

"How many are left?"

She couldn't answer, but Beccaroon spoke up for her. "Three."

She heard Librettowit's sharp intake of breath and looked up. Fenworth waggled his eyebrows and wobbled his head back and forth. The action dislodged a bird and several bugs. The sparrow snatched a flying insect and flew out the window.

The wizard watched the bird's departure. "Harrumph! What were we discussing? Three? Ah yes, three! Odd number. But odds are the three are not the right three."

Tipper pulled away from her father to look him in the eye. "What is he talking about?"

"We are looking for three statues in particular. They were carved out of one piece of marble, and in my cleverness, they will fit back together." He did not look particularly pleased as he boasted of his skill. In fact, Tipper thought he looked considerably more downcast than before.

Her father wiped a hand over his face. "They cannot be rejoined as they originally were, one solid stone, but the sculpted pieces fit together as if three figures embrace one another. In my ignorance, I did not realize that the rock I sculpted was one of Wulder's foundation stones."

"Wulder?" Tipper asked. "Who's he?"

"Ignorance!" The wizard slapped his hands on his knees, and small beetles scuttled out of the folds of his robe. "Like father, like daughter. Librettowit, what are we doing in this heathen land?"

"Unheathenizing the populace." The librarian sniffed and turned his gaze back to Verrin Schope.

Beccaroon cast the two men an outraged glare. Tipper waited for him to issue a scathing retort over the nonsense of their country being uncivilized. But he shook his feathers and settled them, obviously controlling his indignation.

"Is it possible?" The wizard's glower swept over the inhabitants of the bedchamber. "Will the populace learn? I hate to spend time on unprofitable ventures. Trailing truth before lovers of deceit. Offering light to those who relish dark. Admit it, Librettowit, some minds are too little to hold even a drip of a big concept. We can avoid the sea of explanation and not dip into futility."

"Verrin Schope realized the truth," said Librettowit.

"But he is an exceptional man. Brilliant! Talented! Sensitive! Like me. Absorbing knowledge like a sponge."

Librettowit rolled his eyes. "Thank Wulder you are not a lake wizard." His shoulders rose as he took in a deep breath and drooped as he expelled it in a sigh of excessive patience. "The simple can detect the truth. Wulder does not wish to be out of reach."

Tipper shook her father's arm. "There's that name again. Who is Wulder?"

Verrin Schope beamed. "Longing to know, aren't you? Caught me that way too." He tapped his finger on her brow. "Now smooth out those worried wrinkles, and I'll tell you." He winked at Beccaroon. "You'll be interested in this as well."

Wizard Fenworth leaned back in his chair and closed his eyes. "I've heard it before." He snorted twice and commenced a rhythmic breathing, indicating he'd fallen asleep with no more ado.

"We refer to Wulder as Boscamon, but our perception is incomplete." Verrin Schope tapped his daughter's forehead. "You're frowning again."

"Tell me, Mistress Tipper," said Librettowit, "what do you know of Boscamon from your childhood?"

"He is the one behind everything. Before there was anything, he conjured up all that we see." She looked at her father and he nodded, so she continued. "He keeps each thing in balance with the others. He arranges elements of our world, taking away one thing and replacing it with another."

"That covers the temporal," Verrin Schope prompted, "but what of the nonphysical?"

Tipper thought for a moment. "Part of his realm is to see that goodness is rewarded in time and evil is punished."

Verrin Schope nodded and turned to face Librettowit. "In pictures drawn for children, Boscamon is often depicted as a magician or a juggler. But unlike Wulder, he is mysterious, unknown, beyond reach."

Librettowit shifted on the footstool. "Not much use, is he?"

Tipper knew her frown had returned, but she could not figure out what her father meant or why it should be important enough to discuss. Surely the statues and the ramifications of her selling them were more to the point than fables.

Beccaroon shook his feathers. "Boscamon has never been sufficient for me. There have been times I've looked at the magnificence of my jungle and known I should give thanks to Someone for its existence. It is rather disconcerting not to have anyone to whom I may express gratitude."

Verrin Schope scrunched his expression as he grasped for words. "Bec is right. Our people give Boscamon no homage, nor do we worship him. He is just a hypothetical power. Something that might explain what has not been explained."

Librettowit pinched his lower lip between his thumb and finger and nodded, a look of concentration on his face. "Your Boscamon is a fairy-tale figure. Storytellers have woven his existence out of a dim understanding of how things must work without any real knowledge to give weight to the theories."

"Exactly!" Verrin Schope grasped his daughter's hands and shook them slightly to secure her full attention. His face shone with excitement. "The marvelous thing is that Wulder has revealed Himself to the people of Amara, and we can introduce Him to our civilization."

"If," said Librettowit in a deadly serious voice, "we can secure the three statues that make up the foundation of your corner of the world before irrevocable damage is done."

"Which statues do you need, Papa?"

"*Morning Glory, Day's Deed,* and *Evening Yearns.*"

Tears welled in Tipper's eyes. "All gone. Among the first to go."

Verrin Schope cupped his hand around his daughter's chin. "Still no need to despair, my dear. Just tell me who you sold them to."

"I never know." She let her head fall onto his shoulder, hiding her face in his robe.

Beccaroon tsked. "She gives them into Hanner's care. He takes them to Tackertun, and Dodderbanoster sells them locally and to distant art dealers. They are spread all over the fair land of Chiril and quite possibly beyond our borders."

"We shall start with Dodderbanoster, then," said Verrin Schope. "He's an old friend and will help us, I'm sure." He patted Tipper on the shoulder. "Brace up, girl. All is not lost."

Tipper sobbed and managed to squeak out an answer. "Hanner told me that Dodderbanoster said the artwork often trades hands many times as greedy patrons endeavor to collect the most valuable pieces." She hiccuped. "The three statues could be anywhere. Nobody can tell us exactly where each piece is."

Beccaroon shifted from foot to foot. "Not true. There is a possibility."

"Who?" asked Librettowit. "A cataloger?"

"No, an artist."

Tipper wailed.

"There, there," said her father with more ineffectual patting of her shoulders. "Speak, Bec. Who?"

"Bealomondore."

Tipper raised her head. "Yes," she managed to say. "But no!"

"Why not?" Verrin Schope asked.

Beccaroon shook his tail feathers. "Tipper managed to alienate the young artist's goodwill."

"This is the young man who painted the fountain?"

"Yes." Tipper sniffed and wiped her face with a handkerchief.

Verrin Schope released her. "Oh, busted banderilles."

She hung her head. "I know. I have been deceitful, and the worst is the spite I felt at having to sell them. I knew you would be displeased."

"Well, yes, there is that anger of yours. Your mother has mentioned it," said her father. "But that wasn't the cause of my oath."

"It wasn't?"

"Decidedly not."

"Then…?" She looked straight at him and realized the problem. "Banderilles, broken, bashed, and blitherated. I'm fading again."

10

Changes

And so it falls to me to usher these odd fellows to hidden statues in my beloved forest. Beccaroon strutted through the dense undergrowth, following a path the wizard and his librarian would never have been able to discover on their own. He glanced over his shoulder and realized they had stopped again. The tumanhofer wrote in his notebook as he examined the leaf of an ordinary sputzall vine. The wizard appeared to be talking to a striped monkey. Beccaroon tsked and flew up into a tree to snack on boskenberries while he waited.

Tipper and I informed them that the statues are not those they seek, but do they listen? No.

The librarian took a few steps and examined another bush. Wizard Fenworth sat down with a "tut, tut" and became very still. Soon a flatrat peeked out from the underbrush and sniffed the air. The furry shadow scuttled across a bare patch of ground and poked its nose under the hem of the wizard's robe. To Beccaroon's amazement, the timid beast disappeared into the folds of the cloth.

After a moment, the wizard stood. "Sir Bec, where are you? Shouldn't we be on our way?"

Beccaroon tsked again. *As if I'm the one stopping every whipstitch to examine the flora and fauna.*

He spread his red wings and glided to the forest floor. "This way," he said and parted the branches obscuring the path.

If he'd flown, the journey would have taken three minutes. If he'd walked with Tipper, it would have taken ten. But guiding the two men from Amara through the jungle, prodding them past mundane foliage that the librarian declared "exquisite," and getting the wizard back on his feet after his many stops for "a bit of a rest" lengthened the expedition to an hour and three-quarters. Wizard Fenworth and Librettowit exhausted all of Beccaroon's patience.

"We're here," he announced and gestured toward a vine-covered statue only two feet tall.

The wizard glared at the overgrown vegetation. The branches loosened their hold on the sculpture, dropping to form a circle at the base of a carved boy hunched over an animal in his cold hand.

The wizard raised an eyebrow at his companion. "Well, help me lift it, Librettowit."

Beccaroon eyed the heavy stone and the two old men. "You can't possibly carry that statue."

The wizard grunted as he leaned over the boy. "Not in our arms, of course." He spread his cloak around the statue. "There, I've got his head in the opening, Librettowit. Just tip him in."

The librarian took hold of the base of the statue and thrust it upward and over, sliding it into the opening. The cape bulged momentarily, then hung flat again. Both men straightened.

"One down," said the wizard.

"Two to go," said the tumanhofer.

Wizard Fenworth took a step, and his robe flowed as it had before. No lump or sagging in the cloth indicated that a heavy statue was stored within.

"What did you do?" asked Beccaroon. "Where is Verrin Schope's sculpture?"

"In a hollow," answered the wizard, holding his cloak open so the bird could see the lining. "It looks just like these other pockets, but the opening leads to a…hmm. How to explain it? Librettowit?"

The tumanhofer stroked his beard. "If you were to open a cupboard door and place an object, say a cup, on the shelf and close the door, you would know that the cup is in that cabinet, on a shelf." He pantomimed putting a cup into a cupboard. "When you put an object in a hollow, the object is still there but not just on the other side of a door."

"Confusing!" The wizard waved his hands in front of him, and a myriad of creatures escaped his sleeves, some dropping to the forest floor and scurrying off, some flying to nearby branches. "Are you talking about a pocket or a cabinet?"

"A hollow," stated the librarian.

"You're making things altogether too complicated." Wizard Fenworth turned to Beccaroon. "When we put the statue in my pocket, we more specifically put the statue in a hollow. Therefore, it is *there* but not there. It is essentially far away in another place but quite positively *there* instead of the there you expect. Understand? It's simple."

Tired of the muddled rhetoric, Beccaroon nodded. "I see. Shall we go on to the next hiding place? I assume another statue will fit in this hollow."

Wizard Fenworth waved one hand as if dismissing any doubts. "A hollow will accommodate any number of things as long as the thing initially fits through the opening."

"The openings do not stretch," said Librettowit.

Fenworth grinned and held up one finger. "But I have more than one hollow with varying sizes of openings."

Librettowit spoke softly as he shuffled away from his tall friend. "And even I have a hollow."

"He does indeed," said the wizard with his face pulled into a frown. "But he has odd notions."

"Precautions," objected the tumanhofer.

"Worrywartish, unscientific, unfounded superstitions. Comes from sitting with books too much."

"Maybe so, but I've never reached my hand into my own hollow and pulled out a full-grown centimonder."

Fenworth blustered. "And you are implying—"

The shorter man seemed to grow a bit as he stood up to his companion. With one eyebrow cocked, he glared at the old wizard.

"Ah yes," said Fenworth. "I remember being bitten."

The tumanhofer agreed with one emphatic nod.

Beccaroon ruffled his feathers. "Shall we proceed, gentlemen?"

Ushering the two visitors farther into the tropical forest to the second and then the third hidden statue proved to be just as strenuous on Beccaroon's nerves as the first leg of their journey. As they headed back, he took them a shorter route.

"That's an odd tree," said Wizard Fenworth. He moved off the path to examine his find. "Librettowit, take a look at this. We have nothing like it in Amara."

His curiosity aroused, Beccaroon doubled back to see what his followers had found. He landed on a branch close to the librarian's hat.

"What do you call this tree?" asked Librettowit.

"I've never seen it before, and it's dying. It looks somewhat like a bittermorn tree, but it is so disfigured and twisted..." Beccaroon leaned over the tumanhofer's shoulder and nipped a leaf. He spit it out after a second. "Awk! It's a bittermorn for sure. Tastes awful."

Librettowit scowled. "I'm afraid this tree may have dissipated as Verrin Schope does."

Fenworth nodded. "And come back together every which way." He scrunched his brow and looked askance at Beccaroon. "I would assume that this tree, in the normal way of things, is not sapient."

"I beg your pardon?" Beccaroon knew the man was touched in the head, but sapient? "Do you mean you have trees in Amara that think, plan, and converse?"

"We have some that are emotional, but few are thinkers."

"As far as I know," said Beccaroon, "this type of tree has shown no sign of being able to reason."

Fenworth nodded as he considered the parrot's words. "Didn't have the sense to guide its reassemblage so that it would turn out a tree as it had been before."

"This is proof, then?" asked Librettowit.

"We'll discuss it with Verrin Schope, but I believe our theory of the effect of the foundation-stone fiasco is correct."

"What?" squawked Beccaroon. "What are you talking about?"

Librettowit cast him an apologetic look as Fenworth returned to the path and started on. "If more things besides your sculptor friend start dissipating and reforming, we may have a landscape covered with these abnormalities."

If he had not been looking at evidence of disaster, Beccaroon might have scoffed. Instead, he grew silent and got the two foreigners back to Byrdschopen as quickly as possible.

By the time they returned to Verrin Schope's mansion, exasperation quivered at the tip of every feather of the grand parrot's spectacular plumage. The men had expounded on every possible mishap that could possibly come about as objects passed through the process that ailed their apprentice wizard.

Tipper rushed onto the back veranda as soon as the men stepped into the fountain garden.

"Did you find them?" she called.

"We did," Beccaroon muttered.

Fenworth patted the sides of his robe. "Magnificent work. Your father is a genius."

Tipper merely nodded. "Do you want to send someone out to fetch them?"

The old wizard laughed, jarring loose a few leaves clinging to—or were they growing from?—his robes. "We brought them, my dear. Now where is your father?"

She frowned, looking at the two old men as they climbed the three stairs to the veranda and then at her friend perched on a balustrade. Beccaroon shrugged.

Tipper glanced over her shoulder to the second-story windows. Her father looked down from her mother's chamber.

"He's still upstairs. I've been sitting with him ever since you left. He has spent the day going into the closet as he fades and then coming out, whole and happy again, a few minutes later." She smiled wanly at Sir Bec. "It makes a conversation rather disjointed."

Beccaroon cleaned his wing feathers and made no comment.

"Let's go see if he's in or out," said Fenworth. "I'll carry the statues, Librettowit. No reason to bother yourself."

"I hadn't intended to." The librarian trudged toward the door without waiting for the others.

Tipper paused to speak to Beccaroon. "Are you coming, Bec?"

"Awk." He shook his head. His feathers ruffled. "I've had enough of those two. You go along. I'm going to seek seclusion in my forest. I have some thinking to do."

"Oh, Bec." Tipper brushed her fingers softly from his shoulder down one scarlet wing. "I'm sorry."

"Awk! Hurry along. Maybe some good will come of all this. If not—and I, for one, am not expecting easy outcomes—you know where you can find me. And Tipper…tell your father about the rocks by the fountain." He shifted away from her, spread his wings, and flew off.

Tipper wondered for a moment over his parting words but had something else to catch her attention. She wanted to see the statues and verify that the ones the men sought had been indeed sold. She easily caught up with Wizard Fenworth and Librettowit. Neither of the old men moved faster than a steady plod.

They entered her mother's chambers just as her father opened the door of the closet and stepped out. His smile encompassed his two old friends, as well as his daughter.

He clapped his hands together. "You're back. I trust you found the three remaining statues."

"We have," said Librettowit, "and I believe your daughter is correct. These are not the statues we seek."

Wizard Fenworth unfastened the string at his neck that held his cloak in place. He removed the cape with a flourish and spread it across the bed inside out.

"Here we are," he said.

Tipper gasped as he and Librettowit pulled a bulky stone figure from the flat material. Verrin Schope came to their aid and helped hoist the crouching boy onto a nearby table.

"Aha!" exclaimed her father. "I called this one *Protector*. See, the child has a young pippenhen in his palm. He's covered the bird with the other hand to shield it from harm." He stood back and frowned. "All wrong, all wrong. See how the lines curve in? See the darkness at the center of the piece? This is about withdrawing from life. Not at all what I intended. But then that was before Amara, so of course, I have a better perspective now."

He gently placed his fingers under the boy's chin and coaxed the stone to move. Tipper put a hand on the back of a chair to steady herself. She blinked and looked again. Her father stroked the features of the now upturned little face. Concern eased out of the statue's expression. A brightness, a sense of wonder, appeared, especially around the eyes, as her sculptor father reworked his art.

Verrin Schope once again stepped back and eyed the statue. "Yes, better."

Tipper sat down with a whoosh on the cushioned chair.

Absorbed in his task, her father didn't glance at his mystified daughter. "Now for this tiny chick."

He rubbed the rigid wrist of the boy's top hand for a moment, then gently turned it over so that both hands now cupped the tiny bird. Verrin Schope got on his knees and plied the material that made up the half-formed chick.

Tears welled in Tipper's eyes as she watched her father transform the rough rock into a lifelike image of a pippenhen. If he were to add color, Tipper would expect the figure to peep.

"I don't understand," she whispered.

Librettowit came to her side and put a gentle hand on her shoulder. "Your father's talent has multiplied as he has come closer to Wulder. This increase is not unusual. The Creator first gives the gift, then perfects the gift if the recipient is willing. Your father has told us he always knew there was more and found his work frustrating instead of satisfying because he perceived the lack."

Tipper sniffed and retrieved her handkerchief from her pocket. "Everyone proclaims his genius."

"But they don't know, do they? How could they? Only the individual can recognize the potential that is yet unfulfilled. Only the individual can stand on what has been given and reach for what is offered."

"You're talking about this Wulder? He's the Creator, the Giver, the...what?"

The old tumanhofer smiled and patted her back. "Wulder. He is Wulder."

11

To and Fro, Back and Forth

The broot made an excellent swing. Tipper leaned back on the thick vine that looped toward the forest floor. Her perch swayed forward, lifting her into the cozy clearing. She breathed deeply, trying to relax. Beccaroon sat in the branches of a sacktrass tree a few feet away.

With his head tilted, he looked like he focused only one eye on her. But she knew he had been listening intently to her description of what had passed during the last twenty-four hours. The debate at the mansion covered every aspect of a proposed quest.

Beccaroon flapped his crimson wings and settled them against his blue sides. "So the major flaw in their plan is that your father cannot accompany them."

Tipper gave an extra shove with her foot to make her swing scoot higher into the brush behind her. "I see flaws all over the place. Too much of what they think is speculation."

"Your father always exhibited extreme intelligence and good sense. If he says the three statues reunited will stabilize his condition, then…"

"The two foreigners and Papa admit this reuniting idea is just a theory. Wizard Fenworth says if combining the stones doesn't work, they will just rethink their hypothesis and see what new ideas they can come up with. Apparently he doesn't feel it necessary to 'attack an adversary not posing a threat.' It sounded like a quote when he said it. He's a confident one." She held up a finger, imitating Fenworth. "'But not to worry now, because our design hasn't yet failed.'"

"I haven't known him long, but I can hear the words flowing from his mouth as frogs hop out from under his robe."

Tipper giggled. "I think that time it was a small green garter snake."

"Letting your father live in a perpetual state of disappearing and coming back together in your mother's closet is not an option, Tipper. Something must be done."

"But their strategies involve too many unknown factors. They don't know how much time they have. They hint that Papa is just the first sign of an unstable environment. Perhaps the problem will spread. They didn't like that tree you saw in the jungle, and they had me go get one of the rocks that changed color. Librettowit thinks more dire things will happen. The house could disappear and try to reassemble in the closet, which would, of course, be gone as well. Even Fenworth thought that might be an inconvenient occurrence."

Beccaroon's head bobbed. "That explains the urgency to begin the search for your father's sculptures. They plan to leave tomorrow?"

"And they don't know where the artwork is."

The grand parrot clicked his tongue and let out a whistle. "But Bealomondore does."

Tipper shook a stray lock of fine hair away from her face. "Perhaps, but we don't know where the artist went. Probably back home, and that is too far away to even consider."

"He's in Temperlain, staying at the Boss Inn."

Tipper dragged her foot in the dirt and came to an abrupt stop. "How do you know that?"

Beccaroon lifted one shoulder in an understated shrug. "I am a respected leader of the community. Most people treat me as such and take the time to keep me informed."

Tipper reacted to a tangent thought. Her mentor again brought up how people usually regarded him. He did it to point out her shortcomings. "Your veiled allusions to my impertinence are annoying. I'm never sure if you mean what I think you mean. Couldn't you just be blatant about it and shake a wingtip in my face?" Tipper hopped out of the swing and put her hands on her hips. "And besides, I treat you with respect. At least I think I do."

"Awk! You treat me with affection." He gave her a disgruntled look. "Affection suitable to a doddering old uncle. At times your conduct is extremely flippant."

Her heart seized up as she studied his demeanor. Her old friend truly resented the manner in which she loved him. "Is that so bad, Sir Bec? You practically raised me, and many times you've been the only one to give me comfort." She cocked her head. "Does it wound your pride for an emerlindian girl to dote on you?"

"It is not that you bruise my dignity, my dear. I have enough self-confidence to be able to sustain a few callous blows." Bec sidled along the branch. "But you act as if I am not worthy of your regard. Your offhandedness reflects on you, showing a lack of discernment." He tossed his head and looked into the rich green canopy above them. "I thought I had taught you to be more adept at judging the appropriateness of any chosen behavior."

Tipper twisted in the corner of her mouth and bit her lip. Having a grand parrot as her guardian for all these years had been as much a trial to her as it had been to him. At times she could not seem to please the fussy bird, even though she loved him dearly. And that was the problem. He accepted her love, but not the demonstration of it. He was not a father who would hold her in his lap or swing her up in his arms. She missed that. But if she could reason out why their relationship scraped along a bumpy road from time to time, why couldn't he? Why did she always have to be the one to apologize and make adjustments?

Beccaroon hopped off his perch and landed in front of her. His beady eyes narrowed as he gazed into her face. "Perhaps it is your lack of social interaction with the outside world. Perhaps it would be good for you to travel with this wizard and his librarian and be exposed to a more sophisticated population."

As if he'd punched her, Tipper's answer whooshed out in a shriekish whisper. *"What?"*

"Your father can't go. You would benefit from an introduction to the world outside your secluded niche. And you need to make peace with Bealomondore." He smoothed the feathers on his chest with his beak. "You should go."

"I can't leave." She found her arms flailing in the air, emphasizing her objection. She pinned them to her sides. "Who would run the estate?"

"Your father."

"From a closet?"

"He isn't always in the closet."

She crossed her arms over her chest, trying to shield herself from his absurd suggestion. "I don't want to go." She pointed her chin at him. "Why don't you go?"

Beccaroon wagged his head back and forth. "I don't want to go."

"You're Father's best friend."

"You are your father's daughter."

Tipper stiffened. "I'm tired of being his daughter. I'm tired of responsibility and impossible circumstances."

"Then run away from home and have an adventure."

She growled in her throat but not loud enough for her mentor to hear. "You taught me not to run away from my obligations."

"Then go with Wizard Fenworth and Librettowit and fulfill your obligations."

She whirled, stomped away, then turned back. "You're more suited to accomplishing tasks of great importance."

"You have more at stake and are therefore more motivated to achieve."

"I don't want to go with those crazy old men."

"And you think I do? Three hours in my forest convinced me I didn't want to travel to the neighbor's fruit stand with those two." He bristled. "If you play your cards right, you can have Bealomondore come along."

"I don't want to go with two crazy old men and one fanatical artist." She spoke through clenched teeth. "You go. You know how to discern the proper behavior appropriate to any given situation."

"Don't throw words of encouragement and instruction back in my face, you ungrateful whelp."

Tipper relaxed as a wonderful idea blossomed. "Rolan."

"Rolan?"

"Let's send Rolan."

Beccaroon clicked his tongue against his beak. "Now that's an idea. We can stay here and pretend our secure little life hasn't been bopped with a rolling pin."

Tipper shook her head and waved her hands in the air in protest, but the bird continued. "I can see plainly that Rolan will be able to talk Bealomondore into aiding in the search for the three statues. He has a smooth way about him."

"Oh, do stop."

Beccaroon flew the short distance to another good perch and stared down at her. Sarcasm laced his words. "Also, Rolan is loyal and trustworthy. I can't think of a better person to be an emissary for Verrin Schope. Our neighbor, at least, looks the part." He shook his head. "Tipper, be reasonable. Rolan looks like what he is—a farmer."

She lifted her chin. "True, but a gentleman farmer."

"He'd be uncomfortable in crowded city streets."

"He's a valiant man. He'd cope."

"His harvest would suffer while he was away."

"You could offer to take over the management of his farm."

An unladylike snort escaped as Tipper remembered the withering of her father's productive land under her guiding hand. The crops had dwindled from a thousand acres to a garden plot. The grand parrot magistrate might solve disputes among the neighbors, make judgments on behalf of the less fortunate, and order changes made for the safety of the population, but he was not gifted with agricultural wisdom. Sir Bec had not provided wise counsel in this area. If it weren't for Gladyme, the garden would be thistles.

She sighed. "We can't send Rolan."

"Then you should resign yourself to going. You must save your father. And perhaps even save our world from whatever happens to a world that dissipates and then regroups in a closet."

"I can't do this, Bec. You try to make me believe I have done a good job taking care of my mother and our estate." She gestured as if evidence sprang up around her, illustrating her speech. She flung one hand out, pointing. "Ruined crops." Her other hand waved. "Destitute peasants." With her arms spread, she turned in a circle. "Can't you see it, Bec? Be honest!"

She clenched one fist and shook it at an unseen list detailing her ineptitude. "Mother is more flighty than ever. Her behavior is a direct reflection of the security she does not feel. Our once-beautiful home is falling into disrepair. The former staff of eighty servants now consists of two old people who stay because they love me. I've put scores of people out of work by not being able to maintain the crops and industry that was derived from the land."

She paused, all the fire going out of her argument. "I'm not suitable for a quest to find lost treasure, to save a man's life, to save the world. Someone else will have to do it."

"Someone like me?" Beccaroon asked.

"Someone exactly like you."

"Fine, I'll do it."

"You will?"

"Yes. I've never saved the world before. Such an accomplishment will look good on my gravestone. 'Here lies Beccaroon, a worthy steward of the forest, a steadfast friend, a considerate and honest neighbor, and saver of the world.' "

"You're joking."

"Yes, but I will go on this quest." He shuddered. "With Fenworth and Librettowit."

"You are a good friend, Bec."

"On one condition."

Tipper stiffened. "There's a condition? What is it?"

"That you go too."

"I thought we established that I am good for nothing."

"Never, my dear." He cocked his head in a gesture that always warmed Tipper's heart. "I would never acquiesce to such an idea. You are undoubtedly good for something."

Oh, the doubt again. Tipper struggled to keep a firm hold on the positive. She managed to speak without sounding defensive. "What?"

"A buffer. The one person who will keep me from deserting the worthy wizard and the gloomy librarian. You may keep me out of jail for pecking them when their constant nonsensical patter drives me mad. You might even save me from the hangman's noose should I be trapped in a room with them for more than an hour."

Her heart lightened. Bec's presence would make everything all right. She kept her somber tone. "In a quiet room, there's always the possibility that the wizard will sleep."

"And what will crawl out of his clothing while he snoozes?"

She shrugged and let a smile escape the control she had maintained to be serious.

Beccaroon pointed a wingtip at her and shook it. "We both go on this quest, or your father scatters one time too many to be put back together. The quest is imperative."

The smile deserted her face. "On that I agree."

12

Boss Inn

Tipper stepped down from the back of Rolan's wagon onto a busy street in the center of Temperlain. She had been to the larger town twice in her life, but never to this corner of affluence. Surely this section of Temperlain rivaled Ragar, the capital city of Chiril, for cosmopolitan sophistication. The bustling atmosphere, with men dressed to impress fellow merchants and women dressed to impress each other, made Soebin seem like a backwoods hamlet. Even the hawkers and errand boys were better dressed than the average citizen of her hometown. On the other side of the cobblestone street, the Boss Inn loomed large and elaborately elegant.

Backwoods. Tipper would have giggled if her throat had not been so tight with apprehension. Soebin did inhabit the edges of a tropical forest. Not exactly backwoods, but close enough. Yes, she was definitely out of her element and with an unpleasant task ahead of her as well.

On the wall behind her, a town bulletin board displayed sketches of young people. Curious, Tipper moved closer to read them. The posters depicted those who might have been abducted by slave traders. She scanned the faces and saw strong, healthy males and females. If the posters were right in their assumptions, then those happy faces were happy no more. She turned away.

On top of that unsettling discovery, the constant movement of goat-pulled carts, quick pedestrians, and hawkers with their wooden trays jarred her nerves. A boy bumped into her.

He turned, walking backward at what she deemed a dangerous pace, doffed his soft, flat hat, and grinned at her. "Sorry, miss." He slapped his cap back on his head and trotted off.

Beccaroon left his perch beside Rolan on the driver's seat and landed next to her. Several passersby slowed long enough to take a second look at the grand parrot. Few of the great birds came into cities.

Wizard Fenworth and Librettowit remained on the sofa situated in the wagon's hauling bed. Junkit and Zabeth lay on the wizard's shoulders. He'd surprised Tipper by insisting that the minor dragons come along. He said they were eager to see Temperlain and scolded her for being neglectful of the little beasties' desires. Tipper listened now as the wizard spoke to her dragons. Junkit and Zabeth did appear to be listening. But then, all animals seemed to listen when the wizard spoke.

Fenworth tilted his head up and peered down his nose as he took in the surrounding area. "There's a predominance of wood in their architecture, isn't there?"

Rolan looked over his shoulder. "What do you build with?" he asked.

"Wood, lumber, timber, and hewn boards."

"I see." Rolan nodded and quirked an eyebrow. "Then our homes and buildings are constructed much like your own?"

"Different!" proclaimed Fenworth, loud enough to turn the heads of those in the street.

Tipper fixed her attention on the wizard, waiting for him to elaborate on the difference in buildings. He didn't continue but began gathering town birds, pigeons, sparrows, and grackles around him. The variety of birds soon covered the wagon. Junkit and Zabeth flew to sit with Rolan. More townspeople stared.

Fenworth smiled at Tipper. "I have an owl at home. I do believe I miss the placid fellow."

Beccaroon reclaimed her attention by nudging her with his wing. "Shall we go into the hotel?"

Tipper looked into her friend's beady eyes and then up at Fenworth.

"I'm staying here," said the wizard. "I find dealing with disgruntled tumanhofers to be tiring."

"Horsefeathers," grumbled the librarian. He climbed down from the wagon. His weight tipped the vehicle dangerously to one side. He took Tipper's elbow in a firm hand and steered her across the street. "Always confront a tumanhofer head on. Don't beat around the bush. We don't like wishy-washy ways." They paused to let a dogcart pass. "Tumanhofers are solid folk who like to deal with facts, not emotion."

The temptation to inform Librettowit of Bealomondore's disposition parted Tipper's lips, but before she could utter a word, the steps to the front of the inn loomed before them. She held back, and Librettowit pushed harder against her arm.

"You'll get us run over in the streets, young girl. Let's get this meeting with the artist behind us."

Beccaroon's wing came around her back. He tsked. "Your home is much grander than this. Quit dragging your feet."

With Librettowit on one side and Bec on the other, the two ushered Tipper up the painted white stairs. She felt trapped, and the urge to escape increased. If she focused on something minor, perhaps she could make it. If she could explain…

"It's not the pomposity of the building that's bothering me," she said. "It's the bombastic attitude of the man I must humble myself to."

"Don't," said Librettowit, stopping before the elaborate wooden door of the inn and staring seriously into her eyes. "Don't ever end your sentences with prepositions."

Beccaroon clicked his tongue. "Before. I believe the preposition she should not have ended that sentence with would be *before* instead of *to*. One humbles oneself before another person, not to."

Tipper glared at her friend. "Have you gone mad?"

"No." The parrot's skin lifted in a ridge above one eye, like an eyebrow arching. "I think I have caught on to the rhythm of our guests' conversational pattern."

Librettowit patted her arm and propelled her gently toward the door. "He ended two sentences with the preposition *to.* Two prepositions incorrectly positioned." He reached forward with his free hand and twisted the brass knob. "I must confess, in the past I've committed the two *to* transgression too."

A ripple of laughter quivered in Tipper's stomach and rolled up to her throat. "You're doing it on purpose to make me relax."

"Yes, my dear," said Beccaroon, "and here we are."

They proceeded to the front desk at a quick pace. Obviously, her escorts did not want her to have time to devise a means of escape.

An o'rant commanded a position of authority behind the wide, highly polished, wooden counter. "Welcome to the Boss Inn, Temperlain's most prestigious hotel. May I be of service?"

Beccaroon cleared his throat. "We're looking for the artist Graddapotmorphit Bealomondore."

The clerk drawled, "He's here." He returned to his task.

Bec tilted his head forward. "May we see him?"

"If you take a room." The clerk turned a heavy book with lined pages so that it faced the three.

Librettowit examined the register. "Why do we need a room?"

"Bealomondore is an employee of the Inn. He does not render his services to anyone outside our patronage."

The tumanhofer picked up the pen and scratched in his name. "We'll take three rooms. One for the young lady and two for myself and three traveling companions."

The o'rant bowed slightly and pulled three sets of keys from a board on the wall.

Librettowit took the offered keys. "Now, where is Bealomondore?"

The man pointed a long finger to a hallway. "Last door on the left. You'll make your payment for the artist's work through the front desk."

"Payment?" Tipper whispered as they moved away from the desk.

Librettowit jingled the keys in his hand. "Thought you said this man's family is well-to-do."

"He dressed well," said Tipper. "He spoke like a gentleman. He said he was Graddapotmorphit Bealomondore from Greeston in Dornum. He sounded like his family held a position of prestige."

Beccaroon clicked his tongue against his beak. "And *he* supplied all the knowledge we have of him."

"Papa knew of him. Mother said so."

"Now, how is that?" asked the bird, turning an eye to the tumanhofer.

Librettowit paused in the hall. "For quite some time, we made attempts to return Verrin Schope to your country. Seven out of ten times, he landed in his own home. On the other three occasions, he popped up in the most unusual places. We often worried whether he would return to us. During these misplacements, he explored cities, mountains, isolated grasslands, and islands."

Tipper gasped. "He could have landed in the ocean."

Librettowit shook his head. "Highly unlikely. The mechanism, even when faulty, is strongly attracted to solid objects. He was in no danger of drowning."

"But you had to wait longer for him to return?"

"Yes." The librarian rubbed his fingers over his mustache. "The longest he was gone was nine days. By then we'd given him up entirely. Each time he visited your mother at the original entry of the gateway, he was gone from Amara for only six or seven hours." He shrugged his shoulders. "We tested theory after theory and could only surmise that the weave of the gateway burst in places, and he could not be readmitted until that rip had repaired itself."

"Awk!" Beccaroon halted. "This gate fixes itself?"

Librettowit resumed walking, and Tipper and Beccaroon followed. "It's not made out of brick and mortar, you see. Not even wood or thread. But time! Strands of flowing time and light. I've said *mechanism,* and that has given you a poor picture in your mind. I apologize."

He tapped a finger against his chin. "The product of our manipulation of strands of light and time is more like a living thing than a watch that merely counts minutes and hours. The gateway flows constantly."

He abruptly stopped, and Bec and Tipper had to retrace their steps to where he stood.

The tumanhofer changed from finger tapping to mustache stroking. "Ah! If you toss a rock into a stream, the water is only momentarily disturbed." He shook his head. "Bah! Another bad example."

He thought, his eyes squinted, then held up his finger. "If you scratch your skin, the abrasion allows blood to escape, but shortly thereafter, the small wound closes and eventually heals." A grin parted the mustache and beard.

To Tipper his smile looked more like a grimace. "The gateway is like that."

Beccaroon stared for a moment, then began walking once more. "That doesn't make a bit of sense. If this theory of putting three bits of stone back together is based on the same type of logic, Verrin Schope is doomed."

Tipper scampered to catch up. "Oh, Bec, please don't say such a thing."

His pace slowed. "Now, Tipper, don't fret. If this wizard and librarian were the ones we rely on, I'd be worried. But throw your father into the mix, and I have more confidence that all will turn out as it should."

"Wulder," said the tumanhofer, again walking by their sides. "Wulder is for us, as well."

Beccaroon didn't answer. Neither did Tipper. Trusting for aid someone who was like the fable of Boscamon didn't seem something to rejoice about. According to her father, this Wulder was real. But what did that mean? A real juggler was not much improvement over a storybook juggler.

They came to the door on the left at the end of the hall. Librettowit knocked.

"Come in." It was Bealomondore's voice.

Tipper allowed Librettowit and Beccaroon to lead the way. She hung back in the doorway to see what their reception would be. The much shorter bird and tumanhofer afforded her no shield, and they didn't block her view either.

Bealomondore sat with his back to them. An easel before him bore a black-on-white sketch of a marione. This person, apparently a businessman, raised his eyebrows at the intrusion, but when the artist made a hissing noise, he composed his expression with a flinch.

"I'm almost finished here," said the artist without turning his gaze. "Sit down. Shouldn't be long."

Bec remained standing, but Tipper and Librettowit sat on the soft sofa along the wall.

Tipper watched as Bealomondore's charcoal scraped lines across the paper. Occasionally, he stopped to deliberately smudge an area, creating shadows. The likeness to the man posing was remarkable, almost breathtaking, considering the artist worked only with black.

Bealomondore signed his name with a flourish, put down the charcoal, and stood. "Done!" He turned the easel with an ostentatious gesture and beamed when his patron exclaimed his astonishment.

"Marvelous! Incredible! You're a genuine genius."

Bealomondore nodded without a trace of humility. He then frowned as the man pulled out his leather purse. He shook his head. "You pay at the front desk, then the portrait will be mounted, framed, and delivered to your room."

"Yes, yes. I remember now." He gestured toward his likeness. "I can hardly take my eyes off it. My wife will be very pleased. Thank you, young man."

The marione businessman tore himself away from admiring his face on paper and scurried out of the room, evidently eager to pay the commission.

Bealomondore wiped his hands on a gray cloth as he turned to his waiting subjects. His eyes popped open at the sight of Beccaroon. He squinted and glared as his gaze swept over the tumanhofer and came to rest on Tipper.

"You," he thundered and pointed a blackened digit. "You are the cause of this humiliation. You have stripped me of my pride. You have reduced me to such circumstances."

Tipper couldn't see how she had caused anything. "Me?"

His nostrils flared. His head reared back, and he looked down his nose with exaggerated indignation. But he spoke with subdued rage. "Yes. You."

"Bah!" exclaimed Librettowit as he jumped to his feet. "Is there no normalcy in this confounded country?" He shook a finger at the offended artist. "You're a tumanhofer, aren't you? Act like one."

"I am an artist first," said Bealomondore, but the stab to his ego by a fellow tumanhofer had diminished his huff to a whisper.

Librettowit walked over to the younger man and put his arm around his shoulders. "You are a great artist, it is true."

Bealomondore perked up.

"But you are a lousy tumanhofer."

Bealomondore drooped.

"Never fear." Librettowit squeezed the artist's shoulders and shook him. "You have before you the opportunity to win fame and recognition, not only for your own talent but also for your acumen in the recognition of another."

Confusion wrinkled Bealomondore's face.

Librettowit continued. "Because you had the foresight, the ingenuity, the sagacity to seek out the work of the acclaimed sculptor and artist Verrin Schope, you are in the position to retrieve three priceless works of art. In doing so, you will save not only the artist's life but also the world."

Tipper managed to feel sorry for the man. He looked totally obfuscated by the charge to save his icon, Verrin Schope, and the world.

"Me?" asked one tumanhofer.

"Yes," said the other. "You."

13

Unexpected Alliances

"I'll do it!"

Tipper gasped at Bealomondore's proclamation. "What?"

He frowned at her. "I said I'd do it. Did you expect me to refuse to come to your father's aid just because you treated me shabbily?" He straightened his back, appearing to stretch at least an inch. "I consider myself above petty retaliation."

Librettowit nodded sagely as he stroked his beard. He turned to Tipper with a hint of amusement in his eyes. "I see what you meant in your earlier assessment."

Tipper hid her smile. Sometimes she liked the librarian very much.

To Bealomondore, Librettowit said, "Fine, fine. I'm glad you wish to join us."

Tipper arched her eyebrows. They would have no direction at all if the fanatical artist chose not to cooperate. That "glad you wish to join us" was an understatement.

Librettowit cleared his throat. "What will it take to get you out of your obligation to the hotel?"

The young tumanhofer seemed to consider his answer, then sighed, all the stiffness leaving his posture. "Four hundred mikers."

Librettowit arched his eyebrows. "I'm unfamiliar with your money system. That sounds like a lot."

"It is," said Tipper, trying not to stare at Bealomondore. She'd be able to keep the household finances afloat for three months on that much money.

Bealomondore shrugged. "I stayed here for several weeks before I followed through on my plan to seek Verrin Schope's benefaction."

"You waited until you were broke," said Tipper.

He hung his head. "A combination of motives. Empty pockets stoked my nerve to approach your father."

"So," said Beccaroon, "we need to pay the bill you ran up with the hotel, and you will be free to join our quest."

With narrowed eyes, Bealomondore studied Tipper. "Is this her plan? Is her father still inaccessible?" He crossed his arms over his chest. "Is he truly in danger?" He turned slightly away from Tipper and addressed Beccaroon and Librettowit. "Forgive me if I want proof that I will be engaged in an endeavor for Verrin Schope."

The grand parrot nodded. "That's understandable. We'll take you back to Byrdschopen and introduce you to the man you will save."

"Bec," Tipper objected.

He cocked his head at her. "It will be a while before the young man trusts you."

"But I didn't ask him to help. I didn't explain things to him. Why is he doubting Librettowit?"

A rare chuckle escaped her friend's throat. "Librettowit and I are painted by the same brush with which the artist depicts you. We walk in with you, and therefore we are as untrustworthy as you."

The parrot eyed Bealomondore and laughed again. "Wait until you meet the wizard, sir. I'm fighting my better judgment to trust this team of world savers. A fuddy-duddy, eccentric old man who says he is a wizard. We have no wizards in Chiril, and I am quickly learning that is a good thing." He nodded to Librettowit and winked. "The librarian seems steady but is prone to grouchiness."

Beccaroon suddenly sobered. "But I've seen evidence with my own eyes as to the seriousness of Verrin Schope's situation. We'd best join forces and set forth to find the three statues."

"What three statues?" asked Bealomondore.

Tipper placed her hand on Beccaroon's back. "I believe we forgot to tell him about the quest and Papa's need for the statues."

"Can we do that over dinner?" asked Librettowit. "I'm starved."

Tipper couldn't bring herself to blow out the candle. She'd never slept in a hotel room. Hostels, yes. Roadside taverns on the way to visit her mother's sister, yes. In the homes of people her parents knew, yes.

Of course, it had been years since she had traveled at all. Back then, she'd had some experience in sleeping places other than her own home. Their travels had been clandestine and therefore all the more adventuresome in spirit. Technically her mother was exiled to Byrdschopen.

Tipper had traveled some, but never alone. Never in the middle of a noisy town.

Junkit and Zabeth perched on the four-poster's footboard like sentinels. The light from one candle did not reach the shadowy corners. A town clock struck two. Even at this hour, carts rattled through the back street. Their rooms were at the side of the hotel, near the rear, and three stories up.

Tipper sat in the large bed with the covers pulled up to her chin and the pillows stacked behind her. Her weight on the soft mattress made a dent big enough for a bird of Beccaroon's size to nest in. If she stretched out, would the stuffing swell over her and bury her alive? She envisioned being pushed down into risen dough and disappearing like her fist did when she punched down the yeast dough for kneading.

A shout from the alley jerked her attention to the window.

"I wonder if that window's locked." She turned her head. "I locked the door." She reassured herself that the chair wedged under the doorknob hadn't fallen. "Oh, I need company. My mother. Gladyme. Somebody!"

Junkit flapped his wings, but Zabeth turned her head away and lifted her chin as if she had taken offense.

Tipper let the abundant covers drop into a pile in her lap. "Oh, I know you're here, but you can't talk to me. And I don't know if you really know what I'm saying."

Zabeth glared over her shoulder, then resumed pointedly staring out the window.

"Now don't get your feelings hurt," begged Tipper. "It's just that I can't expect…" She stopped to study the two animals. Zabeth clearly ignored her. Junkit returned her gaze as if waiting for her to continue.

Tipper blinked. The two minor dragons remained in their positions, one offended, the other alert and paying attention. "If my words hurt Zabeth's feelings, then she must understand what I say. Papa was right!"

Junkit flew from his perch and landed on the mountain of covers in front of her.

Tipper scrutinized his small, intelligent face. "You do understand me, don't you?"

His mouth didn't open. His lips did not move. But as clear as if the word had formed on his tongue, she heard *"yes"* in her mind. She pulled back, eyes wide and mouth open.

Old Junkit jumped into the air. Chittering, interspersed with squeaks, accompanied his rather clumsy airborne dance of glee. Zabeth flew to sit in front of Tipper. The minor dragon eyed Tipper just as warily as Tipper eyed Zabeth.

"Are you going to speak to me?" Tipper asked.

Zabeth whipped her tail from side to side. From Junkit Tipper received the impression that Zabeth was "talking."

"But I don't *hear* her."

The dragons chittered, squeaked, twittered, and cheeped back and forth. Tipper recognized a conversation when she saw one. She realized she had seen this many times before and just dismissed it as the same type of noise birds make. Even when her father had made it clear that the dragons were capable of communication, she had dismissed the idea. "Just because talking dragons are something I didn't accept as a reality, I ignored what I could see. Hmm…Bec would say there is a life lesson here."

Junkit clambered over the blankets and sat in her lap.

Tipper stroked his blue back. "I understand you, Junkit, but not Zabeth."

The green dragon unfurled her wings and snapped them shut. Her head bobbed and her tongue flicked out.

Tipper held Junkit to her chest. "She's going to bite me!"

The blue dragon scolded her.

"Well, I thought she was going to."

Zabeth sat back and looked pleased with herself.

"I understand." Tipper gasped. She understood. She really understood the female dragon. She wanted to prove it to Junkit. "Zabeth was thinking she would like to nip me because I'm so—" She glared at Zabeth. "I am *not* dense."

Zabeth collapsed and rolled over on her back. She clicked deep in her throat and quivered, her small arms crossed over her front.

"Is she all right?" Tipper leaned closer.

Junkit popped out of her arms and went to his companion. He unceremoniously poked her with his foot.

"Laughing? She's laughing?" Tipper picked up the squirming

Zabeth and set her on one of her knees. "Stop that." She shook her finger in the small creature's face. "Here you tell Wizard Fenworth we never talk to you, and now that I attempt communication, you laugh!"

Zabeth stiffened, pulled a straight face, then fell apart in another fit of giggles.

Tipper put her down on the covers. "I'm going to sleep."

She wallowed around in the mushy bed until she got to the edge. With one big puff, she blew out the lone candle, probably splattering wax on the stand. But Tipper didn't care. She threw herself back on the bed, sinking deep enough to give her a moment of panic. When she knew she wasn't going to be submerged in mattress, she yanked up the blankets.

Zabeth still chortled.

"Good night!" Tipper whispered between clenched teeth.

In a moment, silence permeated the room. A lone set of footsteps passed by the hotel. The man whistled a slow tune as he walked away.

Junkit came to lie on the pillow next to her head.

"You've never done that," she said.

She squeezed her eyes against tears when she understood he'd never felt welcome before. With a finger, she rubbed the top of his head.

Zabeth crawled to her shoulder and settled down in the covers.

Tipper giggled in response to the dragon's concern. "Don't worry. I won't roll on you."

She sighed and closed her eyes.

The clomping of heavy boots passing her room in the hall jerked Tipper out of a sound sleep. Rattling, banging, clattering, and loud voices drifted up from the street behind the hotel. Bealomondore had said the rooms facing the front were quieter because the genteel people used the main street. Tradespeople used the side streets and alley.

"Delivering milk makes noise," he'd said.

Evidently, friends of the artist did not rate the best rooms.

Tipper sat up. The dragons perched on the windowsill, watching the city chaos below.

"Good morning," she called as she rolled onto her stomach and wiggled loose from the heavy blankets and off the edge of the bed.

They greeted her with silence.

"What are you looking at that's so interesting?"

Stretching, she crossed the room and looked over their heads. A man lifted bags out of a cart and hauled them into the hotel's back entrance.

"Is that all?"

She picked Junkit up and cuddled him under her chin. "Did you get enough sleep?"

He chirred and responded with a friendly nudge against her cheek, but no thoughts came into her mind that she could identify as his.

She held him out and studied his face. "I can't hear you," she said.

Junkit's expression changed to one of woe.

"What happened?" she asked. She didn't get an answer.

14

Transportation

Beccaroon circled the sky above Rolan's overcrowded vehicle. The wizard and Tipper chose the sofa. Junkit and Zabeth settled on Fenworth. Librettowit sat on the front seat with Rolan. The tumanhofer artist balanced on a couple of bags of grain, the most comfortable arrangement among the supplies the farmer had purchased.

Beccaroon glided in a lazy circle back toward his companions. If all the passengers of the wagon could fly, he'd be roosting in his home tree by now. However, his obligation to keep pace with the group did not mean he must keep them company. He chose to meditate high in the air rather than be shaken to pieces riding on that glorified farm cart.

He tsked at the clumsy vehicle below. "Listening to blather as well. Watching that wizard sleep. Counting the varmints escaping from his clothes." He shuddered and looked for somewhere else to spend his time.

He landed in a boskenberry tree and nibbled a snack while he watched the horses clump across the wooden bridge, pulling the creaking wagon. Bealomondore looked bored. The wizard was asleep. Librettowit had twisted in his seat to talk to Tipper. Beccaroon saw her smile and felt a lifting of his concern. She'd been pensive and withdrawn all morning. He hoped Verrin Schope would have good news when they got back to Byrdschopen. His old friend had been spinning theories through his head, trying to solve his problem of being tied to a closet.

Bec chortled. Verrin Schope could always find a fix to get in. But he was equally capable of getting out of it. This predicament continued to try the artist-inventor-explorer's mettle, but Beccaroon knew he'd solve the problem.

The wagon passed under his tree, and Tipper waved to him.

"I know you're anxious to go home, Bec. We're all right. Go on and check your territory and how things are progressing at Byrdschopen." Her smile didn't shine with its full brilliance, and an unsettled expression hung in her pale blue eyes.

Beccaroon nodded his agreement and launched into the air. If she didn't tell him over breakfast what was troubling her, she wasn't going to blurt it out on a country road in a wagonload of farm supplies and strangers.

He flew straight to the location where he'd seen the vagabonds' encampment, the ones who had convinced Helen the cow to go for a stroll. The rangers had arrested or dispersed them. Some of the villains, he knew, were in jail in Temperlain since the smaller towns did not hold prisoners. He made a careful inspection of his borders, then zigzagged from east to west, gradually working his way south to where Verrin Schope's mansion nestled against his forest.

The peaceful atmosphere ruffled his feathers. By appearances, he could take off and no disaster would disrupt his home ground. He pondered the issue. He'd contemplated how to avoid the discomfort and inconvenience of leaving. His chief excuse for backing out of this quest caved in on itself with the revelation that life went on smoothly without his direct supervision. Served him right for organizing his underlings in a tight-knit network and enlisting dependable allies.

He landed on Verrin Schope's roof and entered by way of the cupola. As soon as he opened the door to the third level, he heard hammering. He followed the sound and a few minutes later entered Lady Peg's chambers. Her dresses and cloaks covered the bed. A pile of shoes occupied a chair. Paneling, elegant trim, rough boards, and the door to the closet lay on the floor, along with a good deal of dust and splintered wood.

"As long as I've known you, I've never seen you destroy anything," he called to Verrin Schope, who wielded a hammer inside the spacious clothes cabinet. "I honestly expected to find you sitting in a chair, thinking." When his friend issued no answer, Beccaroon tried harder to draw his attention. "Awk! What are you doing?"

"Searching for the spot." The sculptor hammered against an upright board, loosening it from the frame of the wall.

"What spot?"

"The exact spot where the center of the gateway is focused."

Beccaroon flapped his wings. "Why?"

"If my theory is correct, the anchor is portable."

"Ah," said Bec, nodding his head. He strolled forward and peered into the partially dismantled room. "And if you locate this portable anchor to a nonfunctioning gateway, you can go with us on this preposterous journey?"

"Yes."

Beccaroon took a turn around the bedroom. "Then there would really be no need for me to go. And every reason for me to stay here and continue to employ a vigilant eye toward the safekeeping of your estate."

Verrin Schope stopped hammering. He leaned against the doorjamb, his breath heavy from exertion, his shirt-sleeves rolled up, and sweat dripping down the side of his dark face. "There's not much left of the estate to supervise. I would prefer that you join us but will understand if the quest is too much of an imposition."

He straightened and let out a loud sigh. "Good! I'm fading. When I reassemble, old Bec, take careful heed of the exact location where you first catch a glimmer of my return."

By the time Beccaroon ambled forward, Verrin Schope had disappeared. The bird stuck his head through the closet door and saw a spot on the wooden floor darken as if something cast a shadow there. In the next moment, Verrin Schope stood before him.

"Ah yes," he said. "Here I am again. Always in this corner." He took a step forward, turned, and surveyed the area from the ceiling to the floor. "Tell me, old friend, what did you see first?"

"A shadow."

Verrin Schope frowned. "Here?" He pointed to the disassembled wall.

Beccaroon shook his head. "On the floor."

"Odd." He cupped his hand over his chin and peered down. "I expected to come forward, not upward. I had even thought I might descend." He glanced at the ceiling. "But I think ascending might prove to be a better circumstance to deal with." He clapped his hands together. "It will be some time before I fade again. Shall we call Gladyme to bring refreshments? I'm curious, of course, to know if you have attained the cooperation of Graddapotmorphit Bealomondore."

"I'm not hungry, but I could use a drink."

Verrin Schope arched an eyebrow. "And the fanatic artist?"

"He'll come with us."

"Us? You are coming?"

"Awk!" Beccaroon shook, sending his feathers into a quivering display of indignation. "You wouldn't let me rest if I said no. And besides, the last time you went off without me, you got yourself in this impossible condition."

The tall emerlindian went down on one knee so that he was at eye level with his friend. The grin on his dark face dispelled any notion that he had a serious thought to relay.

"It will be like old times, Bec."

"Old times were before you married. Before we both had responsibilities."

The smile disappeared, and Beccaroon wished he hadn't spoken.

Verrin Schope nodded with rapid, sharp jerks of his head. He pressed his lips together as if to squelch the strength of his emotion. "We have responsibilities, my friend. To Chiril. To our world. To Wulder. I've been given a task, and I appreciate that you are one of those who will help me fulfill my duty."

After Verrin Schope had a substantial lunch and Beccaroon sipped frissent juice from a wide goblet, the artist again attacked the closet. He brought out the floorboard Bec had identified as the spot where the shadow first appeared.

The artist held the one-by-eight-inch plank in his hands. He'd sawed it to a length of only eighteen inches.

Beccaroon shifted from one foot to the other. "What if you've made your base too small? That's hardly enough for a man your size to stand on."

"You said the first spot of shadow only covered a space the size of my palm, right?"

"Right."

"Then quit worrying. I'm more concerned with whether the board has to be lined up with certain gravitational pulls." He waved a hand in the air. "Polar influence and all that."

Beccaroon knew when to pursue further explanation and when it was futile to try to untangle his friend's brilliant line of reasoning. He shrugged.

Wheels grating on the entrance to Byrdschopen's driveway caught his attention. "The travelers return."

"Fetch them, Bec. I want to meet this new comrade, a tumanhofer artist with airs. He'll make our quest that much more interesting."

On his way to the door, Beccaroon threw another comment over his shoulder. "I did tell you, didn't I, that the wizard and the artist aren't getting along?"

Verrin Schope laughed. "It takes talent to get along with Fenworth, and this Bealomondore seems to have an abundance of talent."

"Fine." Bec paused in the doorway. "The wizard will pose for the artist, and the painting will be named *Outrage.*"

Beccaroon stood aside and observed with little pleasure as preparations for dinner were made. With help from their guest, Gladyme served the evening meal in the upstairs sitting room. She didn't fuss over the inconvenience. Watching the wizard transport trays up the stairs without touching them stole her breath away and, with it, her voice. When she squeaked out a concern that her dishes would be cold when they finally got everything arranged to serve, the old man chuckled and said he'd heat anything that cooled.

Beccaroon tsked, shaking his head. The unnatural things this man could do made his feathers sit uneasily along his back. All thoughts of abandoning the quest and sending Tipper off with this trickster vanished. He'd protected his girl for fifteen years, and he was too much in the habit to turn the privilege back to her father. Would Verrin Schope be wary? That was doubtful.

Even the house dragons accepted the strange man without a hint of disapproval. They flew among the floating trays, chittering happily over the phenomenon. Verrin Schope's dragon perched in the straggly hair on the wizard's head.

Beccaroon growled in his throat. No one seemed concerned that their comfortable existence had been mangled beyond recognition.

Verrin Schope and Librettowit had their heads together, discussing the sculptor's new theory. When they consulted the wizard, he announced that he didn't approve or disapprove scientific advancement on an empty stomach.

The wizard had balked at carrying tables. "I'm an old man. It's not good for my back to lift heavy objects."

Beccaroon ducked, walked under a table, and rose up to balance it on his back. He could not strut and abhorred the undignified waddle necessary to move, but he managed to move two small tables.

They sat down to dinner, and Verrin Schope bowed his head, thanking Wulder for the food and friends and asking that He bless their endeavors to unite the three statues.

This launched the conversation into all that had been explained before, but this time for the benefit of Bealomondore.

Beccaroon pecked at his food and didn't pay much attention. Irritation spoiled his meal. He felt uncomfortable when they mentioned this Wulder. He resented the presence of three men who should not be admitted to the crucial scheme to save Verrin Schope. He doubted the world was at peril. These scoundrels exaggerated, tended toward affected behavior, and flaunted tricks and chicanery. He was tired of them.

Verrin Schope's voice abruptly stopped. Beccaroon glanced his way.

Verrin Schope grinned. "I'm fading."

He disappeared. Beccaroon expected a few minutes to pass before his friend would come through the door from the hall. Instead, that shadow he'd seen in the closet formed on the empty chair, and Verrin Schope reappeared.

"Remarkable," said Librettowit.

Bealomondore remained silent, his eyes large and his complexion pale.

Fenworth brushed a bug off the table. "You did that quickly."

"I've been practicing," said Tipper's father with the humility he had displayed more often since his return.

Beccaroon narrowed his eyes. "Practicing what?"

"I've found that once I feel that first tingle that signals I am going to fade, I can hurry the process. The faster I disappear, the quicker I reappear. I hope to develop the process so that I only flicker." He puckered his lips. "The time between fadings is lengthening. I'm hoping this is a favorable adjustment, as I seem to have no control over it."

"Yes," said Fenworth. "Quite so. But why aren't you in the closet?"

Verrin Schope reached under his seat and pulled out the floorboard. "I've got the only piece of the closet that connects to the gateway."

Fenworth chewed and nodded his head. When he swallowed, he spoke. "Always knew you were an intelligent fellow. Hang around, and we'll make a first-class wizard out of you. I must say, this disappearing business had me doubting the steadiness of your character."

"Papa," said Tipper.

"Yes, dear? You've been quiet tonight. Are you troubled?"

"No more than usual."

"That's good."

"Papa, are you coming with us on the quest?"

"Yes, I wouldn't miss it for the world."

"I would," said Wizard Fenworth emphatically. "Quests are uncomfortable things. Villains pop up. People, things, memories get lost. Hard beds, cold food, grouchy individuals griping about inns, hiccups, and misplaced necessities."

"That would be you," said Librettowit. He winked at Tipper. "Horrible traveler."

Fenworth pointed his fork at his librarian. "You'd rather leave me at home. But if I were at home, you'd stay at home as well."

"And you'd be complaining about this and that at home. I might as well go with you."

"Harrumph! I wouldn't mind missing this quest." Fenworth scowled, and the emerlindian artist caught the glare full on. "Uncomfortable, long, full of frustration." He let out a dramatic sigh, and the stiffness of his shoulders fell away as he nodded toward his protégé. "But Verrin Schope here is in a fix, and we must put personal comfort aside."

Librettowit held his hand before his mouth and spoke in solemn tones. "There is that detail about the world crumbling."

Fenworth looked at him from under his bushy eyebrows. "I'd forgotten that." He tapped the table with the handle end of his fork. "It's starting already. Lost a memory. Next it'll be something I really value…like my hat."

15

Slight Change of Plans

"You can just go sleep somewhere else," Tipper whispered.

Zabeth flew to the windowsill, but Junkit stayed. Cloud cover hid the moon and stars, but Zabeth's green scales caught the glimmer from Tipper's branch of candles. Junkit's blue wings looked almost purple in the dim light. Tipper frowned at his expression.

"Don't look hurt. Last night you 'talked' to me. This morning not one single impression. You spent the whole day ingratiating yourselves to the wizard." She wrapped her arms around her middle and squeezed as if the pressure would lessen the hurt she felt. "I've never seen such smarmy behavior in all my life."

She raised her chin and glared at Junkit. "*Now* you come looking for a place to roost. You can roost wherever you used to before you decided to be more than house dragons. You can roost in the barn with Trisoda and Helen."

Heedless of Junkit's precarious perch on her blankets, Tipper blew out the candles, burrowed under her covers, and pulled them up to her chin. Junkit turned around several times beside her knees, then flew to join Zabeth at the window.

She heard them "discussing" something and assumed it was her behavior. She had been less than gracious. Both her mother and Beccaroon would have chastised her.

She stretched out on her back and stared into the dark. She should apologize, now that she knew the dragons understood her and had feelings to be hurt. She sighed.

The soft chittering quieted, then Zabeth chirped, a short note that sounded like a summons. Several times the coaxing trill wafted through the night. Wondering what the dragons were up to, Tipper rolled on her side.

On the windowsill, Zabeth and Junkit became quiet, their attention riveted on the sky outside. Tipper heard a flutter of wings first. Then two more dragons landed next to her own. One was her father's dragon, Grandur. The other was a darker, smaller dragon. All four flew to her bed.

She sat up abruptly, panic energizing her muscles. "What's this? Are you ganging up on me?" She started to jump out of bed, but her eyes had adjusted to the dim room, and she saw their faces. The quartet of minor dragons looked happy, not threatening.

She crossed her legs under the covers. "What do you want?"

Grandur settled on her calf. The dark dragon perched on her knee. It tilted its head and gazed into her eyes for a moment, then began to sing. The sounds coming from its little mouth were merely notes, but within her head, Tipper heard the words. A lullaby, one her father had sung to her when she was very little.

Astonishment gave way to peace. Tipper leaned back against the pillows. Grandur scampered up to her right shoulder, and Zabeth claimed the left. Junkit sat on her stomach and swayed back and forth in time with the music. The two green dragons, Grandur and Zabeth, lay down, stretching their bodies along a line from the base of her neck to the top of her arms. Warmth flowed down Tipper's back, through her arms, and up the nape of her neck to soothe even her tight scalp. The singing dragon settled on her leg.

She drifted off to sleep, content to have four minor dragons snuggling her like kittens.

Four passengers—Tipper, Fenworth, Librettowit, and Bealomondore—
sat in the crowded coach, one arranged through a rental agency in
Temperlain. Four minor dragons slept on laps and shoulders. In the
light of day, the new dark dragon's scales glimmered a rich shade of
purple. At breakfast, her father had said his name was Hue. Verrin
Schope sat on the top with the hired coachman.

The carriage rocked, and Fenworth jerked awake as his body hit the
side. "Confound it! Doesn't this heathen land have any decent dragons?"

The minor dragons lifted their heads and scowled at the wizard.

"Tact," said Librettowit. "Doesn't have it."

Bealomondore looked pointedly at the small creatures riding with
them. "We have four dragons. Are they not decent?"

Tipper noticed Zabeth stiffen her neck and peer over her shoulder at Bealomondore.

Librettowit stroked Junkit, who perched on his knee. "Yes, they
are fine, decent minor dragons."

"Exactly," grumped Fenworth. "What we need is riding dragons
or even a couple of major dragons."

"Larger dragons?" Bealomondore scoffed. "Large dragons fly over
the Sunset Mountains, but I've never heard of anyone riding one."

Wizard Fenworth rubbed his hands together with glee. "Yes, yes!
Where are these Sunset Mountains? Wait until you've ridden one, boy.
You'll never want to be trapped in one of these confounded boxes
again. Your grand parrot has the right idea. Fly!"

"It's out of the way for our first stop."

"But we'll make better time, more comfortably." Fenworth leaned
back with a contented sigh. "Tap on the roof, my good tumanhofer.
We'll inform the coachman and Verrin Schope of our change of plans."

Bealomondore looked at Librettowit. "Does he mean you or me?"

"Has to be you," said Librettowit. "He hasn't called me a good
tumanhofer for a century and more."

Bealomondore raised his cane and rapped on the ceiling. The coach slowed, and Fenworth grinned. "Ah, I look forward to the luxury of a dragon's wings beating a slow rhythm, a cool breeze in my face, the smell of clouds, the thrill of looking down from the sky upon the vista of the world—green pastures, rolling hills, ribbons of water, dark forests." He closed his eyes, his lips frozen in a lopsided grin.

Bealomondore gulped and ran a finger around the inside of his collar. "Looking down from the sky doesn't sound like an advantageous viewpoint to me."

"Nonsense, boy," said the wizard without opening his eyes. "Think of the paintings you can do."

"I'd rather have my feet on the ground when I paint. Actually, I prefer a wooden stool to sit on."

Fenworth's eyes opened. He nodded as he stared at the young tumanhofer. "You see? It's happening."

"What?"

"Memory loss."

"I haven't lost my memory."

"But you realize it will happen. You will witness vistas of incredible beauty but be unable to paint them. Why? Loss of memory. You will have forgotten the spectacle. You know it even now."

He leaned forward and spoke in a more confidential tone. "Quests do that, make you forget your everyday accomplishments. Foil logical thinking. Stymie progressive thought. In short, memory loss."

Bealomondore scowled and pursed his lips. "And why is this?"

The wizard sat back and resumed his normal volume. "The inconvenient necessity of expending energy to stay alive. One engages in fighting grawligs, beating back bisonbecks, ascending and descending mountains, traversing deserts, and the like. Very tiring. Also very absorbing occupations. Doesn't leave much time for cogitating."

Bealomondore rapped the ceiling of the coach again. The man's face showed nothing, but his knock to draw the attention of someone outside the carriage sounded desperate.

The coachman hollered, "Whoa!" They gradually came to a stop. The carriage dipped to one side as someone climbed down. The door opened, and the sight of her father's face took Tipper's breath away. He looked healthier, happier, more eager than the first night she saw him beside her bed.

But it wasn't his present state of health that overwhelmed her. Of course she was glad for that. The astonishment came from the mere fact that he was here. The wonder of it still gave her goose bumps, stunned her, stopped her breath. She'd done without him for so long.

Her mother should be enjoying his presence as well. But apparently she had, to some extent. A tingle of resentment prickled Tipper's joy.

Verrin Schope grinned at the passengers. "What can I do for you?"

"Dragons," barked Fenworth. "Riding dragons."

Verrin Schope's gaze slipped from one occupant of the coach to the next. "I'm sure Tipper and Bealomondore have told you that in Chiril, the larger dragons and people do not mix."

"It's high time they did."

Verrin Schope looked down the road on which they journeyed. Tipper could see by his expression that he was pondering the possibilities. She knew exactly when he decided they would get riding dragons. A light came to his eyes, the same light her mother had described shining when her husband was about to do something outrageous. Her mother exasperated her, but still Tipper wished Lady Peg traveled with them. She longed for both quizzical parents to travel on this quest. Oh, how her mother would love the adventure.

Tipper smiled to herself. Some things remained constant. Her bouncing back and forth from irritation to delight over her mother's antics didn't change. The thought of conversations between Lady Peg and Wizard Fenworth made her giggle. All eyes turned to her.

"I can't help it," she gasped. She fumbled for a rational explanation for her laughter. "I've never been on a quest before." She hiccuped. "And it's exciting."

The wizard harrumphed.

"And I just thought about riding on a dragon…"

Bealomondore said, "The idea makes me queasy. Humorous is not a description I would apply to such an 'adventure.'"

"It will take us two days to reach the Sunset Mountains," said Verrin Schope. "We'll overnight in Cambree."

He started to close the door, but Fenworth stuck his foot out. "Just a moment, young wizard."

Librettowit stirred. "What are you up to, Fen?"

"Just a cloud suspension, nothing fancy." He climbed down the two steps to the road.

Librettowit followed, grumbling. "Are you sure that's wise?"

"Necessary."

"Luxury."

Tipper leaned out of the carriage window to watch the two men.

Fenworth scowled at his librarian. "Don't be such a worrywart, man!"

"Don't you remember the last time?"

"I might." Fenworth pushed back his sleeves, dropping a lizard and a string of beetles. The lizard licked up a couple of bugs before slipping away. "Then again, I might not. Memory is never a reliable thing on a quest."

Librettowit put his hands on his hips. "There are some who would argue that we are not properly on a quest as of yet."

"There are some," Fenworth bellowed, "who would argue that the sky is not blue."

"There are some who would use a flimsy excuse to do something foolhardy and then not accept the consequences of their folly."

Fenworth tromped the few steps to stand directly in front of Librettowit. He leaned over so his straight, pointed nose pressed against the shorter man's bulbous snout.

"There are some," said the wizard in low tones of rumbling thunder, "who would arrive at their destination battered and bruised by the very seat they sat upon. Pummeled by the walls meant to protect them from the elements. There are some who would not deem to use an innocuous solution because of slim possibilities of error."

He suddenly grinned and clapped Librettowit on the shoulder, turning him to face the coach. "Done!"

Tipper looked down. What looked at first like a dust cloud surrounded the wheels of their vehicle up to the hubs. She blinked and remembered the wizards saying *cloud.* Yes, the turmoil beneath their coach looked like a billowing, stormy cloud. Smaller, of course. And flatter.

Librettowit clambered aboard. "Let's get going before this convenience becomes decidedly inconvenient."

Chuckling, Fenworth mounted the steps and entered the carriage. He sat and peered out the window. "Move, Verrin Schope. Librettowit is correct in saying we should make haste. Close the door and take your perch."

Tipper's father gave the old man a slight bow of obeisance as a servant to his master and closed the door.

When Beccaroon spotted his friends' coach, he thought the vehicle kicked up an amazing amount of dust. As he drew nearer, he realized the disturbance under the wheels stopped at the back and didn't trail off as road dust should. He narrowed his eyes. Some trick of the wizard's, no doubt. He continued to examine the phenomenon as he approached. Just as he leveled off to fly beside Verrin Schope on the driver's seat, he decided it was not dust at all but something like a cloud in the sky, a very turbulent cloud.

"What are you doing?" he called to his old friend.

"Floating." Verrin Schope grinned, clasped his hands behind his neck, and leaned back.

"Awk!" He looked down once more and decided to make no more comments on the cloud. "The Ciskenner Bridge is out. You'll have to turn at Daynot Corner and go south to the Moot Mooring. They'll ferry you across."

"That'll be a delay." Verrin Schope frowned and sat up. He peered over the edge.

"Is that a bad thing?" asked Beccaroon.

"Could be."

"Why?"

"Fenworth's manipulations have a habit of taking on unexpected characteristics."

"I knew it!" Beccaroon flew off to find a tree to roost in, a sip of warm nectar, and perhaps a few nuts. For the moment, he could not help those in the coach. "That wizard will do us in."

16

Baaa!

The detour to Moot Mooring required that they spend the night in Fox Ears instead of Cambree. The people of Fox Ears demonstrated a distinct distrust of the strangers.

"Why are they so standoffish?" Tipper asked Beccaroon.

He ruffled his feathers. "They've had kidnappings of their youth in this area. Everyone is on edge."

Tipper nodded toward a sinister-looking man standing near the door of the tavern. "I don't like that sheriff hanging around and giving us suspicious looks."

"He's doing what he should. If he were under my command in the Indigo Forest, I would commend him for a job well done."

In the morning, Tipper noticed the man scowling at them from the edge of a crowd that had gathered to see the strange visitors. She could almost feel the curiosity among the townspeople heighten as the wizard approached with what appeared to be a vine trailing off his robe.

Beccaroon strutted around the carriage, inspecting the wheels and avoiding the cloud. The grand parrot received a few glances, but most of the villagers were fascinated by the sight of more than one minor dragon in one place. The colorful dragons stretched their wings, zooming over the spectators, swooping down on Fenworth, and putting on quite a show.

As the wizard drew near the coach, the door popped open on its own accord. The crowd gasped. Fenworth ignored them and climbed in. "We're late."

"Make haste," said Librettowit. He put his hand on the back of Bealomondore's arm and urged him toward their conveyance.

Verrin Schope bowed to the watching sheriff and then to the crowd. Following her father's lead, Tipper curtsied. He took her hand and placed it on his arm. They walked to the carriage like a lord and his daughter.

Tipper's heart skipped a beat. She could not remember a time when she had paraded before a crowd as the daughter of the esteemed Verrin Schope. She grinned up at him, and he doffed his hat first to her and then with a gesture to the villagers.

Inside, she relaxed against the cushions as the horses pulled the carriage out of the small village.

"I have a feeling," she said, "that we are going to have a glorious quest. This day is the beginning of a great adventure."

Librettowit uttered what sounded like a growl. Surprised, she turned to look at him and felt her eyes open wider at the stern look on his face.

"Whatever is the matter?" she asked.

"The cloud's wet."

"The one underneath us?" asked Bealomondore.

"The very same."

Tipper leaned a little toward the window and looked down. "Aren't clouds supposed to be wet?"

Fenworth nestled back against the soft cushions of the carriage seat and crossed his arms over his chest. "My librarian is worried."

Tipper almost relaxed. By her observation, the librarian carried a load of anxiety with him. But on the other hand, the wizard often seemed out of touch with reality. She tensed. She had a lot of experience with what happened when a person in authority didn't correctly interpret her surroundings. Tipper's mother was capable of causing all sorts of difficulties.

Librettowit glared at Fenworth. "You should be too."

"Should be what? Wet?"

"Worried."

"Why?" asked Tipper and Bealomondore in unison.

Librettowit broke off his glare at the resting wizard to explain. "The cloud absorbed water as we crossed at Moot Mooring. Last night, the coachman had no idea he should keep the carriage at a distance from any body of water and left it smack-dab between the stream and the water well. The cloud took on even more water."

"Will that slow us down?" asked Bealomondore. "Because of the weight of the water, I mean."

"No," said Fenworth emphatically.

"Not because of the weight, Bealomondore," explained Librettowit patiently, "but because of the irregularities that are bound to erupt because of the changed nature of the cloud."

Apprehension crowded out the last lingering pleasant feelings that had bloomed in Tipper's heart as they began this leg of the journey. "I don't understand."

Librettowit sighed, leaned back against his seat, and closed his eyes. His voice sounded weary. "When Wulder creates a cloud, He has all things in control. Everything. In total. No room for variance. Complete control is not possible for a wizard."

Fenworth snored. Amazed, Tipper studied him to see if he had actually fallen asleep. He certainly appeared relaxed, and the nasal breathing continued. The man was a paradox she could not explain.

Bealomondore peeked out the window. "What do you think might happen?"

The sour look on Librettowit's face deepened. "Who knows? Thunder. Lightning. Whirlwinds. Hail. Mayhem of some kind, for sure."

The day passed without incident. Occasionally, Tipper felt a buzzing in her feet. If she lifted them off the carriage floor, the sensation ceased. As the day progressed, a drone accompanied the feeling.

She sang for a while to mask her discomfort. Hue and Librettowit joined her. The librarian had a fine voice and shared a few songs from Amara. As she listened to Hue and the older tumanhofer, she had the odd sensation of remembering tunes she could not possibly know.

Librettowit laughed. "Hue is delving into my mind to get the words and music and sharing them with you. It is part of his talent. He would be able to remember for you the lyrics of songs you have forgotten."

"He did that the other night." Tipper looked at the small purple dragon with amazement. "It was a lullaby Papa sang to me before he went away."

Librettowit stroked Hue with a finger. "It's a soothing talent but not one of the more practical ones." He looked Tipper in the eye. "Practicality is not always the most important element in a situation."

Their day of traveling stretched through long hours.

Bealomondore looked out the window and down at the road beneath them as often as Tipper did. His constant vigilance reawakened her apprehension each time she caught him peering downward at their buffer. The haze remained beneath them, and their ride was as smooth as boating on a calm lake. Only the darkening of their cloud caused Tipper concern. But surely dirt mixed with vapor would naturally be dark.

She couldn't ask Fenworth since the old wizard slept. She didn't want to ask Librettowit. Once he ceased singing, his dour attitude resurfaced. A pessimist would not relieve her fears. And her strained relationship with Bealomondore prohibited a chatty discussion of impending doom.

The sun dropped beyond the rolling hills, the air cooled, and field flowers gave off an intoxicating fragrance. Tipper leaned against the side of the coach with her face close to the window.

For long periods of time, her exciting adventure seemed more like a pleasant dream than an important life-or-death quest. When she remembered the rocks and the tree, she had to push away panic. Her father seemed healthier and happier than when he'd first returned, but the whole situation was odd and unsettling.

Her niggling doubts arose. A sleeping wizard might be leading them to an unpleasant destiny, her father might be ensnared by some evil influence that occurred while he was dealing with these men's foreign ideas, and Bealomondore might be in cahoots with art thieves. Anything horrendous was possible, including a storm manifesting itself between the wheels of their carriage. She fluctuated between ease and dread as the day drew to a close.

She heard the bleating of sheep and a shout from their coachman. The carriage came to a stop.

Bealomondore leaned out and reported. "There's a narrow pass between two cliffs. A shepherd is moving his flock through. Why didn't he go over the hill? Isn't that what sheep usually do?"

The wizard snorted and sat up. "Sheep?"

Librettowit cast him a nasty glare. "Wool!"

"Static." Fenworth pulled his hat off his head and plunged his fist into the depths of the crown. "Blast!"

As annoying as the brooding silence of the librarian and the snore-punctuated snooze of the ancient wizard had been, this agitated air between them made Tipper's skin crawl.

"What's wrong?" she whispered.

"Lightning," said Librettowit.

Fenworth tilted his head and raised both eyebrows. "Maybe not."

Librettowit rolled his eyes and reached for the door handle. "I, for one, am not going to wait and see." He hopped out of the carriage, then turned to extend a hand to Tipper. "Coming?"

Tipper took his hand, holding her long skirt aside with her other hand, and descended. As her feet passed through the cloud surrounding the steps, a chill swept up her legs.

With more speed than grace, she climbed a small knoll beside the road. Librettowit continued past her and stopped on a higher mound. From her vantage point, Tipper watched the fluffy backsides of the sheep crowd through the gap between the cliffs. The hill looked like it had split in half, one side sliding away from the other and sinking into the ground. She contemplated for a moment how such a rock formation could happen, but the plight of her father and the coachman distracted her.

She cupped her hand to her mouth. "Papa, are you coming?"

Verrin Schope waved at her. As she watched, he faded and reappeared in less than ten seconds. Was it right to say he was getting better? Could one get better at limping, or coughing, or this physical disposition of coming apart and reforming?

Bealomondore joined her. She shifted her attention away from her father. He and the coachman didn't seem worried about their predicament. She smiled at the young tumanhofer. Her nose crinkled against a disagreeable odor. "Their smell is a bit strong."

Wizard Fenworth labored up the incline. "I told you quests were unpleasant. Odors. Beasties carrying odors. Not exactly wild beasties, however."

The din from bleating sheep increased.

He covered his ears. "Noise. Raucous. Beasties or not, the bleating is bothersome." He frowned at Tipper. "Better than bellowing or roaring, I suppose."

Bealomondore straightened and peered around. "It seems to me that the cacophony is coming from more than one direction."

He turned toward the crest of the knoll, and Tipper followed his gaze.

Dozens of fluffy heads appeared first. The heads were, of course, attached to heavy bodies. At the bottom of each wooly leg was a dark, hard hoof. From directly in their path and looking up, Tipper decided these animals were huge.

The sheep charged down the hill.

She grabbed her skirt with one hand and Fenworth's sleeve with the other. "Run!"

17

Baa-Baa-Boom!

With a strong grip and a jerk, the wizard pulled Tipper next to his chest. She gasped but was so surprised that she didn't struggle. He wrapped his arm around her so that the wizard's cape he wore enveloped her.

"Steady, girl." His voice rasped in her ear. "None of your theatrics."

Before she could protest the slur against her character, air began to circulate as if a wind wound itself around them. The little she could see dimmed to darkness. She smelled biscuits and the flowering vine outside her bedroom window. She heard whistling and water pouring into a glass.

"There, there now." The wizard patted her arm. "We're almost there. Hold on a second, and we'll make a grand landing."

With a start, she realized her feet did, indeed, dangle into nothingness. The wind ceased, and she dropped with the wizard. A hard surface jarred her soles, and she sat down hard. Her vision cleared, and she found herself on top of the carriage, seated on a trunk, behind her father and the coachman.

"What are we doing back here?"

The wizard sat beside her on another trunk. He patted her back. "Better here than under the hoofs of rampaging sheep."

Shock registered on the hired man's face, but her father smiled a greeting. "Rampaging?" He frowned at Fenworth. "Do sheep rampage?"

Fenworth nodded decisively.

Tipper looked back to where she had just been standing. Bealomondore struggled to stay on his feet as the sheep plunged down the hill around him.

"Tut, tut, oh dear," said the wizard. "I seem to have forgotten something."

A large ram clouted Bealomondore's side. He spun and lost his balance, toppling forward. A full-coated ewe broke his fall. The tumanhofer wrapped his arms around her middle and kept himself from falling beneath the hoofs of the throng of sheep.

"Do something!" Tipper pulled on the wizard's sleeve.

"Something besides sitting?" asked Fenworth.

She let go of his robe and growled, "Oh, you!" She grabbed her father's shoulder. "Bealomondore is in trouble!"

Verrin Schope nodded. "I see that."

The minor dragons screeched and hopped into the air, batting their wings but doing nothing helpful.

Tipper stood and peered around. The carriage swayed under her. She spotted Librettowit, sitting on a round boulder at the top of another hill. With his hands folded between his knees, he calmly watched the drama being played out on the adjacent slope.

A shepherd and a younger version of himself came over the top of the hill, and for a moment, a surge of relief flowed through Tipper. But when the shepherd spotted the ewe plodding down the hill with Bealomondore clinging to her back, he dropped his staff and bent over double, laughing and slapping his knees. The son fell on the ground, rolling back and forth. Two dogs bounced beside the shepherd.

The herd reached the bottom of the hill. With the encouragement of another herding dog, the sheep turned toward the narrow way through which the road passed. In a moment, they would sweep past the carriage.

Tipper pounded her fist on the closest part of her father's anatomy. She could only reach his head from where she stood among the trunks. "Do something! Do something!"

"Excitable child," barked the wizard.

Verrin Schope ducked away from the onslaught and grabbed his daughter's hand. "He'll be all right as long as he stays on top of the ewe, Tipper. Danger awaits under the sheep, not on top."

"What if he falls?" she wailed.

Fenworth cupped his hand next to his mouth. "Hold tight!" he yelled.

The coachman joined in with further encouragement. "Hold on, man!"

While the uproar of cheering erupted from her companions, Tipper collapsed, sitting back down on the trunk strapped to the roof of the carriage. She refused to watch. Covering her eyes, she moaned over the fate of poor Bealomondore. The bleating of the sheep rose in volume, and their pungent odor increased as the matted, field-dirty animals swarmed around the carriage and pushed on toward their destination. They bumped against the vehicle, jostling the passengers.

"Tut, tut, oh dear."

She peeked at the wizard.

He shook his head. "This is not good."

She bit her lip, angry that the strange old man worked up concern for himself but callously ignored the tumanhofer's more precarious situation.

"Hurrah!" exclaimed Verrin Schope. "Here comes Beccaroon."

Tipper looked in the direction her father pointed. Her parrot friend approached and swooped down on the sheep.

The herd must have sensed an attack from above. Panic raised the volume of their grating voices. The forward flow of their charge broke into a mad dash for safety. Disorder multiplied in the narrow pass between cliffs, and the sheep thrashed against one another, trying to escape.

Beccaroon caught up with the flock. His claws snatched and held the fabric of Bealomondore's jacket. The tumanhofer had the presence of mind to release his death grip on the ewe. Bec delivered him to safety, setting him gently on the hilltop next to Librettowit and then landing a few feet beyond.

The shepherds, all mariones like Rolan, appeared. One came from ahead, and the man and his son descended the hill to offer direction from the rear. Several herding dogs contributed to compacting the panicked herd into the small natural pen provided by the pass in the road. The shepherds and dogs set to work restoring order to their flock.

Tipper covered her ears against the torrent of orders from the shepherds, barks from zealous dogs, and bleats from worried sheep. She looked down and saw that Wizard Fenworth had clapped his hands against the sides of his head as well. She jerked her arms down and frowned.

The man was useless in an emergency.

Reason poked a hole in her criticism. The wizard had whisked her out of harm's way. And he was a very, very old man. Perhaps she needed to adjust her attitude to include some gratitude and forbearance.

The clamor from the flock subsided, and Tipper contemplated what words she could say to express thanks for her rescue. Bealomondore sat on the hill, drinking from a flask Librettowit must have provided. Beccaroon stood beside them. She knew her guardian would expect her to quickly fulfill her obligation. She turned to the wizard and found him observing her with a gleam in his eye.

She drew in a breath, but before she could speak, the old man chortled. He clapped his hand on her father's shoulder.

"You've a good girl, Verrin Schope. Good heart. Loyal. Dutiful."
He winked at Tipper. "You're welcome, child." He slapped her father's
back. "You squeeze that tendency toward hysteria out of her, and she'll
be a good comrade on our quest."

Tipper bristled, but Wizard Fenworth paid her no mind.

"Excitable!" he exclaimed. "Prone to exasperation."

Tipper tamped down the words of vexation that perched on her
lips, ready to explode.

"Impatient too. Ought to wait a minute to see how things are
going to unfold. The quest is just the thing to knock some of that im-
petuousness out of her. Uncomfortable things, quests are, but great
for training the young."

His gaze shifted, leaving those who sat on the carriage. "Tut, tut,
oh dear. I imagine this fellow is ill-pleased."

The oldest shepherd approached. Tipper tried to read his expression. The minor dragons slipped behind her father and Fenworth.

"Greetings, friend!" Her father jumped down and extended his
hand.

The dragons scrambled to find cover behind Tipper.

The marione took Verrin Schope's offered handshake.

"You're on the road to Tallion," the shepherd said with a grunt.
"Did you know that?"

"Yes, we did."

"There's nothing beyond Tallion except the Mercigon territory of
the Sunset Mountains."

"We know that too."

The shepherd glowered. "You've business in Tallion, then?"

"No," answered her father, shaking his head as if to express his
regret.

"I thought not." The shepherd examined each of the travelers in turn, even the three on the hill, before he spoke again. "The road stops at Tallion. There is no road beyond."

"Ah," returned her father, this time nodding sagely. "We know that as well."

"There're dragons in the mountains, fierce dragons. Occasionally they pillage our crops and herds." He eyed Tipper. "Now it hasn't happened in centuries, mind you, but in the days of old, dragons captured fair maidens and took them off."

"Tut, tut, how rude." Fenworth patted Tipper's arm. "Perhaps they've learned some manners." He peered over the edge of the carriage top. "Do they breathe fire, young man?"

The shepherd snorted and turned to leave. "You'll find out, now, won't you?"

Fenworth's bushy eyebrows shot up. "Perceptive man. Of course we will." He clapped his hands together. "Sort yourselves out. Who's in the coach? Who's on top? We've a quest to undertake."

Fenworth decided to ride with the luggage on top, and Tipper chose to sit right behind her father. The wizard from Amara amazed her once more by wedging himself between two trunks and falling asleep. The minor dragons came out. Tipper delighted in being able to decipher bits and pieces of their outrage over the shepherd's slur on dragons. Bealomondore and Librettowit trudged down the hill and reluctantly climbed into the coach. The air had cleared of the odor of sheep but not of the disgruntled attitude of the two tumanhofers.

The sun began its descent behind the distant mountains, tinting the sky with pink and orange.

Tipper sighed as she observed a large bird circling above one snow-capped peak. An eagle? No, too large from this distance to be a bird. Her breath caught in her throat. A dragon! Dragons *did* fly over the Sunset Mountains.

She put her hand on her father's shoulder.

He patted it, and she looked his way to see that he, too, had spotted the dragon.

"You are in for an adventure, my dear."

A laugh bubbled up and poured forth. "I know. I know!"

18

A little Trouble Here

They reached their destination after dark and came to a halt at the crossing of the only two streets in Tallion. A bailiff came out to meet them, holding a torch aloft. He had no official badge but announced his position as he approached the carriage.

"Bailiff Tokloaman here. State your business."

Verrin Schope nodded to the fellow. "We need accommodations for the night and supplies for a quest tomorrow."

"We've got no inn, but the mayor will put up two of your people. Master Stone will put up the rest." He paused. "Do you know there's a light flickering under your coach?" He scratched his head with his free hand. "And there's rumbling, even though your wheels aren't turning. Maybe you should get down from that contraption and unhitch your horses."

Librettowit opened the door and hopped out in a hare's breath. Bealomondore scrambled out next but had the courtesy to turn around and offer Tipper assistance. She stepped down and peered beneath their carriage. Miniature bolts of lightning flashed through the cloud. After each glimmer, thunder vibrated the chassis and wheels. With every flicker, the resulting atmospheric growl grew louder. Several villagers appeared to gawk at the sight.

The minor dragons flew up to perch on the gable of the tallest building, a two-story home. They hopped up and down, screeching a stream of alarm. Her father and the coachman passed the luggage down to villagers on the ground.

Tipper gestured to the old gentleman who had ensconced himself in the carriage at the first sign of nightfall. "Do come on, Wizard Fenworth."

He grumbled and moved toward the door. A scattering of old leaves fell from his beard and robes. Both Tipper and the tumanhofer artist helped Fenworth negotiate the small steps through the cloud and onto solid ground. He groused about unnecessary panic as they urged him to hurry.

A crowd gathered in the cross streets. Every villager—man, woman, and child—must have turned out of their beds to see the phenomenon. They pressed their backs against the buildings but stared with fascination at the now empty carriage and the storm cloud beneath it. With the luggage piled at a safe distance, Tipper's father and the coachman helped the two lads unhitching the horses. As the boys led the tired sister mares away, a flurry of lightning crackled under the coach.

Through the open coach door, Tipper watched tiny bolts pierce the floor of the carriage and dance among the leaves left by the wizard. In the wild swirl of activity, one of the dry leaves ignited, then two. The lightning disappeared, a series of thunderclaps echoed through the street, and the burning leaves set aflame the others. The fire flowed across the floor and licked up the seats. With a pop, the vehicle flared into a bonfire blaze.

"Botheration," muttered Fenworth. "I hate it when that happens."

Tipper held on to his sleeve. "Can't you put it out with the water in the cloud?"

The wizard's eyes widened. "You have potential, my dear. Something I'd expect from Verrin Schope's daughter."

She tightened her grip of his sleeve and gave it a little shake. "The cloud. Water. Fire."

He patted her hand. "Yes, of course, but the cloud is under the coach, not on top. Rain doesn't fall up. You see the problem, no doubt."

"Buckets!" yelled a man.

The bailiff added his voice to the order. "The mayor's called for buckets. Step lively, folks."

Villagers scattered and returned to form a water line, passing buckets from the well to the fire. The coachman and Tipper's father joined the line. Tipper and Bealomondore looked at each other, nodded, and jumped into small openings between villagers.

Tipper noticed when Beccaroon joined the dragons on the rooftop. The townspeople saw him as well and pointed out the grand parrot to their friends. Everyone was too busy to stop and gawk.

With teamwork, they put out the fire, but not before the tinderbox coach caved in on itself and the four wheels folded, leaving charred circles of wood. A cheer greeted the last sizzle when the mayor himself poured out a bucket and proclaimed the emergency over.

The hired coachman stood between Tipper and her father. Sweat dripped down from his brow. He pulled a rag from his back pocket and mopped his gloomy face. "This is going to be hard to explain."

Verrin Schope clapped a hand on his shoulder. "You are a valiant man. We thank you for your heroic efforts to save our belongings. We will pay for the coach. Wizard Fenworth has the coins to pay for your service and to take back to your employers."

The *whoosh* of a relieved sigh changed the coachman's anxious demeanor. "You've been a strange crew to cart from one place to another, I'll say. But it's been an adventure I'll be recounting to my kids for years to come." He grinned.

Tipper giggled at Verrin Schope's expression, but her father chose not to take offense and changed his gasp of surprise to a congenial laugh.

The coachman walked off to see to his horses.

Tipper touched her father's arm to draw his attention. "Where did the wizard get money? Surely he can't spend coins from Amara in Chiril?"

"The wizard's hollows are full of marketable merchandise."

She smiled. "More than bugs and birds?"

"Yes. He said he sold all manner of things at a shop in Temperlain while you went in to discuss the journey with Bealomondore."

Now a sigh escaped Tipper.

"What's wrong?"

"I've been worried about expenses. I'm used to worrying about expenses."

Verrin Schope kissed the top of her head. "I know, my dear, and I am truly sorry."

To Tipper's surprise, no one left to go back to their beds. A party sprouted out of the aftermath of excitement. Women brought sandwiches and drinks, men appeared with tables, boys came running with wooden chairs, and a group of musicians gathered with their instruments and began to play. The old and young villagers, in their nightgowns, robes, slippers, and in some cases nightcaps, danced through the street. Tipper drank a sweet juice she couldn't identify and tapped her foot to the music.

She glanced at her father and saw him blink out, disappearing so suddenly that she doubted anyone noticed. Her eyes sought out the pile of luggage, and sure enough, he appeared, sitting on the trunk that held his piece of closet flooring. A sudden rush of gratefulness swelled in her heart. She was thankful the coachman had helped remove the trunks.

A muscled young marione pulled her cup from her hand and set it on a table. He caught her by the arm and dragged her into the merriment. She had never been to a dance, though her mother had taught her the most common steps. She whirled around with the exuberant young man and didn't mind a bit that he hadn't bowed before her first and asked, "May I have the honor of this dance?"

Bealomondore stole her from her first partner, and she soon realized this was a game played by all the men dancing in the street. She'd be whirled away and, when she finished the turn, would find a different partner greeting her. Sometimes the young man who had spun her lay in a heap, suggesting he had been forcefully removed. But no one was hurt, and Tipper thought she had never spent such a happy hour. She looked up and grinned at her parrot friend. He nodded his approval.

The bailiff sounded a horn, and the festivities came to an abrupt end. Tipper's father stood on a barrel and thanked the people for their aid in putting out the fire and for the fine food and dance. He thanked the music makers in particular. The villagers gave a last cheer, then set to work putting all to rights. A group of men shoveled up the coach debris.

"Come this way," said the mayor to Tipper and her father. "You may spend the night with my family."

"Thank you," said Tipper, suddenly exhausted and almost too weary to walk. Fortunately the mayor's house stood on one of the four corners of the crossing.

She opened the window of the room given to her as soon as the mistress of the house closed the door to the hall.

"Here," she called softly.

Hue, Junkit, Zabeth, and Grandur flew in the open window and found comfortable perches. She knew Beccaroon preferred to be out in the night.

Tipper scrubbed the smell of smoke off her skin and put on a fresh gown. She crawled between the sheets and barely noticed as the minor dragons settled on the bed around her.

"Questing is a wonderful occupation. I wish I'd started sooner," she whispered. Only the snores of four dragons answered her.

A small crowd of villagers marched along beside them as they hiked toward the Dragon Valley of the Mercigon Range. Each of the questing party carried a knapsack provided by the Amaran wizard. The bags were hollows, and Tipper had marveled as she transferred all her belongings from her large trunk to the small knapsack.

Fenworth declared as they left the town that this was "the beginning of the proper quest." Tipper felt a thrill of excitement, especially since the townspeople celebrated the occasion by trooping along.

Midmorning, the questers reached a ridge that provided a natural borderline between farmland and the mountains beyond.

"A break!" declared the mayor. "The women have brought refreshment, and then I'm afraid the people of Tallion will have to return and allow our esteemed visitors to resume their journey alone."

Enough rocks jutted out from the grassy ridge to provide seats and make-do tables. The village women produced a meal from their knapsacks.

"Enjoy this," said Librettowit. "Food on a quest can sometimes be a hit-or-miss ordeal."

"Harrumph." Wizard Fenworth glared at the librarian. "I've brought provisions. You'd think I didn't know what to pack for a quest. I've been on a few, you know."

"And I've been with you. Your idea of a tasty dinner is sometimes different from my own."

Tipper caught sight of a brilliant bird approaching and ran to greet Beccaroon with a hug when he landed.

"I've missed you," she said into his neck feathers.

"We left Tallion two hours ago. How have you had time to miss me?"

"I wish you'd stay with us."

"I am a more valuable companion in the air."

"But I'm more comfortable with you than with any of the other companions."

Beccaroon's gaze passed over the villagers and examined the questers. "Awk! Against my natural inclination, I've decided to mingle with you unfortunates restricted to walking."

Tipper offered him food and drink, and they enjoyed the conversation of the people from Tallion. The villagers enthusiastically offered advice and warnings. She decided that most would have enjoyed joining the quest, and she couldn't blame them. Tending crops and livestock could not be as pleasant as seeking dragons to ride and visiting intriguing cities to find lost art.

After a substantial noonmeal and a few speeches by the mayor, the Tallion citizen escort bade the questers farewell, replete with even more suggestions, cautionary counsel, and well wishes.

"No fire," said Wizard Fenworth as they waved to the last stragglers descending the hill. "None of the villagers remember ever seeing a dragon scorch a field. And we all know dragons love braised corn."

Bealomondore leaned toward Tipper. "We all knew that, didn't we?"

"Oh yes." She grinned at him. Since the dance last night, the wall between them had crumbled. She'd watched him be kind to old women and young, fair and not-so-fair. He danced with all, acting gallant to an old and rather smelly hag as well as to a gangly girl who wished very much to be counted as a young lady.

Tipper wanted that kindness to extend to her. The debonair tumanhofer's approval became important. "Am I forgiven?" she asked.

He looked at her with one eyebrow quirked, but the twinkle in his eye relieved any apprehension she had.

"Yes. I admit there were extenuating circumstances." His expression sobered. "But you understand that I will always examine what you say, wondering if circumstances are pushing against your ethics."

Tipper pursed her lips. "That doesn't sound like you've forgiven me."

He picked a cluster of purple grassblooms and handed them to her. "Forgiven you? Yes. Forgotten the offense? No. I won't act as if you lie at every opportunity, but I won't be caught again by any prevarication on your part."

Tipper sniffed the flowers, giving herself a moment to absorb what Bealomondore said. "I guess I deserve that."

"You do."

He didn't have to agree so quickly. Who was he to point out her shortcomings?

Words surfaced on her tongue. The words sprang from deep inside her. Sharp words, ready to wound. Strong words, tasting bitter in her mouth. She wanted to spit them out, but instead she swallowed, as if that would force them down. But these hateful words still clung to her lips. She swallowed again, but the action forced open her mouth. A hand gripping her elbow stopped the flow before it began.

"Tipper." Her father pulled at her arm. "Come walk with me." He nodded to Bealomondore. "Excuse us."

The tumanhofer bowed and strolled up the hill toward the other members of their party, who led the advance.

Verrin Schope pulled his daughter closer and tucked her hand in the crook of his arm. He gestured toward the grassblooms in her hand with his chin. "You've mangled the stems."

Tipper gasped at the mashed leaves and slender stalks. The heads of the purple blossoms drooped over the outside of her fist. Unclenching her hand, she let them drop. She stared at her palm covered with green goo. Her father flicked a cloth into her hand, and they stopped while she scrubbed away the evidence of her anger.

When they resumed their walk, Verrin Schope patted her arm.

"The Amarans have tomes written to record things that Wulder has proclaimed. Incidences in history, too, that reveal His wisdom. But I especially appreciate the pithy sayings that put into words exactly how things work—how we think and act and speak in a general sense. And how those processes influence our circumstances."

Tipper nodded, not really interested in what her father meant to tell her. Her heart still thumped in uneasy resentment of the fancy-mannered tumanhofer.

"Here is one of the principles you almost acted out in your dealing with Bealomondore."

He'd caught her attention, but she wouldn't urge him on. Instead she looked down, concentrating on the rocky path as it narrowed. Her father let her proceed and followed.

Even from behind, his voice sounded warm and close, personal and kind. " 'My mouth says what I have told it not to. My tongue spits the poison I would not swallow. Later is remorse, but now is the sweetness of one barbed morsel after another.' "

They walked on in silence. Tipper tried to repeat Verrin Schope's words in her head, but they didn't come out right. "Say it again," she requested reluctantly.

" 'My mouth says what I have told it not to. My tongue spits the poison I would not swallow. Later is remorse, but now is the sweetness of one barbed morsel after another.' "

"It means…?"

"You tell me."

She shook her head. She wouldn't attempt rephrasing the quote. Warring feelings of resentment and chagrin ruled her answer. "I wanted to blast Bealomondore with words that would hurt him. At the same time, I didn't want to allow those words out of my mouth. But I almost said them. You stopped me."

"Yes, and another principle in Wulder's Tomes is this: 'I stand. I fall. Another and another stand together. We do not fall. I stand. I fall. Another and another raise me to my feet. We do not fall.'"

"That means…?" She glanced back at her father.

He winked. "Another principle: 'The urge to do good blossoms in the company of those who also choose good. The urge to do bad can be multiplied by the influence of just one with evil intent.'"

Tipper laughed. "Do these people in Amara ever just say something like 'don't steal' or 'don't lie'?"

Verrin Schope caught up with her and draped his arm over her shoulders. He squeezed. "Yes, but apparently Wulder prefers His people to puzzle over things and deepen their attachment to His truth."

"Sounds like a lot of work."

"If you consider pondering to be laborious, then yes." He looked back over his shoulder and turned her to face the fertile valley behind them. "'A field tilled, a seed planted, the ground tended—the harvest repays each moment of care.'"

"Let me guess. That's in Wulder's Tomes."

"That's in Wulder's heart. Written as a promise and shared with His people."

"Does it help to know these things presented this way, Papa? After all, we have similar sayings. 'A cock crows to launch the day. A dove coos to ease the night.'"

"Yes, my dear. Truth exists in many Chiril sayings, but Wulder's equivalent goes beyond the stating of truth and reveals wisdom. That is an important difference."

At some point, as they climbed the steep hill, Tipper's reluctance to engage in this conversation had flown. Eagerly she asked for more insight from these tomes. "And what is Wulder's equivalent to the rooster and the dove?"

" 'Begin a day with vigor, and give the night the simplicity of rest. The day and the night will be similarly productive. One generating satisfaction, the other yielding peace.' "

"It sounds like a lot to learn."

"Like a song, dear Tipper. Like a song."

Tipper didn't ask what he meant. She knew. Songs had always been her comfort, like the lullaby she remembered from the days before his departure.

19

A Little Trouble There

Beccaroon plodded along beside Tipper and Bealomondore, listening to his girl's bubbly prattle.

Tipper gathered her skirt to avoid a row of prickly weeds. "I don't see what Fenworth objects to. He's always saying that a quest is a bother, an inconvenience—uncomfortable and fraught with danger. I disagree. Traveling by foot in this glorious weather isn't a hardship, and when our feet get sore, Grandur heals them."

Bealomondore nodded in enthusiastic agreement.

She gestured to the towering peaks. "The scenery among these majestic mountains is inspiring. You've scouted out easy trails, Bec. The whole venture has proven that questing is a marvelous enterprise. Why does anyone ever stay at home?"

"And I," said the tumanhofer artist, "am storing up memories of landscapes that will cover more canvas than I could possibly purchase. Despite what the wizard says about questing robbing me of recollection, I look forward to capturing these memories. I don't believe I will lose even one impression with the passage of time."

"At the risk of prying," Beccaroon began, "you are a paradox to me, Bealomondore. Your clothing, your manner, and your education all speak of being raised in an affluent home. But every now and again, you say something that speaks of poverty."

This time Bealomondore gave a somber nod. "I did not have the money to pay my bill at the hotel."

Tipper placed a hand on his arm. "You don't have to tell us if you'd rather not."

"And just now," he continued as if she had not spoken, "I mentioned more canvas than I could possibly purchase."

"Really," insisted Tipper, "we respect your privacy."

Beccaroon chortled. "Oh, let him say it, girl. You're as curious as I am."

She dropped her hand from the artist's arm and placed it on her hip, stopping to glare at her friend. "I'm trying to be more attentive to what my thoughtless words might incur. You know—embarrassment, regret, things like that."

"Well, it's not your wayward tongue, but mine." Beccaroon hopped over a half-hidden boulder. "Come on, Tipper, you can walk while you listen. No need to stand there in a pose of righteous indignation." He peered at Bealomondore, who looked to be at ease and ready to talk. "Go on, man. If she's determined not to hear, she can fall behind and walk with Fenworth and Librettowit."

Just as he suspected, the suggestion did not sit well with Tipper. She clamped her mouth shut and strode beside them.

Bealomondore did not seem at all nonplussed by having to explain his lack of funds. He strode along the path with the same jaunty air he always assumed.

"Well, as you have guessed, my childhood was spent in a comfortable home. My father is the head of a mining company. I have three sisters and one brother—an older brother, one who pleases my father in every way. I am the delight of my sisters and basically ignored by our mother. This is not a sore point, for my mother ignores us all equally."

Bealomondore tucked his thumbs under the straps of his knapsack. "My mother's sister, Aunt Eireenangie, cared for us as a governess.

She more than made up for our mother's neglect, and her strongest influence was in the area of art. My sisters are all accomplished watercolorists."

"And your brother?" asked Beccaroon, ignoring Tipper's glare of reproach. "His talent is in another form?"

"Talent?" The tumanhofer pursed his lips. "I've never thought of Araspillian as having a talent. My brother was and is attached to my father's coattails. Or perhaps I should say, he's walked with his hand in my father's pocket for so long he can no longer tell which set of trousers is his own."

The tumanhofer warmed to his descriptions and grinned with glee. "He treads so closely in our father's footsteps that at times he is wearing the same shoes." He chuckled. "The hat on his head is greased by my father's hair. He sees not with his own eyes but through my father's spectacles."

Beccaroon cleared his throat. "I think we get the idea."

"Ah yes, I suppose you do. The long and short of it is that my brother has won my father's favor, and eventually my father noticed that I was nowhere to be seen. He came looking and found that I was cultured. Not only was I cultured, but I was remarkably adept at the social arts. This might have been tolerated, but I painted. What male tumanhofer paints?"

He hunched his shoulders. "I was thrown out. My aunt gave me a small purse filled with coins. My sisters cried. My brother gloated. I have often wondered if my mother discovered the hullabaloo and made inquiry as to the source. Or if she did not, does she to this day not know I have been banished?"

Beccaroon noted the look of sympathy that Tipper cast the tumanhofer, and so did Bealomondore.

"Ah, Mistress Tipper, do not feel sorry for me. For quite some time, I dallied about in society. I am an entertaining character and contribute to any festivity with my sparkling conversation and uncommon wit. And I am knowledgeable in the fine arts. Hosts and hostesses like to be told that their collections are exquisite. Don't forget, I am also the premier expert on Verrin Schope's works."

His expression became serious. "But my passion is my painting, and one day I decided to establish myself as an artist. The same people who courted me and cosseted my whims when I was merely a decoration to their social revelry scorned my talent. Thus, I came to Byrdschopen."

Beccaroon bobbed his head. "Boscamon took with one hand and gave with the other." He nipped off a flower bud, chewed it, then spit out a hard black seed. "It's the way of things. Bealomondore is blessed with talent, then cursed with condemnation from his father and peers.

"And the juggler performs once more. We need help in finding the three statues, and while that ball is in the air, Boscamon slips in Bealomondore, who wants to study under Verrin Schope and just happens to know the whereabouts of the statues." The parrot tilted his head at Tipper, who obviously had something to say.

Her eyebrows lifted, accentuating her pointed features. "But you don't really believe that Boscamon exists."

"I believe there is something that acts to balance forces in the world. A juggler depicts the action as well as any other."

"You said you thought it would be nice to be able to thank whoever provided us with the beauty of your forest, of our surroundings." She stopped but moved again when Beccaroon prodded her with his wing.

He tamped down his irritation and strove for a calm voice. "And that is Boscamon, the conjurer. He pulls something out of nothing, much like your trickster wizard."

Tipper's eyes flashed with as much portent as that confounded cloud Fenworth had put under the coach. "Do you think my father is a trickster as well?" Her tone of voice dripped icicles.

Beccaroon almost chuckled. She sounded remarkably like her mother when Lady Peg chose to be affronted. He considered himself a wise old bird and did not hint that he found his girl amusing.

"Papa became a wizard while he was in Amara, and he's training to be a better one." She stopped again, and this time Beccaroon did not urge her on.

He no longer found her amusing, for she harped on the same things that worried him. He marched in silence.

He hadn't decided what he thought of this Wulder concept that Verrin Schope embraced. Indignation caused his feathers to fluff out, and that annoyed him. He'd rather carry his concern without exposing it to Tipper. He stewed over the whole business of his good friend's return and the nonsense he'd brought with him. Nonsense that included Wizard Fenworth and his librarian, as well as some astonishing philosophies.

Tipper came up beside him again, and he struggled for words that would say what he wanted to clarify but reveal nothing more of his turmoil.

"Of course, I don't take the tales of Boscamon seriously. No one but a very young child does. And that is why it bothers me so much that your father is committed to this Wulder. If he is intelligent enough to see through the fable of our own making, why has he chosen to be gullible where this other country's fable is concerned?"

"Perhaps," said Tipper, "because this Wulder is not a fable."

"Awk!" Beccaroon spread his wings and left the troubling band of fellow questers below, seeking clearer vision in the blue skies above.

The questing party sat along a stream in the second valley they'd entered that day. Tipper pulled off her soft leather boots and silky stockings and plunged her aching feet into the cool water.

"Good idea," announced her father as he sat beside her on the grassy bank. He took off heavier footgear and socks, then rolled up his trouser legs. He splashed as he plopped his feet into the stream up to his calves.

Tipper laughed. "Be careful."

He leaned back, supporting himself on his elbows, and gazed into the branches of a bentleaf tree. "Fenworth and Librettowit have decided we should camp here."

"Shouldn't we wait for Beccaroon to come back and report? He would know if this is the best place."

Her father frowned. "Do you really want to put your shoes back on and walk even one mile farther?"

"Ummm…" She pretended to think about it. "No."

They laughed and sank back on the soft grass.

Tipper put her hands behind her head. "Oh, this almost feels like a mattress."

"Wait until Fenworth pulls our bedding out of his hollows. You will not believe how comfortable you can be in a sleeping bag."

"A bag?"

Her father rolled on his side, propped himself up on one arm, and poked her, making her giggle. "A sleeping bag is like your softest down quilt at home. It's folded over and fastens up the side. You'll be warm and cozy, and these sleeping bags are even more rest-inducing than the beds we slept on in the mayor's house."

"I can't wait." She pulled her feet out of the water but did not get up. "I'm sorer than I've ever been. Will Grandur help ease my aches?"

"As soon as he and Zabeth have had some time together."

Tipper rolled to face him and gave her father an inquisitive look. "Romance?"

Verrin Schope slapped his knee and sat up. Chortling, he managed to speak. "No, no, not that." He stopped. "Well, I don't think so, at least. Grandur is trying to help Zabeth awaken her skills as a healer."

The thought brought Tipper to an upright position. "Zabeth is a healer?"

"She's green." He stood and gathered his boots and socks.

"What does that have to do with anything?"

He extended a hand to help Tipper up. "Green dragons most often are healers. Purple dragons like Hue are usually singers."

Tipper stood with her hands on her hips. Verrin Schope snatched up her footwear and held them out. After a moment, she took them. "Maybe just dragons from Amara do this kind of thing."

"Hue is from Beccaroon's forest."

"He is?"

"Yes. He didn't come through the gateway. Grandur found him in the forest and brought him to you to help you transition to being able to mindspeak with the dragons."

"I've only been able to do this 'mindspeaking' a very little."

"I know." He put his arm around her shoulders and started toward Fenworth, Librettowit, and Bealomondore.

"How do you know?"

"Junkit told Grandur. Grandur told me."

Tipper leaned against her father. "Why could I do it well only the one time at Boss Inn?"

"You were in just the right state of mind. And you had a need, probably an emotional need, that made you even more receptive."

"I have *almost* heard them since then, but not quite. I did hear the lullaby."

"That is exactly why Grandur brought Hue into our midst."

Bealomondore stood close by with wooden stakes and a tangle of ropes in his hands. He looked up as Tipper and her father approached. "I hope you know what to do with these things. That wizard's in a foul mood. I thought he'd turn me into one of his toads when I asked him to explain again what I was supposed to do."

Verrin Schope strode to the young tumanhofer's side and took the knotted ropes. "I've never known Fenworth to turn anyone into anything. I've seen him convince a snake that it was a stick. And I've heard him teach an owl to howl. But I think you're safe from toadhood, Bealomondore."

The ropes had fallen into straight lines while Tipper's father held them. "Come," he said to the tumanhofer. "I'll help you put up the tents." He gazed around at the slope of the land and pointed to one level area. "There. Tipper, see if you can help our wizard with our meal."

The aroma of roasted chicken still mingled with the smoke of the fire when Beccaroon returned. He strutted into their cozy circle and perched on a fallen log. The questers voiced their welcome.

Tipper didn't get up to greet him. "Bec, I'm tired and full and wonderfully content to just lie here. Have you eaten? What did you see?"

"I've eaten. And I've seen two things of interest."

The murmuring between camp members ceased. Even the minor dragons gave Beccaroon their attention. Tipper licked her lips and gave a quick glance around at the others, all stilled by anticipation.

"What did you see, Bec?" asked Tipper.

The parrot's eyes creased at the corners, the closest he ever came to a smile. Tipper felt a warm glow at the sight. Everything—well, almost everything—had been astounding. And Beccaroon had good news.

"I've spotted the dragons."

Tipper clapped. Bealomondore squirmed. Librettowit, Fenworth, and her father exchanged satisfied smiles.

"Far?" asked Fenworth.

Beccaroon shook his head. "No, but the other thing I saw isn't far either."

"What is that?" asked Verrin Schope.

"In this unpopulated mountain range, where only animals are said to dwell, there is a man-made tower."

"An ancient edifice?" asked Librettowit.

Bec's voice dropped. "Undoubtedly."

Tipper's skin crawled. "It's old and abandoned, right?"

"I saw no one, but there is evidence that someone has been concerned with the upkeep. A well-tended garden circles the base, the windows are clean, and a square on the roof has been recently patched."

"Found the dragons?" Fenworth rubbed his hands on his knees, and lightning bugs swirled around his hat. "Our course is plotted."

"What about the tower?" asked Bealomondore.

"Tower?" He pinched his chin, pulling that scrap of beard into a tight cluster. "I've never heard of a tower attacking anyone. We shall proceed."

Bealomondore came to his feet, and he paced back and forth beside the fire. He abruptly stopped. "I don't know that I want to ride on a dragon."

"That's not such a big problem, son," said Librettowit. "There's a much weightier problem to consider."

Bealomondore's expression looked even more morose. "And that is?"

Librettowit rubbed his nose. "What if the dragons don't want *you* to ride on *them*?"

20

Dragons!

If Hue hadn't sung her to sleep, Tipper might have been awake all night. Grandur eased her sore muscles, and Zabeth decided to be cuddly, curling up next to her inside the sleeping bag. But Hue's soothing tones pulled away the tension and then calmed her anticipation. Still, she awoke when the first morning bird trilled and the dawn light barely gave color to the festoon of yellow and orange mountain lilies.

She stood as she ate breakfast, unable to contain her excitement and sit serenely with the others. She studied the happy faces of her companions. Bealomondore alone exhibited a thwarted spirit.

"I'm off." Beccaroon shook his tail feathers. "I want to scout for the inhabitants of the tower. Perhaps this early in the morning I will catch them close to home."

"Well, then," said Bealomondore with an uneasy smile, "we can wait for your return before embarking on our search for the dragons."

Beccaroon laughed. "I'm sorry, dear tumanhofer. I've given directions to Verrin Schope. You'll reach the meadow where the dragons rested last night before I will."

The young tumanhofer held a spoonful of porridge aloft. "Perhaps they moved on this morning."

"I doubt that you shall be so fortunate." The big bird stretched. "The area looked like it was their usual residence." He moved away from the fire, flapping his wings. "The sun is up." He took flight as he bade them, "Fair weather and good progress, my friends."

Tipper smiled as she watched her feathered friend fly away. His colorful form grew smaller and smaller until he appeared as a large black dot and then vanished behind a hillside. In spite of his doubts, he seemed to be enjoying this adventure.

The sky was clear and crisp and, to her way of thinking, absolutely astonishing. But she turned from the enjoyment of her surroundings to the work they all must do. She helped gather their paraphernalia as quickly as she could and took it to Fenworth. She didn't even pause a moment to gape with her usual fascination as the wizard slipped object after bulky object into his cloak.

When their campsite was restored to its natural state, Verrin Schope led the way, following the stream to a small lake. From there they traveled west to a narrow valley that served as a passage between two larger mountain peaks. By midafternoon, they reached a spot where the trees thinned and revealed a spectacular view of the expanse between the lofty peaks. Tipper gasped at the beauty of the landscape. She'd never been able to see so far from anywhere near Byrdschopen.

"It must be miles to the other side," she said.

No one responded. The panorama created a feeling of awe. Tipper sensed something far more imposing than the vista. She looked around, wondering if a large and magnificent beast watched them.

Her father stood closest to the edge, where the ground dropped off in a gradual decline. He flickered, faded out, and returned almost too quickly to notice. If Tipper hadn't been looking directly at him, she would have missed it. Her father had come close to mastering his problem. With him as their leader, she knew everything would turn out well.

Large, flat boulders, laid out like a grand staircase, provided an easy path down the gentle slope to the massive valley floor. The surface of the vale rippled in gently rolling hills. Streams crisscrossed the entire region, small stands of trees dotted the expanse, and a lake sparkled at the southernmost end.

Directly across from their vantage point, a pale stone tower pointed to the sky. Numerous colored windows reflected the rays of the sun, glistening like jewels set in a scepter. Red and blue swirls decorated the bulbous top, and an emerald green band circled the base of the roof globe, shimmering as if made of some metal.

"There!" declared Wizard Fenworth.

Tipper followed the line of his pointing finger.

On one of the hills, three large dragons stood at attention, obviously watching them, strangers that dared enter their valley. Tipper blinked. Was the splendid awareness she'd felt earlier generated by these creatures? She willed herself to evaluate the atmosphere surrounding her, but that elusive presence from before was gone. She realized the mysterious sensation had nothing to do with the dragons.

Still, they were not ordinary animals. Their scales shimmered in the sunlight, one predominantly blue, one purple, and the last, shades of scarlet, gold, and cream.

The minor dragons piped a rumpus of shrill chatter. Grandur flew off in the direction of the large dragons. Junkit, Zabeth, and Hue hesitated for a moment and then flew after the Amaran dragon.

"Those huge beasts have seen us," squeaked Bealomondore. "Don't you think we should hide?"

"Harrumph!" said Fenworth. "Dragons don't have to see you to know where you are."

Librettowit scowled. "That's not exactly true, Fen." He turned to Tipper and the other tumanhofer. "Dragons can make a bond with one of our kind, then they know exactly where their partner is. All dragons do not know where all people are at all times. One dragon may know where one person is, but only if he has that special rapport with that person. But we are in no danger. Dragons are passive creatures unless connected with someone evil or driven to defend something or someone of importance to them."

"Oh," said Tipper, still unraveling the information.

"They're far too interested in us for my comfort," said Bealomondore.

Fenworth charged forth as fast as the old man could travel, using his walking staff and almost hopping from one flat stone to the next.

"Wait up, Fen," called Tipper's father. "We're not going to get there any faster if we have to pick up your broken body and carry you."

The old man called over his shoulder, "Insolent pup!" and kept up his breakneck pace.

"Fortunately," said Tipper's father as he took her arm. "His fast isn't too fast for us to catch up."

They scrambled down the massive steps while the dragons watched them with interest. Once in the basin, the questing party had to trudge through several pastures of waist-high grass and cross three streams. They could no longer keep an eye on their target with the landscape serving as an obstacle.

The pace of the two old men amazed Tipper. She expected Fenworth to demand one of his "rests," but the wizard tramped forward with a steady flow of energy.

She didn't worry so much about the wizard and Librettowit since she could see that neither man looked in distress, but she wondered about Zabeth and Junkit. They were old, too, and only accustomed to trials that might arise in a household, not the wild.

"I wish our dragons would return."

Her father glanced her way. "They can take care of themselves."

"You don't think those big dragons will hurt the little ones?"

"I shouldn't think so. I can't recall ever hearing of such a thing."

Tipper concluded that her father's knowledge of what dragons did in Chiril was as limited as her own, so she clarified his statement. "In Amara."

"Well, yes, of course, in Amara," replied her father, his tone a bit impatient. "Why should it be different in Chiril?"

Tipper saved her breath for hiking. Her father did not choose to be worried, and neither did Librettowit and Fenworth. Librettowit would most certainly worry if there was a need. Since the librarian did not perceive a danger, she resolved to be optimistic. She glanced back at Bealomondore. His reluctant trudging looked anything but confident of their reception.

His apprehension rubbed off on her, and she wished Beccaroon would return soon. With the big bird by her side, she would be braver in confronting the enormous dragons. He'd always stood with her when she had to do something difficult.

As they got close to their destination, they chose to go around a little wood rather than through it. After the stand of trees, they climbed one last hill before Fenworth called a halt. On the next knoll, the three dragons munched on grass and scrutinized the intruders with no particular alarm.

Next to Fenworth, a mound of grass-covered dirt pushed up out of the earth until it was the proper height for a seat. Fenworth perched on it.

"Now there's a fine sight," he exclaimed. "Three healthy riding dragons. Not a bit skittish around people. This should be an enjoyable interlude. Then we shall be on our way. Questing for the real objects of our quest instead of questing for a means of questing more efficiently, not to mention in comfort."

Fenworth reached inside his cloak and pulled out a tall glass filled with a ruby liquid. He took a drink and smacked his lips. "A quest can be so irritating, but with proper planning and cooperative dragons, *our* quest shall progress quite well."

Librettowit sat on the ground. "I wouldn't say we've properly tested the theory of cooperative dragons, Fenworth."

"Hungry?" asked the wizard. "I am too. Gather round, everyone. Let's feast before we play."

Verrin Schope's new custom of thanking Wulder for their provisions included gratitude for a snack from the wizard's hollows. Tipper paused out of respect for her father's little speech, then bit into the flat, circular, crunchy cake called a daggart.

Librettowit passed out flasks of cold milk. The next portion of their refreshment consisted of a handful of nuts and a parnot fruit for each. Tipper particularly liked the green fruit from Amara. And last, Fenworth pulled out sandwiches with crisp lettuce and thin slices of ham. Each piece of the meal was chilled, but Tipper knew that Fenworth could just as easily pull out mugs of hot soup.

Bealomondore wiped his fingers on a handkerchief. "Have we decided not to go any farther? Those beasts look much bigger than they did from the mountain pass."

Fenworth stood up, and the mound flattened back to its original state. "Ah, dragons. Let us go make their acquaintance. These splendid beasts should make cheery, first-rate companions."

"If they don't eat us," said Bealomondore as he rose and halfheartedly dusted bits of grass from his trousers.

Tipper bounced along behind Fenworth, Librettowit, and her father. Bealomondore followed, staying close enough not to be separated from the group but still managing to drag his feet.

A dozen yards from the red and gold dragon, Fenworth came to a standstill. He raised his hand in salutation. "Hello. I'm known as Wizard Fenworth. We've come a long distance to enlist your aid."

The dragon snorted, bent his neck, and ripped off another swatch of tall grass. He chewed and eyed Fenworth.

"Do you suppose," asked Bealomondore in a whisper, "that these dragons are strictly vegetarian?"

Librettowit pointed to a pile of bones. The younger tumanhofer gulped and covered his mouth. From the size of the rib cages, Tipper assumed the animals had been goats and sheep. Most of the bones were cracked and broken. Obviously the dragons chewed on the whole animal and spit out the skeleton. Other animals and birds probably stripped off the remaining meat. Tipper found nothing disgusting in the sight, but Bealomondore paled and turned away.

The wizard edged slightly toward Verrin Schope but kept his eyes on the dragon. "Have you tried to mindspeak to our new friends?"

"Yes, all of them."

"I assume you've had no success."

Verrin Schope shook his head.

"Peculiar." Wizard Fenworth clutched his beard at his chin's point. "Neither have I."

"Each message seems to disappear into a black void." Verrin Schope put his hands on his hips. "I believe they are deliberately shutting us out."

The red dragon stepped toward them.

"He's coming," Bealomondore squeaked and backed up.

"Hold your ground," ordered Librettowit. "The last thing we need is for the creatures to think we're playing a game of chase and they're supposed to catch us."

The younger tumanhofer froze in place.

The red dragon took nine more steps closer and stretched out his neck. His face stopped inches from Fenworth's. They stood looking into each other's eyes. Then the dragon lifted his chin slightly, puffed through his nostrils, and blew Fenworth's crumpled wizard hat off his head. The creature turned, barely missing them with his tail, and loped away.

Knowing how particular Fenworth could be about his hat, Tipper expected one of his tirades. But he remained unruffled. Verrin Schope picked up the hat and handed it back to the wizard.

"Hot breath, but not scorching," said Fenworth. He paused, tilted his head, then grinned. "Did you hear that?"

"I did," said Verrin Schope, smiling as well.

"What?" demanded Tipper.

"A chortle," said her father.

"More than one," said Fenworth.

Tipper glared at them. "I don't understand."

Her father winked. "The dragons are laughing at us."

21

Frustration

Beccaroon circled the knoll, watching the strange dance Fenworth and Verrin Schope performed with the dragons. The men approached, the dragons allowed them to get close, the men held out a hand, the dragons sidled away. The ballet loosely followed the same pattern again and again.

Bealomondore and Librettowit sat beneath a lone tree to one side. Tipper had claimed a boulder in the midst of the action. Beccaroon landed beside his girl and noted that she looked bored. She held a flower chain made from wild mumfers. She greeted him with a wan smile, picked another bloom, and split the stem.

"What are they doing?" Beccaroon asked.

"Trying to establish communication." Tipper sighed. "We've found a difficult watch of dragons."

"Watch?"

"It's a grouping like a herd or a swarm or a flock."

Beccaroon eyed the three dragons and two men. "The dragons don't seem aggressive. Very placid. They don't seem to mind being approached."

"Papa says they're playing a game and laughing at us."

"So they *can* communicate."

"He's sure of it, though they won't cooperate. He and Fenworth have caught bits and pieces of their thoughts but mostly the sound of them laughing."

Beccaroon watched them for a minute more, then turned to study Bealomondore and Librettowit. The older tumanhofer appeared to be asleep. The younger sketched on a large pad of paper.

"Where are our dragons?" he asked.

"I don't know." She waved a mumfer in the air. "They flew ahead of us with Grandur in the lead. They headed this direction, so I assumed they would be here."

Beccaroon saw the concern in her eyes. "And you are worried."

"Yes! And everyone else says they're all right and not to fuss. Except Bealomondore, who says nothing." She paused. "I don't think he likes dragons. Not our little ones and certainly not the big ones."

"He appears to be drawing them."

Tipper looked from the artist to the scene around her. "They *are* lovely."

Beccaroon studied the dragons and then the young tumanhofer. "Perhaps his aesthetic sensitivities will be aroused by their beauty, and he'll begin to appreciate them."

She joined the beginning and end of her string of blooms and hung it around her neck. She picked a pink mumfer and started another chain.

They sat in silence, Beccaroon watching the play between man and beast. Tipper concentrated on her fragile jewelry, making a crown, another necklace, and a bracelet for each arm.

Beccaroon nudged her with his wing. "One of the dragons is coming this way."

The blue dragon approached. His chest scales glistened turquoise, and his darker sides looked like the gray blue waters of a deep lake. Pale blue wings furled and unfurled as he strode closer. His intelligent face glittered with a pattern of three shades of blue. White circled his eyes, making them look larger than they were.

Beccaroon straightened his legs from his resting position, and Tipper stood.

"What should we do?" whispered Tipper.

Beccaroon glanced at Verrin Schope. The sculptor didn't appear to be alarmed for his daughter's safety. "I assume imitating what that wizard and your father have been doing would be our best choice."

"But Papa and Fenworth have been approaching the dragons. This dragon is moving toward us."

Dealing with dragons was outside his realm of experience, but Beccaroon decided that the dragons should behave as many wild animals do. If not threatened, the dragon should remain nonviolent.

"Just be still." Too late, it occurred to him that the smaller birds of the mountain forest might be a food source for the big creatures.

Tipper spoke softly, her voice full of wonder. "Oh, he has kind eyes."

Kind eyes? Beccaroon looked away from the sharp teeth that had captured his attention and allowed himself to gaze into the dragon's expressive face. "He certainly looks like a thinking animal."

"I dare not reach out to him," said Tipper.

"Why not?"

"Haven't you noticed that when Papa and Fenworth try to touch the dragons, that is when they move away?" She smiled up at the beast. "I want him to stay."

With a tongue that was just as blue as his wings, the beast licked his lips.

"I don't know that I like that gesture," said Beccaroon. "Do you suppose it's hungry?"

"Not it, she."

Beccaroon jerked, then wished he hadn't. The dragon switched her attention from Tipper to him. "How do you know it's a she? You've been saying *he*."

"I know, but now I know she's a she. I think she told me."

The dragon's attention returned to Tipper. She pushed her snout against the emerlindian girl's stomach, then her feet, sniffing with a soft whuffing sound.

Tipper giggled. "That tickles."

The dragon nosed her from bottom to top. She backed up a bit, eyed Tipper, then came forward again with her lips parted.

Beccaroon scooted closer to Tipper and stretched a wing between his girl and the huge beast.

"She's not going to bite me," Tipper reassured him. "She likes my flowers."

In a manner similar to the way Beccaroon had seen horses eat from the hands of small children, the dragon placed her lips around the crown of flowers and pulled them out of Tipper's hair. She closed her eyes and chewed, then nuzzled Tipper's neck and got hold of the two garlands there. The blue tongue slipped out and wrapped around the delicate chains. With one tug, the dragon broke the necklaces and then slurped in the lovely blooms.

She sat back on her haunches, closed her eyes, and lifted her chin as she chewed. A throaty thrum issued from the beast.

"She's humming." Tipper clasped her hands together and bounced on her toes.

Verrin Schope's voice startled Beccaroon. "Tipper, my dear, you seem to have developed a rapport." He came along the side of the blue dragon and looked under the creature's chin at his daughter. "See if she will allow you to touch her."

Tipper slowly lifted her hand. The beast did not move. She stretched out her arm and laid her palm on the blue scales covering the dragon's foreleg. The emerlindian girl's face beamed. "Her name is Merry."

"She's given you her name. That's significant." Verrin Schope laughed. "And very humbling. Here Fenworth and I have experience with riding dragons, and the least likely among us has made progress."

Beccaroon cleared his throat. "Pardon me, but I believe I am the least likely. I do not find these creatures as fascinating as our girl does. And I'm certainly not interested in bonding with a dragon."

Merry opened her eyes and stared at Beccaroon. She lowered her head and gave him a push on his brightly feathered chest.

"Awk!" He fluttered into the air and came down again a few feet away. "Rude!"

Tipper put one hand on her hip and pointed a finger with the other. She shook it at Beccaroon. "It seems to me she would be justified in saying *you* are rude." She changed her voice to match the parrot's. " 'I'm certainly not interested in bonding with a dragon.' "

She rammed her other hand onto her hip as well and waggled her head at her mentor. "I was taught to be more considerate of others' feelings. Particularly when meeting someone for the first time." She lifted her chin. "*And* I seem to be able to remember my manners even though I have lived a secluded life and not had the infinite opportunities to practice as you have."

"All right, all right." Beccaroon came back to her side and looked up at Merry. "I beg your pardon. My remark was thoughtless."

Tipper whirled around to face the blue dragon and shook a finger in her face. "Stop that! The appropriate response is, 'You are forgiven.' Or, 'No harm done.' Or, 'Apology accepted.' "

Beccaroon turned to Verrin Schope and cocked an eyebrow at his friend's amused expression. "What is going on?"

"Merry is laughing."

"I don't hear her."

"She's laughing in her mind," Verrin Schope explained. "And Tipper wants her to be serious about accepting your apology."

"I got the last part." Beccaroon fumed. These dragons were even more trouble than the wizard.

The questers made no further progress with the dragons that afternoon. As the sun lowered in the west, they decided to abandon their efforts for the day and camp in the glen between the wooded area and the dragons' hill.

In the morning, Tipper sat beside Merry and watched the wizard and her father work to gain the other dragons' confidence. Verrin Schope convinced the purple dragon to allow him to put his hand on her leg. He learned the dragon's name, Kelsi.

Kelsi would not mindspeak to him but seemed to understand everything Verrin Schope said…to a point. She allowed him to stroke her scales. She accepted a token gift of muffins from Fenworth's hollows. She didn't turn her back on him or walk away.

Several times, Tipper's father thought he might be able to mount her from the side and sit as a rider. Each time he made the climb, he reached a spot closer to the top. Then the obstreperous dragon shed him. She either leaned her bulk to one side so the slope of her flank became a perpendicular wall of slippery skin, impossible to hold on to, or she gave a gentle shake that dislodged the climbing emerlindian. After each unsuccessful attempt, the dragons chortled.

Fenworth went through all sorts of procedures to ingratiate himself with the red and gold dragon. He lectured, he hummed, he meditated, he danced, and he massaged the creature's toes. The dragon seemed to like the massage and the humming best. The old wizard never attempted to climb aboard the dragon, and eventually he and his nemesis curled up together under the lone tree and took a nap.

The noonmeal included a variety of sandwiches and two kinds of soup. Fenworth grumbled about wasted time. Beccaroon left on another search for the mysterious and evasive inhabitants of the tower. Bealomondore displayed the sketches he'd been making, and Verrin Schope gave him some pointers about light and shadow when dealing with a vast landscape. His drawings of the dragons were more comical than realistic.

After the meal, they all—except Beccaroon—went back to the dragons on the hill. As they stood at one edge and contemplated plans that might win the dragons' favor, Beccaroon returned, flying in at a speed he normally reserved for emergencies. He landed beside them.

"I've found an emerlindian," he said through panting breaths.

"Where?" asked Verrin Schope.

"Right behind me." He looked up at the sky.

A dark spot grew as it neared.

"A dragon," said Bealomondore.

Wizard Fenworth nodded with satisfaction. "And a dragon rider."

The dragon zoomed over the meadows, and his yellow and white wings stilled as the creature glided toward Merry. The dragon rider stood on the flying dragon's back. The air rushing past rippled his loose-fitting tan tunic and trousers. The light material pressed against his tall, thin form. As rider and dragon crossed over the blue dragon, the pale emerlindian flipped himself into the air and landed on Merry's back. She spread her wings and launched into the air, following the yellow and white dragon.

"Did you see that?" Tipper exclaimed.

"Imprudent," said Librettowit.

"Astounding," said Bealomondore.

Merry circled and landed so abruptly that the young man on her back somersaulted down her outstretched neck, came up on his feet, and ran to Kelsi. Her purple tail lined up with Merry's head. Tipper realized the dragons must have done this on purpose.

The rider ran up the incline of Kelsi's tail, and as soon as he stopped on her back, she took off. Tipper smiled at the intent look on the rider's face. A band of green material wrapped around his head kept his longish blond hair out of his eyes. A glint of gold on the band reminded Tipper of her mother's royal circlet.

The young man did a flip in the air and landed with one of his feet on each side of the ridge running up the dragon's back. The first dragon caught up with Kelsi. When they were neck and neck, wingtip to wingtip, the emerlindian raced over Kelsi's wing and jumped to the white dragon's wing. Both dragons on the ground trumpeted, then launched into the air. All four dragons flew toward the eastern range, then circled back. The rider ran and jumped across all four dragons.

"He's crazy," said Bealomondore.

Tipper twisted her lips. "Show-off."

When the dragons returned, the rider sat on the white dragon's neck. The three others veered off in different directions, but the white dragon pointed his head upward and began a vertical climb. The young man, his blond hair blowing in the wind, leaned forward and wrapped his arms as well as his legs around his neck. The dragon went over backward and completed a loop in the sky, returning to an upright flying position with the rider still attached to his neck.

"Aha!" said the wizard. "We've been talking to the wrong person— or persons, one might say."

Tipper huffed. "You mean we have to talk to that flashy show-off?"

"Indeed," said the smug wizard. "*That* is a dragon keeper. And a dragon keeper will solve our problems."

"How?" asked Bealomondore.

"By convincing the dragons to cooperate."

The young tumanhofer scowled. "And what assurance do we have that the dragon keeper will cooperate?"

The smirk fell from Wizard Fenworth's face. "Young man, you have listened to Librettowit for too long. Problems are not problems before they occur. After a problem has sprouted, it is indeed proper and prudent to address the problem. But to attend to a problem before it has manifested as a problem is foolhardy. Kindly refrain from attempting to present problems that are, at the moment, nonexistent."

Librettowit gave the younger man a sympathetic nod.

Bealomondore sighed. "Yes sir."

"Quite proper, that!" Fenworth clapped his hands together and disturbed a bat sleeping in his sleeve. The little beast flew away in a staggered path, evidently bewildered by the bright day. "A good 'yes sir' strategically placed is a gem, a diamond, a jewel set in gold."

The young tumanhofer leaned toward Tipper's ear.

"What is he talking about?" he whispered.

"Nothing," she said, then shrugged. "Or maybe everything."

Verrin Schope came to stand behind them and draped his arms over their shoulders. "You'll get used to him."

Librettowit smiled, and the strange grimace of widened mouth and large, square teeth made Tipper laugh. He chuckled, then laughed with her. They ended up sitting together on the grass while the four dragons and their rider circled above them.

22

Uncooperative

"Look," cried Tipper, pointing to the sky. "Are those our dragons?"

She knew they could be. Their bodies hung under the wings rather than being positioned between them. The small airborne creatures couldn't possibly be birds. But the minor dragons flew too far from where the questers stood. Tipper could not determine if they were Grandur, Hue, Junkit, and Zabeth.

She turned to her father. "Can't you mindspeak with Grandur? Is it him? What are they doing?"

Her father's frown grew fiercer. "It is Grandur, and I can mindspeak with him, but the conversation is not going well."

Bealomondore came to Tipper's side. "What's going on?"

"I don't know, but I don't think it's good." She turned back to Verrin Schope. "Can't you order Grandur to come back?"

"Order a dragon?" He snorted. "No, my dear, one does not order a dragon to do anything. I think I've mentioned this before. One seeks to acquire his cooperation."

"But doesn't Grandur enjoy doing things with you? I thought he liked you."

The four large dragons circled and headed toward the high end of the valley, where the tower stood. The minor dragons followed.

A light breeze skipped across Tipper's bare arms, and either that or her father's cold expression made her shiver. She turned to see Wizard Fenworth leaning over Librettowit, engaged in a serious conversation.

Tipper scurried over to find out what the men knew about the little dragons defecting from their questing party.

A word exploded from the wizard. "Young!"

"Inexperienced," the tumanhofer barked back.

"Needs to learn a thing or two."

"Now," said Librettowit with a grin, "isn't it fortunate that we've come along to give him the benefit of our vast knowledge?"

Tipper stopped and waited for them to see her. They were too engrossed in their own discussion to notice.

"I," said the wizard, "am not opposed to aiding a youngster in bettering himself."

"Surely there is a mentor somewhere."

"If there is, he has been most ineffectual."

"We shall see. This is a strange country with strange customs."

Tipper cleared her throat. Both men turned toward her.

"That dragon keeper has our minor dragons. What are we going to do?" she asked.

Fenworth straightened. He left Librettowit and came to her, putting his arm around her shoulders. With gentle pressure, he turned her and guided her back toward their camp.

"Why, we're going to go calling on the inhabitant of the tower."

"That dragon rider?"

"Yes."

"How do you know he lives there?"

Fenworth stopped and turned shocked eyes to examine her. "You really don't know, do you?" He patted her shoulder and sighed. "I'm a wizard, dear child."

Tipper fought the urge to stamp her foot and answered as calmly as she could. "I am aware, sir, that you are a wizard."

"Well, wizards do things, you know. And we know things as

well. And, of course, wizards aren't in the least bit timid about saying so."

He turned to shout to the others. "Hurry, my friends. We have an appointment with the local dragon keeper."

Tipper ran down the hill and began disassembling her tent before the others caught up with her.

"What's the hurry?" asked Bealomondore.

"That boy has our dragons."

The young tumanhofer stood looking at her until she cast a glare over her shoulder. He shrugged and then scooped up a pile of blankets. He divided them and poked them into their hollow knapsacks. Then he tackled the equipment Tipper gathered at a furious rate. He kept an eye on her frenzy with a scowl on his face.

Tipper rounded on him, placed her hands on her hips, and scowled back. "You can quit staring at me as if I'd suddenly grown another nose. What is your problem?"

"Are you mad at the dragon rider, the dragons, me, or the whole world?"

Her hands flew up in the air, expressing her outrage in a flurry of flapping fingers. "I was learning to talk to them. I was getting better at interpreting the impressions I got. I thought they liked me."

"Who? The big dragons or the little ones?"

"Both!" She plopped onto the folded tent, put her elbows on her knees, and hid her face in her hands. "Who does he think he is?"

Bealomondore shuffled his feet. "The dragon rider?"

She nodded and sniffed.

"I guess he thinks he's a dragon rider, or keeper, or whatever Fenworth called him."

Tipper heard Beccaroon's claws scratch the dirt as he approached. She quickly sat up, scrubbing the tears off her cheeks with the sleeve of her blouse. She stood and snatched up the canvas tent but over-balanced when she rose. Staggering under its weight, she tried to keep from falling. Bealomondore rushed forward, grabbed the other side of the bulky tent, and steadied her.

She looked into his face, attempted a smile, and mouthed, "Thank you."

He winked.

"Tipper," said Beccaroon. "I'd like to talk to you."

Bealomondore pulled the bundle from her arms. "I'll take this over to Fenworth."

She let him go and turned to face the inquiring eyes of her mentor.

"Talk to me." He settled on a fallen log.

She sighed and sat beside him. "The ease and comfort of our journey has been destroyed. That one ill-mannered ruffian, that dragon keeper, had the power to turn the tide."

Beccaroon chuckled and shook his head. "You amaze me, my girl. We've had a sheriff look down his nose at us, we've dealt with frantic sheep and a catastrophic fire, and you label this quest with words like *ease* and *comfort*."

"This quest has been a lot more fun than figuring out where to get more seeds after an insect infestation, or how to get a new pane of glass for a broken window, or how to pay the butcher. Climbing a mountain trail is more exciting than hoeing the garden. Sleeping under the stars is better than mending old, old tattered sheets. Dancing in the streets is definitely preferable to dusting a whole library full of books that nobody reads."

Beccaroon held up the tip of one wing and silenced her outpouring. "I have explained to you the way of life, and you have experienced it on a small scale at Byrdschopen. Our quest will involve the same things. Beauty and ugliness. Feast and famine. Fortune and misfortune.

A balance. Why do you expect life with no death? Why do you welcome rain and curse the flood? You must accept both the good and the bad to claim maturity."

"I could quote that speech, Bec. You've said it often enough."

"Because it's true. If you struggle against truth, you will be dissatisfied and, ultimately, unhappy."

"It all seems so haphazard. We should have more control over... everything." She hung her head, knowing Beccaroon would likely point out the futility of such a desire. Her bird friend said nothing, and Tipper peeked at his face. He stared off into the nearby woods.

Tipper examined the trees but saw nothing. Nervous twinges pulled at her, making her tense, ready to run. What had captured Beccaroon's full attention? She searched the trees again.

"Do you see something?" she asked.

"No, I don't see at all." He shook out his feathers. "And that bothers me." He hopped off the log and strutted to where the others worked.

Tipper looked back at the small forest, then at Beccaroon's retreating back. She tilted her head, puzzled. "I don't think he was talking about things you *can* see." Her head bobbed a nod as she came to a conclusion. "He's bothered by Papa's ideas."

Thinking about their conversation, she could not determine what had reminded Beccaroon of her Papa's strange devotion to that Wulder. She pulled in a deep breath and let it out, wishing there was someone to question besides herself.

Bealomondore walked alongside Tipper, and she marveled that he had chosen her as a companion on their hike. She also wondered that he turned out to be the one she preferred as well.

Glad that her mother was not with them to complicate matters, she kept pace with the shorter man. With mother safely at Aunt Soo's, Tipper didn't have to explain over and over that she and the tumanhofer were not stepping out together. Just walking. She grinned.

"What are you thinking?" asked Bealomondore.

"That walking is pleasant. We've only had small knolls to trudge up. Some of those mountain passes were too steep to be enjoyable."

"Ah yes, but the views!" He smiled in memory, then gestured back toward Librettowit and Fenworth. "I wish we could get them a ride. They're too old to be tramping through mountains. And I don't think it's right that the wizard carries so much of the camping gear."

Tipper watched Fenworth for a moment. The old man leaned on his walking stick and breathed heavily. Birds circled his head from time to time or rested on his shoulder. She knew that bugs of all kinds, and even snakes and lizards, roamed through his clothing with the same comfort with which they inhabited the alpine terrain.

She turned back to the tumanhofer. "I don't think he really carries it. I know he puts it in those pockets—"

"Hollows."

"Hollows. But I don't think it exists until he takes it out again."

Bealomondore chuckled. "That doesn't make any more sense than his explanation." He winked at her. "Or the librarian's."

Tipper grinned. "Not much those two do makes any sense to me."

He squinted at the long narrow meadow through which they traveled. "We aren't going to reach the tower tonight."

She agreed, and the idea worried her. "Do you suppose the longer he has our dragons, the harder it will be to get them back?"

"I didn't see any leashes. I don't think he has them captured. Once we get close to them, they'll want to come back to the ones they know best."

Tipper shook her head. "Papa said that when he tried to get

Grandur to return, the little dragon just acted annoyed to be interrupted. He was excited over the dragon keeper. Fascinated. His little brain frantically reflected image after image of the dragon rider to the exclusion of all else."

"That certainly doesn't sound normal."

"It's not."

"So what are our learned leaders going to do about it?"

Tipper pointed to the tower. "They are going to talk to the source of the problem."

23

Disobliging

"I didn't sleep for more than ten minutes at a time, and I ache all over," Tipper complained as she stood holding two corners of a sleeping bag.

Her father walked toward her, holding the other end. He joined his corners with hers, pulled them out of her hands, and finished making the cumbersome item ready to be stored. She watched as it decreased in bulk each time he folded the material. By the time he handed it back to her, it fit in her hand like a large potato.

She hefted the sleeping bag, testing its heaviness against its small size. The bundle weighed more like a heavy rock.

"Are you going to teach me how to do things like this?"

Verrin Schope continued packing the gear from his tent. "If Wulder has given you the talent, I would be pleased to help you expand your gift."

Tipper thought of all the talents her father exhibited. Painting, sculpting, architecture, languages, music, the analytical sciences. The list went on forever.

"I don't believe Wulder gave me a talent."

Her father stopped putting large objects in a small bag. With his arms crossed over his chest, he studied her. She stood still for a moment, then shifted her feet. He continued to stare, and the longer he examined her, the more uncomfortable she became.

What should she do with her arms? She crossed them in imitation of his stance. That didn't feel right. She clasped her hands behind her back. That was better.

She looked at his face and caught him still looking at hers. She swiftly focused on Fenworth and Librettowit chatting on the other side of the camp.

Her father's voice interrupted her discomfort. "Your most obvious talent is singing." He picked up his small bag of belongings. "Music is a wonderful tool for so many other endeavors. For instance, a song may bolster a deficiency in the heart. A rousing march builds courage for soldiers headed to war. A ballad may help a frozen heart express grief. Music lifts the spirits, expresses true emotion, heals, and fortifies. Ah yes, your talent for song is an incredible gift and worth investing in to develop."

He held up a finger, indicating he had more to say on the topic. "The quest should bring out more of your talents that are presently unrecognized."

He grinned and made a face that reminded Tipper of Wizard Fenworth, then spoke in the old man's voice. "Quests are uncomfortable. You know that, don't you? But if you're hiding talents, they'll come jumping out of you during a quest. Kind of like bubble beetles when they hear water running. That can be uncomfortable too, all that talent leaping around."

Verrin Schope came to his daughter and gathered her in a tight embrace. He kissed the top of her head. "You're to be careful. Bubble beetles sometimes drown in the water they converged upon with such zeal."

He leaned back and looked her in the eye. "Did you say something earlier about not sleeping? You're sore?"

"Yes. I went to bed without Grandur working his wonders on my poor feet and tired legs. And I missed Hue's nighttime hums. His music is soothing."

"Two weeks ago you ignored Junkit and Zabeth. Now you know our little friends' usefulness. I'd say they spoiled you."

"I didn't totally ignore the house dragons. I think I did pretty much ignore Trisoda."

"Trisoda?"

"The barn dragon. He's new. Beccaroon brought him to us when I was twelve."

"Ah." Sadness pulled at her father's face, making him look older. "I missed a lot." He planted another kiss on her forehead and lightened his tone. "But we shall find the three statues and allow them to embrace, and I shall stay at home, read books, and drink hot amaloot."

"Are you coming?" barked Fenworth.

Beccaroon strutted toward Tipper and her father. "I'm going on ahead. I'll meet you at the tower."

"Be careful," Tipper warned, and the big bird rewarded her with one of his grouchiest looks before he took off.

With mixed feelings, Tipper walked with the others to the beautiful tower. Someone cultivated the land around the tower. Small fields contained corn and wheat, and an orchard lined up in even rows. Closer to the stone building, vegetables grew in neat plots. The place looked more prosperous than Byrdschopen.

Beccaroon waited for them at an arched entryway in a thick hedge. A few feet beyond, a moat surrounded the base of the tower. When they crossed a dainty wooden bridge over the circular splashing brook, they entered a flower garden.

Tipper could name most of the plants, but at the far end of the walkway, one unusual shrub caught her attention. The beauty of this bush fascinated Tipper. Tiny dark green leaves provided the backdrop to large, brilliant blooms. She had never seen a plant that put forth flowers in such a variety of colors.

She hurried down the path to examine it and stopped in shock as the blossoms uncurled and flew away. "Minor dragons!"

Dozens of minor dragons inhabited the foliage. She wandered the intertwining lanes in the expansive garden. Birds, butterflies, and dragons flitted from hedges to stands of miniature trees to flower beds.

"Hello!"

The word caused Tipper to jump. She whirled around to glare at the speaker.

The dragon rider stood ten feet away, a smile on his face, blue eyes sparkling, his shoulder-length blond hair combed, his white and tawny-gold clothing neat, and his arms hanging loosely by his side. Tipper caught her breath. The man was stunning.

"I'm glad you came." He walked forward. "I hoped your visit would be today. We're having a sort of celebration. May I introduce myself?" He stopped before her and bowed.

When she first met Bealomondore, he had performed a formal court bow with a flourish, complete with the clicking of heels. The dragon rider merely bowed his head and bent slightly at his waist, putting one arm behind his back and crossing the other over his middle. The gesture made Tipper's toes curl inside her boots.

She extended her hand. He took it and clasped it lightly. "I am Prince Jayrus." He nodded to the lone tower. "This is my castle."

Tipper's eyes flitted to the stone wall, where, on a windowsill, sat the four minor dragons belonging to her questing party. She jerked back her hand and used it to point at the deserters.

"What are you doing with our dragons?"

His head whipped around to see where she pointed. "You're speaking of Hue, Grandur, Junkit, and Zabeth?"

"Yes!" She stepped around him, closer to the window. "How do you know their names? Are you a wizard?"

Prince Jayrus laughed. "Being a prince and a dragon keeper is enough to keep me busy. I'm not sure I'd want to add wizard, even if I had a clear idea what one was." He gestured to his home. "The castle is filled with books, and I've seen the term used. But I've never met a wizard."

The gravel crunched as Wizard Fenworth, with Librettowit, came to join them. "I'm not surprised," he said. "As far as I know, there are only two in Chiril."

The dragon rider turned and greeted the old man. "May I get you a seat, sir? Your journey has been long. I anticipated your arrival, and there are refreshments in the castle."

"Castle?" Fenworth looked around hastily. "I seem to have overlooked the castle."

Prince Jayrus pointed out the tower.

Fenworth scratched his cheek through the long beard. "Young man, one tower does not a castle make."

The dragon rider looked confused.

"Tut, tut, oh dear," said Fenworth. "Lots of new concepts for you today, no doubt. I'm a wizard, and my friend here, Librettowit, is my librarian. You say you have books. He'll like that."

Fenworth stepped closer and took Tipper's arm. "And this young lady is Tipper. The two men joining us from that direction," he said, indicating one of the longer garden paths, "are artists. Verrin Schope is every kind of artist. Give him a twig, and he'll whittle a figurine. The man can't seem to leave things alone. Has to create art!

"The young tumanhofer with him paints. Two artists. Oh, and Verrin Schope is a wizard as well. Said two, didn't I? Verrin Schope and I make two wizards in Chiril. Sounds like a musical, *Two Wizards in Chiril*."

Wizard Fenworth hailed the two companions. "Verrin Schope,

Bealomondore, come meet our host, who has offered us a light repast."

Verrin Schope strode up confidently and shook hands with the younger emerlindian. "Pleased to meet you."

"He's Prince Jayrus," said Librettowit.

Verrin Schope's eyebrows shot up. "A prince? I didn't know there were any outside my wife's family in Chiril."

The dragon rider's face shuttered, his emotions suddenly hidden from his guests. Tipper's curiosity tingled. Her eyes widened, and she studied the prince. His proper mask crept back in place, but his hospitable smile didn't reach his eyes.

"This way. My people have been lavish in their preparations. We do not often have guests."

Tipper paused. "Where is Beccaroon?"

"Here I am." He stepped from behind a large bush, and Tipper had the odd notion that he had been standing there watching all the time.

She cast him a puzzled look, and he returned it with a slight shake of his head. Putting aside her question for her old friend, she fell into step beside the prince and quizzed him.

"Why won't our dragons return to us? What have you done to them?"

"Done?" His easy manner returned in full. "I haven't done a thing. I welcomed them just as I have welcomed you. I can see you are encountering concepts that are new to you." His glance toward Wizard Fenworth held a shadow of unease. "I am a dragon keeper. It is natural that the dragons prefer to keep my company."

"You stole them."

"That is absurd." He said the words without rancor.

Tipper changed tactics. "What is the celebration?"

"My ascension to the throne was five years ago today."

She stole a sideways glance at him. His profile was just as striking as looking full in his face. She caught her breath. Not only were his features perfect, but he oozed self-confidence and a dignity that went with self-assurance. How had she considered him a show-off? The memory of his aerobatic stunts brought back the appraisal she'd made the day before.

For a fleeting moment she felt again that irritation. "Prince of what? I know you aren't part of the royal family of Chiril. I've studied the lineage."

He looked her way, caught her eye, and smiled. She recalled his last statement.

"Does that mean your father died five years ago?"

His expression changed, the shadow of sorrow dimming his light-hearted charm. "Not my father."

"Your mother?"

"No." He turned to address the others. "I welcome you to Castle Dragon Eyre."

They entered through an archway that had no door. Odd crystals glowing with a blue light illuminated the cool interior. A long table set with china and silver graced the middle of the round room. A circular staircase followed one wall and disappeared into the ceiling.

"Come." The prince urged his guests to gather around the feast. He seated Tipper in a chair to the left of the head, and the others chose their places. The prince sat in the elaborately carved wooden chair at the end, between Tipper and Wizard Fenworth.

"I do thank you," said the old wizard. "I've grown quite tired of my own cooking. This is far more than refreshments—more like a meal. Nothing looks to be poisoned, so we'll gladly partake."

The young prince raised his eyebrows but made no comment.

"Do you mind," asked Verrin Schope, "if we bless this food and your hospitality in the name of our Creator?"

"This is your custom?" asked Prince Jayrus.

"It is a courtesy to Wulder. It is not required but gives pleasure to us and to Him."

The dragon keeper nodded. "This, I understand."

Although Tipper bowed her head as her father had instructed her, she watched Jayrus out of the corner of her eye. He stayed alert and turned his eyes to one after another of his visitors. When he came to the grand parrot, he found Beccaroon staring back at him. With remarkable composure, Jayrus nodded and continued his scrutiny until the brief prayer ended.

The delicious food occupied much of their time, and their host asked many questions, keeping each of them talking in turn. Tipper found herself relaxing and enjoying his enthusiasm. He graciously inquired of their homes and expressed such a genuine interest that even Librettowit and Beccaroon returned amiable answers.

Librettowit fell into a long description of his bookrooms. Tipper had to grin when he revealed that the wizard's castle was a hollow tree. The prince looked with interest at Fenworth, but the wizard made no comment. Perhaps one tower wasn't a castle in Amara, but a hollow tree did not make a castle in Chiril.

"This meal was delicious," said Bealomondore, dabbing his mouth with a linen napkin. "Where are your servants? I'd like to express my gratitude."

"I don't have servants," said the prince.

"You said—" Tipper felt her new trust in their host evaporate.

"I used the word *people*. Just as the dragons are mine by their choice, the kimens work the land and keep the castle because they derive pleasure from their tasks. I have never demanded a chore performed.

"This is a concept I see you do not understand. I am the prince. My relationship with dragons and kimens is a natural result of my position and their perception of what is expected of them. They fulfill who they are by what they do. Just as I fulfill who I am by what I do."

"Service!" said Fenworth, banging the table. "An admirable staple to a code of ethics. Service smooths deficiencies. Service stimulates the economy. Service incapacitates hopelessness. Service makes barreling catastrophe inert. Service, Prince Jayrus, comes in handy."

The dragon rider's eyes had narrowed during this speech. He nodded warily.

"Our request of you is merely a request for a service."

The prince's body stiffened, and he placed both hands on the edge of the table.

"We require speedy transportation in order to save a man's life," the old wizard continued. "Will you oblige?"

"What do you mean by speedy transportation?"

"The loan of five riding dragons."

"Then I must disoblige," said the prince. "My dragons stay here in Mercigon."

He rose and left the room. Hue, Zabeth, Junkit, and Grandur followed.

Tipper jumped to her feet. "Wait!"

Neither the dragon keeper nor the dragons paid her any heed.

24

Contrary

The room filled with silence. Tipper plopped back into her seat. "Now what?"

Fenworth stood up. "Did that young prince offer us a room? I could use a nap."

Librettowit pushed out his chair. "No, he did not, and I thoroughly agree with you. What do you say to putting up a couple of hammocks in that orchard?"

"I suppose," said Bealomondore, grinning as he carefully placed his used napkin beside his plate, "that we shall have to abandon our attempt to acquire dragons and resume our quest without them."

"Oh no, not at all." Fenworth stopped on his way out, turned to look back at the table, and leaned on his walking staff. "Tipper will go have a talk with the young prince, and all will be well. Get some rest. We continue our journey in the morning."

Tipper's mouth fell open, and she couldn't gather her wits fast enough to object to the old man's plan. He and Librettowit walked side by side through the broad archway and into the sunshine.

"Well," said Bealomondore, "you need not try too hard on my account. We can ride horses, ride in a carriage, ride in a boat, ride a big sheep, anything but fly high above the ground. Go talk to Prince Jayrus, but don't feel I will condemn you if you do not succeed in persuading him to lend us a speedy form of transportation."

Verrin Schope reached for a pitcher and refilled his goblet. "I, on the other hand, would appreciate the use of his dragons to speed our journey. We've interacted with these dragons long enough to know that the creatures are gentle. We've seen their cooperation with a rider and know they are adept at carrying our kind. And not to alarm you, my dear, but I'm experiencing some physical difficulties that can only mean my time is running short. We must reunite the three statues."

Tipper took a long look at her father, saw the black circles under his eyes, noticed then how he had become thinner, and realized his general air of vitality had diminished. She swallowed the urge to cry and stood.

"I'll see what I can do." She walked out the same door the prince had used.

Tipper followed the only path that led away from the back door of the tower. She crossed the moat and passed through another arch in the hedge. On this side of the prince's castle, a lawn dotted with small lavender flowers rolled away and ended at the base of a hill. Wild-flowers covered the rise to one large tree. The prince sat on a bench under the widespread branches. Minor dragons flew around him, catching insects but also playing with each other.

Without waiting to formulate some kind of persuasive speech, Tipper began the long walk. As she trod on the ankle-deep grasses with tiny flowers in profuse numbers, a spicy-sweet fragrance rose around her. Phrases popped into her head.

Service to mankind.
For the good of all.
Life or death for my father.
Selfish, stingy, unfeeling, mule-headed…

Well, the last certainly described his attitude. But he didn't know the circumstances, and once he did, surely he'd see the need and agree to help. She panted as she climbed the hill.

No one allows another to suffer if aid can be given.

Your help is needed.

No one else can come to my father's rescue.

Do you want something in return?

Are you a beast with a heart of stone?

He stood as she came into his circle beneath the spreading tree and gave her his polished bow.

She liked the way he did that. For some reason, it made her feel very special. But he didn't speak. When he looked her in the eye, she saw he'd frozen his face into a noncommittal, though pleasant, mask. And that made her feel like kicking him.

She tamped down her ire. For her father's sake, she must be diplomatic.

"I need to talk to you."

He gestured to the bench. "Please, have a seat."

She sat and waited, expecting him to urge her to begin. He didn't. She looked down at her hands to hide the fierce scowl she knew occupied her face. She wished she had the same control over her features that he maintained over his.

When she felt she had her face schooled and her voice under control, she looked up at him.

"We are on a quest," she said. "Years ago, my father accidentally stepped through a contraption called a gateway. He ended up on the other side of the world where Wizard Fenworth and Librettowit live. The gateway was an experiment and never very stable. My father was trapped in Amara. For years, the three men—Fenworth, Librettowit, and my father—have been trying to fix whatever it is that went wrong. I'm not very clear about the technical things."

She gave a sigh and studied his face, hoping to see some interest in his expression. He still wore a cool, polite mask.

The urge to show her impatience almost got the better of her, but she continued in an even tone. "They were able to repair the gateway to the point that my father could visit home, but after a few hours, he was pulled back through the hole to Amara. If he didn't go willingly, he came apart. He still comes apart, but now the gateway is entirely shattered."

Surely Prince Jayrus would ask how someone came apart. But he remained silent. Tipper balled her fists in her lap. Rather than look at his incredibly handsome and nonexpressive face, she stared at one of the minor dragons sitting on a limb of the tree. At least the little pink dragon looked interested in her tale.

"The problem is a marble stone my father used to sculpt three statues. The wizard had tied the framework of the gateway to that stone, and since it is in three pieces, the frame didn't hold."

The pink dragon tilted his head, and Tipper felt him urging her to continue. "I sold the three statues, so we have to find them and put them back together. Not like they were, of course. My father created the statues so they stood separately, but if you place them together, they look like three people dancing in a ring while embracing one another."

She smiled at the dragon, a young male named Vanz. "Yes, yes," she answered him. "Very clever. My father works wonders with stone and clay." She paused and spoke again. "I sold them because, without my father there to make a living, we had no way to support the manor and the people who lived there. Eventually most of the servants had to seek employment elsewhere."

She nodded. "Yes, he still comes apart. He looks like he's fading. Then he comes back together in the vortex of the gateway, which fortunately he is able to carry with him. The problem is that it is not good for his health to be coming apart two or three times a day."

She stood and walked over to speak directly to Vanz. "I totally agree with you. An extremely unpleasant business. I must do something to help my father, and although Bealomondore knows where he last saw each statue, traveling by conventional means is much too slow. He says we must get to Fayetopolis, Hunthaven, and Ohidae. Ohidae is very far away. It will all take too long."

Movement in a far field caught her eye. Several huge dragons grazed peacefully. "No," she whispered. "I've never ridden a dragon."

"It's impossible," said Prince Jayrus, his voice like another whoosh of the breeze through the leaves above them. "I would break a covenant generations old. Those who are given dominion over the Mercigon dragons are charged to keep them here and keep them safe. I and the dragons will never leave this valley."

She turned to face him. "My father will die. The world is in danger as well. Librettowit says the gateway is trying to fix itself. It reaches out and takes hold of something physical, dissolves it, then reforms it in a ludicrous copy. This is done at random and will ultimately destroy everything. Everything, Prince Jayrus."

"I did not cause this. I'm not the one to fix it."

She believed his regret. His face had lost the cold, hard, closed expression. His warm voice and sincere eyes said he felt for her cause. Just one more push, and perhaps he would agree.

She touched his arm. "But you can prevent my father's death."

His gaze dropped to her pale fingers resting on the amber-colored cloth of his sleeve. "It is not allowed."

"Who stops you?"

He turned and walked away.

"Where is the prince?" Beccaroon asked as soon as his girl reentered the central garden.

"Out in a pasture, talking to his dragons. At least I assume that's what he's doing. He was certainly finished listening to me." She detailed her conversation with him. "I actually spoke more with the pink dragon, Vanz. He seemed to understand our dilemma." She looked over her shoulder toward the back pastures of the tower. "I'm sure there is a reasonable explanation for why Prince Jayrus won't help. I think he's a good person under that royal standoffishness."

"Arrogance."

Tipper looked back at her friend. "I don't think it's arrogance."

"Then what is it?"

"I don't know."

"Awk! I'll go talk to him."

Tipper shrugged. "Thank you, Bec. I don't see that it will do any good. But please try."

Beccaroon couldn't decide which emotion reigned as he flew across the fields between the tower and the meadow where Prince Jayrus sat with his dragons. These were not the same dragons they had met earlier. He wondered how many occupied the high mountain valley. The scarcity of people baffled him. Apparently, there were kimens who served the prince, but where were they? He knew a few kimens from his own forest, and although shy, they were never invisible.

Through the tangle of mystery, a thread of distrust colored his analysis of the situation. And he knew it. He brought with him doubts about the wizard and the librarian. Although Librettowit had gained some respect, Beccaroon held on to his skepticism toward the leaf- and varmint-shedding wizard. He even doubted Verrin Schope's good judgment in this affair.

Now they had to deal with a prince with no ancestry that he knew of and dragons that enjoyed toying with their attempts to develop a partnership.

Frustration grew in his chest and stirred up anger, an emotion

Beccaroon rarely had to deal with. And the realization that Tipper obviously could be smitten by the young prince's courtly ways and handsome face fueled that ire. For the most part, she behaved with the correct amount of reserve, but he'd seen a look of admiration come over her when she sat talking to this self-proclaimed monarch. Having some time alone to talk to this rapscallion suited Beccaroon's protective instincts. He'd get to the bottom of things.

He landed next to Prince Jayrus. The young man stood, showing good manners but not impressing Beccaroon. Even a dolt could imitate a gentleman given the right instruction.

"Perhaps," said the grand parrot in a controlled voice, "if you were to tell me something about yourself, this valley, and your kingdom, I could understand your perversity."

"I think not."

One of the large dragons lumbered over to them. The prince mounted the steed, scaling its side by putting one foot after another in convenient folds of skin and clinging to a wing that the beast had put within his reach. As soon as he sat astride the dragon's shoulders, the beast took off.

"Well, he can't fly away from me." Beccaroon launched into the air and caught up to the bigger animal with ease.

The prince looked over at him with surprise first in his eyes, and then a smile curved his lips, demonstrating that he'd seen the humor in the situation.

A sense of relief eased Beccaroon's irritation. At least the young man was a good sport and took the thwarting of his plans with grace.

They flew on together for some time. When they reached the lake, the prince pointed to an island and led the way to a landing.

Beccaroon didn't waste any time. He was growing tired of the young man avoiding the subject. "Are you going to tell me why you will not aid our quest?"

He nodded. "I am charged to hold the fort, not to lead the advance."

"I suppose that means something."

"It does to me."

"And why are we here?"

"To consult the oldest dragon in the valley. Let me go first. He's a bit blind, and I don't want him to mistake you for a plump pheasant, one of his favorite meals."

25

Old Sage

"I'm not all that fond of water in dark places," Beccaroon said as he peeked into the gloomy opening. Hot, moist air hung in the mouth of the cave, and in the distance he could hear a constant drip.

"Sage lives in here because of the moisture. And because it is warm year-round." The prince moved inside.

"Fed by a hot spring?"

Prince Jayrus nodded. "I apologize, but if you want to go with me, you will get wet."

Beccaroon shrugged. "I live in a tropical forest. We have showers frequently, but I can see where it is coming from and know where it will go."

"I understand." Prince Jayrus glanced into the recesses of the dark cave. "There's no standing water and only a trickle about an inch deep that we will have to cross. And we have lightrocks positioned along the way."

"Those were the glowing blue crystals in the tower hall?"

"Yes."

The prince's comments showed real consideration for Beccaroon's concern. The bird pushed aside the feeling of relief and, along with it, appreciation for the young ruler's compassion. He wasn't ready to concede that Jayrus might be a suitable companion for his girl.

"Well, let's get on with this. How far behind do you want me to be? Now that I know I won't drown, I want to be assured I won't get eaten instead."

The prince chuckled, and Beccaroon saw his charm, that intangible quality that toyed with his girl's sensible heart. This young man had better watch his step. Neither he nor Tipper's father would let a ne'er-do-well tamper with her happiness.

"A few feet," the prince answered. "Not more than ten. I don't want to lose you down in the part that twists and turns."

"I will keep you in sight. I have no desire to be lost."

Prince Jayrus now sang as they made their way through the narrow corridors of the cave.

"Is there a reason for your song?" asked Beccaroon.

"Yes, Sage does not like to be startled. He was a fire-breathing dragon, and although his flame is but a sputter, it still singes."

"By all means, sing."

Beccaroon followed the tall emerlindian, grateful that he did not have to bend over to keep from scraping his head on the ceiling. He did have to remember to keep the tip of his tail raised a tad to keep it from dragging on the wet floor.

"We've gone down quite a bit," he remarked.

The prince interrupted his song to answer. "Yes, we're probably under the lake now." He resumed singing.

Beccaroon concentrated on the words of the ditty. He preferred that over contemplating whether or not the sodden rock walls would hold.

The merry tune brightened the atmosphere more than the blue crystals. And the prince had a very fine voice.

Three sailors, three, went out to sea
In a slip of a ship meant not for the deep.
They sailed away for many a day, many a day, many a day.
Maidens they sought that they might keep.

Trillalee, trillalee, a wife for me.
Chugaroo, chugaroo, wives for me and you.
Chugaroon for a wife, the love of my life, to cuddle 'neath the
    moon, 'neath the moon, 'neath the moon.
Chugaroon, chugaroon, chugaroon, chugaroo,
a wife for me and you and you.

The first sailor man bent iron in his hand,
Into bows and shoes and frilly pans too.
He found his girlie to be his sweet, be his sweet, be his sweet.
And she spoke in naught but tweet, tweet, tweet.

Trillalee, trillalee, a wife for me.
Chugaroo, chugaroo, wives for me and you.
Chugaroon for a wife, the love of my life, to cuddle 'neath the
    moon, 'neath the moon, 'neath the moon.
Chugaroon, chugaroon, chugaroon, chugaroo,
a wife for me and you and you.

The song went on to a second sailor who found a woman who
knitted shoes and a third whose love attracted a host of animals. Just
when Beccaroon gratefully assumed there was no more story to tell,
Prince Jayrus began the verses about the progeny of the sailors. Even
a golden voice couldn't smooth out the rough spots of this nursery
tune. Surely this inane ode to the absurd wasn't sung in music halls.
No, nurseries would be the proper place to perform the mindless
words. The babies probably went to sleep to avoid the torture of more
lyrics.

Beccaroon's impatience grew. "Are we going to the center of the
earth?"

"No, only one more turn." The prince did not begin his song again. "Sage, I've brought company. May we enter?"

"Yes, enter, dear boy."

Flabbergasted, Beccaroon blurted, "He spoke!"

Jayrus nodded, a smile on his winsome face. "Many of the older dragons did. But Sage is the only one I know of who does now."

"Why? I mean, why not? I mean, why do the dragons not talk?"

"Sage says it is because they are a lazy generation, and it takes years of training to develop the skill."

The noise of the dragon shifting positions scraped through the entry. His deep voice echoed against the stone walls. "Are you coming in, or are you going to lallygag in the hallway?"

Prince Jayrus gestured for Beccaroon to follow and went around the bend. The big bird trailed behind, wondering how he had managed to come to this place. His intention had been to cross-examine a young emerlindian, not converse with an ancient dragon.

The cavern sparkled with over a thousand colored crystals. Not just the blue lightrocks Beccaroon had seen before, but golds, greens, reds, and purples dotted the walls and cast a lovely glow in the room.

The dragon lay on a bed of straw, bony elbows and knees pressing against baggy red skin. Sage was no bigger than a draft horse and didn't rise when they came in.

"Welcome, stranger. It has been a very long time since I have seen a grand parrot."

"I am pleased to make your acquaintance." Beccaroon bowed. "May I ask what type of dragon you are?"

"I was a major dragon, but I am nearing the end of my existence. I no longer eat, and my body is diminishing."

"I am sorry to hear that." Beccaroon cast a chastising look to the young emerlindian. There had been no chance of Sage pouncing on a feathered visitor and devouring him as a tasty morsel. Much like the prince's dragons, the boy enjoyed mischief.

Rather than looking abashed, Prince Jayrus returned Beccaroon's glare with a cheeky grin.

The red dragon allowed his eyes to drift closed, and a smile lifted his lips. "It is of no matter. I am assured of my existence beyond this world."

Sage opened his eyes and looked at Jayrus. "Why have you come, boy?"

"The people who came to the valley with the parrot have a great need, but to answer that need would break the covenant I made before Prince Surrus died."

Sage held his head higher and, with bright eyes, examined Beccaroon. "Where have you come from?"

"Indigo Forest."

The dragon's head drooped. "No, Jayrus, this is not the time."

"But some of his questing party come from much farther away."

The dragon raised his head again and quirked an eyebrow at Beccaroon.

"A place called Amara." Bec watched enthusiasm take hold of the old dragon and boost him to his feet.

Sage wobbled and sank, but his voice still held energy. "I had begun to believe that I wouldn't be here, even though the Creator told me I would."

Jayrus stood straighter. His face glowed with anticipation. "Am I the one to leave?"

"Yes, Prince. You shall become the Creator's herald. Aid these travelers. Learn from them and be ready."

"I can go?"

The dragon chortled. "I've said so. Did you not suspect when the guardian allowed these outsiders into Mercigon?"

"Wait!" Beccaroon ruffled his feathers and glared at the prince and the dragon. "Explain. Explain in detail. Ever since that wizard and his librarian walked into Byrdschopen, everyone has talked in circles or in cryptic nonsense that sounds like it might mean something if someone would just elaborate. So elaborate!"

Prince Jayrus nodded, the serious look on his face once again tempting Beccaroon to reevaluate the young man's mettle.

Sage grumbled. "It is too much work for me." He lowered his head to rest his jaw on his front legs. "You do the honors, Jayrus, and I shall correct you if you err."

"Have a seat?" Jayrus pointed to a long quartz formation that resembled a fallen log.

Beccaroon perched and looked pointedly at the prince, hoping he wouldn't try to evade the subject.

Jayrus rested against an uncomfortable-looking boulder. "For generations, the dragon keeper has been chosen by the previous dragon keeper. I was chosen by Prince Surrus when I was seven. He found me in a marketplace and persuaded my mother to send me away for an education with him. We came to the tower, and Prince Surrus instructed me. He groomed me to be his successor, understanding the dragons, establishing a relationship with the kimens, and preparing to be the champion of the Creator should this age be the one in which He chose to bring Chiril to Awareness."

Beccaroon squinted his eyes against the image forming in his mind. This Wulder that Verrin Schope spoke of sounded suspiciously similar to the prince's Creator.

Jayrus rubbed his hands back and forth on his thighs. "No dragon keeper truly believes… I mean, no one expects to be the one… My expectation was to live and die in the valley, except for my one journey out to choose a successor."

He sighed and focused on Beccaroon. "My charge is to hold the fort, take care of the Mercigon Range and the dragons that live here. To lead the advance would surely fall to some dragon keeper born generations from my time. But I…" He looked at Sage. "I am the one to complete the mission."

Beccaroon's claws tightened, but unlike a perch in his forest, the stone did not yield to his claws. Pain jabbed at his feet, and he loosened his grip. "And what exactly is that mission you are to lead? What is the advance?"

Sage spoke up. "He is the bridge. He will carry knowledge, words, and enlightenment from the Amaran people to the citizens of Chiril. You could liken him to a town crier who not only relays the good news that all is well but will also be able to explain why this is so."

Jayrus stood. "I get to leave the valley."

Sage laughed and wheezed. "Yes, I believe we have established that fact."

26

Going Places

In the tower's Great Hall, Prince Jayrus announced that the dragons would go on Verrin Schope's quest and he would come along. A thrill raced through Tipper, leaving goose bumps in its wake. Her father could be saved. She would ride one of those magnificent steeds. And…

Perhaps some of Prince Jayrus's finesse would rub off on her. When he turned those blue eyes on her and spoke with that slow, low, and soothing voice, her hands trembled, her mouth went dry, her heart pounded, and she couldn't think of anything to say. When she was mad at Prince Jayrus, she could think of exactly what to say. When he irritated her, his manner didn't stop her body and mind from functioning. But she couldn't stay mad at him for long.

If she studied him, maybe she could learn his tricks. Twenty-two years living almost exclusively at Byrdschopen had not prepared her for the rest of the world. As they had ventured out on this quest, she'd become painfully aware of her lack of sophistication. The Boss Inn, the dance in Tallion—both had proven she needed a different education. She grinned. Boscamon provided one more person in this juggling act. And whether she believed in the old fable or not, she was pleased with the additions to the questing party.

Prince Jayrus invited the travelers to have another meal in the tower and to spend the night in his castle. To Tipper's disappointment, the young emerlindian cornered her father and the two men from Amara. He seemed intent on learning everything they knew about life in the foreign land. He showed particular interest in Wulder.

Tipper grew tired of their intense conversation and went outside to sit on a wooden swing in the garden. Beccaroon perched in the tree. Crisp air shivered her skin, and the view took her breath away. The evening sky shone with bright stars, much brighter than they were at Byrdschopen. The moon rose over a ridge of mountains, tinting the silhouette with a pale blue glow.

"It'll be cold out here tonight. Don't you want a chamber in the tower?"

The big bird tsked and shook his head. "I'd feel like I had taken refuge in a blinker owl's nest."

"Yes, the rooms are small." Tipper kept herself from elaborating. Beccaroon had already seen one of the tiny rooms with only a bed and a chair in it. "But the bed is soft, and the linens are wonderful."

"Kimen-made."

She nodded. She recognized the finely woven texture that only the kimen people could produce. "I wonder where they are."

"Another odd occurrence. Do you ever wish, dear Tipper, that we could just go back to trying to figure out how to pay the village shop-keepers on your father's behalf?"

"Sometimes, Bec. But really, I do want my father back whole and hearty. That would make Mother happy too."

"I imagine Lady Peg would also be happy if the world didn't fall apart."

Tipper rolled her eyes. "Yes, that would be a good thing."

Tipper's excitement flowed through her, making her want to jump about, hug everyone in sight, and sing at the top of her lungs. Instead she stood with Bealomondore beside Wizard Fenworth and her father and listened as the two experienced dragon riders gave out advice.

"Your dragon will be aware of your thoughts," said Verrin Schope. "The dragon will open up communication. You need not worry about that."

Fenworth held up one finger. "Speak kindly to your dragon carrier. One tip, and you'll be lost forever."

Librettowit rolled his eyes.

Verrin Schope continued as if there had been no interruption. "Wear warm clothes, as the higher you go, the colder it will be. And breathe deeply—the air is thin."

"Clothes! Tut, tut, oh dear. I wonder if I packed clothes." Out of the folds of Fenworth's cloak came dragon saddles and riding clothes. "And this," said the wizard as he pulled out a long leather strap, "is especially made for one such as our young tumanhofer friend."

"What is it?" asked Tipper.

"It's a belt for holding someone in his seat while dragon riding."

Tipper burst into laughter, but Bealomondore sat on a rock, groaned, and buried his face in his hands.

When the dragons were ready, Prince Jayrus paired up rider and steed. Librettowit and Bealomondore rode together on Kelsi. A black dragon named Ketmar would carry Wizard Fenworth.

Prince Jayrus stood before Tipper, bowing with the air of assurance she envied. She felt her smile grow and listened raptly to what he had to say.

"My dragon is Caesannede, and we would be honored if you rode with us."

Before she could answer, Verrin Schope stood beside them. "That is very kind of you, but my daughter will ride with me."

Her father smiled graciously, but Tipper saw his ears twitch. The situation amused him.

Jayrus bowed to the older emerlindian. "Gus has agreed to accommodate your needs."

Verrin Schope lost his composure. "Gus?" he sputtered as he laughed. "You have one dragon named Caesannede and another named Gus?"

The prince's brow lowered. "I don't name them, you know."

"Yes, yes, I know. Forgive me." Verrin Schope took Tipper's arm. "Come, my dear. I'll show you how to saddle a dragon, if you can lift the contraption onto his back."

"Her," called Prince Jayrus.

"If you can lift the saddle onto *her* back."

"Flying is the best part of questing," Tipper told her father. She sat facing backward with her shoulders resting against Verrin Schope's back. She had a good view of the land below. Trees looked like splotches of green. Animals appeared as dots against the grass. Rivers flowed through the land like strings of blue yarn.

She breathed deeply. The cool air tasted clean and somehow lighter. She enjoyed the feel of the dragon's muscles powering her great wings and relished the bond with the dragon. Through that connection she knew that Gus delighted in carrying her passengers. Tipper felt as if she were born to fly and wished her new friend felt the same way.

"I hope Bealomondore hasn't thrown up again."

"It's good he emptied his stomach before we left the ground. Fenworth gave him a flask of medicated water to drink. That will soothe his nerves. Perhaps he will even sleep."

"What type of medicine is it?"

"Ground momile shells."

Tipper pictured the small yellow beetles that ate aphids in the garden. Momiles were useful for several things. "How did you convince Bealomondore to get on Kelsi?"

"Both Grandur and Zabeth are riding with him. His fear brought on a physical reaction, and the healing dragons will help him."

"You did something else, didn't you? I saw him before you talked to him and after. Before, every muscle twitched. Afterward, he seemed asleep with his eyes open."

Through her back, she felt a huge sigh from her father.

"It's something a wizard can do, although we consider it cheating. But our poor young artist's sensitivities were overwrought, and I mesmerized him as a compassionate means to dull his suffering."

"Mesmerized?"

"Entered his thinking and suggested he calm down. The suggestion will not last forever, but by the time it wears off, he will have seen that no harm is going to come to him. And the two healing dragons are working on him, to keep his physical reaction to fear under control. They will be tired tonight."

"The dragons?"

"Yes." He sighed again. "We will be in Fayetopolis this evening."

"Papa, are you all right?"

"Yes, yes, of course. We will have the first statue by this time tomorrow."

Tipper had been so delighted over the prospect of flying that she'd only partially listened to the dinner conversation the night before. "Bealomondore saw the statue in the home of a wealthy lawyer in Fayetopolis less than six months ago?"

"Yes, but immediately afterward, he heard it was sold to Bamataub, a man Bealomondore does not like."

"Why doesn't he like this man? I thought anyone who admired your work would be considered a fine fellow by our tumanhofer friend."

Verrin Schope coughed, and it took him a moment to get his breath back before speaking. "Bealomondore says that this man is not worthy of owning an exceptional piece of art. A lump of clay molded by a toddler would be more equal to Bamataub's capacity for appreciation. That is, according to Bealomondore."

"Bamataub must have liked *Morning Glory* to spend all that money to buy it."

Verrin Schope shook his head. "People buy art for the strangest reasons. The color goes with the draperies. A person he hates desired the same painting. A neighbor has two good sculptures, so the man acquires three. The space in the corner looked empty."

"That last one is true in our house." She paused. "I am sorry, Papa, that I sold so many things. Beccaroon and I tried many schemes to bring coins into the coffers, but I'm not very good at that sort of thing, and as it turns out, neither is Bec."

Verrin Schope laughed, which made him cough again. He wheezed when he spoke. "I never expected Beccaroon to manage Byrdschopen. His estate, the Indigo Forest, does not run on commerce." He panted for a moment, then continued in a stronger voice. "I trusted the parrot as my good friend to instruct you on ethics and morals and integrity. And I believe he has succeeded in instilling in you the basics of what is right and wrong."

Guilt swept through Tipper as she thought of all the times she'd not heeded Beccaroon's teachings.

Her father's voice interrupted the flow of condemnation before Tipper had even listed a dozen instances in her mind.

"Don't wallow in regret. I learned while I was in Amara that it is impossible to always choose right without the friendship and guidance of Wulder. And even with His backing, handling life in an upright manner is still a struggle."

"So everyone, even this Wulder, fails from time to time?"

"Wulder defined what is good and bad, right and wrong. He

doesn't make mistakes. Fenworth told me it is impossible for Wulder to choose to do wrong. Can you imagine that?"

Tipper leaned her head back so that it rested between her father's shoulders. "No, I can't."

27

Fayetopolis

They landed in a valley outside the city as the late afternoon air began to pick up the chill of evening. Tipper's legs surprised her by refusing to provide support. She and Bealomondore were labeled "novice riders" and told to sit under a tree and gently massage their legs while Grandur and Zabeth worked healing on their stiff muscles. The others busied themselves with removing the saddles and rubbing down the dragons in appreciation for their cooperation.

"You're better off than I am," Tipper complained. "You, at least, walked over here by yourself."

Bealomondore laughed at her. "The prince did not insist on carrying me. You probably could have walked had he given you the chance."

"I don't think my father and Beccaroon appreciated the prince's gallantry."

"They probably thought of it more as presumption."

"Well, Beccaroon couldn't carry me, and my father—" She stopped. She didn't want to voice what had come to her mind.

"I know," said Bealomondore in a low voice. "I'm worried too. Even in the short time since I met your father, I've seen a drain on his energy."

Tipper felt a buzz in her head. She concentrated. "Oh! Oh! Grandur says to bend our legs and flex our ankles to help speed the recovery."

"You heard him?"

"I did." She paused to listen to her father's healing dragon. "He says Papa is much weaker than he is letting us know."

Bealomondore struggled to his feet. "Then we should hurry. I'll go to that building over there. It looks like a tavern. Perhaps I can procure a conveyance to take us the last mile or so into town."

By the time the young tumanhofer got back with a volunteer, Beccaroon and the dragons had made themselves scarce. The big dragons would certainly cause a stir in the neighborhood. Prince Jayrus felt more comfortable leaving them when they promised to stay out of sight. And Sir Beccaroon had no desire to spend the night in a noisy city. A wooded area nearby would provide shelter from prying eyes for the night and for as much of the next day as the questers needed to secure the first statue. The minor dragons would accompany the party that went to town but stay hidden in the pockets of Fenworth's cape.

"They can go into your hollows?" Tipper felt a tremor of fear. "Couldn't they get lost or hurt?"

"Nonsense," said Fenworth. "She picks sheer nonsense out of the air and panics over it. I do have normal pockets, flighty girl. Try not to get flustered over every little thing. Going to pieces on a quest is most undesirable."

The jolting of the wagon proved ten times more uncomfortable than gliding through the air on a dragon. Tipper had felt the muscles of the creature flex beneath her, but the motion was never jarring. She thought she might break her teeth in the back of the large farm cart if she was not careful.

The marione driver stopped in front of The Moon and Three Halves Inn. Prince Jayrus, Wizard Fenworth, and Librettowit jumped down immediately, but Tipper stretched out her legs and wiggled her feet to be sure they were ready to support her. Bealomondore cautiously climbed down, then turned to help her father.

Tipper craned her neck to look up at the building they would sleep in that night. The Boss Inn had impressed her, but this edifice left her speechless. Carved wood emphasized every line of the hotel. Gilding accentuated most of the windows.

Numerous patrons went in and out through the door. She saw a sign that gave dining hours and realized they had arrived at the peak of that busy time. Then she saw the placard that displayed the words "The Moon and Three Halves Inn."

"What an odd name," she said.

Fenworth scowled and pulled his beard. "Should have named it Two and a Half Moons. Would have made more sense."

Librettowit stamped his feet, knocking bits of hay from his trousers. "I don't see that either name makes sense. We've only one moon on any given night. Why mention more?"

Fenworth tapped his shoulder and pointed to the front window of the establishment. "A bow window sticks out. That one is backward, sticks in. But look in the three panes of glass."

"By my list of great ancestors, I wonder how often that occurs."

Tipper hopped off the wagon and came to see what they were looking at. The single moon in the sky reflected off a window nine feet above the front porch. One moon gleamed in each of the first two panes. The last section angled in such a way that the glass only revealed half the reflection.

Bealomondore stepped closer with his head tilted back to scrutinize the window. He started to laugh. "It's a painting. A very clever painting. If we'd seen this in the full light of day, we would not have been fooled."

Tipper and Prince Jayrus clambered up the stairs, their boots making a racket in the quiet evening.

Jayrus, with his emerlindian height, had no trouble reaching up and touching the picture. "The wall isn't even curved in. The surface is perfectly flat. Could you draw something like that, Bealomondore?"

"Yes, and I have many times. This type of false impression is all the rage in Greeston. Many times this was the reason behind my being invited to stay. The hostess wanted something clever on the walls, something different from the art collected by her friends."

"Two and a Half Moons is still a better name," grumbled Librettowit. "Fenworth is right. Three half moons would be a half moon, a half moon, and a half moon, separated. Not two halves making a whole."

"Now, Wit," said Fenworth, "don't get too melancholy over the folly of these Chiril citizens. We've already noted that their quirks and idiosyncrasies are abundant. Must tolerate the natives, after all. We are the guests in their fair land, and to point out the silliness of some of their ways would be discourteous. Who's got the money to pay this farmer for the ride?"

Librettowit pulled out his coin purse and shook out the coins acquired in Temperlain. As he reached up to put a sum in the driver's outstretched palm, the man leaned over to speak.

"Seems to me," he said in quiet tones, "that these guests are the ones with the quirks."

The librarian looked around at the questing party. Only Beccaroon was missing. Librettowit raised an eyebrow at the farmer. "I agree," he said. "Bealomondore and Jayrus are odd, but these quirky ones are yours. We didn't bring them from Amara."

The driver frowned, sat up, and tucked his pay into a small pocket in his vest. Snapping the reins lightly, he called to his horses to get a move on.

Wizard Fenworth led the way into the inn. A crowd of milling people obstructed their way in the foyer. Off to one side, double doors opened into the dining area. Tipper rose up on her toes and looked over the heads of most of the people. The restaurant appeared to be filled to capacity. The sound of quiet conversation, music, and dishes clinking floated from the dimly lit room. The smell of meat roasting and savory spices awakened a ravenous hunger in Tipper.

She squeezed her father's arm. "How do we get in that room and seated at a table?"

"We ask," answered Prince Jayrus.

Fenworth made for the restaurant, and people stepped aside to let him pass. Bealomondore put Tipper's hand on his arm and managed to stay behind Fenworth.

"Must be a wizard thing," he said. "I don't think they'd part for us, so let's follow in his wake."

They reached the door, and a man in a fancy suit stood in their way. Tipper looked down at her clothes. She still wore the riding clothes Fenworth had pulled from his hollow. The loose fit looked rumpled. She reached up and touched her head. Stray hair blown from her braid stuck out around her face. She tried to smooth it down.

"Are we expecting you?" asked the door guardian with a skeptical smile.

"You should be," said Fenworth.

"Your name?"

"Fenworth."

The man looked at a list in the book at his side. "No Fenworth is listed."

Prince Jayrus stepped forward. He greeted the man with one of his most charming smiles. "Hello. You are?"

"Sabatin, sir."

"Sabatin, from Little Liscover?"

"Why, yes." The man's tone warmed.

"Sabatin, my guests are from a great distance, and I would like to show them the best of our country. Naturally, we arrive at your doorstep. Where else would we go?"

The guardian nodded.

"There are five of us. While you are preparing a table, would you send someone to acquire rooms for the night?"

"Oh, sir, I would like to oblige, but—"

Prince Jayrus looked the man in the eye. "That's fine, Sabatin. I know you will do your best. Travel-weary though they be, the dignitaries from Amara are first of all gentlemen. I have no doubt they will wait for you to work wonders on their behalf."

"Yes, yes." Sabatin turned, raised a hand, and snapped his fingers. Another well-dressed man appeared. "Calros, mind my station." He turned to Prince Jayrus. "Right this way, sir."

Tipper transferred from Bealomondore's arm to her father's. She stood on tiptoe to speak in his ear. "Was that the mesmerizing thing you spoke of?"

"It had some of the trappings of mesmerization, but I can't be sure. It certainly isn't the way I influence a person's mind. Too much talking for my taste."

Tipper realized her father leaned on her. She started to say something but glanced up at his face. She read more than fatigue. Her father was in pain. She shifted her arm to support him and guided him to the table where they would eat.

28

Bamataub

Fenworth decided he was too tired to find and visit the owner of *Morning Glory* that night. Tipper saw him cast a glance at her father and wondered if the wizard aimed to protect Verrin Schope from becoming overtired.

At breakfast the next morning, Beccaroon strutted through the door in time to sip from a cup of amaloot. The hot, sweet beverage usually calmed Tipper's nerves, but today her anticipation was beyond taming.

They rented a carriage to take them to Bamataub's estate. Beccaroon rode on top, but the other six in their party fit comfortably in the spacious carriage.

Their driver maneuvered through the busy city streets. The noise and confusion bothered Tipper, and she wondered about Beccaroon on his perch above. He wasn't fond of hustle and bustle either. He'd probably fluffed himself up, pulled his head down, and closed his eyes. For a moment, she wanted to be up there with him, but a harsh exclamation from someone in the road reminded her of the safety the carriage provided.

Eventually they reached a less crowded area, where other vehicles no longer jockeyed for the right of way. Businesses gave way to homes. Modest homes gave way to larger houses. Bamataub lived in an affluent part of town where all the residences sat back from the road, massive lawns and groomed flower beds showing off their wealth. The branches from tall trees arched over the lane, creating a pleasant shade. Breezes rippled the leaves, creating an ever-changing, lovely dappling on the fine gravel road.

Tipper's nerves prickled as they moved farther out of the city. Wider spaces separated the homes. The trees thinned, and glaring sunlight beat on the carriage. The atmosphere became stifling, hot, dry, and still. Bealomondore and Jayrus opened the windows on either side.

Tipper tried unsuccessfully to squelch an uneasy feeling that had begun when Bamataub's name had first been mentioned. When they stopped before a heavy wrought-iron gate in a high brick wall, she wanted to tell the driver to turn back. The atmosphere of their destination contrasted with the sunny estates they had passed.

"No one else lives in a fortress," she pointed out.

Bealomondore shifted in his seat. "He has his reasons. Although everyone in Fayetopolis respects him, it's a respect born out of fear, not admiration."

Tipper remembered the look on the concierge's face when they asked for a vehicle to take them to Bamataub. "So that's what was behind the concierge's expression? I sensed he didn't approve, but I thought he didn't approve of us, not Bamataub."

Prince Jayrus's blue eyes looked thoughtful. "This would be a circumstance when those who have no power are very careful to guard themselves from incurring the wrath of he who is in power. Those who work at the hotel dare not voice a warning or disapproval of any kind."

"You are correct," said Bealomondore.

Tipper eyed the prince. "How did you know that? Do you come here often?"

"I never go anywhere. You know that. But part of Prince Surrus's instruction included political intrigue. The nature of government, commerce, and greed."

Fenworth laughed out loud. "I would have liked to meet your mentor, boy. Prince Surrus sounds like a man of acute discernment." He laughed again. "Lumping government, commerce, and greed together! Astounding insight."

The driver of their carriage got down and spoke to a man behind the barred entry. As he climbed back up, the iron gate opened. The horses pulled them into a dark lane. Thick trees cut off the sunlight. The harnesses jingled harshly in an unnatural stillness.

Tipper peered out the window on her side and thought she saw hideous shapes dodging between the tree trunks in the surrounding forest. She swallowed and chastised herself for being the panicky, flighty alarmist Wizard Fenworth already claimed her to be. The shadows among the trees were merely that—shadows. The absence of sound only meant that the birds… She couldn't think of a reason the birds would not chirp.

She took her father's hand. His long fingers were cold and dry. Her father's health was in real danger. She must concentrate on their quest, not on imagined terrors.

Wizard Fenworth growled in his throat. "This place holds evil."

So much for convincing herself she had an overactive imagination.

From among the trees, a woman screamed in stark terror. Everyone in the carriage jumped.

"A bird," said Fenworth. "A peacock. Wretched squawkers."

Tipper let out a sigh of relief simultaneously with most of the other occupants of the coach.

The drive from the gate to the house continued. They passed out of the forest and obtained their first view of Bamataub's mansion. The huge stone manor squatted like a massive, warty toad on the hillside.

"Well, Verrin Schope," said Librettowit, "it is safe to say that it wasn't good taste or an eye for beauty that led Bamataub to purchase your statue."

Tipper's impression of the house and its owner did not improve when a gnarly-looking marione opened the door. He dressed the part of a butler, but his mannerism reminded Tipper of those men she'd seen hanging around The Other Boot, a tavern in Soebin with a reputation for gambling and fistfights.

The man showed them to a large room decorated with dark purples, greens, and browns. The heavy curtains kept out the sun, and a thick rug muffled their steps.

"Master Bamataub will be with you in a moment." The butler bowed stiffly and left.

Bealomondore walked to the center of the room and turned slowly, looking at the art on the walls. "Does anyone else feel like we were expected?"

"Yes," said Verrin Schope. He walked to the nearest chair and sat down. "Our host needs some tips on displaying his collection."

Prince Jayrus walked around the edge of the room, examining the many paintings. "A little light would be helpful."

Beccaroon, Fenworth, and Librettowit stood together, talking in low voices. Tipper tried to hear but couldn't and decided to move closer. She heard Librettowit say, "…with the proper medicine…"

Then the door opened and their host arrived.

"Hello, I am Bamataub, and this is my wife, Orphelian."

Bamataub's short legs brought him into the room swiftly, with his much shorter wife trailing behind. He approached the men standing together first, shook hands with Librettowit and Fenworth, and bowed to Beccaroon. "You are visitors from Amara? Extraordinary! Welcome. You, Sir Beccaroon, I understand, are from our own Indigo Forest. I'm pleased to meet you. Not many grand parrots deign to gift us with their delightful presence. I am honored to have you in my home."

They muttered responses, but Bamataub was not interested. He whirled and advanced on Prince Jayrus and Bealomondore, who had reached a point where they both examined the same painting. "Bealomondore, I have heard of you, both of your talent and your obsession with the artwork of Verrin Schope. Welcome, welcome. Jayrus of Mercigon? Welcome."

Again he ignored any comment they made and went on, swooping down on Verrin Schope, who rose to his feet to receive the man's greeting.

"I hardly know what to say." Bamataub pumped Verrin Schope's hand. "The great Verrin Schope, a master of all that is acclaimed as art, a world-renowned authority on countless subjects, a confirmed recluse, and a member of the royal court, visiting my humble household. Amazing!"

Verrin Schope extracted his hand and gestured for Tipper to come forward. "My daughter, Tipper."

Bamataub nodded in a perfunctory manner. "Yes, perhaps you would like to sit with my wife. We will have refreshments shortly."

He proceeded to steer his guests to chairs he designated, chattering all the while of his great honor in entertaining them. Tipper sat on the sofa next to Orphelian and took stock of their host.

He was a shorter emerlindian, quite dark, with close-cropped hair, an overly wide, thin-lipped smile, an ordinary nose, and small eyes. For all his overt congeniality, Tipper thought of a rat. Busy, busy, busy, but looking out for his own advantage.

Orphelian patted her hand. "Do you enjoy traveling, Mistress Tipper?"

"Oh yes." She turned her attention to the plump woman sitting beside her.

Sad eyes gazed at her out of a typically square marione face. Tipper thought the matron of the house must have been a pretty young woman. Life in this gloomy mansion must have depleted the woman's vivacity. Her lined face definitely showed years of strain. Tipper felt an urge to comfort the old soul and be a friend.

She smiled. "I do like traveling. But the reason we are on this journey is not too agreeable."

Sympathy invaded the woman's expression. "What is it, dear?"

"My father is ill, and we must buy back some of the statues I sold."

Terror replaced sympathy. Orphelian's eyes darted to her husband and then to Verrin Schope. "Is he very mad? Are you in danger?"

"No, no. I'm just worried about his health."

"But you sold his art!"

"He understands."

"Understands?" Her eyes flitted to her husband once more. "I see." She turned back to Tipper. "His health?"

"The story is complicated, but my father desires to have the three statues carved from one stone back together as he meant them to be when he did the sculptures."

Bamataub stood and gestured to his wife as the tea tray came into the room. Several servants followed Orphelian's instructions to pass out the small cakes and cups of steaming tea. When her hostess duties were performed, she returned to her seat beside Tipper. All the servants save one slipped out of the room. Tipper eyed him. He had the look of a thug, not a refined manservant.

Bamataub prodded the conversation toward the upcoming festivals that would be celebrated in Fayetopolis. Since he never addressed the women, Tipper and Orphelian did not participate. Several of the other members of their questing party remained very quiet, though the general talk during their refreshment covered an assortment of pleasant topics. Prince Jayrus spoke little, but Tipper thought he was studying the different speakers, especially their host. Her father didn't join in the banter.

Tipper watched Bamataub. He seemed interested in keeping the conversation directed toward his choice of topics and avoided conversing with her father. Several times, the dialogue would have naturally included Verrin Schope, but Bamataub deliberately drew someone else's contribution instead.

The servants came again and cleared away the remnants of their tea.

Wizard Fenworth waited until the door shut behind the last servant and turned purposefully to their host. "Do you mind explaining how you knew us?"

"I am a leader in the community." Bamataub's tight-lipped smile widened. "Of course I am kept informed of who comes and goes in Fayetopolis."

Fenworth did not return the smile. "Do you know why we have come?"

Their host tilted his head and lifted his hands in a disarming gesture. "That I do not know."

Librettowit scooted forward on his chair. "We came to buy the Verrin Schope statue *Morning Glory.*"

Bamataub sat back and placed his hands on his lean stomach. "I believe *Morning Glory* is one of three statues that belong together. Do you possess the other two?"

The librarian's eyes narrowed. "No."

"A shame." He straightened. "I do not wish to sell my statue."

"We have not yet named a price," interjected Prince Jayrus.

Their host bestowed a look of scorn on the young emerlindian. "Price is irrelevant. I will not sell."

Tipper clutched the arm of the sofa. "But—"

Verrin Schope held up a hand. "Tipper."

She fell silent.

Her father rose to his feet and nodded to Bamataub. "We have no more business here. Thank you for your hospitality." He came to stand before the ladies and bowed to Orphelian. "Thank you, Madam." He gestured to Tipper, and she stood beside him. He placed her hand on his arm and started out. She heard the others behind them, shuffling as they made their farewells to host and hostess.

"What are we going to do?" she whispered.

Verrin Schope did not answer as they approached the front door and the butler rose from his seat and opened it for them. The carriage still stood in the drive.

Tipper waited until they were all seated and the horses given the command to go. "What are we going to do?"

Verrin Schope leaned his head back against the cushion and closed his eyes.

"The evil was oppressive in that house," said Prince Jayrus. "I couldn't discern from where it came."

Bealomondore cast a glance upward to where the coachman and Beccaroon sat on the outside. He lowered his voice. "The rumor is that he deals in slaves."

"Surely not," whispered Tipper. "No one owns slaves. That practice was forever banished when my great-great-grandfather was king."

Bealomondore nodded. "No one owns slaves in Chiril, but women and children and sometimes young men are kidnapped and sold in other countries."

Jayrus lifted an eyebrow at the tumanhofer. "Perhaps the dealing in fine art covers the transport of slave cargo."

"That would be my supposition."

Fenworth leaned forward and slapped the prince on the knee. "Again you astonish me, lad."

Jayrus looked at the toad that had hopped out of the old man's sleeve and now sat on his leg.

"Oh, sorry about that," Fenworth scooped the critter into his hand, and it disappeared. "Rupert becomes confused easily."

"The toad?" asked Jayrus.

"Yes. Shy, you know." Fenworth patted his chest and butterflies poured out from under his beard. They flew out the window. "As I was saying, your acumen astonishes me."

A hint of pride colored the prince's features. "Prince Surrus was a thorough teacher."

"Yes, well, ahem, tut, tut. He could have worked more on your humility." He tapped Tipper's leg. "Now as to what we are to do. We will come back and try again. Perhaps we will even go and acquire the other statues first, before we return."

His gaze fell upon Verrin Schope, who hadn't moved since they entered the carriage. "Right now it is imperative to find a rare insect containing a certain property that will be beneficial to your father's health. Beccaroon, Librettowit, and I discussed this earlier. Your feathered friend should have directed the coachman to take us to the nearest medicinal bug shop. He assures us that quality insects can be found in the larger cities of your Chiril. I hope he is correct. I don't carry a *Fineet fineaurlais* on my person. And I haven't had one in storage for ages."

"Interesting," said Jayrus. "Even as a street urchin, I never visited the bug shop. I was afraid I'd be made to eat one."

"Nonsense." Fenworth gave him a scouring look, making Tipper believe the young man had fallen out of the wizard's good graces. "They come powdered. One does not eat bugs."

"In Chiril one does," said Bealomondore.

"Harrumph! Heathen country."

29

The Bug Shop

Beccaroon swayed on top of the coach as they came again to the thoroughfares marked by crowding and noise. He felt like the congestion of the city could permeate his feathers, and he'd instinctively fluffed up against his surroundings. He'd also scrunched his neck, pulling his head down. This would never do if he were to help spot the medicine shop Fenworth needed. He shook his feathers, straightened, and watched the signs ahead.

With relief, he read "Insect Emporium" in big green letters, outlined in gold. A bit ostentatious to his way of thinking. Underneath, "Remedies for Common and Uncommon Ails" scrolled out in red on a brown background. A bit more tasteful. In even smaller letters, this time brown on red, the owners proudly displayed their names—Rowser and Piefer.

Beccaroon nudged the coachman and nodded toward the shop.

"I thought it was along here somewheres," the man answered and edged his horses closer to the side of the street. The driver pulled to a stop and jumped down to help the passengers alight.

"Wait here," said Fenworth. "Verrin Schope is not coming in."

"Yes sir." The driver tipped his top hat and peeked with curiosity into the coach.

Bec flew to the sidewalk and stood beside his girl. He could feel tension radiating from her. He got a glimpse inside the carriage and understood why. As dark as Verrin Schope was, it was hard to see the ashen undertone of his black skin, but his eyes lacked luster. Beccaroon could not miss the lethargy, strong evidence of Verrin Schope's state of health. His old friend looked like a wax reproduction of himself.

Prince Jayrus opened the door to the emporium and stood back to let the others enter. Beccaroon followed right behind Tipper. As she passed the prince, he smiled down at her. She smiled up at him. Beccaroon put his forehead to the small of her back and pushed.

"Close the door quickly," ordered a man behind the counter.

They hustled in, and Jayrus swung the door shut. Worn wood covered the floor of the old shop. Thankfully, the store was spacious enough for all of them. Several lamps hung from the ceiling, and shelves lined the walls. Bags, baskets, bottles, jars, jugs, boxes, and cages filled every nook and cranny. A strong but not unpleasant odor drifted about. Beccaroon decided it smelled like the forest floor after a heavy rain. A cricket chirped incessantly, and tiny feet scratched on paper surfaces. Bec looked around and saw that some of the cages, with their fine wire mesh, contained skittering bugs.

Tipper moved to a cage of exotic butterflies and stood transfixed. Beccaroon didn't blame her. Dozens of species of various sizes and spectacular colors flitted about the floor-to-ceiling structure.

The minor dragons jumped out of Fenworth's pockets.

The marione shopkeeper looked up from the clipboard he held and frowned. "None of that, now." He spoke in an even tone. "They eat the merchandise, you know. And it's a tangle to figure out who ate what and how much is owed."

Fenworth gestured with his hand, and the four dragons came to roost on the wizard, the librarian, and the prince.

The man behind the counter stood, pushing a wooden stool out of his way. "I'm Rowser of Rowser and Piefer. What can I do to help you?"

Beccaroon caught a movement out of the corner of his eye. Another man—a long, lanky emerlindian—crawled from behind one barrel to another. His tan skin and brown hair indicated he was older than Jayrus but much younger than Verrin Schope. He was also thinner than both men.

Wizard Fenworth advanced to the counter. "My friend is falling apart."

Rowser held up one finger. "Nerves. I have just the thing." He looked up at his stock and moved toward a ladder connected to a rail. With one push, the shop owner could move the steps to any section around the outer wall of the shop, providing access to the topmost shelves.

"No," said Fenworth, "not nerves."

"Falling apart?" Rowser snapped his fingers. "Dollopsy." He turned and walked the other direction, looking on the lower shelves.

"No, not dollopsy." Fenworth picked up and examined a cloth bag from the counter. He read the label, then continued his response. "Glad of that actually."

The crawling man came out from behind the barrel, slapped his hand against the wooden floor, and yelled, "Gotcha!"

"Good going, Piefer," said Rowser. "How many does that make?"

"Eighty-six."

"Only fourteen to go."

The emerlindian shook his shaggy hair. "Unfortunately, that was a gross of grassbenders, not a hundred pack." He began his search again, peering behind a stack of crates.

Fenworth looked down his nose at the bags on the counter. "Had a mishap with your grassbenders?"

"Yes," said Rowser. "When we opened the shipment this morning, one of the bag clasps had come loose in transit."

"Have you got a sugar lickick around?"

Rowser looked doubtfully at the old man. "We don't sell lickicks that aren't medicinal." He pointed to a stand on the counter that held colored sugar globs on wooden sticks. "We have lickicks for oral pain, toothaches, and sore throats. We have lickicks for calming nerves, upset stomachs, and fierce headaches. Also lickicks to obliterate cravings and aid in the loss of weight."

Wizard Fenworth held up his hand to stop the flow of information. "This would be a lickick for the sake of good taste, not good health. A red one, if you have it."

Rowser looked at Piefer. The emerlindian sighed and pushed up from his crawling position but did not stand. Still on his knees, he poked around in his pockets. He came up with a blue lickick first.

"That'll do," said Fenworth, "if you don't have a red."

After producing a green, two yellows, and a broken orange, Piefer held out a red lickick.

Fenworth took it and turned to the other owner. "A small bowl of water, a pinch of salt, and straw from a broom, please."

Rowser pulled the bowl from under the counter and a bag of salt from a shelf, and brought the broom from the back. Piefer got to his feet and stood with his hands on his hips, watching the old man.

Fenworth raised his eyebrows. "Water?"

Piefer leaned over the counter, his long arm easily reaching underneath, and retrieved a clear glass jug. "Water." He put it down in front of the wizard.

Beccaroon edged closer to get a better look, as did the prince and Bealomondore. Librettowit had taken out a piece of paper, and as he roamed the store, he scribbled a list. Tipper pulled herself away from the butterflies and stood next to Beccaroon.

Fenworth poured water into the bowl. He took a pinch of salt from the bag and sprinkled it in, then stirred the concoction with the red lickick. When the water turned pink, he set the stick aside and pulled straws from the broom. He constructed a grid by placing the straws across the bowl from rim to rim.

"That's so your grassbenders don't drown," Fenworth informed his audience.

He handed the broom to Piefer. Two green bugs landed on the straw topping the bowl, stuck their heads through the grid, and began drinking the beverage provided by the wizard. Piefer set the broom aside and scooped up the bugs. Another landed on the trap, and he collected it.

"Thank you," he said, grinning. "This should save my knees."

"Think nothing of it. A trick from Amara."

Rowser plucked another bug from the top of the bowl and put it in Piefer's bag. "Amara. That's a far distance."

"Yes. We've come on a quest, and one of our party is having trouble."

"The one who falls apart?"

"Yes. Do you happen to have a *Fineet fineaurlais* in your stock?

Rowser looked up at his partner. "Piefer?"

The emerlindian scratched his head. "I don't think so. But could you draw us a picture? Perhaps we call it something else."

Fenworth shook his head, and a string of insects dropped onto the counter. The multitude sat for an instant and then charged the bowl.

"Oh, sorry." The wizard plucked Hue off his shoulder and put him down. "Clean that up, would you? But don't eat the gentlemen's merchandise. Junkit, Zabeth, give a hand. Where's Grandur?"

The healing dragon flew from Librettowit's shoulder.

Fenworth grinned. "Ah, that should take care of the problem. Remember, don't eat the grassbenders. Not ours, you know."

Beccaroon watched with fascination as the dragons efficiently sorted the bugs. Using their front claws, they captured insect after insect. The dragons handed grassbenders to Rowser and Piefer and ate the others. Fenworth's bugs were gobbled up until none remained. Beccaroon saw a couple he knew to be tasty but refrained from barging in on the minor dragons' feast. A stray that fell to the floor was, however, a different matter. Tipper had no interest in the bugs and wandered around the shop.

Soon the little dragons rolled onto their backs, stomachs protruding in a very full state. Bec felt lighthearted, surprised by the pride he had for Junkit, Zabeth, Hue, and Grandur.

Piefer and Rowser exchanged puzzled looks.

Piefer cleared his throat. "Amaran dragons, I assume."

Beccaroon chuckled. "Grandur is, but the other three were born in Chiril, either in or near the Indigo Forest."

"They're very intelligent," said Rowser.

Hue lifted his head from the counter and winked at the marione, then collapsed again.

Wizard Fenworth coughed. "Well, getting back to the *Fineet fineaurlais,* I can't draw one, but I imagine my librarian can. Librettowit?"

"Got it." The older tumanhofer came over, waving a paper from his tablet. "Knew you'd want it as soon as the young fellow asked for it." He put a drawing on the counter.

Piefer and Rowser studied the black lines of a beetle.

"*Cranicus batteran?*" asked Piefer.

"*Cranicus albatteran.*"

"Ah yes, the elongated thorax."

"Is this your family?" asked Tipper.

All heads turned in her direction. Fenworth shook his head, very gently, only dislodging a couple of leaves from his beard.

"I beg your pardon," he said. "She's excitable and sometimes doesn't follow what's going on. I'm sure she didn't refer to phylum, classes, orders, *families,* genera, species. She's been well educated and knows mariones and emerlindians are not classified in the same order as *Fineet fineaurlais.*"

Beccaroon wandered over to where Tipper studied a painting on the wall. "She means this family portrait. It appears to be Rowser, his wife, and many children. Piefer has a dog."

"And a wife," said the emerlindian.

"Do you have a dozen?" asked Librettowit. "Are they fresh?"

"Wives?" said Piefer. "It's against the law."

"Children?" said Rowser, at the same time. "Only nine."

A moment of silence followed. Beccaroon closed his eyes. That this type of discussion was beginning to sound normal to him caused a certain amount of trepidation.

"Fineet fineaurlais," clarified Librettowit.

"Powdered and hermetically sealed," said Rowser.

Piefer vaulted over the counter and pushed the ladder. "I'll get the jar." The old steps rattled and banged as they coasted along the rickety rail. Piefer stopped it and climbed up faster than a monkey. Beccaroon squinted, trying to read the words on the jars.

Piefer scanned the labels on one row, climbed a few steps to examine the next, pulled on the shelf to move the ladder, and finally located the container he wanted. "Here it is. We've only used this for closing wounds. What is it you need it for?"

"My friend has molecular malocclusion distress syndrome."

As he climbed down, Piefer looked at Rowser.

Rowser shrugged. "How much do you need?"

"We'll take the bottle," said Librettowit, "and here's a list of other insects. We are in short supply of medicinal bugs at this time." He glanced at the four sated dragons and handed the paper to the marione shopkeeper.

Rowser's eyebrows lifted. "This will take some time to fill."

Librettowit took the bottle from Piefer. "We'll pay for it now and ask you to deliver the rest to The Moon and Three Halves Inn. Can you have it ready by this evening?"

"We can," said Piefer.

Librettowit waited for them to tally up the cost while Fenworth and the others left the shop.

Prince Jayrus grimaced. "I'm not sure I liked the odor in there, but we managed to escape without eating any bugs."

"Speak for yourself," said Beccaroon with a laugh. "I managed to snag one of Fenworth's beetles that fled from the minor dragons."

Bealomondore opened the carriage door, and Tipper gasped. Beccaroon hurried to her side. No one sat where her father should be.

Bec looked up at the driver. "Did Verrin Schope get out?"

"No sir, not that I saw."

"Did you go anywhere?"

"Just to get a pint. I asked the gentleman if he wanted a drink, and he said no. I didn't check on him when I came back."

Tipper twisted one hand against the other. "Where can he be?"

Fenworth quietly stood by, rubbing his finger against his chin whiskers.

The door to the shop opened, and Librettowit stepped out. "What's happened?"

"Verrin Schope is gone," said the wizard. "We shall have to attempt a rescue."

"A rescue?" Tipper screeched. "He's been kidnapped? How? How can we help him? We don't know where he is."

Beccaroon put a wing around her shoulders.

Fenworth tapped the side of his nose. "There is the slight odor of the house we just left. I believe some of Bamataub's men have been here."

"Couldn't we have carried the odor?" asked Bealomondore.

"We did! But I dissipated the scent before we passed out of Bamataub's gates."

"Let's go." Tipper jumped onto the coach's step and stopped. "Oh no!"

Fenworth let out an exasperated sigh. "What is it now, child?"

"His board. His board is still here."

"Well, that *is* cause for alarm. In his present state, he won't be able to do any long distance incorporation."

"You can do something, right?"

"Can't say that I can. No, this could get messy." Wizard Fenworth pushed her toward the carriage door. "Get in and don't start hollering. We'll work on the problem. Maybe even find an answer. Hopefully before your father finds himself floating on the wind."

30

Plots and Plans

Tipper argued all the way back to the hotel, but the men around her proved stubborn and mule-headed. Even Beccaroon had crowded his tail into the coach so he could help hash out the probabilities. They talked around her, over her, and sometimes, she felt, even through her. None of them listened to her plea to go immediately to save her father. When they reached the hotel, Prince Jayrus picked up Verrin Schope's piece of the closet floor and tucked it under his arm.

"What are you doing?" she shrieked.

Fenworth put his hands over his ears and muttered something. Tipper ignored him. She tried to grab the board and got a splinter for her trouble, but she held on and tugged.

"Calm down," said Jayrus. Even irritated with her, his voice remained quiet and steady. "If you had been listening instead of scolding and wheedling and yakking a mile a minute, you would have heard the plan. I'm taking the board and the minor dragons to Bamataub's. I'll wait outside until dark. If your father comes apart, I should be close enough for him to reassemble on his focal point."

"How do you know you'll be close enough?"

"That's why I'm taking the minor dragons. They can fly into the house unseen and report to me when they know which part of the house he's in. I'll situate myself and the board as close to him as I can."

Tipper thought about it. Junkit and Zabeth could be very sneaky. And if what she'd learned about dragons was true, then Grandur, in particular, would know exactly where her father was hidden.

"It's a good plan," she said.

"I'm glad you think so," said the prince.

"I'll go with you."

Outrage flared across his face. "What? You can't go with me."

Tipper bunched her hands into fists and planted them on her hips. "Why not? He's my father."

"Because one person is less likely to be seen than two."

"I'm going." Tipper glared at him, hoping her eyes would show her determination or perhaps drill holes in the know-it-all prince.

Beccaroon stood on the sidewalk watching them. He moved closer. "Tipper, you are not going. Your father would not allow you to go off alone with any young man. It is improper."

She started to voice her opinion, but Beccaroon held up one wing. "Stop, Tipper. We must not be overheard. It is quite possible that one of Bamataub's spies is nearby. We do not wish to expose our plan."

The bird turned to the young emerlindian. "Go. Be sure you are not followed. We'll join you after dark."

Tipper looked into the prince's startling blue eyes and saw a flicker of sympathy. He lowered his voice to just above a whisper, and his tone undermined her resentment. "I'll do anything I can to assure his safety."

She nodded, swallowing the lump in her throat. He leaned over and kissed her cheek. Tears she'd kept at bay fell down her cheeks.

"First woman I've kissed, and she cries." He winked and left, melding into the crowd of people.

The afternoon took forever to pass. They congregated in the largest suite of the hotel, which had a sitting room attached. Bealomondore sketched. Beccaroon sat on the arm of a chair with a large book on the table beside him. He turned the pages with his beak and seemed perfectly content to forget for the moment that her father was in dire straits. Tipper waged a campaign to be allowed to go with the men when they stormed Bamataub's mansion.

"We're not storming a fort," said Fenworth, settled in a comfortable chair with a strange cube in his hand. He twisted the parts of the puzzle in different directions. "Our attack will be genteel, quietly orchestrated, and an operation of finesse. No storming."

"I can do all those things."

"No, you can't." Fenworth leaned back again in his chair.

"I can."

"Can't."

"Can."

"Genteel. Quiet. Finesse. It's the middle one of which you're incapable."

Tipper opened her mouth to argue the point and slammed it shut. If she continued to bombard the wizard with her reasoning, she proved his point. She crossed her arms over her chest and paced to the window. On the street below, many city dwellers hurried hither and yon. One man looked out of place. He stood at a corner of an alleyway, leaning in a shadow, hardly moving at all. Tipper stepped back from the window and motioned to Bealomondore to come join her.

"See that man?" She hung back to the side, hiding behind the curtains.

"Which man?" Bealomondore looked back and forth.

She pulled him back. "Be careful. He'll see you and know we know he's watching us."

Bealomondore approached the window more cautiously. "What man?"

"Across the way, in the alley. He's wearing a black hat."

"I see him." He sighed. "And I've seen him before."

"Where?"

"Driving a carriage in which Master Bamataub and Madam Orphelian rode."

Fenworth snored.

Bealomondore turned to Librettowit. "We shall have to plan more thoroughly how to leave the hotel tonight and reach our destination unseen."

Librettowit pulled his beard. "Perhaps we should take a walk."

A look of delight came to the younger tumanhofer's face.

Beccaroon pushed the book he was reading aside. "An excellent plan." He hopped down from the arm of the chair.

"What?" cried Tipper. "What plan? Where are you going? Why?"

Fenworth snorted. "Does she ever maintain silence?" He shifted and returned to the heavy breathing that rattled his nasal passages.

"I'm going too," she whispered.

The men moved toward the door. Tipper grabbed her light cape and started after them.

"No," said Beccaroon. "This might be dangerous."

She forgot the sleeping wizard and shrieked. "*What* might be dangerous?"

"No," said Fenworth, "she doesn't." The sentence hardly disturbed the resonance of his sleep.

Tipper rolled her eyes and swung the cape over her shoulders. "I'm going."

Beccaroon stepped closer. "You are not, Tipper."

She looked into his serious eyes, sighed, and took the cape off.

Bealomondore clapped his hat on his head. "We'll be back as soon as we have something to tell you."

She nodded and watched them leave. She eyed the snoozing wizard for a moment, then went to peek out the window.

Her three friends walked across the uncovered portion of the sidewalk and crossed the street. The two tumanhofers were taller than the grand parrot by a head. Each dressed differently. Librettowit wore robes, a tunic, soft leather boots, and a hood that covered his grizzled head. He had a leather pouch slung under his arm.

Bealomondore wore what Tipper called "town clothes." His tailored fawn trousers hung over polished boots. His shirt ruffled at the chest and stuck out of a close-cut maroon jacket with tails. Of course, Beccaroon's tail was more impressive. The younger tumanhofer carried a cane, though he didn't need it, and wore a fancy felt hat with a feather in the band. Tipper wondered what Bec thought of that. Bec had his own glorious plumage, and Tipper caught people giving him a second look, although her bird friend never acknowledged the unwanted interest.

She straightened as she saw the suspicious marione come out of his corner and follow discreetly behind the three men. Was that their plan? To lure him away, then lose him? They had succeeded in luring him away, and that left the coast clear for her to slip out.

Tipper tiptoed to her cape and draped it over her arm. With her eye on Fenworth, she reached the door, turned the knob, and eased it open. Her skirts swished as she moved too quickly through. She froze, but apparently she hadn't awakened the wizard. She stepped into the hall and pulled the door softly into the frame. The latch scratched shut.

Fenworth whispered. "Do tell the prince we'll be there about a half hour after dark."

She pushed the door open and stared at the old man. He snored. But she'd heard him. She closed the door again without as much care, shook out her cape, and flung it around her shoulders.

Going to Bamataub's manor was a great idea. Staying in that room, just waiting, would have driven her mad.

In the lobby, Tipper asked the concierge to find a taxi for her. The man hailed one of the waiting vehicles, and a small carriage, pulled by a very old nag, jostled up to the hotel entry. The concierge opened the hack's door and assisted Tipper as she climbed the two narrow steps.

"May I tell the driver your destination, miss?"

Tipper had a mental picture of the concierge telling her destination to Beccaroon and decided not to reveal that information. "I'm going shopping. I'd prefer an outlying district instead of the middle of town."

"Just as you wish, miss." He relayed the information to the coachman, and the carriage jolted as the horse responded to the driver's voice.

After a few blocks, Tipper knocked on the front of the cab. A little door opened, and the driver peeked through. "Yes, miss?"

"I've decided I'd like to shop in the northwest part of Fayetopolis."

"Aye, miss. That's a nice part of town. I know just the street—"

"I don't have much money. Do you know of a reasonable marketplace?"

"I do. Have a sister who works out a ways, in one of the big houses, and I know where she does her own shopping. Lean back and relax, miss. It'll be a while before we get there."

"Thank you, sir."

He winked, and she thought that such a familiarity was perhaps not acceptable, but she didn't know for sure. She smiled instead of frowning at him.

As they passed into the more residential streets, a nanny pushing a baby in a perambulator gave Tipper an excellent idea. She rapped on the front again, and when the driver opened the little door, she asked him to take her to a secondhand shop. He nodded his agreement and continued on.

She'd have to be careful not to overspend on her disguise. But walking down that long lane to Bamataub's house in the lovely cloak Verrin Schope had purchased for her would be foolhardy. She smoothed her hand over the soft, peach velvet cape and sighed. The serviceable blue or brown of a nanny would not be so conspicuous and would be so much better for hiding at night in the shrubs. The thrill of participating in the venture gave her goose bumps, and she couldn't help the smile on her face. Then the thought of her father suffering wiped both the smile and the giddy anticipation away.

At the row of shops, Tipper dismissed the driver, giving him some of her precious Chiril coins. One shop had odds and ends in the way of household items. She asked for a baby carriage and was told they'd sold three last week but didn't have one at present. In the next little store, hardly bigger than her mother's closet, she found a used nanny's cape, a pair of breeches for her to wear when they climbed the wall, a shirt, and better shoes for walking. The clerk glanced oddly at Tipper as she totaled the cost.

Tipper smiled. "Boys are so rough on their clothing, aren't they?"

That seemed to satisfy the woman. Tipper spotted a man's tunic and thought of Jayrus in his princely garments made from kimen cloth. She added a rough pair of trousers and a larger tunic, both dark and very ugly. As soon as the clerk had the garments wrapped in brown paper and tied with a string, Tipper realized her mistake. She couldn't carry the load.

"May I leave the package here and pick it up in a little bit? I have more shopping to do."

Again the clerk gave her a suspicious look but agreed.

"Phew," Tipper exclaimed under her breath as she closed the shop door behind her. She could imagine that woman being Queen Gossip of the lane, probably relating in detail everything Tipper had said and done in her shop to the very next person who entered.

She visited three of the open-air booths but refrained from buying anything, even though she saw a little reticule that would go well with her new cape. At last she found a perambulator that hadn't sold yet because the price was too dear. She haggled the price down and pushed it back to the used clothing shop to retrieve her parcel.

The next part of her plan proved difficult. None of the taxis that sat idle around the hotel district moved up and down this market street. She finally paid a delivery man to allow her to ride along as he went in her direction.

She sat on the back of the open cart, dangling her feet and counting herself well off. A taxi would have been five times what the ride in this conveyance cost her. She allowed herself to be "delivered" with her baby carriage and bundle to the back of one of the mansions on the lane to Bamataub's. The man had no idea she wasn't a guest at the home.

"May I take your purchases to the front door or the kitchen door, miss?"

"No, I'm fine. Someone inside will be more than willing to help me," she said and added under her breath, "if I were to ask them."

She doled out the coins and gave him an extra since she felt very pleased with herself. He waved farewell, and she stepped inside the back gate until he turned at the end of the alley. Then she hopped back into the narrow drive and looked down at her purchases.

"Almost there," she congratulated herself. "And almost no snags in my plan at all. I think I'm quite good at adventuring."

31

Calm Before the Storm

Tipper longed for Beccaroon's thick forest of tropical foliage. The sparse accumulation of trees behind the house where she had been dropped off provided little cover. She changed quickly in the densest stand of trees she could find. With her dress, shoes, and cape rolled up and placed in the baby buggy on top of the clothes for Jayrus, she strolled down the lane with the dark blue nanny's cape covering her breeches and shirt. The hood covered her hair and allowed her to pull it forward to hide her face. Her sensible walking shoes felt good, and she thought that all her purchases showed her aptitude for scheming and subterfuge. She would be useful in helping her father escape.

The walk to the last house on the lane seemed longer than the ride in the carriage. She finally reached the forbidding manor and walked right past the gate. Jayrus was nowhere in sight.

She chastised herself for thinking she would spot him right away. After all, he wouldn't be standing in the road, waiting for one of Bamataub's henchmen to jump on him and drag him inside.

The thought of the villains lurking around made her scurry down the lane. The road went on into the countryside, and she had no desire to walk to whatever village sprang up next. After turning around, she ambled back the way she had come. Her legs complained by the time she had passed the fortified mansion again and two houses farther on.

Where could she go? Where was Jayrus? What should she do until the others came?

"Walk this confounded baby until nap time is over," she answered herself and turned around once more.

Tipper admitted that her preparation hadn't been complete since she didn't have any water. Then she thought of dinner and wondered how long it would be until the others came and if they would bring something for Jayrus to eat. And if they did, would they remember her? If they didn't remember her, would Jayrus share?

The heavy nanny's cape locked in her own heat and absorbed the heat of the afternoon sun. Her arms went through slits in the front to hold on to the perambulator's handle. The cape parted, however, when she lifted her sleeve to wipe her brow.

She pulled the cape closed in front of her. "Oh, dribbling drummerbugs!" She'd exposed her very improper and not nannylike outfit beneath. Looking up and down the lane, she couldn't see that she had done any harm. No one walked, rode, or drove down the lane. She passed the mansion once more.

This time she walked farther into the countryside. At one point, a bridge passed over a large stream. Tipper peered over the wooden rail and thought the water looked cool and clear. Then a turtle plopped off his log and into the slow current.

Tipper wrinkled her nose and gave up the thought of taking a sip. Bees buzzed around a flowering casting bush. The blooms looked like tiny lures on the end of a leafless stem, much like a fishing rod. She picked one and sucked out the nectar. Several blooms provided enough to make her want more, but the bees became territorial, and she decided to move on.

Before she reached Bamataub's manor, one patch of road passed under some trees. From here, no one would be able to see her from the distant mansion. Tipper pushed the hood off her head and slowed down to savor the shade. A movement above made her look up just as the prince dropped off a branch onto the road beside her.

Tipper jumped and screeched. "Jayrus!"

"What are you doing here?"

"I came to save my father."

"By walking back and forth, pushing a baby?" He peeked into the baby carriage. "Pushing a bundle of your clothes?"

"I've got clothes for you too."

"Me?"

Tipper could not decipher the expression on the prince's face. Amused? Astonished? Annoyed? She lifted her bundle of clothes as if cradling a baby and revealed the stack of tunic and trousers beneath.

"I thought your clothes would be too fine for climbing walls and too visible in the dark, so I bought something else at the same time I got this outfit for me."

Now Tipper was sure amusement had won out over the other emotions. She prepared to trounce him with as many words about ingratitude as she could muster.

He held up his hand. "I appreciate the thought, Tipper, but the kimens make my clothes out of fiber from a special plant. I won't be seen."

Tipper's eyes narrowed as she examined his jacket of finely woven threads. The material looked soft and had a sheen that enhanced the intriguing color, a green-tinged off-white. She touched his sleeve, which felt smooth and cool, much nicer than her heavy, hot cape.

She shook her head. "How is it special?"

"You didn't see me watching you from the tree, did you?"

"No. You were watching me?"

"I wasn't sure it was you until you put the hood down."

He smiled, and his enchanting demeanor almost distracted her from her purpose. Irritation at herself spiked her questions. "Where's my father? Aren't you supposed to be watching for any sign of him?

Where's his board? You're too far away from that despicable man's house to do any good. Where are Junkit and Zabeth and the others?"

Prince Jayrus took the bundle of clothes from her arms and put them back in the baby buggy. "Your father's in an upstairs bedroom, which makes it simpler to rescue him. The board is on the soil outside the grounds' wall closest to the bedroom. Zabeth and Grandur are with your father, healing him. Or at least trying to keep him stable. Junkit is watching the front of the mansion. Hue is watching the back."

"Could we wait until Papa fades and reforms on the board?"

A look of concern passed over the prince's face. He placed a hand on her arm. "Grandur is not sure your father is strong enough to pass through one of his fadings safely."

Tipper swallowed the panic and willed herself to ask a sensible question. "Why is it easier to rescue Papa from an upstairs room?"

"Because I'll be going in on a dragon." Prince Jayrus flattened his hand and used it to demonstrate a dragon gliding in over the house. "From above."

Tipper nodded. "We'll be going in on a dragon."

"You are the most exasperating woman I've ever known."

Tipper grinned. A white dragon in an area where no dragons were known to exist. A man, probably standing to show off, riding the white dragon where no one ever rode on dragons. This prince must believe the world wore blinders. She shook her head the tiniest bit, afraid she'd burst out laughing. "And you won't be seen?"

"While we're flying in, I won't be seen because I am careful. In the house and on the grounds, I won't be seen because of my apparel."

She tilted her head and eyed his clothing.

"Watch." He walked a few feet into the woods, between several slender trunks, and turned around, placing his hands behind his back.

Tipper blinked. It was as if she saw right through him. The colors of his clothing matched perfectly the foliage around him. His head appeared to float over nothing.

She frowned. "That's…I don't know what that is. Eerie?"

"Practical," said Jayrus as he returned to her side, all of him visible as he moved. "Are you hungry? thirsty?"

"Oh yes."

He bowed. "Mistress Tipper, may I escort you to afternoon tea?"

She curtsied. "Yes, Prince Jayrus."

Tipper kept sneaking glances at the handsome man walking beside her. One part of her gladly trusted him. Another part reacted with the same cautious emotion that sprang to her throat when she witnessed his uncanny disappearance. This man could unsettle her whole world if she let him.

Jayrus accompanied her to a point just outside the manor's line of sight.

"Keep walking," he instructed, "and when you get to the turnoff that is the service lane to Bamataub's house, follow that path a dozen feet, and I'll rejoin you there."

"You don't want to be seen with me?"

"Definitely not." He backtracked and disappeared into a copse.

His words didn't upset her. In fact, she pushed the perambulator around the bend in the road with an extra-light step. She now guessed why Beccaroon didn't want her going off with the prince on her own. He was altogether too charming. One minute she wanted to flee his presence for her sanity's sake, and the next she was willing to depend on him no matter what. Realizing this was not a good state of affairs, she determined to proceed with caution.

Less than fifteen minutes later, Tipper sat cross-legged on the ground while the prince served her sandwiches and juice. A hedge as tall as the wall grew along this side of the manor. In a hidden bower between the shrubs and the bricks, Jayrus had set up a comfortable blind from which he ventured out to observe the house. Jayrus left her there with strict orders not to move.

The evening chorus of insects and birdsong created a restful background as Tipper leaned against the wall and slowly chewed her meal. She didn't feel peaceful. Now that she sat in the shadow of the villain's fortress, the seriousness of their undertaking gripped her heart. If they failed, her father might die. If they were discovered, injury or death for one of the rescuers was a possibility.

Before he left the enclosure, Jayrus had sent Zabeth to the hotel to inform the others of Tipper's whereabouts. She was grateful he didn't take the opportunity to lecture her about her thoughtlessness, but she'd read the displeasure on his face. As the time approached for them to risk life and limb to rescue her father, he became less social. Tipper watched as confidence replaced charm. She thought a self-assured champion was more to be desired than a debonair companion. The prince's composure did much to bolster her assurance that all would go well.

He and Junkit were making a tour of the grounds as darkness set in. Tipper sat waiting, wanting to talk to someone. She realized she wanted her father there so she could confide her concerns. Her father had been absent for many years, and she had not had the luxury of his support and guidance. The hole seemed darker now that she'd had a taste of his presence. She wanted Beccaroon beside her for the same purpose. He had experience as her stalwart advisor.

To voice her expectations for the evening and apprehension over the problems that might arise to someone she knew to be constant and wise would ease her tension. In the absence of advice from her father or Beccaroon, steady reassurance from Prince Jayrus would be welcome. The urge to reach out and connect with someone trust-worthy overwhelmed her. She quit eating and put the sandwich in its wrapper and back in the basket.

She remembered Beccaroon saying he often regretted that he could not voice his gratitude for his beautiful forest to whoever created it. Now she groped for some entity who was the guardian behind those she could see with her eyes.

Shadows deepened. A cool wind rattled the leaves around her. Tipper crawled to an opening and looked out at the countryside. Great clouds billowed in a menacing sky. A streak of lightning revealed a threatening storm rolling in from the west. She shivered and retreated to the haven within the hedge. She'd been sitting on her blue cape, but now she wrapped it around her as the air became colder and wet. A rumble of thunder accompanied the soft patter of raindrops on the leaves overhead. She pulled the hood over her hair.

"Where is that prince?"

32

Nefarious Affairs

"I will explain how I am going to arrive on the roof of the house, and then maybe you will concede that I best go alone."

Jayrus spoke patiently, and Tipper wanted to run away, leaving him to yammer on about his plans. She could bolt and find her father on her own. But that was a ridiculous plan that would end in disaster. It would only make her look foolish. And both Beccaroon and Bealomondore huddled between her and the means to get away from the obnoxious dragon-keeper prince. The perambulator also stood in the way.

Librettowit and Wizard Fenworth whispered together, trying to work out the details of a "keeping dry" spell. Her cape was far beyond any hope of being dry again without a couple of days hanging in the sunshine. What did it matter if they were wet or dry? They needed to get on with the business of rescuing her father. Instead, Jayrus droned on about his plan.

"I summoned Caesannede, and he is nearby. He will glide over the mansion." He demonstrated with his hand. He put a rock on his fingers. "I will be lying on one wing. At a precise moment, he will tilt, and I will slide onto the rooftop." He tilted his hand, and the rock fell to the ground.

Tipper did not comment.

"Grandur has located an unlocked window on the top floor and will be waiting for me there."

"How are you going to get from the roof to the window?" asked Bealomondore.

"I have a rope." He seemed to think that was an adequate response.

Tipper admitted to herself that she did not relish the idea of sliding onto a roof. "What will we be doing?"

"Waiting outside. I'll bring your father to you or send one of the dragons for help if I need it."

Tipper hunched down in her sodden cape. At least the prince acknowledged that he might need help.

She looked up at him and caught him watching her. "Be careful," she said.

"I will."

After his departure, the wizard brought out umbrellas from one of his hollows and passed them around.

Beccaroon declined but took over leadership and gave each of them a post at a different location around the wall. "The idea is to be ready when Prince Jayrus brings Verrin Schope out. Right now we have no way of knowing what avenue they will use to escape the house, so we will have help located on each side. We'll get Verrin Schope to the coach as quickly as possible and spirit him away."

Tipper followed Bealomondore to the northwest corner, where they could watch both directions at once. A tree grew inside the grounds, and a large branch hung over the wall.

Tipper put down her useless umbrella and took off her cape. "Boost me up," Tipper commanded.

Bealomondore didn't move.

"I'm sorry," said Tipper. "Would you please give me a boost?"

"It's not that," explained the tumanhofer. "I'm not sure it's safe for you to be up there."

"Why?"

"Rain. Lightning. Tree."

As if to accentuate the logic of Bealomondore's thinking, a flash quickly followed by a crack of thunder made Tipper jump and cringe. When the tingle left her skin, she opened her eyes.

Bealomondore pointed. She followed his finger and saw the white dragon approaching, gliding noiselessly through the rain. He passed directly over them.

Bealomondore sighed. "I wish we could see Prince Jayrus make his landing on the roof."

Tipper sighed as well, but said nothing.

A dog barked within the grounds. Then another. A frenzy of barking erupted.

Tipper wrung her hands. "Nobody said anything about dogs."

"It's too soon for Jayrus to be leaving the house with your father. Something else must have disturbed them."

"Perhaps they see the prince dangling from a rope next to the unlocked window."

The tumanhofer rubbed his chin. "That could be."

"Well, I hope it isn't!" Tipper snapped.

"No need to get testy."

Thunder rolled, and the skies let loose with a torrent of rain. Tipper looked down at the black mass that once was her nanny cape—clean, dry, and respectable.

"You're cold," said Bealomondore. "Take my coat."

He handed her his open umbrella and peeled off his outer jacket. He took the umbrella back and handed her the coat. She shivered and plunged her arms into the sleeves, then gathered the material close around her front. "Thank you."

They stood close under their inadequate shelter.

"I don't hear the dogs anymore," said Tipper.

"I can't see beyond the waterfall coming off the umbrella."

"Prince Jayrus should be inside by now."

The tumanhofer shifted and held the umbrella up a bit higher. His height made it a stretch for him to keep it from knocking Tipper's head. "He'll probably wait a bit for the rain to let up."

"That would be sensible." She grasped the handle. "I'll hold the umbrella for a bit."

"It's sopping wet and leaking."

"I know."

They stood in silence for a long while.

"Did you hear something?" asked Tipper.

"I think the rain is abating."

"I did hear something."

"Probably an animal." But Bealomondore glanced around.

"Aren't animals likely to be holed up, waiting for the storm to pass?"

"Just keep still, and be quiet."

A scuffling noise indicated something large moving through the bushes. Tipper's hand tightened on the umbrella handle.

Bealomondore leaned closer. "Perhaps we better move."

"Where?"

"To a better hiding place."

A male voice, gruff and commanding, interrupted the constant drone of the rain. "You will come with us. Do not try to escape."

Through the curtain of rain, Tipper saw a half circle of men closing in on them. Some of them brandished swords. One stepped forward with a lantern in his hand. Scars distorted his tumanhofer features, twisting what would never be a smile into a menacing sneer.

Tipper and Bealomondore didn't resist. There didn't seem to be much point. Tipper fumed. Her companion darted glances one way and another.

"Don't try to run," she whispered. "Once we're inside the house, maybe we can help rescue Papa."

"Be quiet!" barked the man with the light.

A flutter of wings, the thud as Beccaroon struck one man from above, and a shout sent the men scattering. Bealomondore grabbed the umbrella and closed it, then used it to bash and batter those men who barreled toward them.

Tipper had no weapon. She dropped to her knees and came up with the first stick she could find. Waving it like a sword, she kept the men at bay on her side.

Beccaroon dove again, and another ruffian screeched as parrot claws tore at his face. One of the thugs grabbed the umbrella, pulled Bealomondore close, and punched him in the face. The tumanhofer went down. Another brute rushed Tipper. Her stick broke against his chest. He captured her, pinning her arms tightly to her sides.

"Get the bird," ordered the leader.

On his next dive, Bec aimed for the man clutching Tipper. She ducked, and he delivered a good blow to the man's head. Wet feathers encumbered his flight. As he flapped away, two men swung their swords. The first one landed a glancing blow to Beccaroon's leg. The other struck the base of his tail.

With a shriek, the bird flailed against the rain, then fell into the bushes. The two men crashed into the shrubs with swords raised.

"Beccaroon!" Tipper cried.

"Move!" ordered the man holding her, and he dragged her toward the front gate.

Tipper struggled, trying to get loose, trying to get back to Beccaroon. Another man pulled Bealomondore along behind her, but she hardly noticed.

They entered through the gate and marched between the sinister trees. The man hauling Tipper lost his grip once, grabbed her arm, and walloped her across the face before throwing her over his shoulder and trudging on.

She grunted, stunned by the blow. She hurt in so many places that she couldn't focus.

"Somebody grab her legs," he grumbled. "She weighs a ton and is way too long to carry alone."

Another of the short thugs hoisted her legs onto his shoulder and walked behind her captor.

Someone else opened the front door of the mansion, and the henchmen tramped through the foyer to the same room in which Tipper and her friends had been served refreshments. Her captor abruptly dumped Tipper on the floor. Bealomondore landed beside her.

She heard a gasp and looked up into the eyes of Orphelian. Bamataub's wife clutched the arms of her chair but did not move to aid the prisoners. Tipper turned her head and, through her tears, saw the master of the house, standing beside a roaring fire and laughing down at them.

"I do like gifts on stormy nights. To break the monotony, you know. Orphelian was just reading to me about a man whose life was fraught with trials. So boring. He didn't have the gumption to rid himself of those who amounted to little more than pests."

His wife whimpered, closed the book, and stared down at her hands.

"Now," said Bamataub, "if I could only show the writer of this insipid tale"—he gestured toward the book in his wife's lap—"how a true man of decision deals with irritation, perhaps his next book would be an improvement."

He pulled a poker from the tools beside the fire. "Killing is not difficult. Bloody, of course, but you've already dampened my rugs with rainwater and mud."

"Please, husband," whispered Orphelian, "may I leave?"

A look of disgust flashed across Bamataub's face. "Yes."

She stood, dropping the book, and rushed to the door. She flung it open and stepped through, and a whirlwind entered, flashing two swords. Three of the henchmen fell to the floor before Tipper realized Prince Jayrus wielded the weapons that still blazed through the air and cut down the enemy.

Movement caught her eye, and she saw Bamataub approach Bealomondore with the poker raised above his head. She screamed as the bludgeon descended. The tumanhofer rolled to one side, and the iron rod hit the floor.

Bamataub roared and turned to attack Jayrus. One sword pierced the tyrant through the stomach, and another entered his chest. The prince pulled back, taking his weapons with him. Bamataub sank to his knees, then keeled forward.

Tipper turned away from the bloody scene. Her stomach lurched. She squeezed her eyes shut. Was she sick from her own pain or from the sight of someone else bloodied and killed?

A rustle of skirts at the door brought all eyes to the widow clutching the frame. "He's dead?"

Jayrus put the sword in his left hand down on a table as he went to Orphelian's side. He clasped her arm. "He is."

"Thank you," she whispered, then turned to go. "I must leave this place quickly. He has associates, and I will fare no better with them now than when he was alive. I will be gone before they know of this."

She took a few steps toward the stairs but returned.

"You came for a statue. I am his widow and should own everything in this house. I want none of it, but I give you the statue. It's in the display room. There." She pointed across the hall. "You'd best be quick about taking it and getting out. I assume you've come for the old emerlindian?"

"We have, Madam, and he is already safe."

She nodded, vaguely, as if too many thoughts raced through her mind. "Good, good. Excuse me. I must not tarry. I have only a few things to gather." She lifted her skirts and ran for the stairs leading to the upper level.

Prince Jayrus called after her. "Do you wish to go with us? We will offer you safe journey to your destination."

"No!" She stopped halfway up and stared at him. "They will be looking for you. It is best for me to have nothing more to do with you and your friends. Again, I thank you for my freedom." She sighed. "And I regret, for your sakes, that my chances are much better than yours. Farewell." She dashed up the remaining steps.

Jayrus surveyed the hall. He stood quietly for a moment.

Bealomondore had regained his feet and came to help Tipper. "Can you stand?"

She nodded and allowed him to assist her. The smell of blood nauseated her, and she stumbled toward the door. No one appeared from the many halls to harass them.

She touched the prince's sleeve. "My father is safe?"

"He's in the carriage with Fenworth and the dragons. Librettowit is driving it to the front door."

"Beccaroon is—" She choked on her words.

"We'll not leave until we've located him." Jayrus took her other arm and, with Bealomondore, guided her to the entryway.

Librettowit entered with an empty bag over his shoulder and a short sword in his hand. He looked around and nodded.

"I see you took care of things. I was coming in to help."

"Orphelian has given us the statue," said Jayrus, pointing toward one of the doors. "It's in there."

The librarian nodded. "I'll get it and meet you in the carriage."

Tipper bolted from her two escorts and charged the carriage she could see through the open entry. The rain had stopped, but she splashed through puddles inches deep. She tore open the carriage door and plunged in, wrapping her arms around her father. "Papa, Papa," was all she managed to say. She laid her head on his chest and sobbed.

Her father's hand stroked her back. His voice cooed in her ear. "Here, here. Everything will be all right."

Fenworth harrumphed. "Still a bit dramatic, but not quite so loud in her hysteria."

She ignored him. "Beccaroon?"

Her father patted her shoulder. "I've sent the minor dragons to find him."

Librettowit appeared at the door and climbed in, the limp bag still over his shoulder.

Tipper's heart wrenched with disappointment. "You didn't find the statue?"

"I found it," he said as he sat down next to Fenworth. "It's in the bag."

"Another hollow," explained Bealomondore as he entered the coach.

Prince Jayrus came out of the house. He looked inside, his eyes moving over each of the occupants. "I'll drive." He closed the door and mounted the coachman's seat.

"Do you think he knows how?" asked Fenworth.

"If he doesn't now," said Librettowit, "I'm willing to say he'll know how by the end of the drive."

33

Injury

Tipper raised her head off her father's chest. "Why have we stopped?" She started to sit up, but her father tightened his hold. She could see that his face was lined with fatigue.

"Stay with me."

The coach swayed as Prince Jayrus descended. A few moments passed, and he opened the door.

"Librettowit, Bealomondore, I need some assistance."

Tipper jerked, but her father's arm remained around her shoulders. "Stay with me."

She could barely see the prince's face in the dark of the cold night. "Jayrus?"

"We've found Beccaroon. He's alive. We'll bring him to you in just a moment."

"I like that bird," said Fenworth and followed the two tuman-hofers out of the carriage.

Again Tipper wanted to leave. She leaned toward the door.

Her father breathed deeply. "Stay with me."

"Are you going to be all right, Papa?"

"I don't know. I am more concerned for you and your mother now."

"Why?"

"I assumed I would have time to share with you all I have learned while away." The last words came out in gasps, but he continued. "I've spoken to Peg on my visits, but it takes a long time for her to assimilate something new."

Tipper patted his chest. "Rest. Tell me later."

Bealomondore returned, bringing Tipper's clothes from the baby buggy. Junkit and Hue entered the coach. "They're cold," said the tumanhofer. "Jayrus sent them back to warm up. Can you dry them with these?"

He handed Tipper the trousers she'd bought for the prince. She sat up, and the two dragons landed in her lap, ready to be rubbed dry. Bealomondore draped the peach-colored cape over her father.

Verrin Schope whispered, "Beccaroon?"

"The healing dragons are helping. Librettowit and Fenworth applied some of the powder they got from that bug shop. It looks like those thugs took his tail as a trophy and left him to bleed to death."

Tipper gasped and unconsciously pulled the two dragons into a smothering embrace. They chittered in protest, and she relaxed her grasp.

Bealomondore gently squeezed her arm. "I'll go back and see if they are ready to bring him to the carriage."

Tipper wiped tears from her cheeks and went back to warming the shivering dragons in her arms.

"Put them under this blanket with me." Her father made an effort to move the cape.

She tucked the dragons underneath. "It's my cape."

He leaned his head back and closed his eyes. "Is it, dear? That's nice."

The door rattled and opened. Bealomondore ducked in, turned, and reached to receive Beccaroon as Librettowit and Jayrus passed his unconscious form through the door. He sat with Beccaroon's head and shoulders cradled in his lap. Librettowit climbed in next and scooted under the lower half of the parrot's body. As Fenworth entered, he carefully folded Beccaroon's limp wings so they wouldn't be damaged. A massive, elaborate dressing wrapped the stub where his tail had been. Fenworth sat next to Tipper.

The door closed, obliterating all light.

"Why is it so much darker?" Tipper whispered.

"I'm sitting on something," grumped the wizard. He leaned forward, dug around on the seat, and pulled out a small cylinder-shaped lightrock. The faint glow spread through the gloomy interior of the cab. "So that's where I left that."

They entered the hotel through the back. It took a good bit of Prince Jayrus's charisma to smooth the way. The night clerk had "no authority" to allow guests to enter the establishment other than by way of the customary front entrance. Jayrus offered to escort his mud-splattered, rain-drenched, battle-scarred companions through the elegant grand foyer, and the night clerk relented.

Two bedrooms branched off a sitting room in Verrin Schope's suite. Jayrus put Tipper's father in one room and Beccaroon in the other. Tipper could sleep on the couch, but that night no one slept, not even the wizard.

Fenworth and Librettowit sat with the grand parrot, easing his discomfort with the aid of the healing dragons and bathing his wound with a soothing solution that contained powdered *Fineet fineaurlais* from the Insect Emporium.

Tipper curled up in a chair beside Verrin Schope's bed. The tonic of *Fineet fineaurlais* had also worked well on his ailment, taking hold of his unstable condition sometime during the night. In the morning, Tipper's father sat up, smiled, and offered to help nurse Beccaroon.

Tipper left the room to see how their bird friend fared and found Bealomondore and Prince Jayrus camped in the sitting room.

"You've been here all night?" she asked when they came to their feet.

Jayrus stretched as he stood, then bowed to her. "Yes. We thought we might be needed."

She stared at him for a moment, taking in how, even in a disheveled state, the prince's appeal remained strong. Then his words registered. "Bamataub's men? You were on guard. Orphelian said they would be looking for us."

"Well," said Bealomondore, "they didn't find us last night." He picked up his jacket, which had been draped over a chair. "I'm going to clean up and find some breakfast. Would you like me to bring yours to the room? Does your father feel up to eating?"

"I do." Verrin Schope spoke from the door. "But let's check on Beccaroon first."

Fenworth came out of the bedroom as they approached.

"He'll do," said the wizard, pulling his beard. "He's awake now and not receptive to visitors quite yet. Tut, tut, oh dear. He won't fly, you see. Needs his tail for that."

"Oh, poor Bec." Tipper tried to pass Fenworth, but her father held her arm.

"Give him a little time, my dear."

"Yes," said Fenworth. "He doesn't need sympathy as much as he needs time to deal with his emotions. But something in his stomach would be good. Have Rowser and Piefer made their delivery yet?"

A knock sounded on the door.

"Perhaps that's them." Fenworth started for the door and stopped. "No, it's not. One person, not two. Bent on interrogating our prince." He walked back to Bec's room. He nodded at Jayrus as he passed. "Don't worry over much. The man doesn't want to arrest you if he can help it. Figures you did the city a service, but he has to ask all the right questions. Duty. Procedure. Tut, tut. Botheration."

He took a few more steps, stopped, and groaned. "Oh dear, oh dear. Now there are two. The man who's just joined the first man in the hall is an entirely different sort. He wants you hanged." He sighed and continued on his way. "I do hope the first man prevails. Our prince has turned out to be useful." He opened the bedroom door and walked through, making one more comment before he closed it again. "Quests are uncomfortable things but a bit more tolerable when shared with useful individuals."

Prince Jayrus addressed Bealomondore. "Would you go and procure our breakfast? Also, please see to baths for everyone. I think we'll all feel better with this grime washed away."

"I agree wholeheartedly, but do you want me to leave?" Bealomondore nodded toward the door.

"I don't think this will be a problem. Go take care of the more important things, if you will." The prince moved forward and opened the door. "Welcome, sir." He bowed. "Prince Jayrus, at your service. What can I do for you?"

"A bit of your time?" said a gray-haired marione. He removed his hat.

"Of course." Jayrus ushered the two men in, and Bealomondore slipped out.

The second man, a tumanhofer, moved as if to stop him, but after a brief glaring match, he stepped aside. The antagonistic stranger turned speculative eyes on the prince.

Tipper looked down at her ragged pants and muddied shirt. None of them presented well this morning, but Prince Jayrus carried an air of dignity and appeared half decent even in his mussed attire.

"Please, have a seat." He gestured toward the couch. "I'm afraid we are still a-dither this morning."

Tipper's eyebrows went up, and she turned to her father. His ears twitched. She mouthed the word. "A-dither?"

Verrin Schope choked on a laugh and turned away. "Excuse me," he said, clearing his throat. "Caught a bit of a chill last night."

"Yes, about last night," said the marione, who had seated himself and relaxed into the cushions. He didn't seem threatening, but the man next to him looked like he'd growl at the slightest provocation. "I'm Sheriff Rog, and I'm investigating a disturbance last night. This is Barrister Beladderant. He represents the estate that suffered loss."

"Most interesting," said Jayrus, frowning. "We were attacked last night by a group of ruffians. I had no idea crime ran rampant in Fayetopolis."

Sheriff Rog narrowed his eyes. "We have the same share as most big cities." He fidgeted with his hat. "In a moment, I'd like the details of your encounter. First, let me tell you the reason behind my visit. The home of a prominent citizen was broken into last night, art stolen, the wife kidnapped, and the master of the house murdered."

Tipper did not have to fake the gasp that escaped her lips as she sank onto a nearby chair. Murder was not a crime she wanted any of them to be associated with. "How dreadful," she murmured.

"Yes, miss, it is." The sheriff turned his hat over as if pondering the phrasing of his next question. "The servants say the party of thieves consisted of a gentleman dressed quite well and brandishing lethal swords—two, in fact. Fighting with two swords." He shook his head slowly. "A young lady dressed as a boy, a very ill and elderly emerlindian, two tumanhofers, a kind of o'rant, and a grand parrot." He sighed. "That sort of describes you and your company."

Verrin Schope stood very straight and looked down his nose at both men. "A very ill and elderly emerlindian? I admit to being old, but not elderly. And I am certainly not ill, except for a tickle in my throat from being out in the rain last night."

Prince Jayrus furrowed his brow. "I'm a little confused by your descriptions. 'A kind of o'rant'? Wizard Fenworth is an o'rant, but what does it mean, 'a kind of o'rant'?"

"Apparently one of the servants tried to stop the man as he moved down the lane outside the manor. The servant grabbed the man's arm, and it broke off. He found he was holding a branch of a tree instead of a flesh-and-blood arm."

Amusement lightened the prince's countenance. "First, this servant tries to stop a man walking down the lane. Why bother a man passing the house, no doubt trying to hurry home to get out of the rain? Then he claims this oddity about an arm that is a wooden branch? I think I would toss that witness's story to the side."

"Yes," said Sheriff Rog. "I've already come to that conclusion."

The tumanhofer beside the sheriff growled just as Tipper suspected he might. He leaned close to Rog and whispered something.

The sheriff frowned. "Then there is the matter of the gentleman breaking into the house."

"This was last night, during that dreadful storm?" asked Jayrus.

"Yes." Sheriff Rog ducked his head and wiped a hand through his hair. At the prodding of his neighbor, he continued. "According to the groundskeeper, who'd gone out to silence the dogs, the thieving murderer rode in on a white dragon, landed on the roof, and entered through an upstairs window."

Prince Jayrus sat for a moment, a blank look on his face. "He flew through torrential rain and lightning, and he and this dragon landed on the roof."

"No, the man slid off, and the dragon flew away."

"I've never seen a man slide off a dragon," said Jayrus. "Have you?"

The marione sighed heavily. "No sir, I have never even seen a dragon. Not a riding one, I mean. I've seen the minor ones that hang about from time to time. They live in the alleys if they live in town at all."

"I see. Well, may I tell you of our misadventure, Sheriff? I believe you will find solid evidence to investigate. Our ordeal occurred on the ground, very muddy ground." He looked ruefully down at his clothing.

Tipper thought the mud had not stuck to him nearly as badly as it clung to everyone else. Only her father was decently attired.

Jayrus smiled. "And our mishap involves ordinary thieves who did no more than jump out from behind trees and waylay us. No risky dragon flights."

He proceeded to spin his tale, and Tipper marveled at how close he stuck to the truth. He mentioned the road and the carriage. He talked about the men who surrounded Tipper and Bealomondore, but neglected to say they surrounded only Tipper and the young tumanhofer. He described Beccaroon's brave defense. He talked of his struggle with the ruffians but failed to mention he used swords.

He ended by describing his friend Beccaroon's injury, which made Tipper break down and sob.

Authority braced the prince's voice. "Find the men who have that tail as a trophy, and you will have found the culprits, Sheriff."

Tipper wiped her eyes at that moment and happened to look at the rough man beside the sheriff. Why did he look uncomfortable? Had he been part of the horrors of last night?

As Prince Jayrus showed the two men out, he looked straight into the official's eyes and said, "I wouldn't be at all surprised, Sheriff Rog, if these two incidents were related and the evil perpetrated sprang from the same source."

When the sheriff agreed, Tipper felt like something else had been said between the two men and she had missed it.

34

Flight?

Beccaroon chafed against the confines of his recovery. Verrin Schope irritated him, and the artist insisted on keeping him company. He sat in the chair beside Bec's bed and sketched or played with a small lump of clay, but he never showed Beccaroon the results of his labors. And his old friend talked and talked. The talk was about Amara and Paladin and Wulder. In Amara, they did such and such. Paladin did this. Wulder did that. Unwillingly, Beccaroon learned about the role of this Paladin—not a king but definitely a leader. Apparently someone who always knew right from wrong and didn't mind sharing his wisdom. Yes, Verrin Schope's talking grated on Beccaroon's nerves.

The two pesky healing dragons constantly slept on him or played around the bed. Tipper read to him. Bealomondore told him stories of the houses he had visited. Librettowit and Hue sang to him. Fenworth would sit down to keep him company and then fall asleep. That was preferable to talking, playing, reading, and singing. But the wizard snored. The snoring drove Beccaroon crazy.

The prince, however, left him alone. And if Tipper chose to leave him alone, as well, Beccaroon stewed over whether they were leaving him alone together, in each other's company, without supervision. He warned Verrin Schope. Verrin Schope said his daughter had a good head on her shoulders. Bec wasn't worried about her head. He was worried about her heart.

Beccaroon had to admit that the frequent visits from Rowser and

Piefer amused him. They discussed bugs. Beccaroon knew almost as many varieties as the learned medicinal suppliers did. He enjoyed learning the scientific terms. He taught them the more common names used among the people.

Sometimes he stumped them. Sometimes they stumped him.

And speaking of stumps…the pain didn't hurt as much as the indignity. The indignity did not hurt as much as the future without flight. Beccaroon thought perhaps he'd be able to manage somehow. He'd never regain his grace in the air, but he'd manage to fly at least as well as some of the chickens that roosted in trees. His real desire was to leave this quest, return home, and learn to cope.

But Verrin Schope still needed him—so he said—and Tipper definitely needed him. Her eyes lit up when the prince entered the room, and neither the scoundrel nor Tipper's father seemed aware of the girl's infatuation. Yes, Tipper needed him.

He had to reiterate a thousand times that he was ready to travel before they listened to him. With the help of the healing dragons, his skin had regenerated over the stump, but, of course, it was unsightly. A few of his back feathers dangled down, but not enough to hide the bald spot.

He was ready to face the world with a hole in his plumage. In fact, if he didn't get the initial reentry into society over with soon, he would jump out a window.

When Verrin Schope said one more day, Beccaroon tossed a seed-cake at him. The emerlindian wisely retreated from the room, and neither he nor Bealomondore showed their faces for twenty-four hours.

The next morning, both men appeared. They walked in and stood side by side, occasionally glancing out the door to the sitting room.

Wizard Fenworth followed them a few seconds later, grinning and clapping his hands together more often than usual. The old man even bounced on his toes as he stood waiting, and he also kept an eye on the other room.

Beccaroon suspected something was up. "I thought we were leaving this morning. Why aren't you packing?"

"Tut, tut. Finished. Packing, you say? Not that. The project. I designed the glue. I think it'll work more than adequately. I predict you will be amazed at the comfort."

Verrin Schope nudged the old man, and he fell silent.

Beccaroon heard scuffling noises from the other room.

"Thank you so much," Tipper said, apparently to someone at the door. "Do you want to stay?"

He heard a voice and thought it sounded like Rowser.

Tipper answered the mutterer. "Yes, we hope to have a celebration if all goes well."

Beccaroon strained to hear. People moved around in the other room but had stopped talking. He stood.

Bealomondore actually jumped in front of the door. "Where are you going?"

"To see what they're doing."

"Umm…" The tumanhofer looked to Verrin Schope for guidance.

Verrin Schope chuckled and winked at Bealomondore. "It's all right." He held up a hand to his friend. "Hold on, old Bec. We have a surprise for you, and if you go rushing out there, you'll spoil it."

Bealomondore stepped aside as Prince Jayrus and Tipper entered, arm in arm and grinning. Beccaroon took small consolation in the fact that they were not staring at each other and grinning, just grinning. Still, they looked as if a secret bubbled inside them.

What was this surprise? Was it worth another delay of their journey? His injury had put the quest on hold. They needed to get on with it before Verrin Schope began to show more adverse effects, before more signs of the world crumbling showed up. And the sooner they got the three statues back together, the sooner he could hide in his forest.

Rowser came through the door, holding a bowl-like apparatus covered with red feathers. Piefer followed close behind, supporting the tail—

It *was* a tail! The whole thing was a tail.

Beccaroon hopped across the room to look at it more carefully. The magnificent feathers fanned out from the base perfectly. Glue? The old wizard had said glue. Did they mean to glue this…this…?

"Who made this?" asked Beccaroon.

Verrin Schope stepped forward. "Bealomondore and I designed it. Rowser and Piefer obtained the materials. Then we crafted it between us all."

Beccaroon peered into the bowl. A cloth lined it. He poked it with his beak and found padding underneath.

His friends had worked hard. He looked at the shopkeepers and the wizard. These men didn't even claim longstanding friendship, and they had dedicated hours to make this "thing" a success.

Beccaroon tried not to appear ungrateful. He worked to keep his eyes from squinting and his voice from betraying his doubts. "Fenworth said glue. You're going to glue this on my stump?"

The wizard stepped forward, rubbing his hands, shedding leaves and small creatures. "Yes, a fine glue. It will hold well, then after two or three days, we apply a solvent, right through the porous base. The tail comes off for cleaning and adjusting, and just to give your skin a breather. Then we glue the tail back on when you want it."

Bec looked at the bowl-like foundation, the squishy inside of the base, the long red feathers, and the outstanding craftsmanship and still tried to hide a skepticism he could not eradicate. "It looks longer."

Verrin Schope put a hand on his shoulder. "We can adjust it. But

I think it only looks longer because you are viewing it from the side. You've never done that before."

Beccaroon's head bobbed. "Right. Well, let's try it. We've got a quest to resume." He crossed the room, hopped up on a chair, and turned his back to the others.

First, Wizard Fenworth smeared the glue into the cavity of the base. The glue smelled like some sweet fruit. It took Beccaroon a minute to recognize the fragrance.

"Bananas?" he asked.

"Essence of banana bug," said Rouser. "We tried *fractal appleorreal icknickeous,* commonly known as the apple worm, but the nice odor soured within a couple of hours and was not suitable. Strange that, because the odor remains pleasant when we concoct lickicks for arthritis." He shrugged. "We chose banana bug as the base ingredient."

The smell didn't bother Bec, but he held his breath anyway while they attached the false tail to his stump.

"Now," said Fenworth, "we need only wait three minutes, and the glue should be set."

Bec breathed out and stood still. Having so many people waiting for the results of this experiment unnerved him.

"So," he said into the unnatural silence, "where is our next stop for securing the second statue?"

"Hunthaven," said Bealomondore.

Beccaroon jerked, and Fenworth chided him to be still. "Don't jiggle the glue until it sets up."

Bec bobbed his head, still staring at the wall before him, and addressed the younger tumanhofer. "The celebrated Hunts have a statue? That should make our transaction easier. They are known for generosity and goodwill."

Bealomondore shook his head. "Unfortunately, they only live next door to the manor where the statue resides. The owners of Runan Hill own *Day's Deed*. I have an open invitation to Hunthaven but have never been on good terms with Allard Runan."

Librettowit checked his pocket watch. "Two more minutes."

Tipper quit staring at Beccaroon's back end and turned to Bealomondore. "Does this man, Allard Runan, have an extensive collection?"

The tumanhofer artist considered the question. "It's hard to say what his purpose is. The home does not reflect a love of art, yet he has some astonishing pieces scattered around."

"Don't twitch," said Fenworth.

"One minute," said Librettowit.

Verrin Schope sat down suddenly on the edge of the bed.

"Papa?" Tipper came to his side.

"Just a bit dizzy. I've been very well these last few days. I almost forgot the ailment."

Piefer came over and put a hand on the older emerlindian's wrist. "Pulse is racing."

"A mud-meade moth," said Rowser and reached for a pocket.

"Is it still muddy?" asked Prince Jayrus, his nose wrinkled.

Piefer laughed. "You must think we're very primitive. Nothing in our shop would give offense to your sensibilities. The moth is dried, ground, and put in a lozenge. We use honey to cover the slight taste."

Rowser handed what looked like a wrapped candy to Tipper's father. "Suck on this. Don't chew." He addressed his partner. "Not all of the things in our shop are pleasing to all people."

"You're right." Piefer nodded. *"Gobbilious scrubbugs."*

Rowser returned with *"Morticanicus virtos."*

"Awk! Stop!" screeched Beccaroon. "You forget I know what those are for."

"Proves the point," said Rowser with a shadow of a smile.

"What was the point?" asked Fenworth.

Piefer put his hands on his hips and tilted his head to one side. "Not all of the things in our shop are pleasing to all people."

"Harrumph," said the wizard. "I thought the point was to supply our friend here with sufficient tail feathers to help him toward graceful flight."

"And I thought," said Beccaroon, "that the point was to get the tail on, test it, and get on with the quest."

"Time's up!" said Librettowit.

Beccaroon jumped down from the chair. "Finally!"

"Where are we going to test Bec's new tail?" asked Tipper.

"In the country, where our riding dragons await." Prince Jayrus picked up one of the bags ready to be taken downstairs. "I'll procure transportation."

"No need," said Rowser. "Piefer and I brought our delivery wagon. We would be honored to give you a lift."

"And see the bigger dragons," said Piefer.

Beccaroon strutted to the door, pleased with the way the new tail hung. The weight was a tad more than his old tail, but he'd grow accustomed to that. He moved the stump and found the feathers responded well. Hope put a skip in his step. He looked over his shoulder to see if anyone had noticed. Only Tipper's eyes met his, and she winked.

35

Boscamon Returns

Their questing party strolled through the lobby of The Moon and Three Halves Inn as if they were in no hurry. Prince Jayrus had Tipper on his arm. Fenworth caused a stir. The minor dragons had decided to procure a snack by following the old wizard and snatching up bugs as they fell. Verrin Schope, Bealomondore, and Librettowit carried on a conversation as they walked.

The two medicinal bug merchants had gone ahead to position their delivery wagon at the front door. Tipper giggled at the thought of the uniformed doorman and his stuffy attitude. He wouldn't appreciate the Insect Emporium rig stopped before the grand mahogany and glass double doors.

Tipper wore another new dress her father had purchased. The yellow color accented her fair skin, and the long trumpet skirt made her feel like royalty. It swished. She loved the swish. Normally she would have been proud to display the fancy dress among the haughty clientele of the hotel, but her mind was on her old friend.

She watched Beccaroon as he exhibited poise and self-confidence among strangers. His strut looked natural, not unbalanced and not weighed down by the artificial tail. Sir Bec's squared shoulders and lifted head warmed her heart. Her old mentor might be testy at times, but his ever-present dignity was something she counted on.

In her pleasure, she squeezed the prince's arm. Startled, he looked down at her. When she nodded toward the proud parrot, he beamed one of his dashing, dimpled smiles.

As if the grand parrot could hear the silent exchange, his head swiveled almost completely around, and he latched one beady eye on the couple. He gestured with a nod, and Tipper came to his side.

"Are you all right?" she asked in a hushed voice.

"Certainly, but I have a request."

"Anything."

"See if you and the prince can tone down the brilliance of those smiles. You're blinding the assembly of rich and noble Fayetopolians."

Tipper giggled and stroked the feathers across the back of his neck.

"Tipper!" He hissed.

She pulled her hand back. "I'm sorry."

But happiness prevented her from wiping the grin from her face. To have Beccaroon chastise her for her overfamiliarity proved he was well.

She looked up and saw a man rise from his chair and head toward them. Her smile evaporated. What did Sheriff Rog want with them? And he mangled his hat in his hand again. Was that a good sign or a bad sign?

Prince Jayrus stepped forward and greeted the lawman. Verrin Schope joined them, and as Tipper realized he stood directly beside her, she also realized the others had stopped behind them.

"What can we do for you?" asked the prince.

"I thought you might like news of the mishaps on the night you were attacked."

Verrin Schope raised his eyebrows, which, on an emerlindian, made an upside-down V across the brow.

Prince Jayrus nodded. "I would indeed appreciate your expounding upon the subject."

Tipper heard her father snort and refused to look his way. She didn't want to join him in laughing over the prince's odd choice of words.

"Well." The sheriff cleared his throat and rotated the hat in his hands. "Seems it's most likely some of Bamataub's men accosted you. It's unknown whether your encounter with his henchmen happened before or after the man responsible for Bamataub's death entered the house and scared the ruffians out. But whoever managed to penetrate Bamataub's fortress has done the city a good deed. Apparently no one has stepped up to take over the lead of the evil ring the deceased operated."

Wizard Fenworth bunched his profuse eyebrows in a fierce scowl. "And his brand of evil was?"

"Slavery."

"Aha! I knew it." The wizard tapped his nose. "The house smelled of fear and violence."

The sheriff transferred his steady gaze to the old man. "And when were you in the house, may I ask?"

"The day before. Wanted to buy a statue from the weasel."

"And he wouldn't sell?"

Tipper tensed. Would the sheriff turn on them if he learned a few more facts?

Fenworth laughed. "No, he wouldn't. But his wife gave it to us."

The sheriff looked down at his hat for a moment. "Bamataub's gone, and that's a good thing. I suspect Barrister Beladderant, the man who came with me the other day, was hoping to move up and take his place. Instead, he's disappeared as well. Two self-important rats have left my territory, one way or another. That's a good thing."

He put his hat on his head and snatched it back off, nodding to Tipper. "Sorry, miss." He gestured with the hand that held his hat to include all of them. "I'm pleased to have made your acquaintance."

Once the general pleasantries of farewell were done, they left the sheriff and passed a very disgruntled doorman to climb into the waiting delivery wagon. Rowser handed Tipper up to the driver's seat, where she settled next to Piefer. From that perch, she observed Beccaroon out of the corner of her eye. Prince Jayrus, Bealomondore, and her father stood by, apparently in no hurry to board.

Beccaroon studied the distance from where he stood to the edge of the wagon bed. A shiver coursed through his wing feathers. Then he swatted the air, gave a leap, and fluttered onto a barrel latched sideways to the inside of the cart.

Tipper breathed a sigh of relief and turned toward the front. Rowser climbed up to sit on her other side, and the rest of the questing party took seats among the barrels and crates in the back.

The doorman gladly waved them off, even stepping into the road to hold traffic a moment so they could enter the thoroughfare.

At first, Tipper kept her lips sealed. She had many questions, but the city street echoed with a plethora of noises. When they reached quieter roads, she still held her peace. How freely could she talk with Rowser and Piefer listening?

When they started passing cows instead of people and haystacks instead of houses, she could no longer contain her curiosity.

"Why didn't the sheriff arrest us? He had to know we were involved somehow." She wiggled around to look at Fenworth. He sat behind her and, of course, slept. She poked him. "Why did you tell the sheriff all that about the statue?"

She clamped her mouth shut. She had a whole lot more she could say, and none of it was very respectful to the elderly gentleman.

Fenworth came fully awake as he often did, one minute snoring and the next spouting off whatever was on his mind. He had apparently heard Tipper's question. "The truth wasn't going to hurt us, girl."

Verrin Schope sat up straighter. "Truth is one of the most important tenets of Wulder's teachings."

Tipper smiled at her father, not really listening to his words. "I'm so glad you're back." Her smile dissolved as she thought about all he'd been through. "Why did they kidnap you?"

"Now that's a good question," said Fenworth. "A person who can ask good questions will go far in the world. Provided, of course, she gets answers."

She ignored him and kept her eye on her father.

"Well, as outlandish as it may sound, they wanted to ship me to another country—Maronde, to be exact. King Affron is not above buying an artisan to serve him."

Tipper gasped. "A slave?"

Verrin Schope twisted his face into a grimace. "Yes, and they weren't too pleased that I was too weak to travel."

Bealomondore leaned forward. "How were they going to force you to produce?"

"That didn't come up in their conversations, but I imagine their means would not have been pleasant. I am grateful for the rescue, my friends."

Beccaroon shuddered and unfurled his wings. "It's time for me to test this tail."

He launched into the air and, as far as Tipper could see, had no problems. The men in the wagon cheered, and she clapped.

"That's a good sight," said Verrin Schope.

In the distance, Tipper spotted dark spots flying above the horizon. She stood and pointed. "There are the other dragons."

Piefer slapped his hat on his knee. "Now, that's a sight I've waited all my life to see."

Rowser snapped the reins, and the horses responded by speeding up. Tipper lost her balance and fell back over the driver's seat, landing in Fenworth's lap.

"Umph! Girl!" He struggled to sit up.

"Whoa," said Rowser, and the wagon stopped.

"Prince Jayrus! Verrin Schope! Remove this woman from my lap. She's squishing some furry creature, and it's as frantic as a drowning rabbit." He pushed ineffectively at Tipper's wriggling form. "It *is* a rabbit! Get this girl off me."

Bealomondore grabbed one of her arms and started hauling her upward. Prince Jayrus put his hands around her small waist and lifted her easily. He set her on her feet but did not let her go. The young tumanhofer resumed his seat beside Librettowit, and they exchanged a knowing look.

From the safety of one of the prince's strong arms encircling her waist, Tipper addressed the imposed-upon old man. "I'm so sorry, Wizard Fenworth. Are you all right?"

He threw her a sour glare.

She swallowed. "Is the rabbit all right?"

His expression softened. "You are a tender-hearted gal. Excitable. Clumsy. But tender-hearted." He gave a nod. "The rabbit is fine and has retreated to a hollow."

"I'm glad." Tipper glanced around. "Where's Papa?"

Librettowit picked Verrin Schope's board up off the floor. "He was here when Beccaroon took off."

Fenworth stretched out his hand, and his librarian handed over the piece of closet. The wizard turned it over and over in his lap. "Not here," he said.

A slight pressure to her waist, pulling her back against the prince, reminded Tipper to stay calm.

The wizard placed the board across his knees. "I don't think we need be alarmed." He turned to Librettowit. "Have you been keeping records of Verrin Schope's stability status?"

"Did you ask me to?"

The wizard sat up straighter. "You've been my librarian for hundreds of years. Now I have to start telling you how to do your job?"

The old tumanhofer stood, a profound glower darkening his features. He stepped forward, casting a shadow on the board in Wizard Fenworth's lap. Librettowit didn't move again, but the shadow twisted, thickened, and grew in mass. In another moment, Verrin Schope sat on his board on Fenworth's lap.

The old man bristled. "What is it with you, Schope? My lap is too old to hold cumbersome emerlindians."

With one nimble move, Verrin Schope slipped off the board and stood. Tipper broke from the prince's embrace and threw her arms around her father. "Papa! What took so long? I thought—I thought you were gone."

He hugged her. "No, Tipper, my dear. I've been practicing to slowly dissipate and reform. This time I was taken by surprise in the excitement of your fall. I flashed out, but I was able to slow down the reappearance."

"I thought you wanted to do it quickly."

"My mistake was thinking faster is better. I believe that is what drained me to the point of disability. I believe the combination of low exertion, the remedy Fenworth and Rowser and Piefer concocted, and common sense will keep me alive while we gather the second and third statues."

"You believe? You're not sure?"

He kissed her forehead. "I shall believe very diligently." He leaned back and looked at her face. "I also believe that Wulder will allow me to stay with you long enough to tell you His story."

Doubt seized Tipper's throat. Wulder? They relied on a fable like Boscamon to give her father time? Even children knew the whims of Boscamon were not to be trusted. Children listened to the stories of his trickery and then made up tales of their own. She leaned against her father and melted into his embrace, yearning for facts instead of fairy tales.

36

Dressing Up

Beccaroon could not sustain flight for as long as he had before losing his tail. He hoped that with time, the manipulation of the new tail would become less arduous. For now, he had to think through each motion. He joined the dragons when they landed to pick up the other questers.

Rowser and Piefer were enthralled by the riding dragons. They circled them, drew closer, and ended up helping groom the mighty beasts.

Beccaroon stood to one side, resting after his brief flight and feeling strangely emotional. Gratitude mixed with relief pushed against his chest, making it hard to breathe. If grand parrots were capable of weeping, he would have disgraced himself completely. As it was, the bustle of getting everything ready to depart covered his lack of composure.

Fenworth and Librettowit pulled riding gear out of the wizard's hollows. The prince insisted on a thorough grooming of all four dragons. The minor dragons flew about the field in a wild game of chase, as if energy poured into them through the sun's rays.

Beccaroon needed only to keep to himself and let the others ignore him, but necessity forced him to seek out the only member of the questing party who might be able to help.

"Prince Jayrus." Beccaroon tried to sound casual. "May I have a word in private?"

"Of course, Sir Beccaroon."

The two gentlemen walked away from the others.

Before the prince could deliver his "What can I do for you?" line, Beccaroon jumped in. "I have a problem with which I need your assistance."

Jayrus remained silent. Bec looked up to see concern on the young man's face and a kindness in his eyes that twisted Beccaroon's heart.

Bec snorted and looked away. "My little jaunt in the sky this afternoon has proven to me that I am not up to a long flight. Not yet."

Still the young prince did not speak.

"Neither can I abandon the quest. The two people I care about most need me."

"I agree," said Prince Jayrus. "They need you, and you should not abandon the quest."

His words made it easier for Beccaroon to broach the central issue of his request. "I shall have to prevail upon you to request a dragon to allow me to ride upon his or her back."

The prince's voice returned the answer quietly, with a deep resonance that soothed Beccaroon like a bass tune. "That shall be no problem. I thank you for confiding in me and allowing me to be of service. Will you ride with me? I would be honored, and so would Caesannede."

Beccaroon nodded, cleared his throat, and spoke. "I shall fly from time to time to strengthen my muscles and adjust to the usage of this excellent tail."

"Yes," the prince said somberly, then lightened his tone. "Shall we be off? The next leg of our journey should be interesting. Although I hope it is not interesting in the same perilous way as the first."

They said good-bye to Rowser and Piefer. Beccaroon managed to thank them for their part in acquiring the materials for his new tail. He'd wanted to avoid the emotional encounter, but good manners dictated a formal leave-taking, complete with an expression of gratitude.

He launched into the sky as soon as was politely feasible and flew for the first three miles or so. He then settled behind Prince Jayrus on Caesannede. A ridge on the dragon's back provided an excellent perch, almost as if made for the size of Bec's feet. Sitting directly behind Prince Jayrus gave him some shelter from the wind so that he did not have to expend as much energy to stay seated.

They camped in the countryside the first night. The second night they stayed in a small tavern, The Bell and the Ball. The hostel sat at a crossroads and had a number of customers and patrons who liked the conversation of the brother and sister owners. Even as tired as they were, the questing party stayed up to listen to the tales of the pair.

Two men came in late and demanded the others listen.

"You won't believe what's happened," said the younger man, a marione.

The older o'rant man interrupted. "Over by Bill Gritt's farm, a ridge has just popped up out of the ground."

"And the strange thing is that Bliddye Moscar's got a new ravine." The marione waited for the listeners to encourage him to continue. He took his hat off and thumped it against his palm for emphasis. "Formed right under his barn, so's the animals and everything fell in."

"We've been there all day, helping rescue the cows and pigs."

"But," said the younger one, "here's the kicker. If you were to take that ridge and turn it upside down, it would fit in that ravine. I swear it! We didn't measure or anything, but you could see with the naked eye it was just like someone pulled out a long chunk of earth and turned it upside down two miles away."

The crowd reacted with suitable remarks of amazement.

Librettowit leaned over the table and spoke quietly to his companions. "Just the sort of thing that might happen should a malfunctioning gateway stretch out and try to right itself."

"I don't understand," said Tipper.

"Can't blame you for that," said Wizard Fenworth. "We've been studying it for fifteen years, and our most recent conclusion is that we don't understand either."

The report of the two men gave their quest an added sense of urgency.

By noonmeal the next day, they sighted Hunthaven Manor. From their height, they could see beyond to the stately gray mansion of Runan Hill. When they landed in a pasture near the manor, farmhands came running to see the sight. The master of the house came out to greet them on horseback.

"Bealomondore!" greeted Garamond Hunt. "You of all people, arriving on dragonback! Ho! Ho! I suppose this heralds the coming news."

Beccaroon accompanied the young tumanhofer as he strode across the field with his hand shielding his eyes against the sun.

The bird eyed the man. "Of what do you speak?"

The jolly marione laughed and waved a hand as if to dismiss his comments. "A nursery rhyme, nothing more. Introduce me, please. It's been a long time since I've talked to a grand parrot."

"Garamond Hunt, my friend Sir Beccaroon of the Indigo Forest."

The landowner tipped his hat, and Bec bowed.

"I've heard of you, of course," said Master Hunt. "Are you acquainted with Rudyard of Hollow Hills?"

"I am."

"He's a grand fellow. Quite a wit. I went to school with him a few years back."

The grand parrot nodded, remembering a recent encounter. "I saw him just last summer at my aunt's one hundredth birthday party. He's well and still tells a good joke."

Hunt's smile wrinkled his entire face. A bigger grin would have collapsed his nose between his mouth and his brow. Beccaroon felt the corners of his eyes twitch, which meant his own expression was at its joyful maximum. Recalling Rudyard and his shenanigans brightened an already agreeable meeting.

"Well, Bealomondore, you always keep enjoyable company." Master Hunt gestured with his hand to indicate the others in the questing party. "Who are your other friends?"

"Travelers from afar, Chiril's own Verrin Schope and his daughter, and a prince of dragons."

Garamond Hunt laughed again, loud and hard. "You keep lofty company, as well." He turned and pointed to one of the youngsters in the crowd. "You, boy, go fetch a carriage for our guests."

"Thank you, Master Hunt," said Bealomondore. "First, we'll make the dragons comfortable. They've carried us here from Fayetopolis."

The marione whooped, making his mount sidestep. He brought the mare quickly under control and peered down at Bealomondore. "That's six hundred miles! How long did it take you?"

"The afternoon of the first day, all of the second, and this is our third."

"Amazing, amazing. I'll go tell Gienella you're here. She'll be delighted. My dear wife has had a soft spot in her heart for you ever since you painted her portrait. Silly woman doesn't believe she's as pretty as the gal in the picture. The smile and the sparkle and that bush of red hair make her vastly flattered." Hunt pushed his hat brim so that his hat sat farther back on his gray and flaxen hair. He winked. "You and I know better, though. She's prettier than your fancy painting."

Bealomondore smiled broadly. "That she is, sir."

Hunt turned his horse and waved. "Come up when you're ready, but don't keep my Gienella waiting too long."

"Yes sir!"

Tipper relished the chance to wear yet another beautiful gown. And the room she was given for her chambers had a lovely long mirror on a stand that reflected her image without the splotches that had grown on the mirrors at Byrdschopen. Her mother said the mirrors needed to be re-silvered and that she would have it done as soon as a certain tinker came that way again.

Tipper sat on the edge of a cushioned armchair and held its decorative pillow in her lap. A sense of loneliness descended upon her. She wished her mother could be with them. Even knowing that Lady Peg didn't always understand simple things, Tipper knew her mother and father belonged together.

A knock on the door disturbed her musings. When Tipper opened the door, Gienella Hunt swept into the room, hugged her, then stood back to give her a thorough examination. She clasped her hands in front of her and wagged her head, her face never losing its enthusiastic expression. "You are gorgeous. But how could I expect the granddaughter of King Yellat and Queen Venmarie to be anything else? We go to court twice a year."

Madam Hunt took hold of Tipper's shoulders and guided her to a vanity. Stunned, Tipper allowed herself to be led by her enthusiastic hostess. Her mother had never made a secret of her royal lineage, but since the king and queen had never been a part of Tipper's life and had not once invited her to their home in Ragar, it was hard to relate to being of the royal family herself.

Surely a princess shouldn't be selling off the family heirlooms to pay the butcher. A small coal of anger burned in her breast. Her grandparents could have helped had they so desired.

As Gienella pushed her down on the cushioned bench, Tipper

tamped down her irritating thought and spoke calmly. "I've never been to the palace."

The mistress of the house ignored her comment. "I'm just going to put your hair up, little princess." Gienella's long fingers combed through Tipper's waist-length tresses. "Two—no, four—braids. Then we'll twist them around each other and wrap them around your head like a crown. And I have some jeweled hairpins to hold them in place. You'll look like royalty."

Tipper sat up straighter, stretching her neck in a manner her mother used. "I'm not exactly little. And no one has ever called me princess."

Madam Hunt pulled back for a moment, and her eyes met Tipper's in the mirror. The friendly smile did not change. "My dear, have you not kept track of the lineage of our rulers?"

"Only as a school assignment."

The woman behind her went back to work, separating her hair into even locks. "You are the next in line." She tsked. "Just like your mother and father not to care for such societal conventions. But you have been the talk of the court for years. Your grandfather issued an edict that you were to be left alone. I see Bealomondore broke that quite nicely."

"He came to visit my father."

"Another edict broken. Your father was consigned to solitude as well."

"Why?"

Madam Hunt's nimble fingers ceased twisting Tipper's hair. Tipper looked in the mirror and saw her hostess staring at the ceiling with a puzzled expression on her face.

She clicked her tongue against her teeth and looked at Tipper in the mirror once more. "I think it was a statue. One with a double chin.

Your grandfather took exception to it, but I don't remember if it was a depiction of His Highness or Her Highness." She leaned over and whispered in Tipper's ear. "It could have been either. They both like feasts." She stood erect and resumed the elaborate braiding of the tresses in her hands. "The number of holidays requiring celebration has doubled during King Yellat's reign."

"Do you know my mother?" asked Tipper.

Madam Hunt paused again. Her face reflected what must have been wonderful memories. "Yes, I do." She lightly rapped Tipper on the shoulder with a comb. "Do you sing?"

"Yes."

"Oh, now that is fine. I do too. We shall have a musicale this evening." Holding four long, thin braids in one hand, Gienella searched through the drawers of the vanity with her other. "Aha! Here they are." She pulled out a flat bowl of hairpins, each tipped with a small gem. "This will look perfect."

37

A Blessing

Tipper came down to dinner on her father's arm. Her eyes went directly to the prince, and his beauty took her breath away. She'd always thought his clothing fine, but tonight he wore court dress, which meant his tawny breeches came to his knees and buckled with a gold embellishment. White stockings covered his lower legs. Tipper felt her eyes widen when she saw his shoes. What material would shine gold and still look like leather? His kimen friends must have made them.

His waistcoat looked like spun gold. The flickering candlelight shone with iridescent colors on the shiny white cutaway jacket. Tipper decided the kimens must have worked their skills on all his clothing. Even the cravat at his neck danced with the honey shades of his breeches, coat, and waistcoat.

Bealomondore, of course, wore a colorful costume that spoke of fashionable awareness. Her father looked neat, and Librettowit looked slightly less rumpled than usual. Their host and hostess wore evening dress, but Tipper had already admired Madam Hunt's gown when the woman came to her room and styled Tipper's hair.

Wizard Fenworth walked into the room from a side door and succeeded in tearing Tipper's attention away from the prince. The wizard's white hair and beard gleamed. His wizard's hat stood with its peak straight up and the brim stiff, crowning the old man with dignity. He wore an elaborate robe that sparkled as he moved. A pattern of leafy vines wound through the fabric. The richness in the darker green in the background glinted as if tiny rubies, emeralds, and diamonds dusted the threads.

When Tipper and her father reached the bottom of the stairs, Wizard Fenworth took her other arm, and the two men escorted her into dinner behind Madam Hunt, who had her husband on one side and the prince on the other.

The food looked delicious, but Tipper had a hard time relaxing. Her mother had instructed her on which piece of silverware to use and all manner of things concerning proper etiquette, but she had had very little practice. The conversation, too, seemed beyond her capabilities. Each of the men took part, and so did Madam Hunt. Even the wizard made sense. Sir Beccaroon conversed as if he dined at a table laid with linen napkins and fine china every night. Tipper inwardly groused that he didn't have to worry about which fork to use.

"The Runans are joining us after dinner," said Madam Hunt. "We shall save our dessert to have with tea when they arrive."

They adjourned to another chamber where musical instruments hung on the walls, sat in glass cabinets, and stood around the room. Tipper knew how to play some of these, but others she'd only seen pictures of in the books her father kept in his library.

Master Hunt sat at a keyboard and ran his fingers over keys tinged green and blue, with smaller black keys tucked in the back. He brought a merry tune into the room.

"Gienella, my love, sing for us the lullaby of good news. Our guests remind me of the lyrics."

She moved to stand beside the big black box that framed the strings of the instrument. "A nursery rhyme?" She chuckled and laid her hand on his shoulder. "If you wish." She turned to Tipper. "Do you know it? Can you join us?"

Tipper shook her head and sat on a settee next to her father. Master Hunt's fingers slowly coaxed a melody from the keys, and Madam Hunt closed her eyes as she began to sing the clear, pure notes.

Four and seven and four
Come to give us more
Smiles for frowns
World upside down
Promise of a future great
For those who hear the call.

Dragon's back they ride
Coming to our side
A story told
New for old
Seize the hope and abide
For those who hear the call.

Good news is their song
You sing along
A verse you hear
A voice so clear
Join the music of the throng
All those who heed the call.

"The tune is lovely," said Tipper. "But what do the words mean?" Master Hunt smiled. "I've asked that question ever since I was able to form the words on my lips. My grandmother put me to bed each night and sang it to me. I love the music, but the words make me long for something. As I grew older, I finally decided that all I longed for was to know what the words meant."

"I heard the song as a lad," said Bealomondore. "I told my nurse it made me thirsty."

Tipper laughed. "Thirsty?"

The younger tumanhofer nodded. "She'd bring me a glass of water, and I would drink it straight down. Then I'd ask for more because the thirst had not gone away."

Master Hunt reclaimed everyone's attention with an expansive gesture, sweeping his arm before him to indicate his guests. "I have not, in all my life, seen a riding dragon. And I have certainly never seen four dragons with seven riders. So when you arrived today, I thought of the song—seven on four dragons' backs." He raised a hand and let it drop. "But that leaves out the other four. Our mysterious nursery lyrics are not fulfilled."

Wizard Fenworth shifted in his seat, and the minor dragons popped out of his robe, one by one. Four minor dragons scurried to sit on the back of his high-backed chair.

"Oh!" The wizard lifted Hue off the cushion and put him in his lap. "Come, no sitting on the furniture. We don't know how these people feel about minor dragons in the house." Junkit, Zabeth, and Grandur skittered down to join Hue. Fenworth stroked each one. "Don't take offense now. Let's have Hue join the music, and these Chiril citizens will come to appreciate the talent of at least one of you."

" 'Four and seven and four,' " said Garamond Hunt.

"We once had a house dragon," said Gienella, "but you talk to these creatures as if they understand you."

Her husband dropped both hands on his knees, making a loud slap. "Four and seven and four. Ho! Ho! Who would have thought our Bealomondore would be part of the realization of an old nursery rhyme?"

Tipper shook her head. "Even if we are the four and seven and four, what can the rest of the lyrics mean? Do you know, Librettowit?"

The librarian looked at her with amusement in his eyes. "We don't have that song in Amara. I can't remember ever hearing one remotely like it. But if Wulder originated the verses, and I admit the song does sound reminiscent of some of the prophecies He gifted to our ancestors, then someone someday will figure it out. "

Tipper looked at Jayrus, hoping he would have some knowledge. From visiting in his tower, she knew he read a great many books. But the content expression on his face irritated her. He'd obviously wandered in his thinking and didn't care about the topic under discussion. She asked Bealomondore, "Do you have any ideas?"

"I think there were some more verses."

Fenworth lifted the purple dragon from his lap. "Then Hue should be able to ferret out the other words. He's a musical dragon, after all. Good for that. He can delve into your memory."

This made their jolly host laugh a bit too loudly. "I'm not ready for a house dragon to dig around in my head, even if it's figuratively speaking."

Tipper cleared her throat. "I don't think they like to be called house dragons."

"What do they like to be called?" Still with a twinkle in his eye, he peered at her.

"Minor dragons."

Zabeth flew to her lap.

"Oh! Oh!" Tipper felt her cheeks heat with a fiery blush. "She says she prefers to be called Zabeth. "

The room filled with laughter. Master Hunt slapped his knee and guffawed until he had to wipe tears from his eyes.

Tipper managed a tight giggle but found the attention embarrassing. To move the conversation on, she addressed her host as soon as she thought he could speak.

"Can you tell us what the rest of the lyrics mean?"

Garamond Hunt chuckled heartily. "It's taken me fifty years to see something that resembles the first line. I don't think I can give you any answers tonight. But would you give us a song, little lady?"

Tipper smiled and stood up. The next hour passed quickly. She sang with Hue and Gienella, Hue and Prince Jayrus, and Hue and everyone in the room. Everyone except Beccaroon. Tipper had heard the grand parrot sing and knew her old friend was wise not to lend his voice to the harmony. She could see that he nevertheless enjoyed the music. His head bobbed, and occasionally he did a little dance on the arm of the chair where he perched.

Hue never sang words, but his vocalization was like a fine instrument. His presence enhanced the ability of the others and made every performer more pleasing to the ear. Many of Tipper's fellow questers played instruments. They took turns playing and singing and turning the pages of music Gienella brought from a cupboard.

Along with the night dancing in the streets of Tallion, this experience gladdened Tipper's heart and created a yearning to connect with people through music. A bond formed between the musicians as they shared notes of such beauty.

While they sang a ballad about a sickly bride and a woeful groom, Tipper noticed a couple standing in the doorway to the room. Their blank expressions pulled her out of the fellowship of song.

The music ended, and Gienella crossed the room to greet them. "Allard, Leatte, come in. I'm so happy to see you, and you must meet our guests. Bealomondore, you know." With a natural social grace, she guided them around the room, introducing everyone. Tipper studied the newcomers as she waited her turn.

While Gienella bubbled with delight over everything, this couple slogged through the niceties with no enthusiasm. They discharged their duty with the right words, but Tipper wondered if they retained any of the tidbits of information Gienella offered them. To her amazement, Prince Jayrus's charm had no effect. To resist his smile and attentive demeanor truly revealed a lack of sensibility in the Runans.

As hosts, Garamond and Gienella averted any discomfort that might be felt by the addition of two wooden guests. The conversation continued around a splendid tea. Every effort was made to engage the couple, but their monotone one-word answers made it difficult. Finally, Bealomondore brought up the subject of the statue.

"I've no interest in the thing," said Allard Runan. "You may buy it for what I paid for it." He turned to his wife. "Do you have any objection, Leatte?"

Raising her eyes from her cup slowly, she shifted her attention to her husband. She stared blankly for a moment, then answered, "No, none at all. We will get a different piece to sit on that table."

"Good." Runan put his plate on the table. "I'll have the servants crate it tomorrow and deliver it here." He turned to Garamond. "Do you have any objections, Garamond?"

For once, their host did not answer with a laugh or a wave of his hand. "No, Allard, that will suit us all." He paused. "Did you find the poachers I warned you about?"

Runan looked down at his hands and then back to his neighbor. "I didn't think it warranted any action."

Garamond shook his head, his lips pressed together. "You're wrong there, Allard. Thieves of any caliber warrant action. It's the mind-set that must be eradicated. These people believe pilfering is preferable to pushing a plow. Our duty as landowners is to give them opportunity to do honest work and discourage those who would rather gain by illegal means. To be lax in upholding the law is to invite more serious lawlessness."

Jayrus leaned forward as if to contribute to the line of discussion but then leaned back instead.

Runan made no motion to agree or disagree. He stared at his hands. Then, as if awakening, he addressed Leatte. "Shall we go now, milady?"

She immediately put down her cup. "Yes."

She stood, as did Runan.

"We thank you for your hospitality once again," said the husband with no inflection in his words.

"Delicious," said the wife and moved toward the door.

Gienella rose quickly to see them out, chattering in her usual manner, seemingly undisturbed by her neighbors' lack of social skills. The others in the room bade them farewell, but to their backs, as they were already exiting through the door.

Tipper looked around, trying to gauge the reactions of the others. Wizard Fenworth dozed. Prince Jayrus looked thoughtful. Bealomondore and Garamond engaged in a pleasant conversation about an upcoming feast. Her father and Sir Beccaroon gazed at each other as if an unspoken communication existed between the two.

When Gienella reentered the room, she clapped her hands. "Listen, my friends. I've remembered two more verses of the song we sang first this evening."

"Hue did it," said Verrin Schope.

"She could have just remembered," said Beccaroon.

"That's a possibility, of course, but these minor dragons employ the most wondrous talents." Verrin Schope beamed at the crowd nestled on the wizard's lap. "It's time you recognized how unique Wulder has made them."

Next to Tipper, the sleeping wizard softly muttered. "Bedtime, I'd say."

"Garamond, would you play for me?" Madam Hunt went to the keyboard instrument, successfully cutting off the discussion.

She smiled as her husband positioned himself on the bench and played an introduction. Gienella sang the verses they had already heard, then ended with two new ones.

One of the seven stays on
Guide, servant, champion
Friend to all
All a friend
For us the Paladin
For those who heed the call.

One of our own leads on
To lands of joy beyond
Sweet dreams
And bliss
At the gate of the end and beginning
For those who heed the call.

"Exactly," said Prince Jayrus.

Wizard Fenworth sat up. "Now that makes sense."

Tipper looked from one man to the other. "It does?"

A Pain

The crate arrived in the early morning. The men placed the box on a round table in the foyer, and Verrin Schope pried it open.

He put the crowbar down and leaned heavily on the table. "Oh, I'm dizzy. I better sit."

Prince Jayrus put his arm around the older man and guided him to the wall, where several benches and chairs sat in a row. Tipper followed, but her father waved her back to the task at hand.

"Check the statue."

She returned to the center of the room and peeked inside at the familiar *Day's Deed* and saw the small stone farmer with his arm extended as he scattered seed.

Zabeth and Grandur flew in from upstairs and landed on Verrin Schope. Tipper watched as Jayrus worked to make her father more comfortable. He arranged a cushion he had retrieved from another room behind Verrin Schope's back. When he was satisfied the invalid was at ease, the prince spoke softly to the dragons, as if giving them instructions. His actions mystified Tipper. How did he know what to do?

She twisted her lips. His arrogance still showed in that he took over without consulting anyone, but she couldn't criticize the care he gave the weakened emerlindian. Sighing over her mixed opinion of the prince and her anxiety over her father's health, she purposefully focused her attention on the contents of the crate.

She moved the packing material aside. "I like this one. The person's more practical than *Morning Glory* or *Evening Yearns.*"

Gienella joined her beside the table and moved more of the shredded paper away to get a better view. "Oh my. If he weren't so small, I'd expect him to leap out of the box. He's so lifelike."

Bealomondore passed by and glanced in. "They're all about the size of kimens, but this one has the form of a marione."

Madam Hunt nodded. "Yes, the farmer doesn't have the delicate bone structure of a kimen and definitely has the smooth hair and heavy eyebrows of a marione." She lifted the marble figure from the crate and turned it around in her hands. "Oh my, he's solid. Weighty." She placed the farmer back in the cushion of paper again. "What does the *Morning Glory* statue look like?"

Tipper answered with a smile. "It's a female figure, and her hand is stretched out to the horizon. In her palm is the half-risen sun. The other hand is cupped below the first, and it looks like water flows out of the sun, down to the second hand, then down to the base of the statue. It's"—she glanced at her father—"interesting."

"And what race is she?"

"O'rant," said Verrin Schope. "She represents liquid, among other things. The farmer represents solids." He chortled. "You said he was solid. And the last statue is of a kimen floating above tall grass. She represents air, and since she is floating, she is able to embrace the other two statues at the same height."

"How does a piece of stone float?"

"It only appears to float." Tipper rose up on tiptoe and stretched her arms out, one in front and the other in back. "She looks like she's running in the air, but her toes are in the grass."

"No need to package the statue again." Fenworth came down the grand staircase. "It will be just as easy to place him in a hollow."

Bealomondore looked up from the paper he read. "Why don't those things in your hollow knock into each other?"

The wizard looked over his shoulder at his librarian, who followed him down the steps. "Didn't we explain this?"

"Yes, the cupboard."

"That was an inept explanation." The wizard turned back to glare at the younger tumanhofer. "Things put into a hollow don't all go to the same shelf in the cupboard, so to speak."

Librettowit lifted his chin. "I thought the cupboard was a poor analogy."

"It is," grumped the wizard. "So is the shelf business, but how are you going to explain interdimensional planes to an artist?"

"Verrin Schope understands, and he's an artist."

"Verrin Schope understands quantum shifting particle duality. I don't even understand quantum shifting particle duality. Verrin Schope is something beyond an artist. I think he has imprints from the Creator's thumb on his brain."

Verrin Schope opened his eyes and straightened on the bench where he rested. He shook his head slightly and interrupted his learned colleagues. "Impossible!"

"What's impossible?" asked Bealomondore.

"The thumbprint business. Wulder doesn't need to touch someone to instill gifts."

The front door opened and banged against the wall. "Ho! Ho!" exclaimed Garamond Hunt. "Are you ready? I've got a carriage to take you out to the field where your dragons await." He stomped across the room and bussed his wife on the cheek. "Two carriages because Gienella wants to see the dragons up close." He turned to his houseguests. "I must warn you, the entire village is gawking at the beasts."

The prince shifted, and surprisingly, Garamond picked up the cue.

Their host shook his head as if to rid his ears of water. "Not beasts, I suppose. I'll have to get used to all you've told me. Is *creatures* all right?"

Prince Jayrus smiled. *"Creatures made by the Creator* is quite acceptable."

Librettowit and Prince Jayrus maneuvered the statue into a hollow while Bealomondore and Tipper helped Verrin Schope to the first carriage.

"Why are you so weak, Papa?"

He leaned to one side and kissed her forehead. "Shifting particles." When they had him settled, he winked at her. "You are sitting in the front seat of the dragon saddle on this leg of our journey."

She caught her breath.

"Yes, you," he said, even though she hadn't spoken her thought. "If I dissipate, circle the dragon in the vicinity until I reappear. I doubt that I could follow my focal point any great distance."

This time she couldn't speak past the lump in her throat. Only one more statue to go, and her father would be safe, but would they acquire the last one in time?

Master Hunt had been accurate in stating that the whole village had turned out. He probably could have added "and the surrounding area." Tipper had never seen so many country folk congregated in one place. The crowd was larger than market day at Soebin, but they were orderly and only gaped at the four magnificent dragons in the large pasture. A fence surrounded several acres, and the people stayed on the outside.

As the questing party saddled the dragons and prepared to take off, Jayrus became agitated. He muttered, and Tipper thought she heard him scold Caesannede.

"What is it?" Tipper asked the prince.

"They went out and had themselves a fine meal during the night.

They should have told me they were hungry." He marched away to where Garamond Hunt still sat astride his mare.

Tipper followed, wondering what could ruffle the unflappable prince.

He stopped suddenly, and Tipper almost ran up on his heels. She sidestepped and stood beside him, just a few feet from the master of the manor.

Prince Jayrus gave no preamble to his concern. "Master Hunt, my dragons are accustomed to hunting in the mountains. Imagine their surprise when they found their meal conveniently surrounded by a fence. I fear I owe someone the price of one pen full of mutton."

"Ho! Ho!" The landowner retained his jovial attitude. "I wondered if your dragons nibbled something besides grass. Do you know whose flock they devoured?"

"They foraged to the north, but dragons are not very accurate when you try to pin them down to distance or passage of time. I would guess within twenty to thirty miles."

"I'll make inquiries. I assume you want to offer restitution?"

Prince Jayrus pulled his pouch of coins from his pocket and poured out the contents in the palm of his hand, which he held up to the man on horseback. "Take what you think is fair. If you need more, I'll ask Fenworth for additional funds."

Garamond picked out four large gold coins. "That should be adequate. And should I discover that our long-necked friends ate a bull or two on the way back, I'll cover the cost."

Jayrus poured the money back in its cloth purse. "They would have told me if they had. They do not deceive me."

"Do they not deceive anyone, or is it just you they do not deceive?"

Prince Jayrus flashed him a winsome smile. "Me, and it is because they can't, not because they always choose veracity."

A rumble of laughter escaped their host. "And why is that?"

With nonchalance, Jayrus shrugged. "Because I am the dragon keeper."

"Never heard of a dragon keeper, young prince, but since you have the only dragons I've ever seen, I'll grant you the title if you so desire."

A puzzled look passed over the prince's face, but he must have dismissed the problem readily. "I appreciate your assistance in finding the owner of the sheep and paying our debt."

Garamond bounced the coins in his hand and gave Jayrus a speculative look. "Would you know if I pocketed the coins and never looked for this farmer?"

"Yes sir, I would. But I know that you would never do that, just as I know Runan did not run down the poachers because they work for him."

Garamond barked a laugh. "Runan? The man doesn't have the energy to oversee theft and mayhem."

"In time, I think you will find your assessment of his character to be in error." The prince reached up his hand to shake Garamond's. "Thank you again for your hospitality. Perhaps we will meet again."

Garamond shook his hand vigorously, said his good-byes in a boisterous voice, bade his neighbors to do the same, and beckoned to his wife to come back from petting the mighty creatures.

"I don't want them mistaking you for a fair maiden and hauling you off."

She came toward them, holding up her skirts to keep them from tangling in the long grass. "Garamond, only you would think I still qualify as fair and maiden. And I think you do these fine dragons a disservice by accusing them of such treachery."

"I agree with your husband." Prince Jayrus took her hand and raised it to his lips. "Any dragon worth the name of villainous beast would snatch you away, take you to his cave where he hoards his treasure, and adore you for your beauty."

Gienella's mouth dropped open in momentary shock, then a ripple of merry giggles broke the silence. "You are a flatterer of the worst kind. I almost believed you."

He said nothing, just smiled. Tipper wanted him to turn her way. The profile of his expression warmed her heart. Strangely she did not begrudge Gienella the pleasure of his attention. From the depth of her being, Tipper knew that the more Jayrus encouraged those around him, the deeper his well of kindness became.

Three weeks of travel took them into an area Beccaroon had never seen. The grand parrot gained maneuverability every day and lengthened the amount of time he could fly. However, he realized he would never be able to fly the speed of the dragons for long hours. He also knew they slowed a bit to allow him to keep pace.

From the air, they saw disturbing signs of the land rippling or, worse, segments that looked like they had been bitten out of the earth and spit back out. One section of a forest had sunk so that the treetops barely reached the level of the forest floor surrounding the patch. Beccaroon spotted an odd blemish in the landscape, and upon inspection, he discovered from those who lived in the region that a lake had disappeared overnight. Reaching the city of Ohidae quickly and finding the last statue became more important with each passing hour.

To speed their way, Beccaroon swallowed his pride and often rode on Caesannede's back. His pride also smarted when, every three nights, they soaked and softened the glue so that his tail could be removed. Many times now he had had to endure the indignity, but the blasé attitude of his companions made the ordeal tolerable. And he had to admit that on the third day his skin began to itch and the fresh air felt very good.

They camped mostly, since encountering people required explanations. The dragons, both big and small, attracted attention. Evenings around a campfire at a remote location eased that situation, and Beccaroon loved the music the others performed after the evening meal. Bealomondore sketched. Verrin Schope whittled twigs into objects of art, but the effort seemed to tire him. He put away the small knife and spent more time with a piece of casting clay in his talented hands. Every night, a different miniature creation formed in his fingers. Fenworth tucked them away in a hollow to be used later for making miniature pewter figurines.

Under the tutelage of Hue and Librettowit, Tipper's voice gained strength. Her talent flourished, and Beccaroon marveled that her performance elicited a great range of emotions from her listeners. He began to suspect that her songs did much more than entertain. With Hue's guidance, she seemed to be able to inspire her audience or reveal depths of feeling in the hearts of her listeners. The bird acknowledged that after she sang, he felt more aware of specifics in his own personality—the lofty characteristics of courage, loyalty, and self-sacrifice. The revelations were both humbling and embarrassing.

Tipper asked Beccaroon to tell some of the stories of the Indigo Forest. This developed into a story swap with the librarian. Librettowit would tell a tale, and the others would have to guess whether it was an account from Amaran history or a fiction piece.

Beccaroon soon caught on that if the story related to something done by Wulder or Paladin, the tale was true—that is, according to the three who had been to Amara. Some of Librettowit's reports seemed farfetched, particularly the descriptions of how Wulder chose an individual and imparted talents.

One gift encompassed discernment, truth telling, exhortation, and encouragement. Beccaroon noticed that Prince Jayrus perked up and listened intently to the tale recounting the development of their Paladin, the champion of the people, the emissary of Wulder. Beccaroon expected someone like the young prince, who had been isolated most of his life, to be gullible and ready to believe these fantasies. Librettowit and Fenworth, however, were well educated, yet they believed the Amaran explanations of an absolute power enjoying the fellowship of lesser beings. The details disturbed Beccaroon, but he began to savor the stories as much as he did the music.

Finally they could see Ohidae in the distance. They landed with the intention of setting up camp one last time. Beccaroon flew to the ground and strutted over to have a word with Tipper. She'd become quite an accomplished rider in the past weeks and no longer complained of being sore at the end of the day.

Beccaroon waited as the beautiful dragon with the odd name of Gus folded her wings and legs to the dismounting position. Tipper threw her leg over the saddle horn and slid down the creature's shoulder to the ground. She immediately smoothed the feathers on the back of Beccaroon's neck, and although he enjoyed the touch, he reminded her with a loud tsk not to get too familiar.

She laughed and ignored his sense of propriety. She leaned over to kiss the top of his head. Would she never behave with the decorum he had worked so hard to instill in her?

"Propriety!" he reminded her.

She made a face that was not as contrite as it was mischievous, although he knew she meant to show repentance.

Behind them, Verrin Schope descended from the back of the dragon. Beccaroon heard a snap as his friend slid down in the same manner as all the riders. Bec turned to see that Verrin Schope had slammed into the ground, and one of his legs lay crumpled, twisted at an odd angle.

"Papa!" Tipper rushed to his side.

The minor dragons flocked to the fallen man, and Prince Jayrus appeared beside them, kneeling.

"Papa! Your leg is broken."

"Hush now, my dear." Verrin Schope's smile barely lifted the corner of his mouth. "It's only those shifting particles again."

39

Ohidae Grand Hotel

Tipper paced back and forth in the sitting room of their hotel suite. Wizard Fenworth, Grandur, and Zabeth attended to her father. The dragons had relieved the pain of his injury, but the prince reported that each time he and Fenworth maneuvered the broken pieces of the bone into place, the bone refused to bind. Librettowit, the prince, and Bealomondore kept her company as they waited for something to change.

"This should be an easy procedure," Jayrus told her.

She threw her hands into the air. "Then why isn't it?"

"Fenworth says there are a lot of factors at play here."

"What does Papa say?"

"He doesn't say anything, my girl," said Beccaroon. "The dragons have him sedated so that he doesn't feel the pain involved in maneuvering the bones."

"Is it shattered?"

Librettowit stepped into her path and placed a hand on her arm, bringing her to a stop. "You know that would be a much more serious injury. You're a smart young lady, so I won't try to soften any of the details. Your father's thigh has a clean break in two places. The lower leg is fractured in three. But the bone is not crushed."

He directed her to a chair, and once she sat down, he put an arm around her shoulders. "Fenworth is a skilled physician. It's part of a wizard's job. He's doing his best, and we're fortunate to have a good supply of medicinal bugs."

Out of the corner of her eye, Tipper saw Prince Jayrus shudder. His expression grew serious. "We must not delay in finding the statue."

Tipper glanced around the room at her companions. "I thought we knew exactly who has the third statue."

Bealomondore looked directly into her eyes. "It's been more than a year since I saw the masterpiece in Mushand's collection. He could have sold it."

The seriousness in his tone and expression panicked Tipper. "How are you going to find out? Are you going there?"

Bealomondore's eyes shifted to Beccaroon and back. Librettowit stood and moved toward the door. Jayrus came and stood behind her, placing his hand on her shoulder.

The younger tumanhofer straightened the sleeve of his jacket by giving the cuff a tug. "Mushand's a very rich and influential man. One doesn't just go up to his house and knock on the door." He fidgeted with the lace that edged his shirt at the neck. "I'm going to visit the family who introduced me to Mushand the last time I was in Ohidae. They'll know whether or not he still has *Evening Yearns*. If he does, they may be able to get us an appointment."

Bealomondore took his hat from a side table next to the door. "We'll go now, Mistress Tipper. We'll come back with good news."

He smiled as he put on his hat, but Tipper knew the tumanhofer now, and his expression did not inspire confidence. She nodded and tried to look calm but feared her face froze in a stiff, noncommittal expression. Librettowit, Beccaroon, and Bealomondore each bowed to her as they left the room.

"How odd," she said as the door closed.

Prince Jayrus sat in the chair next to her. "What's odd, Tipper?"

"The way they left." She shifted in her seat to face him. "Sometimes dignitaries come to visit my mother. She gets very royal during their stay. Fortunately, they usually leave after a day or two."

Jayrus tilted his head and watched her, not saying anything but not looking puzzled by this bit of family history that was apparently not connected to anything.

Tipper sighed. "When these men and ladies from Ragar's royal court take leave of my mother, they always bow like our three friends just did."

"Perhaps this action was due to my eminence."

Tipper took in his sincere expression and began to laugh. She tried to talk between giggles but had to wait. Each time she thought she had command of her voice, his puzzled brow set her off again.

"First," she managed to say, "they were taking leave of me, not you."

"I was there."

"Yes, but they were looking at me, and they just nodded to you."

Words didn't come to his lips, but his demeanor shouted, "That can't be right!"

Tipper just shook her head. The prince she admired so very much sometimes acted like he had no clue about the normal world. Perhaps it was a sovereignty thing. Her mother had lost the ability to perceive her surroundings and respond accordingly. She hoped the prince's faculties would not deteriorate in the same manner.

Jayrus touched her arm. "Tipper, have you gone ruminating?"

Her attention snapped back to his face. "And where do you get those words?"

His eyes focused on her, but his befuddlement deepened. "Words? Which words?"

"Ruminating, eminence, a-dither, expounding…you're always using words as if you were part of a book, talking in terms used in Papa's stuffy textbooks."

His eyebrows shot up, but the unruffled calm she expected of him remained. "But, Tipper, books are what I conversed with all the time I lived with Prince Surrus. Of course Surrus talked to me, but he spoke in a similar manner. The only other source I could have emulated is the dragons, and their words are more often pictures. It would be hard to speak aloud the language of their minds."

He stood up. "It is time to attempt an adjustment of your father's leg. Do you wish to help us?"

Tipper nodded and followed the strange young man who flustered her, made her laugh, and confused her.

Beccaroon liked the home of Bealomondore's friends. The large windows almost eliminated the walls that held them and, in some cases, even extended into the roof. Some of the first floor rooms jutted out from the main house. These solariums gathered light from the outside and exposed those inside to the magnificence of crowded trees and bushes growing close together right up to the house.

In the conservatory where he and the two tumanhofers waited for the host and hostess, plants grew in pots. This foliage reminded him of his beloved Indigo, even though the vegetation outside had no resemblance to the tropical plants of his home.

Master and Madam Markezzee entered with servants bearing trays of refreshment. Bealomondore introduced Librettowit and Beccaroon.

"So good to meet you." Madam Markezzee gestured for the gentlemen to return to their seats. "Sir Beccaroon, of course we've heard of you. The grand parrot Dalandoore lives in the extensive woods nestled against the base of the mountains west of Ohidae. He comes to town rarely but visits us when he does."

Beccaroon nodded his head. Dalandoore was somebody's cousin. While he tried to remember who was related to whom, the conversation went on, and tea was served. Librettowit gave a brief account of his visit from Amara, not mentioning the importance of Wulder's foundation stone and their dire need to reunite the three statues carved from that stone.

Master Markezzee sent a runner with a message to Mushand as soon as Bealomondore expressed his wish to see the man's collection again.

"Verrin Schope's daughter is traveling with us," said the tumanhofer artist. "I would like her to see *Evening Yearns* in his magnificent display room."

Their host frowned. "If Mushand is in town, I'm sure he will oblige you. He's proud of his art gallery. But you do realize, Bealomondore, that certain aspects of Mushand's business dealings are questionable. He's never been accused of anything in the courts, but rumors—"

"Really, husband," Madam Markezzee interrupted. "I find him charming. Why do people think he is a scoundrel?"

"Scoundrel is too light a term, wife. Better to label him villain."

She made a face and stirred her tea.

"Wife, when people vanish after a business meeting, when missing people are found dead, when money disappears from a reputable enterprise, and the common denominator is always Mushand, then there is reason for doubting his integrity."

"As you said, husband, 'rumors.' You should have invested in that transportation project he spoke of."

"No, wife, I should not have, and I will hear no more of it."

She pursed her lips and nodded, then sipped her tea.

Bealomondore introduced another topic. He asked about mutual friends, and the tension in the room abated. An hour later, the messenger returned with an invitation for Bealomondore and his party to visit the Mushand house that evening.

"I will go with you," said Madam Markezzee, "to ease the discomfort of the young lady in a house full of men. Mushand has no wife."

Before her husband could voice his objection, Beccaroon reassured her. "Thank you. Our stay will be brief. Mistress Tipper will want to return to the hotel as quickly as possible to be at her father's side. He is too ill to accompany us."

"Oh, how dreadful," their hostess responded, her voice full of sincere concern. "Let me give you the name of our physician. I can have someone fetch him and deliver him to your hotel. How distressing to fall ill in an unfamiliar city."

Librettowit held up a hand in protest. "There's no need, but thank you for your thoughtfulness. Verrin Schope has been ill for quite some time, and we travel with his physician."

"Really?" Madam Markezzee's interest showed as she leaned forward and cast a speculative glance at the librarian. "He brings his own physician with him? There is gossip about Verrin and Peg Schope. I heard she is visiting her sister. Growder is not far from here, and I have friends there and at court. They say she does not remember her father's instructions that she be confined to her property. They say her wits have perhaps…" She paused and took in the glower her husband directed at her. She rushed on. "Perhaps her thinking is permanently muddled by the shock of being rejected by her parents."

"Wife!" Master Markezzee's voice boomed loud enough to cause his spouse's cup to rattle as she set her saucer on the tray.

She primly folded her hands in her lap and meekly bowed her head in silence. Beccaroon suspected there was not an ounce of repentance motivating the pose. She'd said what she wanted to say and would now act the part of a contrite woman, willingly submitting to her husband's rule.

As the magistrate of Indigo Forest, he knew exactly how difficult it was to deal with one who played such tricks. He liked the husband better for his composure—after all, he didn't continue his tirade after his word of warning. And Beccaroon liked the woman less for her chicanery and the smirk she tried to conceal.

An odd thought came to his mind. Would Verrin Schope have a principle from the Tomes of Wulder to address this situation? It seemed his Wulder had a great deal of wisdom concerning the vagaries of people.

40

Mushand's Gallery

Beccaroon rode on top of the carriage. The sun had gone down, and any sensible parrot would be roosting. They were late, but it had taken quite a bit of persuasion to get Tipper to stay at the hotel and not come with them to retrieve the last statue. Master Markezzee sent regrets that his wife would be unable to join them. Her failure to provide a chaperon gave them one more thing to use to dissuade Tipper from coming.

Beccaroon stewed. His companions on this all-important journey were Bealomondore, Librettowit, and Wizard Fenworth.

Of course, Bealomondore had to come. He was their contact, the one who knew Mushand, who'd already been in his house, who appreciated art, and, therefore, who had the art collector's respect.

Librettowit, the librarian, Beccaroon had begun to respect. He enjoyed both his conversation and his singing voice, and the librarian had an excellent stock of folk tales. Now that Bec was getting used to them, even the stories of Wulder were enlightening. Beccaroon didn't see any reason why the old tumanhofer shouldn't come. And perhaps he could temper the wizard's shenanigans.

The third person in the carriage was Wizard Fenworth. The man grew leaves! His complexion took on the appearance of bark while he slept. Critters scurried into his robes and more often dropped out. Or flew out. Or scrambled out. Or slithered out.

The wizard's social skills were nonexistent. He fell asleep in the middle of sentences, sometimes his own. His snores interrupted other people's conversation.

He talked nonsense, but not like Lady Peg. Tipper's mother seemed to follow a jagged line of reasoning that skipped sideways into an unrelated topic. After weeks of being in the wizard's company, Beccaroon had decided Fenworth's words jumped over what others were still pondering. Fenworth landed at a place where the conversation might logically come, if allowed to take a normal course.

Only one thing made the odd wizard more acceptable to the grand parrot. Fenworth, with the help of the two green dragons, had managed to set Verrin Schope's broken leg. Librettowit said the bones would knit quickly now.

Fenworth carried the two statues in the hollows of his cape. Beccaroon wondered if he planned to set up the three in their dancing circle as soon as he had them in his possession. The sooner the three embraced each other, the sooner this whole ordeal would be over.

The prince had stayed to aid the dragons in the healing process. And Beccaroon had felt it was in Tipper's best interest not to go to this notorious man's house. He sighed. Hopefully she was in no danger at the hotel. After all, there were four minor dragons and her father to guard her against the handsome prince. He'd instructed Junkit to come between the two if Tipper and Jayrus became close.

The carriage turned into a lane leading to a mansion. Lights glowed on posts lining the wide gravel path. Many of the windows on the first level of the sprawling house gleamed a golden glow. As they approached, two men came out of the house and two came running from the stable area. Four servants to greet them? It seemed a bit much.

As they pulled up to the front door, Beccaroon got a gander at the greeters. The two from the house oozed sinister, backhanded evil. He could imagine them slitting a man's throat and chuckling as the victim bled. The two from the stables had muscles bulging in their jackets. They'd be more inclined to pulverize their target with their fists. Bec wondered if the daytime crew looked as menacing.

He flew down to an elaborate porch adorned with tall white columns and decorative urns overflowing with cascading flowering plants. The burly servants held the horses even though the coachman told them to leave his team alone. The sinewy house servants opened the carriage door, let down the steps, and waited to escort the visiting party into the house.

Not one surly word was spoken, but Beccaroon's skin quivered, shaking his feathers. Evil lurked in the shadows. Beccaroon examined the bushes, the dark corners, and the distant trees. Whatever watched them did so from secluded vantage points.

The prince would have been a better choice as comrade on this venture. What could two old men, a fashion fop, and a bird do against these ruffians?

They followed one servant into the house to a well-appointed library. At the open door, the servant announced their arrival and stepped back. He didn't leave but stood guard in the hall.

Mushand came forward. "Please, come in. I understand you wish to purchase *Evening Yearns.*"

Bealomondore had warned them that their host would get right to the point and give them only a minimum amount of time.

Beccaroon led the way into the library. Librettowit naturally studied the walls where rows and rows of books lined massive shelves.

Bec studied the owner, a bony o'rant with sloping shoulders. A slender neck and narrow face gave the rich man an emaciated appearance. His arms and legs stretched too long from his short torso. With one more set of each, he'd resemble a spider.

Bealomondore stuck to business. "Yes, Sir Mushand, we have

come with the desire to make a purchase. Verrin Schope has traveled far to collect all three statues."

Sir Beccaroon squinted at the small o'rant and wondered what deed he had done to be given the title. The man's mannerisms indicated that he loved his position of prominence and the ability to wield power. His pleasant form of address and the calm expression on his face did not conceal an underlying contempt for his guests. He had not offered them a seat, and although he held a drink in his hand, he had not asked if they required refreshment. He smiled as if posing for a picture. No warmth touched his eyes.

Mushand moved his glass in a circular motion, swirling the contents. Ice clinked against the sides. "I do not easily part with pieces from my collection. I've chosen them carefully. They attract me, sustain me, invigorate me. Of course, this is what anyone with a true love of art encounters when viewing a masterpiece. But the added pleasure of owning such a work of art is beyond most people's realm of experience."

Bealomondore clasped his hands behind his back. "We are willing to offer you a generous amount. Verrin Schope is ill, and he believes that when the three statues embrace, his health will return."

"If that is what he believes, then it doesn't matter where the statues are displayed as long as they are together and performing their circular dance. I assume you have one of the other statues."

"We have two," said Bealomondore.

Mushand's head tilted, and his eyes widened. "That is astonishing. I also have two of the statues."

Bealomondore shifted uncomfortably. "Which two, may I ask?"

Mushand chortled, an unpleasant sound. "I shall show you." He glided across the room with the grace of a dancer. "Monbull, go ahead of us and light the gallery."

One of the servants outside the room sprinted down the hall.

Librettowit and Wizard Fenworth exchanged a look. Fenworth nodded, and they all followed their unusual host.

Between large, heavy mahogany doors, paintings lined the walls of the corridor. Having been closely associated with Verrin Schope for many years, Beccaroon had a sense for what was quality art and what was second-rate. The landscapes in the hall showed well. Of course, he couldn't distinguish who the artist might be, but he did recognize fine technique and subjects appealing to the eye. Exceptional craftsmanship, but inferior to Verrin Schope's work.

A few statues stood either on the floor or on pedestals. The ones cast in bronze all seemed to have been done by the same hand and were exceedingly well crafted. The style of one set looked to Beccaroon as if the artist had not completed his design, but since there were several, he thought perhaps the approach was an artistic statement of some kind.

They came to the gallery, its door thrown open and the servant still scurrying from light fixture to light fixture, uncovering lightrocks of potent brilliance.

In the center of the room on a raised platform, the kimen runner of *Evening Yearns* raced across the tips of tall grass. One arm reached backward, and her palm rested in the farmer's hand that held sowing seeds.

"Our Verrin Schope is indeed a genius," said Wizard Fenworth as he came closer to examine the two statues. "She looks like an otherworldly being urging the earthbound gentleman to join her in her pursuit of life."

Librettowit nodded. "Clearly the two could be separated and still present a complete image, but together...together the beauty is stunning."

"And this," said the old man, "before he knew Wulder." He sniffed. "Odd that we have the farmer as well."

Bealomondore leaned closer to the statue. "We shall have to compare the two."

Fenworth opened his outer mantle and began to dig in his deep pockets. Beccaroon almost laughed at the horror on Mushand's face as insects, lizards, rats, and birds came in a flurry out of the folds of the wizard's robes. Fenworth located the hollow he wanted and the item within. He gestured to Librettowit and Bealomondore to come help. Between the three of them, they pulled from the opening the statue they had acquired from Allard Runan of Runan Hill.

Beccaroon strutted over and peered at the farmer they displayed.

Bealomondore turned the figure over in his hands. "This one is the fake."

"You're sure?" said Beccaroon. They looked identical to him.

"I am. I created this statue. See?" He pointed to one of the seeds. "Here is my mark."

Wizard Fenworth growled. "You commit forgery?"

"No," said Bealomondore calmly. "A forgery is not signed by the one doing the forgery. I always sign my work. The pay is good for replicas, and I have needed the money."

Irritation loosened Beccaroon's tongue. "Why didn't we notice this before?"

The younger tumanhofer shrugged. "I didn't look at this statue when it was on the Hunts' table. I thought I knew where all my reproductions were. And remember, I'd seen Runan's art collection on a previous occasion. At that time, his Verrin Schope statue was authentic. Apparently that changed."

Bealomondore tucked the fake under his arm. "At Hunthaven, Verrin Schope was too dizzy to examine *Day's Deed,* and I doubt Tipper looked at it with an eye to determining its legitimacy."

Wizard Fenworth turned to Mushand. "It would seem we desire to purchase two statues from you."

"At an exorbitant price," the villain said coolly.

"We are prepared to pay the price you name."

Mushand laughed. Again the grating sound made Beccaroon's feathers ruffle. "I make a counterproposal. I buy your statue. I assume you have *Morning Glory*? I display the three here in my gallery, together as Verrin Schope desires. He regains his health."

Mushand's eyes narrowed. "I possess the most astonishing sculptures of our modern age. Of any age!" His voice rose. "No, I will not sell *Day's Deed* and *Evening Yearns*. But I will offer you a handsome sum for *Morning Glory*."

No one spoke.

Mushand clenched his glass. His cold eyes swept over his visitors. "You may give me your answer tomorrow. I have other business to attend to. Monbull will see you to the door."

Beccaroon glanced once more at the two statues and noted that the unfavorable situation of being owned by a man of corruption did not dim the blissful expressions on their faces. Did it really matter where the three stones stood together?

Monbull hustled them out of the room, down the corridor, and through the front door. Beccaroon climbed into the carriage cab with the others.

Fenworth shook his walking cane. "The man's a villain. His house stinks the same as Bamataub's."

Bealomondore's head jerked. "Slavery?"

"No doubt."

Librettowit rubbed his chin. "We'll have to make calculations as to whether the three statues together, but far from their origin, will indeed influence the fluctuation that decimates our friend Schope."

"You're thinking of selling *Morning Glory* to Mushand?" Beccaroon rocked from one foot to the other, uncomfortable in the cramped

quarters and uncomfortable with the proposed solution to their problem. "I have to admit the possibility had crossed my mind as well."

Bealomondore leaned forward. "It might be for the best. Mushand's pride would be scarred by losing his prized masterpieces. I don't
think he's a reasoning man when it comes to the collection. I don't
want his wrath to fall on any of us."

The carriage slowed, and a horseback rider passed them going up
the driveway they had just exited.

"Tut, tut, oh dear." Fenworth peered out the carriage window.
"That was Runan."

"Allard Runan?" gasped Bealomondore.

Wizard Fenworth glared at the artist. "I don't know many of your
countrymen, young pup. And I'm quite glad that I know only one of
Runan's ilk. One Runan is enough for any country. If Chiril boasts
two, I'm going home."

"Can't go home," said Librettowit. "The gateway's broken."

Fenworth's glare shifted to his librarian. "Fish feathers! If you can't
say anything nice, don't say anything at all!"

41

Falderal?

Tipper listened to the men debate whether to sell *Morning Glory* to Mushand or try to acquire the two genuine statues in some other manner. A bell tolled at midnight, and still no feasible solution had presented itself.

Tipper sat crosswise on the settee, her stocking feet resting on the arm of the chair. Beccaroon, without his artificial tail, perched next to her feet. Prince Jayrus sat on a chair. Librettowit lounged on the window seat, and Bealomondore sat by the second window. Wizard Fenworth stood in the corner, which was odd since he usually sat.

"Won't you sit down, Wizard Fenworth?" she asked.

"Thank you, my dear. I've always said you were tender-hearted, but I'm meditating, don't you see?"

Tipper could see he looked more and more like a tall tree stump the longer he reflected.

The hotel room was muggy even with the windows open and nighttime breezes puffing the curtains inward. Her father lay in the next room with all four minor dragons fanning him with their wings. Tears sprang to her eyes. Could Fenworth and the dragons keep him stable? Would he die before all their efforts brought about a solution?

Hue's soft song drifted through the crack in the ajar door. The melody soothed her fears. She knew the music had a healing quality as well. Her father was comfortable for the moment. She and the others would find an answer.

Bealomondore offered a suggestion. "King Yellat might make a royal decree to save his son-in-law's life."

Tipper tensed. Did the tumanhofer artist know of the rift between the king and her father?

Beccaroon shook his head. "I've made petitions in the past for the king to reclaim his daughter, and he has always refused. I don't see how this circumstance would bring about a different decision."

Tipper looked up at Bec. "You never told me."

He avoided meeting her eye. "It would have distressed you."

"Borrowing them would not suffice," said Librettowit. "We would put the statues together, restore your father, and lose the benefit as soon as we returned the two that don't belong to us."

"Then we should sell *Morning Glory* to Mushand," said Bealomondore. "He's willing to pay a handsome sum."

"It doesn't matter what the sum is," said Tipper. "The point is to unite the statues."

Bec unfurled his wings and brought them back to his body. "Putting *Morning Glory* into Mushand's collection seems to be the only answer to our plight."

Tipper looked from one member of the quest to the next. The burden of what they were about to do weighed heavily on all of them. Except Wizard Fenworth, of course.

She studied the odd tree-man figure in the corner. She could still see his hair, but it was entwined with thin scraggly vines and sparse leaves. A heavier layer of vegetation draped over his wizard's robes. His hat, which sat on a table near the door, had not sprouted so much as a thin green shoot. He looked neither happy nor sad, worried nor carefree. After all, how much attitude could someone in a tree-state emote?

Her eyes moved to Prince Jayrus, the only male in the room who didn't seem to be staring at the floor. He sat with his elbows on his knees and his hands pressed together in front of him. He tapped his two pointer fingers against each other. Again she thought he had mentally deserted them. His look of contentment had to mean he was dreaming about mountains or flying or his perfect tower and garden so far away.

Prince Jayrus focused on her and winked. Maybe he wasn't so far away.

He clapped his hands on his knees and stood. Everyone else in the room jumped at the sudden movement.

"We cannot sell *Morning Glory* to Mushand."

"None of us want to, young man," said Librettowit. "If you have a plan that does not involve chicanery, let's hear it. Otherwise, we are bound to save Verrin Schope's life in the only way we can, by uniting the statues in Mushand's gallery."

"I don't have another plan, but I do know we cannot go against the principles of Wulder."

Librettowit scowled. "What do you know of His principles? I don't believe you have ever seen a Tome, let alone read it, let alone studied it."

Prince Jayrus smiled as he gazed at the arboreal wizard. "I believe that Wizard Fenworth has been sending me messages while he sleeps."

Beccaroon tsked. "Messages? What do you mean by *messages*?"

"Could be. Could be." Librettowit pinched his lower lip. "He has been unusually somnolent."

Bec cocked his head. "Somnolent?"

"Slumberous."

The bird blinked and looked away. "So what did you mean by messages sent by this slumberous wizard?"

"Not messages exactly. More like thoughts being thrust into my memory. It's very much like I'm recalling a book I've read. Probably these Tomes of Wulder our visitors from Amara talk about. Only, of course, I have not read them. But he has."

"Who has?" asked Bealomondore.

"The wizard," snapped Beccaroon. "Pay attention."

"I am paying attention." Bealomondore sat up straighter and addressed the prince. "So you are remembering passages from a book that Fenworth read, just as if you had been the one to read it?"

"Not exactly. I recall the words more precisely than if I had just read the book. Phrases and sentences come to me as if I'd memorized them."

"Interesting." Bealomondore glanced back and forth between the prince and the tree. "What kind of phrases?"

" 'A lit candle in a dark room means there is no darkness. An unlit candle in a dark room means there is no light.' "

Tipper knew her expression was as befuddled as Bealomondore's, but Librettowit's face reflected excitement.

"Here's another one," said the prince. " 'Darkness walks into Light and is no more. Light and Darkness cannot stand hand in hand.' "

Beccaroon stamped a foot on the cushioned armrest where he perched. "Awk! What does it mean?"

The prince paced across the room and back. "It means...it means we cannot deal with Mushand. He is darkness. We are light."

A gasp came from the tree as Fenworth broke free from his wooden form and wobbled to the chair the prince had vacated. "You make me work too hard, boy." He collapsed and leaned his head against the back cushion.

The prince came to his side. "Do you need a drink, sir? Are you well?"

Fenworth waved a hand at him. "I'm old, not ill. Thirsty? I believe I am." He reached under his mantle and pulled out a goblet filled with a bubbling liquid. He sipped, drank more fully, then burped. He tapped his fingers on his lips. "Excuse me." Then he tipped the goblet back and guzzled the rest. "Now what were we talking about?"

"The statues," said Bealomondore.

Tipper spoke at the same time. "My father."

"Awk!" said Beccaroon. "Tomes read and unread. Messages from your Wulder. Mixed memories, yours and the prince's. Falderal. Flimcrackery. Pickles and pudding. Nonsense."

Fenworth sprang from his chair like a young man and embraced the prince. "Librettowit, are you not astounded?"

The librarian nodded. "Definitely astounded."

Fenworth let go of Jayrus and pounded him on the back in a gesture of congratulations. "To think that I would meet you at your conception. Remarkable, isn't it, Librettowit?"

He nodded again. "Remarkable, indeed."

Fenworth swung his head around to look directly at his fellow Amaran. "Explains why we're here. Why Wulder brought us through the gateway. Why we've been stuck here. All of this drama leads to this." He pointed to Prince Jayrus.

Librettowit continued to nod with a controlled elation on his face. "Awk! Leads to what?"

The librarian stood, walked over to Prince Jayrus, and extended his hand. The prince shook it.

Once he had his hand back, Librettowit bowed. "If I can be of service, I am yours to command."

"What is going on?" demanded the grand parrot.

Fenworth raised his eyebrows. "Oh, I see how it is. Yes, dear fellow, it is awkward to be caught with tail feathers down, but you must understand that Paladin does not take such things into consideration."

Bec's neck did a rotation that almost twisted his head completely around. "Your Paladin? The one who comes from Amara?"

"No," said Librettowit. "Your Paladin. The one who comes from the Mercigon Mountains."

Tipper swung her feet to the floor and stood. "Our Jayrus is a paladin."

"Not a paladin, my dear," said Fenworth. "The Paladin. The champion for the people. The educator, encourager, exhorter, spokesman for Wulder, interpreter of the principles, leader—"

"Awk!" Beccaroon screeched. "He's just a callow youth."

Librettowit shook his head. "You mustn't despise him for being young. He will serve a thousand years or more. And you must not think him inexperienced, because his mentor trained him for this task. And Wulder will guide him."

"Surprising," said Fenworth. He moved to the chair and sat down. "After all these years, Wulder still flabbergasts me." He laughed, a soft chortle. The chortle built itself into a more forceful noise and exploded into a guffaw. Fenworth held his side and wiped tears from his eyes. "Remember, Librettowit?"

"I do," said the librarian. "You asked if these heathens could learn. You said you didn't want to waste your time on an unprofitable cause."

Fenworth gasped, still overcome by amusement. "And now a whole country will know Wulder as Amara does. Such an old fool." He slapped his chest. "Such an old fool am I. What a comfort to know that I am still a simpleton and Wulder is not. Ah, should I never make the mistake of thinking it's the other way around."

Tipper stepped forward, determined to bring this chaos back to the problem at hand. "Does this mean that now that Jayrus is a paladin—"

Fenworth held up his hand. "Not a, *the.*"

"Jayrus is the Paladin. Does that mean he can take the statues from Mushand? Or does it mean that he can heal Papa without the statues?"

Jayrus looked from Librettowit to Wizard Fenworth to Tipper. "No, I'm afraid it does not mean I can *take* the statues. But another plan will be revealed to us. Stealing is never Wulder's way."

A hiss came from behind Tipper. She whirled.

Four men dressed in black, faces covered with black silk, and wielding long swords entered the room through the open windows.

"But stealing is our way," one of the men spoke in a breathy whisper. "Once we have the statue Mushand wants, we will find ourselves rich."

"You can't have the statue," Tipper balled her fists and took a step forward.

With her eyes trained on the speaker, she barely saw the man to the side leap forward. He grabbed her and squeezed the air out of her lungs. She felt the sword's tip prick her at the back of her neck. She dared not struggle.

The spokesman for the invaders chuckled. "Now I believe we have a bargaining chip." His voice rasped, barely louder than before. "Will you trade the statue for the life of the lady?"

42

Fair Trade

Wizard Fenworth opened his mantle and started pulling out odds and ends. "That sounds equitable. The life of one beautiful emerlindian for one piece of rock. Yes, I think we can do that."

An unusual amount of crawling creatures came out of the folds of his robes. Tipper couldn't turn her head for a closer look, but one of the black-clad men who stood to the side exclaimed, "I hate snakes. There must be a hundred of them."

"Nonsense," said Fenworth. "Sixty-three at the most. Oh, I forgot the reticulated grossworm. That makes sixty-four. He's really not a worm at all, you know. Misnomer."

The unpleasant man with the husky whisper swished his sword in the air. "Hurry up."

Something slid over Tipper's stocking-covered foot. She squealed, picked up her foot, and shook it. Of course, whatever it was had departed, but now she endured being clamped to a villain's chest with a sword point to the nape of her neck while poised on one foot. Tipper could not contemplate putting her foot back down and stepping on a snake.

She wished she could conjure up something like Fenworth often did. Perhaps lightning bolts or a sheriff's squad. Better yet, she longed for her father to emerge hale and hearty from the bedroom. He could sweep down on this crew and, with the other valiant questers, vanquish the intruders.

The man holding her relaxed his grip a mite and swore under his breath. "I don't like reptiles of any kind. Snakes are the worst."

Tipper felt his leg twitch.

A snake coiled around the ankle of her one foot remaining on the ground. It slithered up her calf. When it tickled the back of her knee, Tipper let out a bloodcurdling scream and jerked away from her captor. She leaped to the settee and landed on the cushions, screeching, and holding her skirts up.

"Excitable," said Fenworth, still pulling things out of his hollows.

Tipper froze. The players in the drama seemed suspended between actions for a moment. The only movement was the constant twisting and gliding of the snakes and Fenworth, who still emptied his pockets.

"Oh, there goes another batch." A knot of larger snakes fell to the floor with a thud and immediately unwound. "Where have they been?"

Prince Jayrus jumped the man closest to him and soon had the man disarmed, knocked out, and stretched across the floor. He whirled through the air and, with a kick to the face, leveled another opponent. He flipped toward the man who had held Tipper captive and landed a fist across the side of the man's face. Since the villain had been pulling a snake out of his pant leg, he hadn't seen the punch coming. He fell with a thud.

Tipper squealed again and, with a glance at the wizard, clenched her teeth against any more *excitable* exclamations. Jayrus…Paladin stood before the last man, the one with the raspy voice. With his sword in his hand, Jay—Paladin presented an alarming picture. Tipper briefly wondered where the weapon had come from, but before she could puzzle it out, the intruder lunged. Paladin blocked the thrust, countered it, and left a hole in the man's chest. The villain fell to the floor.

Fenworth ceased dumping the contents of his pockets. He sighed. "I suppose now I have to clean this mess up." He looked at the fallen rogues, the inert tumanhofers, and Paladin. "I'm only cleaning up my mess. You'll have to clean up your own."

With tears in her eyes, Tipper collapsed on the settee, laughing and crying, sniffing, hiccuping, and wiping her eyes and nose with her handkerchief.

"Tut, tut, oh dear. Don't expect any help from her. Excitable. No good in a crisis." Fenworth lifted an eyebrow as he gazed at Paladin. "Glad you know what to do, boy. Somebody trained you well."

Bealomondore went down to the front desk to report an attempted theft, three injured men, and one dead man. It seemed the Ohidae Grand Hotel did not often deal with thugs, snakes, and swordplay. The night clerk sent for the manager and the authorities. The manager sent for the owner and the mayor, who happened to be the same person. The underlings of the Ohidae police force kept sending for whatever officers held the positions directly above them until the room was filled with medics rendering aid, officials taking statements over and over from the participants, and bellhops collecting snakes. Fenworth soon grew tired of it all and went to sleep.

The chief of police arrived and cleared the room of every superfluous person. By this time, the snakes had been caught and returned to the snoring wizard. They slithered into his robes as if grateful to be out from underfoot. The villains had been carted off. Only the mayor remained. He had not felt he was superfluous.

"So," said the chief of police, "the men in your group overpowered the thieves who came in through those windows?"

Tipper sat prim and proper on the settee, with her shoes on her feet and her hands folded in her lap. "They did come through the windows, but Paladin dispatched them all."

The sheriff's hard face twisted in disbelief.

Tipper continued. "First, Wizard Fenworth let his creatures loose. There were mice, rats, insects, bats, and the snakes. There were more snakes than anything else."

Bealomondore smiled. "There were sixty-four snakes to begin with, all rather small. Nasty but harmless, I suppose. Too small to eat anything but the bugs, and they definitely went after them. Then the wizard found a clump of tangled snakes." The young tumanhofer held out his arms as if he held a huge ball. "They dropped to the floor and uncoiled from one another, and *that* was a disturbing sight. They weren't interested in people but slithered hither and yon, chasing the rodents. Not the bats. The bats went out the window."

"The thieves became nervous," explained Tipper.

"Understandably," said the chief of police.

"Unheard of," said the mayor.

Paladin shook his head. "Not a wise statement around here."

The mayor cast him an indignant look, but Fenworth roused and glared at the town official and owner of the hotel. "I am not a citizen of this land, sir, but in my own country, it is not 'unheard of' for a thief to develop a case of nerves."

The mayor bristled. "I am not referring to the thieves being nervous as unheard of, but to have four ruffians invade the Ohidae Grand Hotel, for snakes of any size to be found in our rooms, for our patrons to have to defend themselves in their own rooms—*that* is unheard of."

Fenworth shook his shaggy head. Tipper watched for leaves or bugs to fall and was amazed when they did not.

"Need to have your hearing checked, Mayor," said Fenworth, yawning. "I've heard of such things. Recently too. By stars and centipedes, I've heard of all that happening just since midnight. But then, I might have better ears than yours." He closed his eyes.

The mayor sputtered, but Paladin came to his side and put a gentle hand on his shoulder. "It won't do a bit of good to answer. The dialogue will just go on and get worse and become completely convoluted and frustrating. Best to just drop it and watch what you say in the future."

The chief stepped in. "Now, the thieves got nervous, and then what happened?"

Tipper cleared her throat, drawing the official's attention. "A snake, a small one, wrapped around my ankle and started to climb my leg."

The raised eyebrows and widened eyes on the man's face satisfied her need for a little recognition of the drama.

"I screamed."

"Always excitable," murmured Fenworth.

She ignored him. "I broke free and climbed up on the settee—"

"Wait," the chief commanded. "He held a sword so that the tip rested against the back of your skull."

"At the base, yes," answered Tipper.

"And you jumped away and didn't get hurt?" Doubt laced his words to the point of sarcasm.

"The snakes were crawling up his pant legs too, and he was distracted and loosened his grip. I suppose the oaf released me more than I struggled loose. And I did get a scratch."

"May I see it?"

"There's nothing to see now."

He cocked one eyebrow.

"Harrumph," said the mayor. "Un—" He clamped his mouth shut and threw a disgruntled glance at Fenworth, who was dozing.

Tipper saw no vines, leaves, or sprouts of any kind on the wizard and decided he wasn't sleeping at all.

The law officer squinted at her. "You heal quickly, Mistress Tipper."

She nodded and tried to sound casual. "We have healing dragons with us."

The chief looked at the hotel owner.

The mayor pulled himself up to his full height. "Ordinarily we don't allow pets in the hotel, especially since there is a city ordinance against stray dragons. But they are housebroken. None of the cleaning staff has complained, and the party gave a substantial deposit against damage to the rooms." He paused. "There are four of them. The dragons, I mean. Four minor dragons."

Tipper tried to read the mayor's face. Was he concerned that he would get a citation for allowing the minor dragons to stay in his hotel? They definitely were not *stray* dragons. She spotted the gleam of avarice in the hotel owner's eye as he surveyed the disorder of the room. Aha! He figured he was going to get to keep the deposit.

The chief's intense gaze returned to Tipper. She refused to squirm.

"And one of these four dragons healed you?"

"Two, Grandur and Zabeth."

"I see." He glanced around the room. "I don't believe I've heard who participated in the struggle to overcome the thieves."

"I did, sir," said Paladin.

"And who are you again?"

"Prince Jayrus of the Mercigon Mountains."

"Never heard of you."

Unaffected by the man's lack of knowledge, Paladin shrugged.

"She"—the chief pointed at Tipper—"called you something else."

"Paladin." Jayrus supplied the answer without hesitation.

"That's your name too?"

"No, that's my position."

"I thought prince would be your position."

"No," said Jayrus, "prince is my title."

"And paladin is your…?"

"Position, charge, calling."

The chief stood still for a moment and just stared at the finely dressed, unruffled young emerlindian before him. A muscle in his jaw ticked. He clenched his teeth, then relaxed. "You were one of the defenders here."

"The only one," said Librettowit. "I'm a librarian, not eager to jump into a fight."

"I'm an artist," said Bealomondore, smoothing the shiny fabric of his coat sleeve. "I would have lent a hand, of course, but Paladin vanquished the lot before I even thought to grab one of the fallen villains' swords."

The chief gave Paladin a hard stare. He looked around the room. "Minimal damage. You say the thieves didn't get the statue they came for. Not one of your party injured."

Tipper started to object but stopped. Something beyond the obvious bothered the city's leading law enforcer.

"I'd say my business is done here." The chief started for the door.

"But," said the mayor as he caught up to him and grabbed his sleeve.

The chief looked him in the eye. "Mayor, the name of Mushand has been mentioned here. The less we delve into this matter, the better."

The mayor swallowed hard. He glanced around the room, nodded, and headed for the door.

With his hand on the doorknob, the chief nodded. "Good morning to you." He closed the door behind him.

Dawn infused the room with light. Prince Jayrus pushed open the door to the bedroom and disappeared into the darker chamber. Bealomondore walked around the room, covering lightrocks and snuffing candles.

Librettowit shoved himself to his feet. "I'm tired." He put his hand to his back. "I'm going to bed. There's nothing we can do right now about the statues."

Tipper peeked in to see how her father fared. Prince Jayrus—no, Paladin—sat on the edge of his bed, holding his hand and talking quietly. Junkit came to her at the door and sat on her shoulder. She leaned her head toward him. He moved his head up and down, rubbing against her cheek.

"Is he better?" she whispered.

Paladin didn't answer.

He didn't hear me.

She decided not to interrupt whatever he was doing. She went to the big soft chair in the darkest corner of her father's room. She cuddled up with Junkit in her lap and watched the handsome young prince soothe her father's restless sleep.

A picture came to her mind of the four dragons standing guard over the invalid. Hue stood at her father's feet on the covers of the bed. Zabeth and Grandur guarded Verrin Schope's head, looking alert and ferocious for such gentle creatures. Junkit positioned himself between the partially opened door and the bed. Outside the door she could hear the conversation, the threats, her gasp as the villains demanded the statue. She realized Junkit was telling her what they had done during the ordeal.

"Thank you, Junkit. Thank you for protecting Papa."

Harsh hands grabbed her as she dreamed. A whispery voice threatened her. She saw Runan and his wife hiding in corners, riding in carriages, and peeking in the windows.

Hue sang on her shoulder, and the dreams settled into more pleasant visions of her father walking through the corridors of Byrdschopen, sitting on the veranda with her mother, chatting with Beccaroon over tea and daggarts, and dabbing at a canvas with a large brush.

"I'm so glad you're better, Verrin." Her mother's voice sounded clearly through the mist in the forest. "However, I think it would have been wiser to tell me we were going on vacation. I had a very hard time finding you."

"I'm sorry, my Peg." Her father's voice rumbled, sounding like a man making amends to his wife, not a man at death's door. "I'm afraid there was a breakdown in communication."

"Yes, your leg. Such a shame it's broken." Lady Peg sighed. "We weren't invited to the Palace Gala anyway. You won't need to dance. Soo was."

"Soo was invited to the Gala?"

"Yes, she always is."

"I know, dear one. But someday your father will relent."

Tipper heard the rustle of silks. "He never will. I don't think so. Not at all. As I understand it, he would have had to lend us something first, and then that something could be re-lent. As it is, he's never lent us so much as the time of day, and he can't re-lend that even if he had the first time, because lending the time of day is such a confusing trial. Trial and error, you know. Error always comes with the trial of lending the time of day, and the clocks are never quite at the same time after that."

Only her mother could have said that. Not even in her dreams could Tipper fabricate that line of reasoning. She opened her eyes.

Mother sat on the bed where Paladin had sat early in the morning.

43

A Shopping Trip

"Mother, where did you come from?" Tipper jumped up and ran to hug Lady Peg.

"Growder, of course. I thought I told you I was visiting your Aunt Soo. Did you not know Soo lives in Growder? Honestly, Tipper, sometimes I think I neglected developing your mind as you grew up." She turned to her husband. "Do you think I've been a bad mother, Verrin? Should I have trained her with mental exercises?"

Tipper's father wore an expression of contented love. "You are the best of mothers, Peg. And I'm sure Tipper has been blessed by your lack of interference in her mental development. Some young minds should be left free to explore their potential."

"That's what I thought," Peg said with conviction. She beamed at her daughter. "Tipper, your dress is lovely, but if you've been sleeping, you should have been wearing a nightdress. But it is day, so I can see how you got confused."

Happiness bubbled inside Tipper, spilling into what was sure to be a silly grin on her face. She couldn't pull back on the smile, even though she tried to be a bit more proper. Her mother liked proper.

Her mother patted Tipper's cheek. "Shall we go shopping? Your father is tired, he tells me. We shall let him nap. And you and I will visit the shops. Mattering Way is right outside the hotel. So convenient. Fashionable, exquisite—"

"Expensive," interjected her father.

Lady Peg patted his arm. "That's all right, Verrin. Give Tipper the purse." She smiled at her daughter. "Be quick now. Change into something less crumpled, and wash your face. I can't imagine all that stretching you're doing with your lips is healthy for your skin. Water should help it shrink back to normal. Don't use too much though. We don't want your mouth to get too small. I hate it when people mumble."

Tipper gave her father a quick look, examining all she could see. Either he or her mother had combed his hair. His eyes were tired but not vacant or feverish. His arms rested on the covers with one hand clasping his wife's hand, and he appeared alert, not lethargic.

He winked at her and nodded. "Go shop, my dears. And when you return, I'll sit in a chair and have dinner with you."

With a glance out the window to note the weather, Tipper scurried off to her own chamber to change. She wore a high-waisted gown of pale pink and a brown pelisse. As she fixed her hair in a fancy braid, the thought crossed her mind that she really did not need more clothing. But she had never been shopping with her mother, and she certainly wasn't going to miss the chance.

"You're disappointed," her mother said as they stepped out into the blustery wind and turned toward the fashionable shops up the street. Zabeth draped around Lady Peg's neck like a colorful green collar for her coat.

Somewhat surprised by her mother's astute observation, Tipper answered, "Just that none of the men could accompany us."

Peg laughed. "So you wanted Wizard Fenworth's fashion advice?"

Tipper felt her cheeks flush. "No."

"The librarian's?"

"No."

"Well, the artist fellow would have given good consultation on matching colors and fabrics."

"Yes, he would have."

"But the prince…ah, the prince would have made our outing so much more enjoyable."

"He is nice, isn't he?"

Lady Peg wound her arm around her daughter's and quickened their pace. "Perhaps we should visit a goldsmith and have your circlet made. It's about time you acknowledged your heritage."

Resentment zinged through Tipper's pleasure. "Mother," she said, "do you know Gienella Hunt?"

"Oh, yes, a very pleasant woman. I haven't seen her in years, of course."

"She said I'm next in line to inherit the throne."

"Did she? I wonder if that's true."

"You don't know?"

"My goodness, Tipper, keep your voice down. Why are you so flapped?"

Normally Tipper could decipher what her mother meant, but this comment challenged her. "Flapped?"

"Yes, dear. It is a good trait to be unflappable. You should culti-vate it."

Tipper accepted the term *flapped* now that she had a reference. "Back to the question, Mother. Do you know if I'm next in line?" She frowned and shook her head. "Why aren't you next in line?"

"I'm not next in line because I was naughty."

Tipper peeked at her mother's face and saw unhappiness there. Her mother's face rarely reflected negative emotions. Even when she scolded, her eyes remained detached from the slight frown of her lips. Now her mother wrapped Zabeth's long smooth tail around one finger.

"I'm sorry, Mother."

Lady Peg's face relaxed, and she squeezed her daughter's arm. "I've been thinking about it, and I think Gienella might be right. Soo and

I are the only heirs. Soo has no children at all, and there is a passel of girl cousins on my father's side. There are male cousins on mother's side, but they, of course, are ineligible. Not illegible. I've never seen their handwriting."

Before her mother could follow that train of thought, Tipper attempted to return her to palace politics. "So I'm the next logical choice."

"Oh, not logical, my dear. Please don't mix logic into this discussion. You are next because there is no one else. At least, no one I can think of. But I don't know what's been going on in the palace since my indiscretion. They don't keep me informed, you see."

"I think that's outrageous, Mother."

Lady Peg beamed. "You're a good daughter. Shall we get you a crown or a dress first?"

"A dress. I have nowhere to wear the crown."

"I know. With your father's broken leg, we will not be going to the Palace Gala that we weren't invited to. So a simple dress—not to say a simple dress, but a plain—no, not to say a plain dress, but a dress not for a ball will be what we should look for. And a hat."

Tipper giggled. "Not a crown?"

"No, a hat."

They gazed in several display windows before they found a shop that seemed to invite them in. They discovered they could make a purchase anywhere on Mattering Way and have the package delivered to the hotel.

At one store, Peg found a delicate bracelet she wanted to buy as a collar for Zabeth. The small dragon didn't want it, and Tipper was pleased she was able to interpret the thoughts that bombarded her mind when Zabeth sent her a torrent of objections. Lady Peg took the dragon's declining the gift in stride and picked out a brooch for a gown she once had instead. Unencumbered by their plunder, they spent more time than they had expected and only became tired when they reached the last shop at the far end of the avenue.

"I suppose we should go back to the hotel now." Tipper sighed.

"Yes, but I'm too tired. My feet ache. Let's get a cab."

Tipper agreed and looked around for some means of transportation. A small two-passenger coach came toward them with the green flag of vacancy displayed next to the driver. Tipper signaled with a raised hand. The coachman slipped the flag out of its holder and reined in beside the two prospective passengers.

He jumped down and opened the door. "Where can I take you ladies?"

Her mother had already settled inside. Tipper turned to answer the man and saw over his shoulder a most confusing sight.

In front of a shop several doors down from where they stood, Runan spoke to another cabman. He nodded, opened the hack's door, and climbed in. Wizard Fenworth had spotted the man riding a horse at Mushand's mansion. What was he doing here?

Tipper pointed to the cab. "Follow him. Follow that cab. I—I know that man, and we've lost contact with him. My—my father has business with him, and I can't let this opportunity pass."

She jumped into the cab while the driver agreed.

"Please hurry," she said and pulled the door shut.

"Where did you say we're going?" asked Lady Peg as the taxi jolted into motion.

"To find out where a man who should be at Runan Hill is going in Ohidae. And maybe we'll discover how he got here."

"Why is that important, dear?"

"It took us three weeks of flying on dragonback to get here, and we see him almost as soon as we arrive. How did he get here?"

"Interesting, Tipper. But why is this more important than going back to the hotel?"

"Well, he probably works for the man who won't give us the statues that would make Papa well."

"Oh, I see. Well, as long as I can rest my feet, I suppose it's all right. I'm going to slip my shoes off, Tipper. This is not something someone ordinarily does in public."

"I won't do the same, Mother. I promise to be dignified."

"You're a good daughter." She patted Tipper's knee. "I hope your father doesn't worry."

Tipper thought of her four fellow questers, who had conveniently found things to do rather than accompany them up Mattering Way. It wouldn't hurt for them to worry just a trifle.

Evening surrounded the coach. Shadows cast by the lamplight mottled the road. Huge trees shrouded large homes by cutting off the moon's milky light. Each house sat back from the street as if the buildings as well as their owners thought too highly of themselves to mingle with passersby.

"I think I know where we are," said Tipper. An ornate sign declared that the property they passed belonged to Mushand.

"Wherever we are, do they serve meals?" Lady Peg asked. "Dinner in particular, Tipper. I'm hungry."

"We can go back now. The cab we were following just turned into Mushand's estate."

"Oh, good. I bet your father is worried about us. He knows I don't like to be late for dinner."

Tipper leaned forward and tapped on the small door behind the coachman. It opened immediately.

"We can go back to the Ohidae Grand Hotel now," she said.

"Yes, Mistress."

The door closed, and the coachman went on to a circular cutaway in the road. In the center, water splashed in a fountain lit by submerged lightrocks. They rounded the decorative structure and headed back the way they had come.

When they reached Mushand's gates, two men rushed out and stopped the horse.

"Here now," yelled the coachman, "let loose my Posie."

Lady Peg sat forward and peered out the side window. "I had a best friend named Posie when I was a child."

"Probably not the same Posie, Mother."

"I daresay you're right. I think the driver is referring to his horse."

"Mother, give me Zabeth."

"Are you feeling unwell?" Lady Peg unwrapped the dragon from around her neck. "Verrin Schope says she's becoming quite good at the healing arts."

"No." Tipper took the dragon and cuddled her close for a moment. "I want her to take a message to Paladin."

"It's very confusing for that nice young man to have two names."

"Yes, it is, isn't it? Zabeth, I hope you can find the hotel. I *know* you can find the hotel. Fly there and tell them what's happened. Tell Paladin or Fenworth or someone to come get us."

She kissed Zabeth on the head and put her out the window. To her dismay, the dragon flew up into the closest tree and perched as if that was all the farther she was willing to go.

The two doors jerked open, and rough hands dragged her and her mother out.

"You're coming with us," growled the one holding Tipper.

She looked around and saw their driver lying beside the road. She gasped.

"That could happen to you if you don't start walking."

"I need my shoes," said Lady Peg.

"That's tough, lady."

"Then you're going to carry me? I don't think that is proper."

"Get her shoes," said the man holding Tipper. "She'll slow us down if'n you don't."

The man hustled Lady Peg back to the open door. She reached in, retrieved her slippers, and brushed off each foot before slipping the shoe on.

"Is there dinner where we are going?" asked Lady Peg.

"I don't rightly know," growled the man who was most given to speaking. The other grunted.

"It would be quite all right," said Lady Peg, "if we could eat the dinner that is left."

Tipper bit her lip, hoping these ruffians wouldn't get annoyed by her mother's skipping conversation. But apparently they were too dense to pick up the right-left reference.

With a shove from behind, Tipper walked through the gates.

"Things have changed so much," said Lady Peg. "An invitation to dinner used to come in an envelope."

44

Help!

Beccaroon saw Zabeth sitting on the outside sill of the closed window at the same time as the prince. Jayrus jumped up and raced to open the window. Zabeth flew in and sat on his shoulder, chittering wildly.

"Here's our answer." Jayrus nodded toward the dragon. "She knows what happened to our ladies." Paladin gently took the frantic dragon off his shoulder and cradled her in his arms. "Slow down." He calmed her with his voice and by stroking her sides. "It's all right. I'm sure you came in time. We'll go rescue them."

He turned to the others in the room, Wizard Fenworth, Verrin Schope, Beccaroon, Librettowit, and Bealomondore.

"The ladies followed Runan to Mushand's mansion and were captured by his henchmen. They are inside his house now."

Beccaroon shook his head. "I would wager that was Tipper's idea."

Paladin focused on Zabeth. "Excellent idea. Take Hue and Junkit with you."

He took her to the open window. Three of the four dragons left in a flurry of wings. Grandur stayed on Verrin Schope's shoulder.

"They're going to scout the house," Paladin explained.

"Help me stand," said Verrin Schope.

Librettowit and Bealomondore came to his aid.

As soon as he was steady, Bealomondore started for the door. "I'll go down and get a carriage."

Paladin eyed their invalid as if assessing his strength. "My dragons will be faster."

Verrin Schope nodded. "I can ride."

"Everyone dress in dark clothing." Paladin surveyed their group. "Meet me on the roof in fifteen minutes."

Beccaroon glanced down at his bright plumage. He had no change of clothing, but he wasn't staying behind!

Paladin left the room, followed by Bealomondore, Librettowit, and Wizard Fenworth.

The wizard had a spring in his step. "What's a quest without a rescue of a damsel in distress? And by the silent stars and singing salamanders, we've got two to rescue." He clapped his hands together and rubbed them vigorously. Critters scattered as they escaped his robes. "Can't say I like questing on the whole, but a rescue! Now there's excitement for you. I just hope that girl hasn't jumped into the excitable nonsense before we even get there."

Tipper sat across the table from her mother in a shadowy little anteroom on the first floor of Mushand's mansion. The meal they had been served was tasty but a bit cold. Tipper nibbled while her mother ate with a subdued appetite. In the shadows next to the door, one of Mushand's big oafs watched them.

Lady Peg took one bite after another, chewing and swallowing but not talking. Tipper knew the signs. She'd taken care of her mother for years. Soon her mother would complain of a headache. Her eyes would lose focus. Exhaustion. Deep fatigue. Once her mother's energy drained to the last ounce, a weariness akin to illness enveloped her. Nothing but sleep would restore her.

Tipper turned to their guard. "If we are staying the night, we will need a bedchamber. My mother is not well and must rest."

Lady Peg glanced up at Tipper but did not contradict her. She folded her napkin and placed it beside her plate. "Yes, I would like to retire."

"Ah, but that will not be necessary." An odd man stood in the door. Backlit from the lights in the hall, his silhouette resembled a round ball for a head, an oval for a body, and legs and arms too long for his frame. He held a drink in each hand. "I am your host, Sir Greystone Mushand. I have a glass of refreshing tonic for you, Lady Schope."

He swirled a goblet, clinking the ice. "I have one of these excellent reenergizers every evening." He gestured with his head. "Come, I wish to show you how your husband's work is favorably displayed in my gallery."

Lady Peg rose. When she reached the door, she took the drink offered her and stepped out into the brighter light. As Mushand turned, Tipper stood and followed. With the light on his face, Tipper thought Mushand repugnant. Straight black hair framed his pallid face. Dark eyebrows slashed across his forehead. His eyes glittered like onyx, with too much white surrounding the pupils and black eyelashes thickly accenting the unusual eyes. He headed down the corridor, her mother trailing behind, sipping her beverage and admiring the paintings.

Tipper caught up with her mother and leaned close. "Don't drink that, Mother."

Lady Peg smiled at her. "It's quite good, Tipper. I don't know why he didn't offer you a glass. Perhaps he thinks you are too young to need a tonic."

Tipper glanced over her shoulder at the guard who walked a few feet behind them. "This is a bad man," she whispered. "We must not trust him."

"He does have very poor manners."

Tipper gave up and followed Mushand. She hoped fervently that the drink was not a potion that would do her mother harm. Mushand drank from his goblet, and the drinks looked the same.

"That doesn't mean anything," she muttered.

"Don't mumble," warned her mother, "or we will have to do mouth-stretching exercises. And they hurt."

They entered the gallery, and Tipper couldn't help being impressed. Not only did Mushand own incredible artwork, but he also knew how to display it for the best presentation.

Lady Peg walked immediately to the two statues. "These belong to my husband," she said.

"They were executed by your husband, Madam, but I purchased them. They are mine."

Lady Peg's eyes widened in horror. "My husband did not execute these people. How bizarre is that? They were never alive, so they couldn't be executed. You have strange beliefs, Mister Mushand."

Tipper examined her mother's face. The lines of weariness had vanished, and since she carried on in her usual style of conversation, the drink must have revived her. Tipper wondered about her mother's use of *Mister*. Mushand had introduced himself as Sir Mushand. Mister, as a form of address, was below Master, and far below Sir.

Mushand's lips pressed in a firm line. He didn't like the slight, whether it was intentional or not.

Tipper's mother pointed to *Evening Yearns*. "You've got her in the wrong place. She's supposed to be in front of the farmer, not behind. You should have put her hand behind her, touching the farmer's outstretched hand, leading him. You've got it all wrong."

Mushand's expression relaxed into a sneer as Lady Peg talked.

Tipper's mother frowned. "She's touching his shoulder, and I'm sure that's not right." Lady Peg shook her head and took another swallow from the glass goblet. "It looks like she's trying to get his attention. I don't like this at all."

Mushand smirked. "At first, I thought as you, dear lady, and had them in the other order. But I have a remarkably intelligent friend— a genius, in fact—and he saw the right of it. I switch them back and forth, but when they are set thusly, the portal opens."

Tipper jerked. Did he mean gateway? The wizard's gateway? She didn't like the smile on Mushand's face. Evil and smug, his grimace made her skin crawl. Out of the corner of her eye, she saw odd lights glimmering in the air just beyond the two statues.

In another moment, Runan stepped out of nowhere, or so it seemed to her.

She blinked. A subtle difference made her unsure if she really did see the Hunts' neighbor and not someone else.

Runan laughed. "Yes, I am the man you met at Hunthaven. At the time, I had to cloak my person so that your nosy wizard would not discover I am his equal."

"Equal?" Mushand's tone dripped with scorn. "You far surpass that clumsy, befuddled wizard. You are brilliant, as you have proven over and over."

The statement inflated Runan. The man looked larger than he had at Hunthaven. Perhaps it was his posture and the arrogant swagger.

Tipper blinked and stared harder. This vibrant personality in no way resembled the unresponsive man who had sat in the Hunts' music room. Even his varied facial expressions demonstrated an incredible contrast to the shell of a man who'd ignored the social interaction around him.

Now he stood as if posing, his hands clasped before him and held at chest level. "It's a nuisance to hide one's true nature. But the rustics would have been overwhelmed by my talents. It was best for them to think I was not only ordinary but perhaps below their level of understanding."

His lips stretched into an unpleasant grin. "And when the wizard appeared…well, there was no sense in revealing my identity until I chose the convenient time."

Runan swaggered across the room, around the statues, and stood before Lady Peg.

He bowed. "Your Highness."

She shook her head. "You've mistaken me for someone else."

"You are Princess Peg Yellat Schope, and as soon as the king and queen are dead, you will rule."

Her lips twisted in annoyance. "I don't know where you get your information."

"I make my information, Your Highness, and I will direct your reign for you. You will find it most convenient to have me as your first advisor."

"I would like to go home now, thank you." Lady Peg put on her most regal stance and looked down her nose at Runan.

"That is no problem." He held out his arm, and she took it.

"Mother," Tipper objected.

"Come along, Tipper."

Runan guided Lady Peg to the spot where he had first appeared. He disengaged his arm and, without preamble, pushed her into the lights. Tipper heard her mother's gasp just before she disappeared. Tipper charged around the statues, only to be intercepted and held by the big oaf of a guard.

"No reason to be alarmed," said Runan. "Your mother is now in the gentle care of my dear wife at the peaceful halls of Runan Hill."

"What happened?"

"The portal," crowed Mushand. "Right now it only allows one person to travel, but Runan assures me that when we get the third figure in place, we can send armies wherever we please."

He turned around slowly with his arms extended as if he would embrace the whole room. "This collection will be nothing compared to what my army will procure for me. And Runan." He gestured toward his cohort. "Runan will maneuver your mother onto the throne and smooth the way for whatever brilliant plans he concocts. He's an alchemist."

He paused to give Tipper a quizzical stare. "Did you even know alchemists still exist? He and his wife are both geniuses, and they won't have to play the boring, nondescript couple hidden away at Runan Hill much longer." Mushand held his goblet aloft. "We have plans."

Tipper saw the disgusted look Runan cast Mushand before he masked it with a polite smile. "And the next part of our wonderful plan is to allow your comrades to break into the gallery. Shall we depart so that their valorous attempts to rescue you are not thwarted by our presence?"

Tipper raised her chin. "How do they know where we are?"

Runan sneered. "You sent word by the green dragon, did you not?"

Tipper tried to think of something to delay the man, upset his scheme, save the day. She could think of nothing, and the oaf who held her too tightly stank. Her stomach roiled.

"Come." Runan gestured, and Mushand's thug dragged her closer to him.

"We must hurry. My wife is to slit your mother's throat if we don't join them at the appointed time."

With that threat dissolving any intention she had of resistance, Tipper allowed the guard to sling her into the portal.

45

Invasion

Beccaroon fumed over the time it took to get ready. Only one riding dragon at a time could land on the hotel rooftop. While one was outfitted with riding gear, the other three hid on the tops of nearby buildings.

Paladin called Caesannede to the hotel last. Beccaroon had come to know the young emerlindian during the long hours of flight as he shared the back of Caesannede. The prince had saddled his dragon only once, when he hoped to persuade Tipper to ride with him. After her father put an end to that idea, he never bothered with the riding apparatus again. Therefore, instead of throwing the pile of saddle and straps over Caesannede's back, the young dragon keeper ran up his tail, along the back ridge, and sat at the base of his neck.

He called to those waiting. "Gus, Ketmar, and Kelsi will land in that order. I'll head on to Mushand's. Your mounts will follow Caesannede."

Beccaroon didn't wait to see the tumanhofers help Verrin Schope onto Gus's saddle nor Fenworth onto Ketmar's back. He flew with Prince Jayrus.

"Do we have a plan?" he asked the prince.

"The minor dragons will be able to tell us where the ladies are. Once we know that, we can decide what to do."

Bec looked over his shoulder. The other three riding dragons followed at a short distance. The flight across the city took much less time than riding through the streets in a carriage. Prince Jayrus chose to land on the grounds of a large house where no light shone.

Beccaroon saw the wisdom of his choice. Hopefully the family had gone on vacation, or perhaps the place was deserted for some other reason. A house for sale? Renovation?

They made a silent descent and soon stood on the extensive lawn.

"We're going to need something for Verrin Schope," said Fenworth, rummaging around in his hollows.

"I'm fine. Let's go get my wife and daughter." Verrin Schope swayed, and Bealomondore reached him before he fell. The short tumanhofer lent his assistance to the tall emerlindian, helping him stand as he waited. He was a convenient height for leaning on. Grandur fussed and wrapped himself around Verrin Schope's neck.

Fenworth snorted. "You can't walk as fast as I want you to go."

"Give me crutches, then. I'll move as fast as need be."

"Tut, tut, oh dear, oh dear, oh dear. I seem to have forgotten crutches, canes, scooters, and—aha!"

He pulled out four wheels, each about twenty inches in diameter. Next he put pieces of a chair on the lawn. Librettowit kneeled on the ground and started assembling the device, which turned out to be an ill-proportioned wheelchair.

"You're going to push me in that thing?" Verrin Schope exclaimed. "Over this uneven surface?"

"Shh! Need for secrecy," whispered Fenworth.

Beccaroon watched as the last nuts and bolts were screwed together. Prince Jayrus stood over to the side, gazing in the direction of Mushand's mansion. Fenworth's assessment of the emerlindian artist's strength had been accurate. He'd never have been able to walk the distance to the wall that surrounded them, let alone traverse the quarter mile to their destination.

Librettowit stood and pushed the chair toward Verrin Schope. A loud squeal ripped through the quiet night.

"Oil, oil," said Fenworth, patting his robes as a man pats his pockets to find a set of keys. He returned to poking around the inside pockets and came out with an oil can. The slight noise of the flexing metal as he pumped drops of lubricant sounded like extra-loud hiccups.

Finally they were on their way. Beccaroon was not surprised that Fenworth's contraption, when outside, floated on clouds. He hoped they would not have to deal with lightning. Grandur settled in Verrin Schope's lap. Bealomondore pushed the wheelchair. Prince Jayrus led. Fenworth brought up the rear behind Librettowit.

The wizard looked very much like he was out for an evening stroll. His lively step, inquisitive, alert demeanor, and pleasant expression belied his usual shuffle and grumbly ways. Perhaps the prospect of a rescue had rejuvenated the old curmudgeon. In general, Beccaroon felt less unsettled by the wizard, but he wasn't ready to accept him and his foreign ideas.

Bec took to the air and scouted, looking for dogs that would bark, people who would object to their skulking through their alleys, and obstacles of any kind. Mushand's house was dark, with only a few lights piercing the darkness.

He landed outside the wall, beside the other men. "The guard at the gate looks like he's asleep. There's a guardhouse, but he's outside the door, in a chair."

Jayrus frowned. "Fallen asleep at his post? That doesn't sound like a very disciplined force to be up against. Still, remain alert. One lax guard does not guarantee an easy entry."

They slipped up to the front gate. Fenworth put his hand on the lock, and Beccaroon heard the latch disengage just as if the old man had used a key. The wizard stepped back, and the prince pushed open the large wrought-iron gate.

He had a sword in his hand, and for the first time, Beccaroon wondered where that sword was kept. Prince Jayrus did not wear a sword belt, yet several times he'd produced his weapon. Did he have a hollow like the wizard? Why had he never mentioned it? Beccaroon had come a long way in trusting these comrades of the quest. He hoped he hadn't been misled. In this dangerous situation, his judgment to follow this new paladin's lead could end in disaster.

Jayrus signaled for them to enter. They passed the guard slumped in a wooden chair. On the ground beside his chair, a plate held the remnants of a large piece of cake, and a dark bottle indicated he'd washed his dessert down with a potent ale. The scent of liquor penetrated Bec's nostrils, and he stifled a sneeze.

Sticking to the shadows, the group approached a side door. Zabeth, Junkit, and Hue waited for them.

The prince whispered to the party of rescuers. "Junkit and the others say Lady Peg and Tipper were led to the gallery. The dragons know they didn't come out of the gallery, but they can't pinpoint where they are anymore."

"What do we do?" asked Bealomondore in a matching low whisper.

Beccaroon detected a tremor of anxiety. He understood. A lot could go wrong here. Beccaroon shivered.

Prince Jayrus seemed unaffected by the tension. "We go to the gallery and see what we find. But we go warily."

He tested the door. It didn't budge. He stepped back and gestured to Wizard Fenworth. The old man came forward and placed his hand on the knob, and the latch clicked. Prince Jayrus led them into the mansion.

Beccaroon thought what an odd bunch of burglars they must appear. He almost chortled, but the seriousness of the mission and his uncertainty of his comrades choked the laugh in his throat.

Their leader, a young man dressed in clothing suitable for a fine dinner, stole through the unlit corridor, heading for a door at the end, beneath which a light shone. Next in line, Librettowit tiptoed. An old tumanhofer tiptoeing was an amusing sight. Beccaroon stifled a chuckle. He needed to get control of himself. His nerves must be making him giddy.

Behind the old tumanhofer, the young tumanhofer pushed the peculiar chair apparatus, which now flickered an occasional light from the dissipating cloud underneath. Fenworth followed, silent and walking as if he were a much younger man. And bringing up the rear was a bright grand parrot, himself, trying not to step on the critters coming out of the wizard's robes. He wasn't dressed in dark clothes like those in the middle, so their procession led off with a prince in finery and ended with a bird in fine plumage.

They would need more than luck to achieve their goal. Perhaps this Wulder would prove Himself trustworthy.

No one offered any resistance to their advance through the elegant hallways of the mansion. That made Beccaroon more nervous. With Junkit and Zabeth sitting on his shoulders, the prince steadily pressed forward. Hue flew ahead and then returned, apparently scouting.

The doors to the gallery stood open, the room half lit by lightrocks. Bealomondore wheeled Verrin Schope directly to his works of art. No remnant of the cloud remained.

The emerlindian gazed thoughtfully at his statues. "What a strange arrangement they've made of them."

"A gateway."

Beccaroon turned at Librettowit's words. The tumanhofer pointed beyond the statues.

Wizard Fenworth took a few hurried steps forward.

From all around them, a hiss disturbed the silence. Billows of white flowed across the floor.

"Gas!" cried Fenworth. His hands twirled around each other, the motion gaining momentum. He threw them out toward the prince. A half sphere spread over the young man like a net. The device quickly expanded and completed a bubble around him, pushing the bad air away from his feet.

Jayrus, sealed in the sphere, battered against the sides. Beccaroon assumed he had not seen who enclosed him.

Wizard Fenworth's hands worked again, but the gas cloud billowed upward. Beccaroon coughed. He saw the two shorter men fall and Verrin Schope slump in his chair. Fenworth's movements slowed.

Beccaroon looked up and saw the minor dragons flying in circles at the highest point in the room. Only wisps of the cloud reached that high, but the white mist was rising.

Each breath Beccaroon inhaled tasted worse than the last and burned his throat. He moved a few steps, realizing he had been trying to escape ever since the first hiss warned of danger, but the heavy mist around his feet felt like thick mud. His muscles ached, and his head swam. He looked at Fenworth. The wizard had ceased spinning his arms around each other. Bec closed his eyes and fell into the poisonous gas.

He made one last effort to spread his wings and move above the foul cloud. His last thought was of Tipper and Lady Peg. Where were his girl and her mother?

Leatte Runan woke Tipper with a couple of rude jabs.

"Get up. You and your mother are going back."

Through the fog of awakening, Tipper took in the strange bedroom. Her mother sat on the other side of the bed, her eyes huge and her complexion pale.

"Back where?" Tipper asked.

"Don't be such a dullwit. You're going wherever you were before." Leatte stomped to the door. "I'll send servants to help you get presentable. Don't try to escape."

The door slammed behind their ungracious hostess. Tipper got out of the huge bed and walked over to put her arms around her mother. "It'll be all right."

Both women wore their slips, having shed their dresses before climbing between the sheets the night before. Lady Peg's hair hung around her shoulders. Her fingers fidgeted with the fringe on the coverlet.

"We can get through this, Mother."

Her mother trembled. "I didn't like going through that hole. It tried to squeeze the air right out of my lungs. And that woman! She grabbed me by the hair, Tipper. She locked me in here."

"I know, Mother." Tipper rubbed her mother's bare arm, surprised at how cold her skin felt and how fragile Lady Peg seemed. "Let's see if there's warm water to wash with."

The basin was empty, but soon a key turned in the locked door and two maids came in with warm water, towels, and breakfast.

Leatte Runan came back too soon and rushed them out the door. She and two footmen escorted Tipper and her mother to a room at the back of the house. She pointed to a spot of rippling air. When Lady Peg held back, the two footmen picked her up and pushed her through. Tipper needed no prodding. Determination to stay by her mother's side hurried her into the gateway.

Tipper saw the statues first when she stepped back through the gateway. *Morning Glory* stood between *Day's Deed* and *Evening Yearns.*

Sun streamed in through the three floor-to-ceiling windows along one wall of the gallery and illuminated the beautiful forms. She heard her mother gasp.

Her mother charged forward, pushing Tipper aside as she circled the display. Then Tipper noticed the peculiar smell and the fallen occupants of the room. Her mother hovered over her father, who sat in an odd wheeled chair. Bealomondore and Librettowit had fallen in two heaps. The four minor dragons looked bad, their skin mottled, each lying in a twist of legs, wings, and tail. Fenworth was stretched out on the floor, his robes spread out around him.

But Paladin stood in the middle of a clear bubble. Angry, his arms crossed over his chest, he made no move to get out and kept his lips clamped in a thin line.

She ran to his prison. "What happened?"

He spoke, but she only saw his lips move.

"What happened?" The scornful voice of Mushand assaulted her ears. He laughed. "Runan's plan succeeded. Your rescuers came. The gas subdued them. Runan was able to plunder the old man's robes. That took a bit of doing, I must say. The wizard's hollows did not like unfamiliar hands exploring their treasures."

Mushand came forward, looking extremely pleased with himself. He circled the globe that held Paladin. "This was the last act of your wizard before he succumbed."

Tipper whirled to examine the fallen men. "Are they dead?"

"No. Runan still has need of them. They sleep." Mushand indicated the bubble before them. "Runan says Fenworth cast a protective shield around this prince of yours. Our question is why would he save this man instead of himself? Runan suggests that the old wizard thought the gas would kill them all and chose to save one man's life."

He turned to stare at Tipper. "Why would he do that, Mistress

Tipper? How is this man so important that Fenworth would sacrifice his own life to assure this man's survival?"

"I don't know."

Mushand cocked his head. "I think that is a half truth. You don't know for sure, but you have an inkling." He gazed into her eyes for a long moment, then shrugged. "No matter. Runan will figure it out. And the act gave something away, didn't it? A totally unnecessary strategic mistake since none of them were going to die from the gas."

Tipper straightened and looked the villain in the eye. "Just why do you need these people alive?"

Mushand shook his head slightly. "I don't, actually. I thought things would be simpler if they were all dead. But Runan decides such things. I believe we need only your mother." He smiled the grimace that made Tipper feel as if spiders had been let loose on her skin. "We don't need you."

Tipper glanced at her mother, who had laid her head in Verrin Schope's lap and spoke to him through her tears. She couldn't hear the words and knew they probably didn't make much sense, but her heart ached for the pain her mother suffered.

"What are you going to do?" She turned back to face the horrible man with his sneer and ever-present drink.

"I am going to collect art," he said. "Runan is going to take over the country."

46

Amassing an Army

Tipper sat with her mother. They'd moved her father onto the floor so they could elevate his leg. Along the wall stood a line of soldiers obscuring the art hanging behind them but, in a way, looking like a display of fashion. Each wore a new uniform of dark green material with gold and purple trim.

Every so often, the gateway crackled and opened. A hundred or more men entered each time, pushing through the lights and stepping into the room. Sometimes their eyes widened, but military discipline stifled their reactions. They didn't stop in amazement as they found themselves in ostentatious surroundings. They marched, eyes forward, following their leader out the side door. During the long wait, she estimated possibly seven hundred soldiers came through the gateway.

Her mother sat with Verrin Schope's head in her lap. Tipper had found cushions on the benches around the room to prop up the injured leg and provide a bit of comfort for her mother. Lady Peg sat in silence, and that worried Tipper a great deal. She spoke soothingly to her mother but got no response. Standing, she searched the room for something she could do that would make her feel useful.

She checked on each of her comrades. All of them breathed, and none showed any signs of waking up, not even when she prodded them, shook them, or called their names. Paladin sat on the floor of his odd chamber, and sometimes he looked like he might be singing. Occasionally, he got up and kicked the side of the bubble. The last time, Tipper thought she heard a twang, but when she came closer to examine the clear shell, she saw no dent. Waving a disappointed good-bye, she returned to sit with her parents.

Fenworth groaned. Tipper sprang to her feet and ran to kneel beside him.

He looked her in the eye. "Have you got a drink, girl?"

She nodded and fetched a glass of water from the tray Mushand's servants had provided. When she brought it back, the old man had managed to sit up. He held his head in his hands.

After he sipped the cool water, he winced. "Breetham gas. Makes one thirsty. Comes with a nasty headache. But I have a powder." He handed her the glass and reached into his robe. His eyes grew wide, and his eyebrows shot up. "I've been robbed. My hollows have been plundered." His eyes narrowed. "Only a very talented wizard could pillage another wizard's pockets."

Tipper nodded. "Runan."

Wizard Fenworth touched the side of his nose. "Now that explains a lot."

The gateway crackled, and the next stream of soldiers paraded through. While they passed, the old man sipped on his water and took in the surroundings. He only glanced at Paladin but studied from a distance each of the fallen questers.

When the last man tromped out the door, Wizard Fenworth moved to get up. "Help me."

Tipper lent support as he rose, but once he was on his feet, he didn't wobble. He walked over to Paladin's enclosure and tapped the side, and the bubble dissolved.

Paladin got to his feet, bowed, and said, "Thank you."

"You and the ladies will be the only ones without headaches for an hour or so." Fenworth gestured. "Come, let's see if we can rouse the others."

Tipper glanced at their guards. They made no move to confine their prisoners' activities. Still, she was glad the usually loud wizard chose to speak softly. As long as those rugged men stood over them, she would whisper too.

Fenworth went first to the healing dragons. He picked up Grandur, kissed him on his tiny green forehead, and cuddled him while he walked over to Verrin Schope. The gesture surprised Tipper, and she realized she liked the old man.

He placed the dragon on the emerlindian's chest and gently touched Lady Peg's shoulder. She looked up, a distant air still claiming her expression.

"It will be all right, Lady Peg. I promise you." He turned to Paladin. "Let's get them some water. A bowl and two glasses."

Tipper followed Paladin as he walked over to the water pitcher. She suspected he was gauging the security of the room as he performed this mundane task, and she expected him to cleverly rescue them. Would he pull out his sword and vanquish the guard? She'd counted them. Twenty-four. Two dozen seemed an excessive security against two women, a man in a bubble, and all the sleeping figures on the floor.

Wizard Fenworth picked up Zabeth next, and after he had her rousing, he handed her to Tipper and told her to take the healing dragon to Beccaroon. "Place her on his neck and stroke the feathers on his back as he becomes conscious. Then get them drinks."

"He doesn't like me to pet him." She sniffed and tried to look like she hadn't. She lifted her chin and batted her eyes against the tears.

Wizard Fenworth cupped her cheek in the palm of his hand. The warmth and smoothness of his fingers comforted her. She detected a strength that she now realized the wizard took pains to mask. She looked into his eyes. A shifting cloud obscured the color. Could he see? Of course he could. How much of this mysterious man was a disguise, an act to shroud his powerful capabilities?

He smiled. "Tender-hearted. I said you are tender-hearted, and you are. And astute. You'll make a good ruler."

He left to tend to Librettowit. Tipper hugged Zabeth as she crossed to her old friend. The gateway crackled, and more soldiers trudged through, but she paid them no mind. She sat with Beccaroon until he could stand. He grumbled, shook his feathers, and complained of a parched throat and a splitting head. Paladin brought them water.

"There were no bowls," said Tipper. "Only glasses."

"I asked for them. The guard wasn't friendly, but he got them."

By the time the next batch of incoming soldiers left the room, all of the questing party had roused from their stupor. Servants brought in tables and chairs, then dishes and silverware.

Tipper concentrated on assisting those who had suffered from the gas.

"Noonmeal is served," Paladin said at Tipper's elbow.

"You startled me."

"I'm sorry. I didn't mean to."

"Do you have your sword?"

"Yes, but I think it is more prudent to leave it concealed."

She glanced around at two dozen guards and the gateway crackling to allow another outpouring of armed men.

"What are they up to?"

"I would surmise they are going to take over the city, perhaps the country."

"Mushand said he would increase his art collection and Runan would rule with my mother as a figurehead."

"Well, there you have it."

His casual tone irritated her, but she kept her voice low. "Aren't you going to do anything?"

He looked down at her, and she read the amused look in his eye. Still unruffled, he found her question entertaining.

She turned away from him and surveyed the scene. Reinforcements poured out of the gateway. Again, the strong young men played follow-the-leader in military style. For the first time she realized they all had a foreign look about them. The hair! These men were all mariones, and mariones in Chiril had blond to sandy brown hair. Yet black hair crowned every one of these soldiers. Chiril men wore their hair longer than these men, some even sporting what she thought of as a mane. The soldiers' hairstyles were not a uniform cut, but even in their individuality, the style was much shorter.

Tipper wondered how far from home these young men were and if they wanted to be here.

She sought out her mother and father. With Verrin Schope awake, Lady Peg smiled and chattered.

"Eat," said Wizard Fenworth, pointing to the two tables. "The food will help the headache go away, and I don't believe our host allowed us to live last night to poison us today."

They settled around the two tables, and Verrin Schope addressed Wulder. "Thank You for this nourishment, and bless our endeavors to honor You."

Tipper sat with her mother, father, Paladin, Beccaroon, and Bealomondore. The minor dragons sat with the wizard and his librarian. They seemed to think dragons eating from bowls at the table quite a normal thing. Tipper watched them for a moment before she picked up her napkin and put it in her lap. "How are we going to honor Wulder, Papa?"

He winked at her. "By overthrowing this unsavory bunch."

Lady Peg stabbed a piece of lettuce with her fork. "Do you think they really throw tossed salad?"

Tipper giggled. Her mother would be fine. She'd recovered from the shock of the night before. Then she remembered Runan. She sobered and looked at her plate. As she slowly chewed her food and forced herself to swallow, she wondered how an army in Ohidae would depose the throne in the palatial city of Ragar.

After their noonmeal, the prisoners roamed around the room, looking at the art, conversing in quiet tones, and waiting. Tipper wandered over to the three statues and studied them. They were backward. *Evening* tapped *Day* on the shoulder. *Day's* hand that scattered the seed brushed *Morning's* arm. *Evening's* other arm reached back as she ran, and her fingers touched the water poured by *Morning*. Instead, *Evening* should touch *Morning*. *Morning* should pour her water on the seed. *Day* should be reaching toward *Evening*.

Tipper's head jerked up, and she searched for her father. He stood with her mother at his side. He and the two Amarans conversed, all three looking serious. But was he well? With Grandur perched on his shoulder, he looked strong. She crossed the room and broke into the conversation.

"Papa, the three statues are joined. Are you all right? Is the problem gone?"

"I believe it is, even with the stones facing the wrong direction."

Librettowit cleared his throat. "We were just discussing the configuration of the gateway. It is not as we originally designed."

Tipper thought for a moment. "You cannot return to Amara?"

The librarian sighed. His shoulders slumped. "Not the way it is set up now. Runan has modified the design."

"Which," said Fenworth, "was already a modification of a variation of a revolutionary device." He pulled his beard. "And we would not go home until Wulder's purpose is accomplished here."

"And what is His purpose?" asked Beccaroon as he joined the circle.

"I believe it is to bring Chiril under His influence," said Verrin Schope.

The bird tsked. "Then He is another conqueror, much the same as our local villains, Mushand and Runan."

Tipper scrutinized the gateway through which more soldiers entered the gallery. "How is it different?"

Verrin Schope wrapped an arm around her shoulders. "Wulder comes with authority as part of His being. These men try to create authority with fear and force."

She leaned her head against his arm. "I meant how is the gateway different from the one Wizard Fenworth and Librettowit constructed."

"I don't do construction. I'm a librarian," Librettowit said.

Fenworth held up his fingers. "Ten. Maybe twelve at the most. You don't bring legions of soldiers through a gateway. A handful of travelers use the passage. Too much traffic tears the delicate fibers of the structure. An ordinary gateway is used sparingly. Of course, Librettowit didn't design an ordinary gateway, but the purpose was distance, not quantity."

Her father looked over Librettowit's head and past the statues to the device. "We'd like to get closer and examine the threads and the weave, but that is one place where the guards will not allow us to go."

"Interesting thing is that those men coming through are not all coming from the same location," said Librettowit.

Fenworth frowned. "And that's something we can't do with our gateways."

"You shall get your chance to get closer, gentlemen," announced Mushand from the door to the hall. He posed, his only motion the swirling of his drink. He wore an elaborate uniform like his soldiers but had given himself a higher rank. "As soon as Runan arrives, we will begin the next phase of our plan. He'll be here shortly. Since we are going to the royal court in Ragar, he felt the need to show off his wizard status in the appropriate attire."

Bealomondore and Paladin came to stand with those surrounding Tipper. The dragons came from various perches. Grandur already sat on Verrin Schope's shoulder. Zabeth landed on Lady Peg. Hue chose Tipper, and Junkit came to roost on Fenworth's head. The wizard didn't seem to think this gave him an undignified appearance. He continued to glower at Mushand.

Tipper heard the evil wizard as he came down the hall. The fabric rustled as he walked. Mushand moved into the room and turned dramatically toward the hallway. Runan stepped into view and paused, framed by the heavy wood casement of the double doors. Vines and sparkles adorned his full garment, and his hat pointed importantly as a wizard's hat should.

"Fish scales in a crocodile's teeth!" exclaimed Fenworth. "He's wearing my formal robes."

47

Going to the Ball

Runan sauntered into the room. "I understand you have not seen your parents in quite some time, Lady Peg."

Tipper's mother did not answer but looked to her husband. His arm tightened around her waist, bringing her closer.

Runan smiled.

Tipper's stomach lurched. The man gloated, and she knew whatever he planned would be evil beyond anything she could imagine.

"I've reconfigured the portal, and our destination is Ragar. The royal palace to be exact. And…" He turned triumphant eyes on Fenworth. "This should be of particular interest to you, my fellow wizard. We shall pass through the portal here in the afternoon and arrive there in the evening."

"First," said Fenworth, "obfuscating time is a bad idea. Second, I am not your fellow wizard. Argumentative, antagonistic, accusatorial, adversarial, combative, oppositional wizard perhaps. Adjectives that still don't pinpoint my aversion at being linked with you. And third—" He paused to glare at Runan. "Third, you have stolen my finest robes. What kind of cheap wizard doesn't make his own clothing? Imbecilic pup!"

Runan raised his eyebrows in mock terror. "You frighten me, old man." He barely pronounced the last word before laughter burst from his lips.

Fenworth's eyes narrowed, and Tipper heard him mutter, "Old?

Experienced is more like it. Messing with time. Imbecile is too kind an appellation."

Mushand ordered a band of twenty soldiers through the gateway. "Secure the corridor on the other side," he ordered, then rocked back and forth from heel to toe as the men marched out of the room, using the crackling gateway.

Turning to his "guests" with a smug look on his pale face, he gestured to the gateway. "After you." He swept an elegant bow. With his extra long arms and legs, the courtesy was more humorous than impressive.

Runan ambled toward the gateway. "Should you be contemplating not cooperating, let me remind you that we only need Lady Peg in order for our plans to play out. And since Fenworth risked his own life to save the young prince, I would choose to eliminate him first. Mistress Tipper would be my second choice."

"Oh, really!" Lady Peg stepped away from her husband and approached the gateway. "Tipper should be first. Ladies before gentlemen. Come with me, dear. Where these people learn their manners, I can't say."

She and Tipper walked into the gateway arm in arm. The device squealed in protest.

Tipper held her breath. The two times she had been through this contraption, the pressure had nearly suffocated her. Three steps, and she pushed her way out of the smothering, thick air.

The guards who had gone before them lined the broad hall. A sandy yellow carpet ran the length of the corridor with shiny, light wood floors showing on either side. A few chairs and tables of the same pale color sat at intermittent distances on both sides. Creamy white walls displayed pictures in gilded frames. Rare yellow lightrocks illuminated the crystal chandeliers. Music played in the distance.

Her mother squeezed Tipper's arm. "This is where I grew up, Amber Palace. Soo and I had so much fun. It's huge and has so many places to play. We'll be fine here, though I'd rather go home. Soo and I hardly ever ran into the king and queen."

"You mean your father and mother."

"Yes, them."

A couple of snaps behind them warned of more people coming through the gateway. Tipper and her mother scooted out of the way. One by one, the others in their party entered the hall. Bealomondore and Paladin came to stand beside Tipper. Librettowit, Fenworth, and Verrin Schope stopped to scrutinize the gateway. Then Runan and Mushand strode through. The minor dragons were the last to pop out, and they flew around in circles, chittering.

"Ah," said Runan. "We won't wait for the others."

Tipper surmised he meant the army at Mushand's mansion. Runan sauntered down the golden carpet, past the men standing directly outside the gateway, past Tipper's small cluster, and between the rows of soldiers.

"Follow him," ordered Mushand. The soldiers brought their hands to their sword hilts in a very threatening gesture. The questers moved to follow Runan. The soldiers fell in behind them.

"Where are we going?" asked Lady Peg as she walked.

"To the ball," answered Mushand from behind.

"The Palace Gala?" Tipper's mother stopped, turned on Mushand, and rammed her fists against her hips. "Do you have an invitation? Because none of us do. Who raised you? Didn't you have a mother who taught you right from wrong? A grandmother? A nanny? Clearly, someone has neglected your manners. We are not going to a ball to which we were not invited, dressed like ragamuffins."

"Your Highness, if you do not continue down this corridor, you will be late for your own coronation."

"There you go with that nonsense again."

"Your Highness, if you do not continue down this corridor, I will have my soldiers kill one of your companions. You may choose the first one to die." He raised a hand and signaled. One soldier drew his sword and stepped toward them.

"Your disregard for propriety is scandalous," said Lady Peg. She pointed to the pale carpet. "Do you know how hard it would be to remove a blood stain from this rug?" She threw her hands up and began walking. "I want to be introduced to your family. Someone should be held accountable for your lack of proper training."

A flush of anger darkened Mushand's unnatural complexion. Tipper tensed and saw Paladin bring his hand to his waist, pulling back one side of his coat. Mushand shook off his ill temper and ambled on, a studied portrayal of a man with an amiable disposition. He passed Lady Peg without a comment.

Verrin Schope caught up with his wife and took her arm. Beccaroon positioned himself on her other side. Paladin took Tipper's arm, and Bealomondore flanked her. The wizard and his librarian brought up the rear, followed, of course, by the soldiers. Tipper heard the popping of the gateway and craned her neck to see.

The influx of "the others" was beginning. Would all of this well-dressed rebel army pour into her grandparents' palace?

The dragons settled themselves on the people in the usual order. Junkit landed with a thump on the wizard's head.

Urgent whispers between Librettowit and Fenworth caught Tipper's attention.

"Fireball, I say," said the wizard.

"That's not any more reliable than those confounded clouds you use to float things. And ten times more likely to go awry."

"Was that figure scientifically deduced, or did you just pick 'ten times' out of thin air?"

"Out of thin air and experience. Concentrate on the time element causing glitches in the gateway."

"It's a fine thing when a mere librarian deigns to advise a wizard of my stature."

Librettowit ignored the jab. "Cosmic whirling might suffice."

"Haven't done it in a while. Risky when you're out of practice."

"You've forgotten how to gain momentum, Fen?"

"I didn't say that."

"Didn't need to. You were always doing it backward anyway."

"Backward, backward. There's something about those pieces of stone being in the wrong order that should be to our advantage."

"Something?" Librettowit growled. "Do you have any idea what this something might be?"

"No, but if you quit yammering at me, I might be able to puzzle it out."

The music grew louder as they continued along the corridor. They passed an archway, and no more lights shone in their brackets on the walls or from the chandeliers above them. Tipper saw a staircase ahead and realized they must be on the second floor. A soft glow barely reached the railings of a balcony that spread out on both sides of the stairs. Had this part of the house been darkened for the party, or did Mushand's crew take out the lights in order to cover their advance?

Two of Mushand's guards passed them from the rear and positioned themselves at the top of the steps. Tipper took a couple of deep breaths. Those men moved without emotion, with speed and a sinister intensity. Fear crawled up her spine.

"Wulder hasn't deserted us." Paladin spoke softly.

Two more guards rushed past them and silently took positions halfway down the unlit stairs. Once they were in place, two more charged to a location ahead of them. When Beccaroon, Lady Peg, and

Verrin Schope reached the top of the stairs, all twenty soldiers lined the path they would take.

Tipper glanced over her shoulder and saw more lurking soldiers. Fenworth and Librettowit discussed something in low tones. Music from below pressed against her ears. The only word she caught of their conversation was "time."

Mushand gestured for them to go down the stairs. Lady Peg lifted her chin and descended the dark steps with a regal demeanor, her two escorts flanking her.

One melody came to an end, and Tipper heard Fenworth say, "He stole my hat too. I could use my hat right now."

She winced. "Our government is about to be overthrown, and he's irritable about his hat."

Bealomondore took her other arm and, with a slight nudge, urged her forward. "Our turn. Mushand is cuing us to advance. Mustn't make our madman angry. And I think a wizard's hat is more than just a hat."

In the great hall below, Runan stood in a large archway. His stolen garb outshone the dazzling gowns of the ladies being twirled around on the dance floor beyond. He smiled congenially and nodded as people passed. He turned and nodded his approval as Lady Peg drew nearer. When she stood behind him, he waited a moment for the others to arrive. Then he snatched off the pointed wizard's hat and, with one hand, made a motion in the air as if he collected something, then thrust his fist into the hat. The music ceased. He put the hat on his head.

"Doesn't fit him," Fenworth grumbled.

Tipper saw the musicians on the platform still playing, but their instruments made no sound. The dancers came to a clumsy stop, gazing around, murmuring and exclaiming.

Runan strolled in among them with his arms raised above him. They backed away, leaving him with an expanse around him.

At Mushand's command, Lady Peg and her entourage followed, and as they got closer, Tipper felt a pulse radiating from the evil wizard. The unpleasant vibration made her want to twitch as if many tiny bugs crawled across her skin.

The king and queen sat in elaborate thrones on a dais. Both emerlindians' complexion had darkened with age and experience, but Tipper noted that her father's skin was much darker. A glow of pride strengthened her resolve to meet these relatives with composure. She wouldn't play the part of a poor country bumpkin. Grateful to her mother for all the lessons in etiquette, Tipper straightened her spine and continued to assess her grandmother and grandfather.

Queen Venmarie's style was elegant without being elaborate. She wore a rich bronze-colored gown that coordinated well with the Amber Palace décor and suited her stout frame. Her grandfather's tall, muscular body belied the many years he had sat on the throne. He obviously did more than just sit. She suppressed a smirk. He did have a double chin.

King Yellat rose. "What is this? Why do you interrupt?"

The queen came to her feet and grabbed her husband's arm. He leaned to hear her whisper, and his eyes locked on Tipper's mother.

"Why have you come, Peg?" he asked.

"Why aren't you dressed properly?" asked the queen.

Tipper saw her mother's back stiffen, but Lady Peg said nothing.

Gasps erupted from the dance floor. At first Tipper thought it was recognition of her mother, the banished princess, but when several women fainted, she realized Mushand's army streamed in through the door in two lines, swiftly surrounding the crowd.

"Where are my guards?" demanded the king.

No one responded. The silence spoke loudly. There were no longer any guards.

King Yellat glared at Runan. "What is this all about?"

"This is about new government. This is about a change. This, King Yellat, is about the commencement of your daughter's reign."

"Tut, tut," said Fenworth. "I disagree. Oh dear, I believe this is about time."

48

Comeuppance

"Stand very still."

Tipper heard Fenworth's command just before things in the room started jerking.

She watched, trying to figure out the meaning of the odd sensation. The fainting lady near her disappeared and then stood four feet from the place she had swooned. A man vanished from beside one woman and reappeared next to another. Careful to move only her eyes, Tipper glanced over at her father. The phenomenon reminded her of her father's blinking in and out—only in this room, everyone but those standing still at Fenworth's command suffered from the rapid, repeated occurrences.

Viewing the constant jerking made her dizzy. It might have been better if they all disappeared in unison, but they did not. The blink-outs staggered. The length of time the person was gone and the distance between where he disappeared and reappeared varied. Tipper closed her eyes against the chaos.

Then she noticed the odd sound effect. If a person started a sentence and stopped, then took up his discourse a matter of seconds later, that would have defined the sound of one person blinking away and returning. Multiplying that by all the occupants of the ballroom added cacophony to chaos.

She opened her eyes again. The sound with the visual was not as disorienting as the sporadic sound alone.

The soldiers along the wall had broken ranks and entered the frenzy. Mushand flickered as he tried to dash from one spot to another and succeeded in actually leaving shadows of himself here and there. The shadows faded quickly, but the sight increased Tipper's queasiness.

She wanted to clamp her hands over her ears but feared that would be too large a motion. She wanted to ask Wizard Fenworth questions but dared not open her mouth. She couldn't see the evil wizard Runan without turning her head, and a chill crossed her skin when she thought of what he might be doing.

Bealomondore had said not to make a madman angry. Every time Mushand crossed in front of her range of vision, he looked redder in the face and fainter in body. Was he like a stain washing away after many trips to the laundry room?

Sweat ran down Tipper's back. The air thickened and felt sticky, like the air within the gateway. Tipper longed to take a deep breath, but would that much movement throw her into the disorder around her? Perspiration trickled down her face and stung her eyes. She fought the urge to lift an arm and wipe the moisture from her brow.

To her surprise, a breeze sprang up and cooled her sweaty skin. No, not a breeze. The movement of air did not fluctuate like the wind. The temptation to move her head grew. What were the others doing? Where was Runan?

Librettowit's voice broke through the pandemonium. "Not a good idea."

He knows I want to move?

"Fenworth, think twice."

He's not talking to me.

The wizard chortled. "Buck up, Wit. It'll only take a minute."

The image of the room around her began to spin. It reminded her of what she could see when she sat on a carousel at the county fair. Only she stood still, and the room revolved.

Runan passed before her, and she saw he was caught in the anarchy of jerking movement and jolted conversation. The revolution came around again, and Tipper saw Runan had lost his hat, or rather, Fenworth's fancy hat. On the next revolution, he'd lost the flowing outer robe decorated with shimmering gem dust and lifelike vines. The third time around, the deep blue underrobe was gone and only a gray shift covered the outraged wizard's body. Tipper determined to close her eyes for Runan's next passing, but it came too quickly, and she was relieved to see he hadn't lost his last bit of clothing.

Thunder rumbled through the room, and everything went black. The wind ceased.

Even though Tipper couldn't see, she felt that the odd motion all around her had stopped. She strained her ears and heard nothing. The darkness faded to gray. Within the blank gray screen, forms began to take shape, fuzzy silhouettes in differing shades of gray. Color seeped into the forms, and the edges became more distinct. Each time Tipper blinked, the scene became more real until she focused on the Amber Palace's ballroom.

Lady Peg's voice broke the silence. "I'm so glad we were not invited to this Gala. I wish we hadn't come."

Tipper whirled to see her mother standing in her father's embrace. Her other comrades seemed to be adjusting to the normalcy with the same blinking fit that had come over her.

Across the open space made by a ring of confused dancers, Fenworth, in his magnificent wizard robes, stood eye to eye with Runan. The sneer on the evil wizard's face made Tipper fear for the confused old wizard she'd grown to love. She took a step toward them and found Paladin at her side. Librettowit stepped between them and grabbed their arms, holding them back.

"No need, children. Fenworth just maneuvered us through a cosmic whirlwind—backward but, still, we made it. And he accomplished this intricate task during a time flux. He can take care of himself." His voice trailed off, but Tipper heard the last sentence. "I wonder if going backward is actually more efficient than going forward."

Runan raised his hands above his head, arched his palms with fingers spread like claws, and uttered something that even without distinguishable words sounded dark and twisted.

In a direct line from his fingertips to the tip of Fenworth's hat, a sizzling bolt of energy zapped through the air. Tipper's eyes widened as she watched a ripple of rainbow colors spread and form a band wrapping Fenworth. The energy ring descended from his hat and widened as it passed over his head and body until it fell to the floor around the ample circumference of his robes. The colors pooled and mixed, muddling into black, and flowed to Runan's bare feet.

"Where are his shoes?" asked Lady Peg.

"The question should be, where are Fenworth's stolen shoes?" said Librettowit. "And the answer is back on Fenworth's feet."

Runan stared at the floor around him, a mixture of puzzlement and horror on his face. The mass of energy bubbled, and as the bubbles burst, rainbows of color escaped into the room. An unpleasant smell like burned fur accompanied the gorgeous display of lights.

"Don't mess with time, young wizard," said Fenworth. "It'll come back and bite you."

The bubbling black puddle shot up like a geyser and covered Runan. He shrieked and dissolved like melting sugar. Even the odor reminded Tipper of the smell of taffy cooking. The second fragrance covered the first, and the room's atmosphere changed from threatening to normal. Fenworth had dispatched the evil wizard.

From the quiet after the storm came a groan. Tipper searched the crowd, as did everyone else. All eyes focused on Mushand. His moan grew louder, changed tone, and became an enraged bellow. The roar ended with a spewing of foul language and evolved into shouted commands.

"Surround them! Execute them! Kill the king! Kill the queen! Destroy these rats dressed in finery. Spare only Queen Peg."

The soldiers in the room drew their swords against the unarmed ballroom. Women screamed. Paladin bolted to confront the line of warriors, his own sword in his hand. He downed three men and took one of their weapons so he could wield two blades at once. A shifting of the crowd brought the ladies to the center with the unarmed men in a protective ring around them. The minor dragons swooped over the men in arms, spitting colorful saliva on their faces. The men dropped their weapons and clawed at the caustic fluid burning their flesh.

The king came down from his dais, swinging his scepter like a bludgeon. The queen grabbed at the bank of candlesticks. She pulled out a candle and threw it to the floor. She then yelled a name. As one of her court turned in answer to the call, she threw him the three-foot-high heavy metal holder. The men soon caught on and dashed over to receive the crude weapons.

Tipper heard a squawk and turned to see Beccaroon in flight, talons extended, battering a group of the men in uniform. Bealomondore and Librettowit fought against the enemy. Her father had a pole with Chiril's flag at one end. As her father thrashed the attacking soldiers, Lady Peg crawled between the scrambling feet.

Tipper wondered what in the world her mother was doing until she saw her come up behind one of the men her father fought. Verrin Schope forced the man back. He fell over Lady Peg, and while he was on the floor, another lady of the court bashed him on the head. Several women then dragged him off to be tied up with whatever they could find.

The king worked his way through the mayhem to stand beside Verrin Schope. Soon Peg was tripping the combatants her father fought as well those who assaulted her husband.

The only two people who didn't enter the fray were the wizard and herself. Tipper assessed the situation. Which group of women should she join: those whimpering in a tight circle away from harm, those ministering to the wounded, or those fighting in their own way beside the men?

She had just decided to find a club when the old wizard gestured for her to come to him. She edged through the terrified huddle of women in the middle of the fighting and went to Fenworth.

"Sing," he commanded as soon as she stood before him. He grabbed her shoulders and whirled her around to face outward, enveloped her in a tight hug, and repeated, "Sing!"

"What?"

"Does Chiril have a national anthem?"

She nodded.

"Sing that."

She opened her mouth, and the first note out astonished her. The wizard amplified the words to resound over the din of battle.

The land of Chiril,
Our home of peace,
Is where the brave
Protect the meek.
Our men are valiant.
Our women strong.
In love and kindness
All the day long,
We stand together

To right each wrong.
We plan together
To make things better.
We live to give
Each other life.
The land of Chiril
Will not bear strife.

Tipper started over at the first verse. Some of the cowering women knotted together in the center of the room joined her song. Their warbling voices became stronger as they made it through the verses.

"Courage! Hope! Determination!" Fenworth hugged Tipper closer to his bony frame. "Your song feeds them what their souls desire."

Many of the men in fancy dress lay bloodied on the once pristine ballroom floor. The women of Chiril knelt beside them, staunching the flow of blood and offering comfort.

As Tipper, within the wizard's embrace, began the anthem for the third time, she noticed that the clamor of battle had subsided. The doors had been barricaded so reinforcements could not bolster the ranks of the enemy. A handful of soldiers still struggled against Chiril men. Librettowit and Bealomondore had just captured Mushand and force-marched him toward Fenworth.

When she finished the verse, Fenworth released her.

"Good voice," he said and turned to Mushand. "Command your men to lay down their swords."

Mushand clamped his jaws.

"Now," said Fenworth in a quiet tone.

Tipper felt energy tingle along her skin. She saw tiny sparks skitter over Mushand's hair and clothing.

Mushand gasped, and his eyes darted around the room.

"Now," said Fenworth in an even softer tone.

Snaps now accompanied an increased frequency of the sparks dancing all over Fenworth's adversary.

Mushand's wild eyes focused. "Put down your weapons."

His soldiers immediately complied, and Tipper wondered if they were relieved. They'd come into the room outnumbering a group of men and women celebrating a gala event. Now they were outnumbered, and the revelers had turned into a formidable fighting force.

Fenworth took Mushand's arm in a friendly grasp. "Now we will go dismiss your army and give them instructions to go home. Perhaps you'll arrange for their wages and an allowance to pay for their journeys."

Mushand nodded.

"Paladin," Fenworth called, "would you join this would-be dictator and me as we seek to undo the mess he's created?"

Paladin sheathed his sword beneath his jacket at the waist, but no scabbard received it. The weapon disappeared at his side. He joined Fenworth and Mushand.

Mushand's eyes pleaded with Paladin. "I really didn't aim to be dictator. That was Runan's ambition. I was to have the art, the art of the entire nation. The art of any world we conquered. I was to build museums. Spacious, filled with light, overflowing with priceless beauty."

Paladin patted his shoulder. "For now, let's send these men home. They clutter up the palace."

They walked to the main entrance, and the men there removed the barricade and opened the doors. Mushand addressed the soldiers waiting. "We are disbanding." He walked on, Paladin and Fenworth flanking him.

"Won't he be punished?" asked Tipper.

Her mother entwined her arm with Tipper's. "He's going to be very poor after paying all that money out for wages and passages and such. Maintaining an army for even a few days has got to be a strain on the household purse."

King Yellat said, "I'll have him arrested, but only after he's done his bit to right some of his wrongs." He looked around the room. "You can't right murder and injury."

The king extended his hand to Tipper's father. "Verrin Schope, it's been a long time."

Her father shook his hand.

"Peg." The king looked sternly at his daughter. "Are you going to introduce me to your child?"

"Where's Soo?"

"She refused to come since you weren't invited. She does so every year."

"I didn't know that. Now why does she do that? She doesn't have to. I'm the one who always got in trouble."

King Yellat nodded toward Tipper. "Your child?"

Lady Peg pressed her lips together. "Father, may I present my daughter?"

The king's face held no warmth, and Tipper had the urge to do something very childish. Kick his shins. Stick out her tongue. Turn her back. But the pressure of her mother's hand on her arm stopped her.

She curtsied as her mother had instructed over the years, a full, graceful curtsy. For a moment, she wished she had the lavish dress that would complete the picture of a dutiful, regal granddaughter. Then she remembered the years of neglect and stood more quickly than was correct.

Her mother did not offer a reprimand. Instead she pulled her daughter away from her royal grandparents and offered their services to the lady who had begun to organize the aid to the wounded.

The king's servants began to arrive as they were released from wherever they'd been captured and held. The wounded were carried away to beds. The royal physician arrived and organized those helping. He sent for more medical aid.

The minor dragons helped where they could. Grandur flew back and forth between two severely injured men, keeping them alive. Zabeth visited the minimally injured, and those men got up, thanked her, and walked away with a dazed look on their faces as they examined a healed wound.

Tipper marveled at her mother's stamina. They worked side by side for two hours before the ballroom began to look less like a battlefield and more like part of a palace. Lady Peg administered aid to nobles, servants, and the fallen enemy, all with a compassionate air and a few words of nonsense.

When Wizard Fenworth appeared at the door, Tipper watched as he silently summoned her father and Librettowit. The men looked up from their tasks, nodded to the wizard, and excused themselves.

Tipper touched Lady Peg's shoulder. "Mother, may I leave you now to see what Wizard Fenworth is up to?"

"Yes, dear. We've got everything under control, I think. Well, not everything, of course. But enough."

Tipper bolted across the room, catching up to the group of three men in the hall.

"Where are we going?" she asked.

Verrin Schope put his arm around her shoulders as they walked. "To put the statues in the correct formation."

She shuddered. "We're going back to Mushand's mansion?"

"No. The statues are here."

"Here? How?"

He shrugged. "Mushand—or more likely Runan—must have had them transferred."

They climbed the stairs, and at the end of the corridor where they had first entered the palace, Paladin stood guarding the three statues. Tipper had always thought Prince Jayrus handsome. He'd matured during their journey and lost some of the arrogance that put her off.

"He used to be a bit bigheaded."

Her father looked down at her. "Jayrus?"

Tipper flinched. She hadn't meant to speak her mind. She nodded.

"Well, he learned most of what he knows from books. He hob-nobbed with one man, who was probably socially inept as well. His other associates were kimens and dragons. But now he is under the direct tutelage of Wulder. He'll improve. You'll see."

Tipper frowned. In spite of all the important, life-changing circumstances whirling through her world, her heart focused on the young man standing at attention at the end of the hall.

"Does being the paladin mean he isn't normal anymore?"

"Normal?"

"Like other men."

"I'm sorry, dear Tipper, I have no idea what you are getting at."

"Can he marry and have a family and live out here, or does he have to go back to that tower castle?"

"Ah." Her father dragged the single sound out. "I see." He patted her shoulder, then stopped.

She stopped as well and turned to face him.

He took her hand, brought it to his lips, and brushed a kiss upon it. "I do not have the answer to that. Paladin who serves Amara is unwed, but I do not recall anything in Wulder's Tomes that says a paladin must remain unmarried."

"Are you coming?" called Fenworth.

Verrin Schope placed Tipper's hand on the crook of his arm and escorted her to where the others waited in a circle around the three statues.

Librettowit pinched his lower lip as he studied the formation. "How shall we proceed?"

Verrin Schope left Tipper to walk around his art, examining the pieces from all sides. "I suggest we move the three statues out of the circle simultaneously, turn them around, then slide them back in place."

"Here in the corridor?" asked Tipper. "Shouldn't they be displayed somewhere?"

"This is temporary," said Fenworth. "Just to right the world so no more damage is done before we make a permanent arrangement."

Verrin Schope, Librettowit, and Paladin each took hold of a statue and hauled the figures out of the backward configuration. A crackling noise filled the air and intensified until at last the librarian edged his statue into place.

Librettowit straightened and frowned. "That took more muscle than I expected."

Fenworth stroked his beard. "There must be an innate energy pulling them toward one another, much like a magnetic force."

Paladin stood with his hand resting on the crown of the farmer statue's hat. He looked at Verrin Schope. "What next?"

"Wizard Fenworth and I will spend a few minutes untangling the weave of the gateway. Runan added some interesting distortions, and we want to break those."

Librettowit, Tipper, and Paladin stood to one side and watched. Tipper saw the two men fingering something in the air but could not see what.

"Can I learn to do that?" asked Paladin.

Librettowit nodded. "If you can see it, you can learn."

He put his hands on his hips and appeared to study the movements of Tipper's father and the wizard from Amara.

Tipper asked, "Why does it matter which way the statues face?"

Librettowit shook his head. "It's all very complicated. The original gateway was constructed for long distance. The weave is strong, but only one or possibly two people could move through the gateway at a time. Runan took the basic framework and improved the function. His configuration allowed the passage of great numbers. However, this new pattern involved reversing the stones. Reversing the stones disrupted the natural energy flow and is as bad a situation as having the stones disconnected altogether."

"They're ready," said Paladin.

He and Librettowit stepped forward, and Wizard Fenworth stepped back.

"Counterclockwise," said her father.

He, the librarian, and Paladin carefully rotated the statues in unison.

"So far, so good," muttered Fenworth. He crossed his arms over his chest and gazed at the procedure with a gleam in his eye.

"Nothing could go wrong, could it?" Tipper's voice squeaked.

The wizard said nothing.

The men pushed the statues into a tight circle.

"Ah, good!" said Fenworth. "Nothing exploded."

Verrin Schope tweaked the arrangement of the statues until the way each touched the next satisfied his artistic sensibilities.

Fenworth leaned closer to Tipper and whispered, "Very important that the energy field aligns perfectly."

"Exquisite!" declared Bealomondore as he came down the corridor. "Divine!" He quickened his step and beamed as he studied the grouping of sculptures. "Magnificent!"

Tipper's chest swelled with pride. The work before her proclaimed her father's talent like no other she'd ever seen. The figures pulsated with an unseen power.

Bealomondore frowned and looked at the others in the corridor. "I apologize, but I've been sent to bring you back to the king. We must drag ourselves away from this splendid display and attend His Majesty."

They started down the hall. At the top of the stairs, Paladin announced that he wanted to go up to the roof to arrange for the reception of their dragons.

"I've called them to come, and I don't want the palace guards thinking this is another invasion. I'll be with you soon."

The king indicated that Lady Peg and her assembly were to move into a private sitting area. Beccaroon followed reluctantly. He found it hard to be civil to those who had caused such unnecessary hardship on the family he loved.

Once beyond the sight and sound of the melee, the king commanded them to sit, and an awkward conversation began. Both Librettowit and Bealomondore were conversant in social situations. Beccaroon contributed, but only to ease the discomfort of Lady Peg and Tipper.

Librettowit, Bealomondore, and Beccaroon gave an account of the unusual happenings of the last few weeks. Lady Peg said nothing. Junkit sat on Lady Peg's lap and looked like a guard. Tipper's mother stroked his back and sides, but he didn't relax. Verrin Schope merely affirmed the more unbelievable aspects of the tale.

Queen Venmarie entered and came to sit by her husband, but she kept her eyes averted and her chin tilted upward. Beccaroon controlled the sarcasm tickling his tongue. He had the urge to ask Her Highness if she found the present company distasteful.

She sniffed. "You've brought a foreign prince to our court?"

Beccaroon sighed. Her tone answered his question.

Paladin appeared at the door as if called. He strode over to the king and bowed. "Your Highness. I have a report from your captain of the guard. He wishes to speak with you when you are free but assures you that his squadron is firmly in control. I offered my services, but he said I might be needed here."

Queen Venmarie clicked her tongue. "I don't see that you are *needed* anywhere."

A thoughtful look crossed Paladin's face. He didn't seem to take affront at the queen's tone. Tipper did not hide her feelings well. The resentment in his girl's heart was etched on her face.

Fenworth, asleep in a chair, snorted. The queen looked down her nose at him and turned away.

Paladin addressed the king. "May I sit with you, Your Highness?"

The king nodded and indicated a chair next to Lady Peg. "You fought valiantly and with great skill. Had you not been present, many more of my people would have been slain."

A smile quirked the corner of Paladin's mouth. "You swing a mean scepter yourself, Your Highness."

King Yellat snorted a laugh. The reaction died quickly. Indulging in merriment lightened the mood only momentarily. The evidence of evil still lingered outside the door.

Paladin sat and leaned slightly forward, glancing from the king to the queen and back. "I will speak of treasure, if I may?"

The queen's eyes narrowed, but the king nodded.

"Mushand's desire for works of art warped his perception of the

world. He thought what he deemed treasure was also desired by everyone else. In his mind, the more treasure he had, the more envy he
generated in all those around him. It never occurred to him that his
servant would rather have a piece of cake than own a picture. He
assigned his values to others."

Beccaroon studied the circle of individuals sitting in comfortable
chairs in a room designed to reflect the name of the palace. Gold, yellow, and warm browns accented the furnishings. His weary friends
were not tidy or even presentable. After all, they'd been through a lot.
The king and queen were haughty even with rips in their lace and
brocade.

Beccaroon had two desires. He would like either to get up and
walk away from this place with his own people, leaving everyone else
behind, or for the cold-hearted royalty to drop their pride and embrace Lady Peg and her family.

And this paladin chose to talk of treasures. Awk!

The room misted, reminding Beccaroon of the gas that had
choked them in Mushand's gallery. But this fog drifted in as naturally
as the morning haze in a stand of trees. No one in the room moved.
No one panicked at the unusual sight.

Paladin's warm voice conjured up a picture in the middle of the
room, in the midst of the fog. Beccaroon relaxed with the other individuals in the room and watched the unfolding scenes with a sense of
wonder.

"Lady Peg as a child used to escape her nanny."

A small child in a dirty dress and pinafore ran through the palace
halls. She burst into a roomful of well-dressed ladies and thrust her
grubby hand in the queen's face. A precious red feather slipped from
her fingers and fell on her mother's lovely silk skirt.

"Mushand thinks everyone admires his treasure. Peg thought the
same. Mushand wants to hoard his beauties. Peg wanted to share."

The fog grew heavy and cleared a bit. In the new scene, the queen promenaded along a garden trail. Behind her trailed three children. One was obviously Soo, neatly attired, walking primly. Beside her was an empty dress with a bonnet hovering where a head would be. The empty dress followed her mother with graceful moves and complete adherence to decorum.

Beccaroon smiled as he spotted the third child. This was Peg, hair in disarray, bows untied, hem of her dress muddied, the fingers of her white gloves black with grime, and the lace of one sleeve torn and fluttering in the breeze.

Beccaroon realized with a gasp that Peg was supposed to be inside the empty dress. There had not been three children. As he watched darling Peg, she skipped into a bed of flowers, picked up a bug, twirled in the sunshine, then began to fade, becoming translucent until her image was gone. In the distance, the queen could be seen following the well-groomed trail with a child and an empty dress stepping properly behind her.

Again the haze grew thick, and this time the air chilled as well. When the mist cleared, a little girl sat in a hayloft admiring a batch of new kittens. She scrambled down the ladder when called and appeared before her father. The child was older by the time she reached her father, but hay still clung to her hair and dress.

Beccaroon shivered as the father pointed to a doll and demanded it be put away. The child hugged it quickly and shut it in a carved wooden box.

"This little girl," said Paladin, "was trained to keep her treasures out of sight."

Queen Venmarie gasped.

"Yes," said Paladin, "she grew to become our queen."

The mist in the room cleared.

"Treasures. Displayed and gloated over. Shared but unappreciated.

Hidden because someone else has deemed them unfit."

"Impressive," said the king, "but what is the value of this display?"

Paladin's eyes gleamed with happiness as he looked from the queen to Lady Peg. The queen no longer kept her eyes focused on something distant. Her eyes were on her child.

"I've got it." Lady Peg held up one finger. "I'm the doll. But when mother grew up, I was me, and she couldn't get me in the dress. When I was a doll, I had to go into the box. When I was real, I was supposed to go in the dress." She turned to smile at Paladin. "Is that right, Paladin? Am I the doll?"

Paladin stood and went to Lady Peg, pulling her to her feet and hugging her. "Yes, beautiful princess, you are an adorable doll." He kissed the top of her head and led her over to the queen.

"Your Highness, I would like to present your daughter, Lady Peg, a treasure. What would you like to do with her?"

Speechless, the queen stood. Beccaroon wondered if she would raise a strident voice or run from the room. He had to do something to sway her. But what? He plucked a feather from his breast and strutted to her side. He offered the plume. For a moment, the queen stared, then with shaking fingers, she took the gift from his beak.

Twirling Beccaroon's soft plumage, she said, "I remember that red feather." Tears ran down her cheeks. She stepped forward and embraced Lady Peg. Her voice scolded halfheartedly. "You crawled on the floor, tripping men with swords."

"You bashed Mushand's men with a candlestick."

The queen leaned back and wiped tears from her daughter's cheeks with a handkerchief she'd kept ready for years in case her royal self ever needed one. She kissed Peg's cheek. "We're feathers."

Beccaroon heard a movement behind him. Fenworth stood beside Librettowit's chair. "I nap, and when I awake, I find everyone crying."

Librettowit sniffed. "I'm not crying."

"The feather story was pretty good."

"How long have you been awake?"

"Long enough. The 'we're feathers' line was good as well."

"If you say anything about birds flocking together…" Librettowit's tone threatened something. Beccaroon wasn't quite sure what.

"Haven't an inkling what you're referring to." Fenworth grinned.

Beccaroon sidled over to stand between the two Amarans.

"Is this the work a paladin does?" he asked.

"No," said Wizard Fenworth, shaking his woolly head and smiling grandly. "This is Wulder's work."

Appendix

People

Araspillian
Brother of Bealomondore

Bamataub
Unscrupulous businessman in Fayetopolis

Graddapotmorphit Bealomondore
Tumanhofer artist

Sir Beccaroon
Grand parrot, magistrate over his district, guardian to Tipper

Caesannede
Prince Jayrus's white and gold dragon

Master Dodderbanoster
Art dealer

Wizard Fenworth
Wizard from Amara

Gladyme
Byrdschopen housekeeper

Gus
Dragon Tipper and her father ride on

Hanner
Go-between for art dealer and Tipper

Hue
Purple minor dragon

Garamond Hunt
Owner of Hunthaven

Gienella Hunt
Lady of Ragar Court, wife of Garamond Hunt

Prince Jayrus
Dragon Keeper, prince of Mercigon Mountain Range

Kelsi
Purple riding dragon

Ketmar
Black riding dragon

Librettowit
Tumanhofer librarian from Amara

Lipphil
Butler at Byrdschopen

Merry
Blue riding dragon

Orphelian
Wife of Bamataub

Lord Pinterbastian
Wealthy neighbor to Byrdschopen

Rolan
Neighbor to Byrdschopen, gentleman farmer

Allard Runan
Country gentleman

Leatte Runan
Wife of Allard Runan

Sage
Oldest living dragon

Brim Schope
Original owner of Byrdschopen

Eldymine Byrd Schope
Wife of Brim Schope

Lady Peg Schope
Mother of Tipper, wife of Verrin Schope

Verrin Schope
Artist, sculptor, scientist, explorer, wizard

Prince Surrus
Mentor to Prince Jayrus

Tipper
Young emerlindian woman

Trisoda
Barn dragon at Byrdschopen

Queen Venmarie
Mother of Lady Peg

King Yellat

Ruler of Chiril, Lady Peg's father

Zilla

Wife of Rolan

Glossary

Amara

Country surrounded by ocean on three sides. Located in the northern and eastern hemisphere.

banana bug

A long yellow centipede.

bisonbecks

Most intelligent of the seven low races.

bittermorn tree

A tree with fernlike leaves which close at the first rays of dawn and slowly reopen during the day.

blinker owl

Small grayish owl. The bird ventures forth during the day and blinks rapidly.

boskenberries

An edible berrylike fruit from any tree of the genus *Bosken*.

broot vine

A tropical plant with a sturdy ropelike stem.

bubble beetles

An insect that gathers around running or falling water.

casting bush

A flowering bush with a bloom that looks like a tiny lure on the end of a leafless stem, much like a fishing rod.

centimonder

An insect with a segmented body and a pair of legs on each segment. The centimonder has large mandibles and a stinging bite.

Cranicus albatteran

The *Cranicus albatteran* has a slightly longer thorax than the *Cranicus batteran*. *Cranicus albatteran* is the Chirilian name for *Fineet fineaurlais*.

dollopsy

A neurological disease that causes loss of feeling in the extremities and, thus, clumsiness.

emerlindians

One of the seven high races, emerlindians are born pale with white hair and pale gray eyes. As they age, they darken. One group of emerlindians are slight in stature, the tallest being five feet. Another distinct group are between six and six and a half feet tall.

fibbirds

A tiny, brightly colored bird with a long slender bill for sipping nectar and narrow, rapidly beating wings for hovering over flowers.

Fineet fineaurlais

An insect that burrows into wood.

flatrat

A rodent that appears to have flattened itself to go under a door but is always in that state.

frissent juice

Juice made from the red tart berry of plants belonging to the heath family and found wild in boggy areas. The juice fizzles slightly when freshly squeezed.

grassbender

A thin, plant-eating, jumping insect.

grassblooms

A plant with long slender leaves growing from a bulb and producing fragile bell-shaped blooms.

grawligs

One of seven low races, mountain ogres.

harpenstead

An instrument usually held in the lap and strummed. Buttons control dampers that form the chords.

hot amaloot

A drink similar to hot chocolate.

Izden glass

An ornately swirled glass, first produced in the city of Izden.

kimens

The smallest of the seven high races. Kimens are elusive, tiny, and fast. Under two feet tall.

lickick

A lollipop.

mannacap shell

A porous shell from a mannacap crab. Momile and mannacap shells should not be confused, especially in the kitchen. Ground momile shells are sweet, and ground mannacap shells can be addictive.

mariones

One of the seven high races. Mariones are excellent farmers and warriors. They are short and broad, usually muscle-bound rather than corpulent.

mikers

A unit of money.

molecular malocclusion distress syndrome

A condition unheard of until a near fatal accident in transportation disrupted a core element of stability in the universe.

momile shells

Porous shells from momile crabs.

mud-meade moth

Powdered, the moth is used for strengthening weak patients.

mumfers

Flowers with small, densely clustered petals.

ninny-nap-conder

A type of con artist who uses the appearance of naiveté to dupe his victims.

o'rants

One of the high races. Five to six feet tall.

parnot

Green fruit like a pear.

pippenhen

A small bird belonging to a variety of tree-nesting thrushes.

pordimum

A flower that has more petals than scents.

quiverbug
A small bug that vibrates violently when atmospheric conditions are right for a storm.

sacktrass tree
A deciduous tree with lobed leaves and fragrant fruit and bark. The fruit is bitter, but the bark is used as a pleasant addition to tea.

sputzall vine
A hardy vine with compound leaves and large purple flowers. The roots contain a nourishing medicinal starch.

swishglimmers
An ornamental fish, with jewel-like scales of brilliant colors, related to carp and minnows.

tumanhofers
One of the seven high races. Short, squat, powerful fighters, though for the most part, they prefer to use their great intellect.

watch of dragons
A unit of dragons (like a gaggle of geese).

Experience the Epic DragonKeeper Series from Adventurous Beginning to Fantastical End

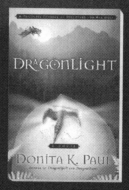

www.donitakpaul.com

 WATERBROOK PRESS
www.waterbrookmultnomah.com

Available in bookstores and from online retailers.

Printed in the United States
by Baker & Taylor Publisher Services